OTHER ST. MARTIN'S PAPERBACKS TITLES BY DIANE KELLY

DEAD AS A DOOR KNOCKER

DIANE KELLY

St. Martin's Paperbacks

This is a work of fiction. All of the characters, organizations, and events portrayed in this novel are either products of the author's imagination or are used fictitiously.

DEAD AS A DOOR KNOCKER

For information address St. Martin's Press, 175 Fifth Avenue, New York, NY 10010.

ISBN: 978-1-250-19742-9

Our books may be purchased in bulk for promotional, educational, or business use. Please contact your local bookseller or the Macmillan Corporate and Premium Sales Department at 1-800-221-7945, ext. 5442, or by e-mail at MacmillanSpecialMarkets@macmillan.com.

Printed in the United States of America

St. Martin's Paperbacks edition / February 2019

St. Martin's Paperbacks are published by St. Martin's Press, 175 Fifth Avenue, New York, NY 10010.

10 9 8 7 6 5 4 3 2 1

*To my mother-in-law, Lucille Mainland Kelly,
for being a role model of hard work,
determination, and thoughtfulness; for raising
the wonderful man I share my life with; and for
her unwavering encouragement and support of
my dreams and those of my children.*

ACKNOWLEDGMENTS

As always, a big thanks to the talented team at St. Martin's Paperbacks who took this book from the first draft to the bookstore shelves. Oodles of gratitude to my editors, Holly Ingraham and Hannah Braaten, who brought this book to life. Thanks to their editorial assistants Jennie Conway and Nettie Finn, as well as Sarah Melnyk, Paul Hochman, Allison Ziegler, Titi Oluwo, Talia Sherer, and the rest of the St. Martin's crew for all of your work in getting my books into the hands of readers, reviewers, and librarians. Y'all are the best!

Thanks to designer Lesley Worrell and artist Mary Ann Lasher for creating such a cute and eye-catching cover for this book!

Thanks to my agent, Helen Breitwieser, for all you do to advance my writing career.

Thanks to Liz Bemis and April Reed of Spark Creative for your prompt and professional work on my Web site and newsletters.

Thanks to fellow authors D. D. Ayres, Laura Castoro,

Angela Cavener, Christie Craig, Cheryl Hathaway, and Angela Hicks for your feedback and friendship. It's great to have such a wonderful support system!

Thanks to my sister, Donna Parsons, RN, for answering my questions about the treatment of cat bites.

And finally, thanks to you wonderful readers who chose this book! I hope you'll enjoy your time with Whitney, Sawdust, and the gang.

CHAPTER I
DEADBEATS

WHITNEY WHITAKER

I grabbed my purse, my tool belt, and the bright yellow hard hat I'd adorned with a chain of daisy decals. I gave my cat a kiss on the head. "Bye-bye, Sawdust." Looking into his baby blue eyes, I pointed a finger at him. "Be a good boy while Mommy's at work, okay?"

The cat swiped at my finger with a paw the color of pine shavings. Given that my eyes and hair were the same shade as his, I could be taken for his mother if not for the fact that we were entirely different species. I'd adopted the furry runt after his mother, a stray, had given birth to him and two siblings in my uncle's barn. My cousins, Buck and Owen, had taken in the other two kittens, and my aunt and uncle gave the wayward mama cat a comfy home in their hilltop cabin on the Kentucky border.

After stepping outside, I turned around to lock the French doors that served as the entrance to my humble home. The place sat in my parents' backyard, on the far side of their kidney-shaped pool. In its former life, it had served as a combination pool house and garden shed. With the help of the contractors I'd befriended on my jobs, I'd converted the structure into a cozy guesthouse—the guest being yours truly. It had already been outfitted with a small three-quarter bath, so all we'd had to do was add a closet and kitchenette.

Furnishing a hundred and fifty square feet had been easy. There was room for only the bare essentials—a couple of bar stools at the kitchen counter, a twin bed and dresser, and a recliner that served as both a comfortable reading chair and a scratching post for Sawdust. Heaven forbid my sweet but spoiled cat should sharpen his claws on the sisal post I'd bought him at the pet supply store. At least he enjoyed his carpet-covered cat tree. I'd positioned it by one of the windows that flanked the French doors. He passed his days on the highest perch, watching birds flitter about the birdhouses and feeders situated about the backyard.

At twenty-eight, I probably should've ventured farther from my parents' home by now. But the arrangement suited me and my parents just fine. They were constantly jetting off to Paris or Rome or some exotic locale I couldn't pronounce or find on a map if my life depended on it. Living here allowed me to keep an eye on their house and dog while they traveled, but the fact that we shared no walls gave us all some privacy. The arrangement also allowed me to sock away quite a bit of my earnings in savings. Soon, I'd be able to buy a house of my own. Not here in the Green Hills neighborhood, where real estate garnered a pretty penny. But maybe in one of the more affordable Nashville suburbs. While many young girls dreamed of beaded wedding gowns or palomino ponies, I'd dreamed of custom cabinets and built-in bookshelves.

After locking the door, I turned to find my mother and her black-and-white Boston terrier, Yin-Yang, puttering around the backyard. Like me, Mom was blond, though she now needed the help of her hairdresser to keep the stray grays at bay. Like Yin-Yang, Mom was petite, standing only five feet three inches. Mom was still in her pink bathrobe, a steaming mug of coffee in her hand. While she helped with billing at my dad's otolaryngology practice, she normally went in late and left early. Her part-time schedule allowed her to avoid traffic, gave her time take care of things around the house, and spend time with her precious pooch.

"Good morning!" I called.

My mother returned the sentiment, while Yin-Yang raised her two-tone head and replied with a cheerful *Arf-arf!* The bark scared off a trio of finches who'd been indulging in a breakfast of assorted seeds at a nearby feeder.

Mom stepped over, the dog trotting along with her, staring up at me with its adorable little bug eyes. "You're off early," Mom said, a hint of question in her voice.

No sense telling her I was on my way to an eviction. She already thought my job was beneath me. She assumed working as a property manager involved constantly dealing with deadbeats and clogged toilets. Truth be told, much of my job did involve delinquent tenants or backed-up plumbing. But there was much more to it than that. Helping landlords turn rundown real estate into attractive residences, helping hopeful tenants locate the perfect place for their particular needs, making sure everything ran smoothly for everyone involved. I considered myself to be in the homemaking business. But rather than try, for the umpteenth time, to explain myself, I simply said, "I've got a busy day."

Mom tilted her head. "Too busy to study for your real estate exam?"

I fought the urge to groan. As irritating as my mother

could be, she only wanted the best for me. Problem was, we didn't agree on what the best was. Instead of starting an argument I said, "Don't worry. The test isn't for another couple of weeks. I've still got plenty of time."

"Okay," she acquiesced, the two syllables soaked in skepticism. "Have a good day, sweetie." At least those five words sounded sincere.

"You, too, Mom." I reached down and ruffled the dog's ears. "Bye, girl."

I made my way to the picket fence that enclosed the backyard and let myself out of the gate and onto the driveway. After tossing my hard hat and tool belt into the passenger seat of my red Honda CR-V, I swapped out the magnetic WHITAKER WOODWORKING sign on the door for one that read HOME & HEARTH REALTY. Yep, I wore two hats. The hard hat when moonlighting as a carpenter for my uncle, and a metaphorical second hat when working my day job as a property manager for a real estate business. This morning, I sported the metaphorical hat as I headed up Hillsboro Pike into Nashville. Fifteen minutes later, I turned onto Sweetbriar Avenue. In the driveway of the house on the corner sat a shiny midnight-blue Infiniti Q70L sedan with vanity plates that read TGENTRY. My hackles rose at the sight.

Thaddeus Gentry III owned Gentry Real Estate Development, Inc., or, as I called it, GREED Incorporated. Okay, so I'd added an extra *E* to make the spelling work. Still, it was true. The guy was as money-hungry and ruthless as they come. He was singlehandedly responsible for the gentrification of several old Nashville neighborhoods. While gentrification wasn't necessarily a bad thing—after all it rid the city of ramshackle houses in dire need of repairs— Thad Gentry took advantage of homeowners, offering them pennies on the dollar, knowing they couldn't afford the increase in property taxes that would result as their modest neighborhoods transformed into upscale communities. He'd harass holdouts by reporting any city code violations, no matter how minor. He also formed homeowners' associations in the newly renovated neighborhoods, and ensured the HOA put pressure on the remaining original residents to bring their houses up to snuff. These unfortunate folks found they no longer felt at home and usually gave in and moved on . . . to where, who knows?

When I'd come by a week ago in a final attempt to collect from the tenants, I'd noticed a FOR SALE sign in the yard where Thad Gentry's car was parked. The sign was gone now. *Had Gentry bought the property? Had he set his sights on the neighborhood?* Time would tell, I supposed.

Turning my attention back to the task at hand, I pulled to the curb next door and glanced at the rental house. While I'd fought a groan minutes before when conversing with my mother, I let out a big groan now. The place bore the telltale signs of having hosted a raucous Halloween party last night. Wispy fake cobwebs hung from the porch railing. Disposable cups littered the yard, scattered among novelty gravestones. A plastic skeleton lay in the neglected flower bed, a bony arm cradling an empty bottle of Jack Daniel's Old No. 7 Tennessee Sour Mash Whiskey.

As my eyes took in the place, they caught movement at the house to the left. The sixtyish woman who lived there peeked out the window, her faded strawberry curls filling the glass. When I raised a hand in greeting, she let the curtain fall back into place rather than return the gesture. Whether she was unfriendly or embarrassed to be caught spying, I wasn't sure.

I climbed out of my car and walked up to the small porch of the stone cottage. An ornate iron knocker graced the front door, the face of the mystical Celtic Green Man deity sculpted into the metal as if he were keeping watch on the world with his deep, all-knowing eyes. The Green Man, which featured carved leaves about his face, symbolized rebirth. The embellishment was an intriguing touch, both decorative and functional. I raised the knocker's ring and tapped it against the plate. *Knock-knock-knock.* When no response came from inside, I lifted the ring again, using it more forcefully this time. *KNOCK-KNOCK-KNOCK.* Still no answer. The Green Man stared at me, as if to ask *What now?*

"They've left me no other choice," I told the knocker. I'd have to barge in.

I pulled my oversized, crowded key ring from my purse and fingered through the keys. *Nope. Nope. Nope. There it is.* I stuck the key in the door and took a deep breath to steel myself. Evictions were the worst part of my job as a property manager. Someone always ended up shouting or begging or crying. Often that someone was *me.* My heart broke when landlords ran out of patience waiting for past-due rent and forced me to put a struggling family or an elderly person with a fixed income out on the streets. Fortunately, the deadbeats *du jour* were a trio of spoiled college kids from wealthy families. Judging from the smell of the place as I opened the door, as well as the bottles and greasy boxes littering the floors, they'd used the rent money their parents had sent them to buy pizza and liquor instead. Several boxes from a mail-order electronics company sat about too, one of them containing a receipt for a two-hundred-dollar virtual reality headset. Needless to say, my heart wasn't breaking this morning. My nose, on the other hand, wriggled involuntarily in protest. The place reeked of stale garbage and beer and young males teeming with testosterone. *Ew.*

You'd never know it to look at the place now, but prior

to the current tenants moving in, the house had been freshly painted inside and out and the wood floors had been refinished. Rick Dunaway, the property owner, was exceedingly cheap when it came to his rentals. I'd managed to convince him to have the house painted and the floors refinished, but only after agreeing to bill him solely for the supplies and do the work gratis myself with the help of my cousins. Call me a pushover, but I didn't want Home & Hearth to gain a reputation as a manager for slumlords. I wanted to be proud of the properties I managed. Of course, there wasn't much to be proud of here now. The walls bore smudges and spots. One wall was freckled with small holes around a hand-drawn bull's-eye that had served as an improvised dartboard. A dart hung from one of the holes. Graffiti covered the rest of the wall, doodles in permanent marker all over it. Several fist-sized holes pocked the drywall. *Hmm.*

I stepped into the small hallway to the left, and addressed the three closed bedroom doors. "Rise and shine, boys! Time to pack up and move out!" Actually, that time should have come weeks ago, but the eviction process in Tennessee required a thirty-day written warning, then a court hearing and delivery of a formal eviction notice.

I strode about, snapping photos with my cell phone to document the damage. In addition to the walls, the floors were a wreck, scratched and scraped and warped where beer and sodas had been spilled and left to soak into the wood. Refinishing these floors had been backbreaking work, and now I'd have to do it all over again.

I closed my eyes and sighed. If I passed my upcoming real estate exam and became an agent, I could leave property management behind. The work paid peanuts, and dealing with problem tenants and penny-pinching landlords was a hassle. Still, I loved the part of the job that involved fixing up properties, turning eyesores into dream homes. After working with owners to set a budget and choose the paint and materials, I'd oversee the contractors, make sure the projects were completed correctly and quickly. As a skilled carpenter, I often did the work myself, earning extra bucks to add to my savings and keep my spoiled cat in tuna treats.

When I finished taking photos in the living room, I ventured into the kitchen. *Cheese-n-grits!* Dirty dishes towered in the sink, while trash and food scraps overflowed the garbage can. Flies buzzed about, enjoying the buffet the boys had left for them. Not to be outdone, a quartet of cockroaches feasted on goo on the countertop, stimulating my gag reflex. *Uck. Should've worn a hazmat suit.*

I turned and headed to the bedroom doors, throwing them open. When sounds of protests came from the bedrooms, I put a quick end to it. "Out of bed now!" I hollered. "Y'all have one hour to get your things out of here before I'll toss whatever and whoever is left out on the lawn." It was bluster, of course. Carpentry work had given me some muscle, but not enough to lift a full-grown male. With that, I walked out to the front porch where the air was fresher.

CHAPTER 2

SUNBATHING

SAWDUST

The small home Sawdust shared with Whitney had French doors in front. The doors faced east, letting in the glorious morning sunshine. Sawdust rolled a quarter turn from his back onto his right side as the sun rose and the sunbeam shifted. He purred in contentment. The only thing that would make this moment better was if Whitney was home.

Sawdust adored Whitney, had since the moment she'd first picked him up, tiny and terrified, in her aunt and uncle's barn. She'd given him a comfortable, if small, home, and all the toys and treats his furry heart could desire. He only wished she wasn't gone so much. He missed her when she wasn't there. His tinkling-ball toy and the birds outside the window only distracted him for so long. He'd discovered that taking a nap made Whitney's absences pass quicker. He closed his eyes and began to doze, dreaming of the time when his mommy would return home.

CHAPTER 3

THREATS AND OPPORTUNITIES

WHITNEY

The three boys ventured out of their bedrooms, half awake and half dressed. They glanced about as if unsure where to start.

"I'd suggest one of you go rent a truck," I called through the open front door. "The other two can start packing."

A beefy, dark-haired boy with scruffy stubble on his face cut me a look so edgy and sharp I could've whittled a stick with it. "You'll be sorry you put us out," he hissed. "Mark my words."

The punk outweighed me by a good hundred pounds. Though my stomach clenched in fear, I mustered up every inch of my height. "Are you threatening me?"

Before he could respond, one of the other boys muttered, "Chill, Jackson. You don't need anything else on your record."

Jackson has a record? He hadn't had one when the boys moved into the place. Home & Hearth ran a background check on every prospective tenant before renting to them.

"Fine," Jackson spat, searing me with another look even as he backed away.

The sullen boys put on shoes and shirts. Jackson left to round up a moving truck, while the other two loaded what they could into the trunks and backseats of their cars. When Jackson returned, they loaded the larger pieces of furniture into the truck, while I carried out lamps and kitchen chairs and other smaller pieces. Not that the boys deserved my help after freeloading and trashing the place, but I wanted to move the process along so I could perform damage control before Rick Dunaway arrived. He'd be none too happy about the condition of his property.

As soon as the boys drove off, I went into whirling dervish mode, moving about the place at a frenzied pace, wiping down countertops and gathering trash. A few minutes later, as I went to wipe down a windowsill in the living room, I spotted Rick Dunaway's silver Mercedes parked in the driveway. Moving closer to the window, I saw Dunaway standing on the lawn, speaking with Thad Gentry. Both wore well-fitting suits, probably custom tailored. But while the men shared a sense of style and a take-no-prisoners approach to real estate, that's where their similarities ended. Dunaway's DNA had made him tall, and his time on the country club's tennis courts had made him tan and trim. Gentry, on the other hand, was short and stocky, his cinder-block physique a telltale sign of deals made over dinners of steak, baked potatoes, and whiskey. Dunaway sported slicked-back, too-dark-to-be-natural-at-his-age hair. Rather than trying to hide his silver strands, Gentry had embraced the timber wolf tones, going so far as to grow a groomed goatee. He looked like a refined mountain man, if there was such a thing.

Seeing the two titans of real estate in a direct confrontation made me curious. Unfortunately, the glass prevented me from hearing their conversation, and their practiced poker faces gave no clue as to the topic of their discussion, either.

Dunaway turned to the house and caught me watching them out the window. But rather than hide like the neighbor had done when I'd spotted her, I raised a hand and offered a forced smile. Dunaway turned back to Gentry and concluded their conversation before heading across the yard and storming up the porch.

I met him at the front door and extended my hand. "Hello, Mr. Dunaway."

He ignored both my hand and my greeting. Instead, he looked past me into the house, his eyes flaring. "It looks like they held a rodeo in there! How could you let this happen?"

My ire rose, my body temperature rising along with it. He seemed to have forgotten that I'd advised him against renting to college students, even if he could charge them more collectively in rent than a single family might be willing to pay. But he'd ignored me, choosing short-term profits over long-term stable income.

"As soon as the rent was late," I reminded him, "I took action. I did all I could, as quickly as I could, while complying with the law."

"The *law*," he scoffed, waving a hand with a telltale pale strip around his ring finger where his wedding band used to be. "If I'd been the one handling things, these boys would have been on their way weeks ago."

And I wouldn't have to stand here and listen to you belittle me. Even so, I couldn't very well share that thought with him. Landing Rick Dunaway as a client for Home & Hearth had been nothing short of a coup. I'd heard through the grapevine that Abbot-Dunaway Holdings was looking at outsourcing management of the company's residential investment properties, and I'd decided to take a chance. After all, the worst he could do was say no, right? I'd put together a proposal that included bios for Mr. and Mrs. Hartley, the owners of Home & Hearth, as well as one for myself. I'd used the skills learned in my college marketing classes to sell our services, promising that if he chose our humble real estate firm to manage his residential properties, he'd be our number one client and receive top-notch service, his calls answered 24/7. The pitch had worked. He'd chosen Home & Hearth over a dozen other contenders, all larger firms with more impressive portfolios.

Dunaway walked into the house and stalked into the kitchen, noting the dripping faucet, the missing cabinet doors, the broken window held together by duct tape. He stomped back across the living room and into the bath. Like the window, the toilet seat had been patched with duct tape, and so much mildew had grown on the shower curtain it appeared to have a five o'clock shadow. At least the claw-foot bathtub appeared undamaged. The classic fixture looked deep and inviting. Someday, when I had a house of my own, I'd have a tub like this installed.

Dunaway opened the cabinet under the bathroom sink, revealing a plastic bucket lodged under the P-trap. Murky water filled half the bucket. Looked like the pipes had a leak. The boys hadn't submitted a repair request. Not surprising. They probably hadn't wanted me to come by and discover the damage they'd caused. I emptied the bucket into the tub and stuck it back in the cabinet.

The bedrooms had fared no better. The folding shutter-style doors on the closets were missing slats and had been pulled out of their tracks, and the blinds on the windows hung askew. The switch plates in two of the rooms were cracked. All of the doorstops were gone, allowing the inside door handles to punch holes in the drywall.

When Dunaway finished his not-so-grand tour, he threw up his hands, the shiny Rolex watch on his wrist giving off a glint as his shirt cuff slid back. "I'm done!"

Uh-oh. Is he firing me? Ending his management contract with Home & Hearth? I gulped to clear the lump of fear in my throat. "What are you saying, Mr. Dunaway?"

He turned to face me full-on. "I'm saying I'm putting this place up for sale."

"Selling the house?" My hand reflexively went to my chest in relief. "That's all?"

His brows drew inward. "What else would it be?"

I shrugged sheepishly. "I thought you were firing me."

He bellowed a laugh. "As hard as you work, Whitney? I'd be a fool to get rid of you."

Thank goodness! I exhaled in relief. Dare I tell him I'd be taking my real estate exam very soon and ask him to give me the listing? Or would that be taking things too far?

My mind performed some quick math computations. Smaller properties in the Belmont-Hillsboro neighborhood sold for around half a million dollars on average. If I could snag the listing, I'd be entitled to 3 percent of the sales price as the seller's agent, or at least fifteen thousand dollars. *Whoa!* It took me six months to earn that much as a property manager. Houses in this neighborhood moved fast, too. With its prime location and historic appeal, the house would practically sell itself—especially if the interior were renovated to provide modern conveniences while preserving the charming midcentury details. *Go for it, Whitney.* "I'll be getting my real estate license soon," I offered tentatively.

"You want it, then?" Dunaway asked.

"The listing? Of course!"

"No. Not the listing. *The house.* I want to get out from under it right away and I'm in no mood to waste time or money fixing it up. Thad Gentry bought the house next door and just offered me four hundred and fifty grand for this place, as is."

So that's what they were discussing outside.

"I'd rather not sell to him," Dunaway added. "Gentry's been a thorn in my side since I got into this business. He's outbid me several times, cost me some good deals. If you want the house, I'll let you have it for four hundred. You could work your magic and flip it for a nice profit."

My mouth gaped. I'd been excited about the prospect of earning $15,000 on the house, but if I bought it at the discounted price he was offering, I could net an easy seventy grand or more after fixing it up. Besides, the fact that Thad Gentry had been interested in the house said a lot. Everything that man touched seemed to turn to gold. "This seems too good to be true!"

"Chance of a lifetime," he concurred. He stared me in the eye. "Look. I like you, Whitney. You've got grit and gumption. Heck, you remind me of myself at your age. Besides, I need some ready cash. My wife's divorce attorney is taking me to the cleaners. My attorney is, too."

My mind spun like a circular saw. Still, as much as I wanted to jump on the offer, there were several ducks to get in a row first. Financing. Insurance. An inspection to make sure I knew exactly what I was getting myself into. An old house like this could become a money pit if it had latent problems. Not that I expected any. Despite the cosmetic issues, the house appeared to have good bones. I'd also need to run the proposition by Mr. and Mrs. Hartley, the owners of Home & Hearth. They hadn't bought and sold houses on their own account in the past, but that didn't mean they wouldn't want to seize this opportunity themselves.

"How long can you give me?" I asked.

"Twenty-four hours," Dunaway said. "Then I'm putting it on the market. Drop an earnest-money check for two grand by my office today. It'll need to be a cashier's check. I need to know you're serious."

"I am," I said. "I'll get right on it."

I stuck out my hand again. This time Dunaway took it, sealing our deal with a firm shake.

CHAPTER 4

CALLING IN FAVORS

WHITNEY

I walked Mr. Dunaway out onto the porch and bade him good-bye. Halfway down the front walk, he glanced down the street and paused in his tracks. My gaze followed his to a white sedan sitting on the other side of the street a couple houses down, parked in the shade of a sprawling tree. The driver's side window was rolled down, an arm clad in a white shirt resting crooked on the frame. Whoever was sitting in the car was obscured by the open newspaper in his hands. *Huh. I didn't think anyone got their news from actual newsprint these days.*

I wasn't sure if the car had been parked down the street when I'd pulled up earlier. I'd been too distracted by Gentry next door and the mess in the yard here to notice. Besides, the vehicle was plain, not the type of car to catch a person's eye. It bore no front license plate—the state of Tennessee didn't require them—so I couldn't verify whether it was a government-issued vehicle, but it looked like the type of car driven by building inspectors, undercover cops, and the like. The driver was probably someone from the city waiting to meet up with a contractor at Gentry's place.

Mr. Dunaway continued on to his Mercedes, climbed in, and backed out of the driveway, heading off in the opposite direction. As soon as he was gone, I locked up the house, hopped into my car, and drove to the Home & Hearth office, located on the east side of the Cumberland River in the Lockeland Springs neighborhood. Home & Hearth was a small mom-and-pop operation. I was their sole employee.

I'd first met the Hartleys years ago, just after I'd graduated from college with a business degree. One of their real estate clients hired Whitaker Woodworking to install a built-in entertainment center in a house they'd purchased. When the Hartleys swung by to bring their clients a houseplant to welcome them to their new home, they'd seen our superior handiwork and asked for our business cards. They'd subsequently recommended us to clients who needed carpentry work done on their homes.

While Whitaker Woodworking had enough business to keep my uncle and cousins busy full-time, it was only an occasional gig for me. I had been on the lookout for another job to fill in the gaps. One day, Mrs. Hartley mentioned that their property management work had become more than she and her husband could handle and that they were looking for part-time help. When she asked if I knew anyone who might be interested, I said I knew someone very well who'd like the job. *Me*. Despite my lack of property management experience, she'd hired me on the spot. She knew from the feedback she'd received from our mutual clients that I was punctual, personable, and paid attention to detail. She and Mr. Hartley had spent a week training me on the ins and outs of property management, then cut me loose. The employment arrangement worked to everyone's benefit. The Hartleys could focus on their clients looking to buy or sell houses, while I could help out the clients who leased their properties. Plus, I could toss even more business to Whitaker Woodworking, and refer carpentry clients to the real estate agency. It was a win-win-win situation.

I pushed open the door and stepped inside.

Mr. and Mrs. Hartley looked up from their desks, positioned side by side in the single room. The two were in their early sixties, pleasantly plump, and gray-headed, but while Mr. Hartley's thinning hair struggled to cover his scalp, Mrs. Hartley's thick, loose waves cascaded past her cheeks. The two greeted me with warm smiles and I returned one of my own.

"Eviction go okay?" Mrs. Hartley asked as I headed to the coffeepot on the corner table.

I refilled my travel mug with fresh brew. "The boys grumbled a little and left a bunch of trash and damage behind, but there wasn't too much drama." No sense telling them Jackson had threatened me. It would only upset them, and it had probably been an idle threat, the twerp's way of getting in the last word. I perched on one of the cushy Queen Anne chairs that faced their desks. "Mr. Dunaway has decided he wants to sell the property."

Mrs. Hartley's face perked up and she sat bolt upright in her chair. "Did you tell him you'll be getting your agent's license soon? That house could be your first listing!"

"Actually," I replied, "Rick Dunaway offered to sell me the property at a big discount. I was thinking maybe I could fix it up and resell it." I said nothing more for a moment, letting the information sink in, eager to see how the Hartleys would respond.

Mr. Hartley spoke first. "Sounds like a good opportunity for you, Whitney."

His wife agreed, her face bright. "It's a great idea! I know how much you like rehab projects, and you'd get a sale under your belt, too."

I looked from one to the other. "So you're okay with me doing it on my own?"

"Of course!" Mrs. Hartley said.

Her husband agreed. "We'd be pleased as punch if you turned a profit on that place. You certainly deserve it."

"Y'all are the best bosses ever!"

We stood and exchanged hugs, an inappropriate gesture in most work environments, but not at Home & Hearth where we treated each other like family.

Having obtained my bosses' blessing, I took a seat at my desk in the back of the room. *Time to call in some favors.*

My first call went to a loan officer at a mortgage company that had financed many a deal for Home & Hearth's clients. After I explained to the woman that I needed a mortgage pronto, she agreed to expedite my application and work on getting me a preapproval letter ASAP. "Send me copies of your most recent pay stub, the last two years' tax returns, bank statements, and a list of all your debts and assets."

I jotted a quick list. Rounding up the documentation would be easy. As for assets, I owned my SUV outright and had forty grand in savings. Luckily for me, I had no debts given my inexpensive living situation and lack of interest in designer apparel or other high-dollar items. My money tended to go to carpentry tools and an occasional new pair of steel-toed boots or coveralls.

My second call went to Bobby Palmer. Home & Hearth hired Bobby regularly to inspect houses for its clients. I often met him at the houses to let him inside. At sixty-three, he had thousands of inspections under his belt and knew his stuff. If there was anything wrong with the house on Sweetbriar, no matter how minor, Bobby Palmer would find it.

After exchanging the usual niceties, I asked, "Any chance you can squeeze in an inspection tomorrow?" I crossed my fingers. Bobby was in big demand and was usually booked days in advance.

"You're in luck," he said. "I had a cancellation tomorrow morning. Financing fell through. I can be there at nine."

"Perfect!"

Next, I checked the balances in my savings and investment accounts. Still being single when I was pushing thirty hadn't exactly been my plan, but the fact that I was single and had no children meant every penny I'd earned was mine. My hourly pay wasn't much to brag about, but I'd managed to save quite a bit of it given that my parents would accept only a pittance in rent for the converted shed. Even so, while I had enough to swing the standard 10 percent down payment on the house, there'd be nothing left to cover the fix-up expenses.

What's a young woman to do? Hmm . . .

My mom and dad would spot me a few thousand if I asked, but I wanted to do this without their help, to prove myself. I wasn't above hitting up my cousin Buck, though. Heck, as close as the two of us were, he was more like a big brother.

I pulled Buck up in my contacts list and placed the call. He answered on the third ring. A saw whined in the background like a monster-sized mosquito. Looked like my cousin was at a job site. "Hey, Nit-Whit," he said by way of greeting.

"Want to make some quick money?"

"Always. You got a job for me?"

"No, Buckaroo. I've got a *house* for you. Well, a house for *us*." I went on to tell him about the property, what a great investment it would be.

"How much we talkin' 'bout makin' on this deal?" Buck asked.

"Seventy grand, more or less. It's been a rental so it needs some work, but it would take us only a month or two to complete the renovations. I don't have enough money for both the down payment and the rehab expenses. I thought you and I could go in together, as partners."

He sounded equal parts incredulous and intrigued. "You're tellin' me we could each net over thirty thousand dollars? In just a couple of months?"

"It sounds crazy, I know, but Dunaway wants to move it quick. He offered me a special deal because I've worked hard managing his properties. He said he sees himself in me."

My chest swelled with pride, at least until Buck brought my ego back to earth.

"Sees himself in you, huh?" He snorted. "Should've plucked that mustache like I told you to."

I treated him to a raspberry in response. *Pffft*.

"I suppose I should take a look," he said, intrigue trumping incredulity. "After all, you and I have always managed to work all right together."

It was true. During our early teen years, my cousins and I earned enough money making birdhouses out of scrap wood to keep us in comic books and candy all summer long.

"What's the address?" he asked. "I'll swing over and take a look."

I gave him the address.

"Sweetbriar Avenue?" he repeated. "I'm not far from there now. What say we meet there in half an hour?"

"See you then."

Things were moving at warp speed. *That's a good sign, isn't it?*

I bade the Hartleys good-bye and drove back to the house. As I waited for Buck, I cleaned up the yard. After yanking the cobwebs from the porch railing and tossing the plastic cups and novelty gravestones into the trash can, I made my way to the flower bed. The plastic skeleton was only partially covered in the loose dirt, as if he'd been buried there and was rising from the dead, like a zombie. The skull stared up at me, its hollow eye sockets seeming to lock on mine. A creepy sensation slithered up my spine. *It's just a goofy toy,* I reminded myself. I pulled it out of the dirt, and shook it off, the plastic bones rattling, the skull lolling to the side. I was wrangling the bundle of bones into the garbage bin when Buck pulled up in his van and slid out of his seat.

Buck's father and mine were brothers, and we cousins looked as alike as most siblings. Like me, Buck had light blue eyes and blond hair the color of pine shavings. But, unlike me, he bore a full beard. He was tall and muscular, years of carpentry work making his shoulders round and strong.

I gestured to the house. "What do you think, cuz?"

His eyes narrowed as he took in the place, scrutinizing it. "Can't go wrong with a classic house like this. The yard needs some work, though."

"True." Like many rentals, it lacked pride of ownership. The grass was sparse, the bushes patchy, and the beds devoid of flowers or ivy to add a splash of color and soften the look. "I can handle the landscaping myself. That part's easy." I enjoyed gardening and would have some fun planting fall flowers in the beds.

I motioned for my cousin to follow me inside. He stopped at the door, staring into the face of the Green Man on the knocker. "It kind of feels like he's watching us."

I chuckled. "I think your imagination is getting the best of you."

We proceeded into the house. Buck grimaced when he saw the doodles on the wall and grunted disapprovingly at the other signs of abuse. He also rapped on the walls, knelt down to run a hand over the floors, and opened the cabinets under the sinks to inspect the plumbing. When he finished, he said, "Far as I can tell, all the damage is cosmetic or easily fixed. Structurally, this place seems to be in good shape."

"Does that mean you're in?"

He raised his brows and cocked his head. "You really think we can spruce this place up for thirty grand?"

"I know we can. Trust me. This is what I do for a living." Of course, I usually made repairs with other people's money. Still, I'd handled enough fix-up projects to become adept at estimating.

Buck's brows lowered back into place and he uncocked his head. "Thirty grand will clean me out, but you're a smart cookie. You wouldn't steer me wrong." He stuck out his hand. "Thanks for bringing me in on this, cuz."

"Not *cuz*," I replied. *"Partner."* I gave his hand a firm shake. "You won't be sorry."

When I released his hand, he glanced around again. "You got some ideas for the place?"

"Sure do." The instant Dunaway had offered the house to me, my mind began designing and decorating the interior. I had subscriptions to every decorating magazine in print, and spent my free time watching HGTV or the DIY network. I also perused home décor sites online. One of my favorite sites was that of designer Isak Nyström, a talented Swede turned Nashvillian. Capitalizing—*literally*—on his initials, he ran a company called INnovations, its slogan *Why just renovate when you can INnovate?* An eclectic, self-proclaimed dumpster diver and garage sale guru, he found rare and intriguing odds and ends that he incorporated into his design work as conversation pieces. But while he might pay next to nothing for many of his decorator items, his services didn't come cheap. What's more, he was in such high demand that he could pick and choose his projects, selecting only those properties he found personally appealing. But as much as I'd love to have Isak Nyström design the house, his rates were way out of our price range, if he'd even agree to work on the place.

"Get Colette's thoughts on the kitchen," Buck suggested.

Colette would be the perfect alternative to a professional designer, at least as far as the kitchen was concerned. "Will do. I bet she'll have some good ideas."

As Buck left, I retrieved my phone from my purse and called my best friend, Colette Chevalier, to share the news. A chef at the landmark Hermitage Hotel, Colette worked mostly in the evenings and would likely be at home now. Her work would give her insights on how we could best fashion the kitchen here. After all, to many buyers, kitchens were the most important room in a house.

My friend answered on the third ring. "Hey, Wh—"

Before she could even get out her greeting, I cried, "Guess what!" And before she could guess, I blurted, "I'm buying a house!"

"You are?" she asked with her New Orleans—*or should*

I say N'awlins?—accent. "Congratulations! It's about time you got out of that tiny pool house. How you've survived with only a minifridge and a toaster oven is beyond me."

My shed also had a microwave and a two-burner hot plate, but her point stood. The makeshift kitchen worked fine for someone like me who relied heavily on frozen foods, but it would never satisfy a professional cook like her.

"I'm not buying the house for myself," I clarified. "Buck and I are going in together. We plan to flip it. It needs some work, but it's in a good area. We think we'll make a nice profit."

"If anyone can do it," she said, "you and Buck can."

My friend's vote of confidence further buoyed my spirits. "Any chance I can convince you to help design the kitchen?"

"No convincing required," Colette said. "That sounds like fun!"

She agreed to come by the following morning, and we spent another minute or two catching up before ending our call.

I hopped into my SUV and headed downtown to the office of Abbot-Dunaway Holdings, Ltd. Their space was in one of the poshest signature buildings downtown, the tallest in Tennessee, what locals referred to as the "Batman Building" due to the dark façade and the two pointy antenna towers at either end of the roof that resembled bat ears.

As I stepped through the door, Dunaway's administrative assistant looked up at me. Presley was around my age, late twenties or early thirties. Dressed in a flattering autumn-gold dress, a print scarf bearing the Versace Medusa logo, and black gladiator heels, she had far more style than I. With mocha skin and dark hair cut short on the sides with a triangle of long bangs angled across her fore-head, she was the epitome of Southern chic. A leather Givenchy tote bag leaned against the file cabinet beside her. My mother had a similar one she'd paid a small fortune for. How Presley could afford designer clothing and accessories was a mystery. Though she served many roles at Abbot-Dunaway Holdings, working as the firm's receptionist and bookkeeper, I presumed Mr. Dunaway was as stingy with his employees as he was with his contract workers like me.

"Hello, Whitney." Presley gave me a tepid smile. She had never seemed to like me. As far as I could tell, the feeling was professional rather than personal. She'd been processing rent checks and handling some of the routine residential property management matters before Dunaway had decided to outsource the work. He'd told me that Presley had asked to be put in charge of the residential portfolio, but he'd turned her down because he didn't want to spend the time training her. His decision to hire me had prevented her from advancing her career, and no doubt she resented me for it. I'd feel the same way if I were in her expensive, ambitious shoes.

I held out an envelope that contained a cashier's check in the amount of $2,000. "I've got a check for Mr. Dunaway."

She took it from me. "Which property does it relate to?"

"Sweetbriar Avenue."

Her perfectly waxed brows lifted in question. "The tenants finally paid their rent?"

"If only," I said. "It's a cashier's check for earnest money. I'm buying the house."

"Wait." Those perfect brows now angled inward, perplexed. "Are you saying Mr. Dunaway is selling the property?"

"Yes. The tenants trashed it. He doesn't want to fool with repairs."

"And he offered it to *you*?"

"Yes."

The twitch about her eyes told me she was irritated that her boss had left her out of the loop. Her mouth then said it outright. "He knows I want to learn the business, that I want to start investing in real estate. Why didn't he offer it to *me*?"

I wasn't sure if she expected a response or whether the question was rhetorical, and I felt a little bad suggesting a possible answer, but I hoped it might make her feel better. "I don't know what he pays you, Presley," I said, though I was pretty sure it wasn't near what she was worth given her dedication. "But maybe he assumed you couldn't afford it. It's in an expensive area."

She reluctantly, and resentfully, acquiesced. "You've got a point. I don't stay in this job for the money. I'm doing it for the experience, trying to learn a thing or two before I venture into the market." She tilted her head and eyed me. "I know what we pay Home and Hearth, and it's not much. How can *you* afford the house?"

"Only because I still live with my parents."

She snickered, but I couldn't much blame her. My living situation was a little pathetic. There was no denying it.

"Thanks, Presley," I said as I turned to go. "Have a good day."

She didn't return the sentiment, but at least she gave me a nod.

I spent the rest of the day dealing with tenant repair requests, processing rent checks, and reviewing applications for prospective tenants. In between my usual property management duties, I gathered paperwork to start the mortgage process and called in favors from contractors with whom I'd done business over the years. By the end of the day, I had commitments from a plumber and a window guy. Buck and I could refinish the floors again ourselves. We could repair the drywall, replace the closet doors, and handle the painting, too.

At two minutes before five, the loan officer called.

"How's the paperwork look?" I asked. "Do you have good news for me?"

"Your down payment is sufficient," the woman said, "but the underwriter is concerned about your ability to make the monthly payments given your limited income."

"I'll only need to make one or two payments before the loan will be paid off," I reminded her. "The house will be sold as soon as we finish fixing it up."

"Even so," she replied, "houses don't always sell as quickly as expected. The underwriter won't issue the loan without a cosigner. Got anyone who'd be willing to be on the hook?"

Buck would do it, wouldn't he? Sure. *In for a penny, in for a pound.* "My cousin Buck plans to help me with the renovations. I'm sure he'd cosign."

"All righty. He'll need to provide the same documentation and information you gave me."

"I'll call him right away." I had to. The twenty-four hours Rick Dunaway had given me would be up by midmorning. No way would I let Thaddeus Gentry steal the Sweetbriar house from me.

As soon as we ended the call, I phoned Buck. As expected, he agreed to cosign the loan. Although he owned three wooded acres north of Nashville, his payments on the land and single-wide trailer he called home were easily affordable on a skilled carpenter's income. I gave him the loan officer's e-mail address. "Thanks, Buck. I don't know what I'd do without you."

"Neither do I," he teased before hanging up.

My mind spun like a socket wrench. With any luck, this venture could be the first of many. Dare I dream I could become a professional house flipper?

CHAPTER 5

QUITTING TIME

SAWDUST

Sawdust sat on the floor, staring out the French doors. He couldn't read a clock, but the fact that it was now dark outside told the cat that Whitney should be home by now. *So where is she?*

If she didn't get home soon, she wouldn't be able to protect Sawdust from the terrifying demon that came to life early each evening and made its way across the floor, searching for prey.

Across the backyard, Sawdust could see Whitney's parents inside their lighted kitchen, eating dinner. Whitney's mom sipped that dark liquid she liked so much. He'd sniffed at her glass once while visiting and the stuff made his nose crinkle. Humans drank and ate some pretty yucky things in his opinion. That red swill. Bananas. Sauerkraut. Of course some of the things they ate and drank weren't so bad. Rice. Cereal. Whitney had left a stick of butter out on the kitchen counter once and Sawdust had licked that. Butter tasted good.

From the back corner where the demon hibernated

came a telltale sound. *Whirrr.* Sawdust bolted across the floor, leaped up onto his cat tree, and scrabbled to the highest perch, putting as much distance as possible between him and the demon as it blindly went about its hunt. He crouched and trembled on the platform. *Where are you, Whitney? Please come home!*

CHAPTER 6

DEAL OR NO DEAL?

WHITNEY

Sawdust met me at the door, mewing and mewling and stretching up on my leg as if he thought I'd abandoned him. "Sorry I'm late." I bent down to scoop him up in my arms and placed a soft kiss on his cheek. "Did you miss me as much as I missed you?"

He rubbed his head on my chin, telling me that yes, my absence had been pure torture for him. Or perhaps I was just flattering myself.

"How about a tuna treat?" I asked, reaching for the canister on the counter.

The cat issued an excited chirp. After hand-feeding him a treat, I set about making my own dinner, a gourmet peanut butter sandwich.

I'd just settled into my recliner to watch the late news when my phone buzzed with an incoming call from Rick Dunaway. Sawdust leaped up into my lap, nearly causing me to spill my mug of hot chocolate as I accepted the call.

"So?" Dunaway asked without preamble. "Are you going to be able to swing the deal on the Sweetbriar house?"

I glanced at the clock. Technically, I had another ten hours before I had to give him an answer, but no sense reminding him of that fact.

"Yes," I told him. "I'll be able to do the deal."

"Good," he said. "Send me the preapproval letter from your mortgage company."

Uh-oh. "I'll have that for you tomorrow."

"Tomorrow? I offered you a fantastic price. I thought you'd got moving on it right away. What's the holdup?"

"I've got the down payment, but the mortgage company wants a cosigner since my income wouldn't be enough to cover the mortgage long term."

"In other words," he snapped, "you might not come through."

I sat up straight, sloshing hot chocolate on my leg with no help from my cat this time. "I'll come through, Mr. Dunaway. I'm a woman of my word. In fact, I've already scheduled the inspection. The guy's coming out at nine in the morning." I fought the urge to tell him we could move even faster if he'd agree to a seller-financed arrangement. *Better not push my luck, huh?*

"Gotta go," he said. "An important call's coming in." With that, he was gone.

Despite Dunaway's doubt, I knew the mortgage would be approved as fast as the loan officer could process the paperwork. Like the inspector, she was a reliable sort.

I set my phone aside and ran a hand down Sawdust's back, igniting his rhythmic, diesel-enginelike purr. *RRRurrr-RRRurrr-RRRurr.* "We're going to get rich, boy. Rich! What do you think of that?"

My cat looked up at me, blinked, and opened his mouth in a wide, fish-scented yawn. He reached up a paw and softly touched my cheek as if to tell me that as long as he had his treats, a cat tree to climb on, and me to love him, he'd be happy, rich or poor.

"You're lucky to be a cat." He didn't have to worry about deadbeat tenants or mortgages or taking the real estate agent's exam. All he had to worry about was rolling over to make sure he was always lying in a sunny spot on the rug. Must be nice to live such a simple life.

At eight thirty the next morning, I turned onto Sweetbriar Avenue. Rather than my business attire, today I sported my paint-spattered denim coveralls and well-worn work boots. Bobby wouldn't be here for another half hour to begin his inspection, but I figured I'd get a jump start on measuring the rooms for the renovations and sanding the wood floors.

As I drew near the house, my eyes spotted Rick Dunaway's silver Mercedes parked in the driveway. At the curb sat Gentry's Infiniti.

"What the heck?" I murmured to myself. *Why are Mr. Dunaway and Thaddeus Gentry here?* There was only one explanation. *Rick Dunaway changed his mind and is going to sell the house to Thad Gentry!*

I braked to a quick stop, sprang from my car, and yanked my toolbox from the cargo bay. I scurried up the porch to find WATCH YOUR BACK followed by the *B*-word scrawled in ballpoint pen on the front door. Jackson's doing, no doubt. I supposed I could call the police, but why take up their valuable time with such a petty crime? Nothing appeared to be permanently damaged, and this could be a one-time thing. Maybe the boy would be satisfied with his little act of revenge and move on. I certainly hoped so.

Stepping inside, I found Dunaway and Gentry in the living room. They stopped talking and looked my way. I plunked my toolbox down on the floor as if staking my claim. *Thunk.* If I were a cat like Sawdust, I'd have raised my tail and sprayed the place, marking it as my territory. My hands reflexively fisted and went to my hips in preparation for the hissy fit I was about to throw. "What's going on?"

Dunaway chuckled. "No need to get worked up, Whitney. I've told Thad the only way he'll own this house is over my dead body."

Gentry grunted. "The place is a dump, Rick. You'll change your tune when things fall through."

Before I could stop my mouth, it snapped, "They won't!"

Gentry tossed me a patronizing look before turning back to Dunaway and talking about me as if I weren't there. "Is she always like this?"

"She can be a spitfire when she needs to be," Dunaway said. "That's why I hired her to manage our residential properties."

Without so much as a good-bye, the two men stepped past me and went outside. I closed and locked the door behind them, the gesture more symbolic than for security. Moving to the windows, I raised them each a few inches to air the remaining beer and boy odors from the room.

I knelt down and opened the latches on my toolbox. *Snap-snap!* From outside came the sound of a car engine. Looked like the men were leaving. *Good.*

Having worked at Home & Hearth for several years, I knew home sales could fall through for any number of reasons and, until all the *i*s were dotted, *t*s crossed, and paperwork signed, this house would not belong to me and Buck. Still, I was too excited about the pending deal to do nothing. It couldn't hurt for me to tackle some of the small, less costly tasks while I was here today. We'd handle the bigger projects once the house was officially ours. And, if the deal fell through, I'd be out nothing more than a few measly bucks and a few hours' time.

I strapped on my knee pads, slid on a pair of canvas work gloves, and knelt down on the floor to start sanding the stained spots with fine-grain sandpaper. I'd been on my hands and knees for a few minutes when a rap sounded at the door.

"Knock-knock, partner!" Buck called to let me know it was him.

I stood and walked over to unlock the door.

He gestured to the expletive scrawled on the door. "What's this?"

I rolled my eyes. "The handiwork of the former tenant. At least that's my guess."

"'Watch your back'?" Buck said, his gaze moving from the words to my face. "That doesn't sound good. You think he's serious? Is this a real threat?"

"Who knows?" I lifted my shoulders. "He could've done a lot more damage here, but he was either too lazy or too cheap to buy a can of spray paint. I can't see him putting much effort into revenge."

"Let's hope you're right." Taking in the pads on my knees and the sandpaper in my hand, Buck said, "You at work already?"

"Figured I might as well make use of this time."

"Good point. Time is money. Best make the most of it."

He stepped inside, tugged a hammer from a loop on his tool belt, and set about removing nails from the walls. I, on the other hand, applied the sandpaper to the front door and rubbed back and forth until all evidence of the nasty threat had been ground into fine dust. Of course some of the paint came off, too, but that was no problem. The door was scuffed and scratched and needed to be repainted anyway.

Colette arrived a few minutes later, when Buck had moved on to the bedrooms. As I let her in, Buck stepped into the hallway and put one arm up on the doorjamb, holding the hammer in the other hand. "Hey, skinny Oprah," he called to Colette. "Long time, no see."

Buck's pet name for my friend was silly but fitting. With her loose curls, brown skin, and broad smile, she resembled the cultural icon, though, as the nickname indicated, my friend was thin rather than curvy. She was over three decades younger than the real Oprah, too.

Colette returned his greeting and jest, giving a nod to Buck's hammer. "Hey, poor man's Thor." Turning back to me, she raised the cardboard tray in her hands. It contained three large coffees. "A little housewarming for the happy homeowners."

I wasn't about to point out that we didn't own the home yet. *Mama needs caffeine.*

She plucked a coffee from the tray and handed it to me. "Vanilla latte."

"You're the best!" I said as I took it from her.

She handed another to Buck. "Black coffee for the purist."

I wasn't surprised my best friend knew how I took my coffee, but she knew how Buck liked his, too? I supposed professional chefs paid attention to people's particular palates.

Buck took the cup and raised it as if in toast. "Just what I needed this mornin'."

Colette pulled her cup from the tray and tucked the cardboard into the tote bag hanging from her shoulder. "Where's the kitchen?"

Buck pointed through the doorway at the back of the room. "That way. Have at it."

Colette blazed a trail through the living room and into

the kitchen. Buck and I followed along behind her. She stopped in the center of the room and looked around, shaking her head at the destruction.

Buck took a swig of his coffee. "You can see why we called you."

While my cousin set about measuring the cabinets and countertops, I picked my friend's brain. "What should we do in here?"

Colette was quiet a moment, her narrowed gaze moving about the space before she walked over to stare down at the oven. "A new gas stove with a decorative vent hood is a must." She turned and ran a hand over the adjacent countertop. "Deeper counters would be a big improvement. That'll increase the space in the lower cabinets, too." Glancing upward, she said, "Glass fronts in a few of the upper cabinets would be a nice touch. You know, for showing off crystal and china." She stepped over to the rust-stained sink. "A wide farmhouse sink would look great. They're handy for rinsing big pots and pans, too. A garden window would be great for growing herbs and letting more light into the room." She turned around from the sink and strode across the empty dining nook, turning around at the wall and squinting into the space. "Is there room to add an island? Maybe a long, narrow one that could be used as a breakfast bar?"

Buck measured from the sink to the wall behind her. "Yup. There's room. Let's do it."

We arranged for Colette to accompany us to the home improvement store after we closed on the house so that she could help us pick out appliances, cabinets, and countertops. As Buck and I walked her to the door, I spotted Bobby's pickup through the living room window. He was right on time to begin his inspection. To my surprise, Rick Dunaway was still outside, too. I'd assumed he'd left when

Thad Gentry had gone earlier. Bobby and Dunaway stood close, engaged in conversation, Dunaway doing most of the talking. A look of concern clouded Bobby's face, but a moment later he gave Dunaway a small nod. Dunaway reached out to give the inspector a friendly pat on the shoulder before climbing into his Mercedes and driving off.

We bade Colette good-bye, and Buck opened and held the door for her. As she went down the porch steps, Bobby came up them, tipping his hat to her. Like me, he arrived carrying a toolbox.

"'Mornin', Bobby." I gave him a smile. "How've ya been?"

"Fair to middlin'," he replied. "That's more than I can say for the Titans. They're having a downright pitiful season."

Forever true to his team, Buck came to their defense. "Can't win 'em all."

"Maybe," Bobby acquiesced, "but they could at least beat the spread once in a while."

Other than presenting an opportunity to gather at home with family, friends, and yummy food, sports weren't really my thing. Still, I had a vague understanding of what a spread was. Some kind of prediction by whoever set gambling odds of how many points the winning team would score over the one that lost.

I introduced Buck and Bobby and the two men shook hands. "My cousin is going in on the house with me," I explained. "We're going to be partners." Moving on to the matter at hand, I said, "I saw you met Rick Dunaway outside."

Bobby dipped his chin in acknowledgment. "He introduced himself."

"Is that all?"

Bobby gestured toward the front door. "He warned me that some of the trim around the eaves might be rotten. Told me to be sure to take a close look."

"Oh." That explained Bobby's expression of concern. But Rick Dunaway was looking out for me? I felt a little guilty about the bad thoughts I'd had about him earlier, especially since he'd offered me such a good deal on the house. "That was nice of him to point it out."

Bobby made an *mmm* sound I took as agreement.

I held up a square of sandpaper. "You don't mind if Buck and I work on the floors while you're checking things out, do you?"

"Go right ahead. I'll get started, too." With that, he set his toolbox on the floor next to mine, retrieved a few tools from it, and got down to the business of inspecting the house.

Over the next few hours, Bobby made the rounds of rooms, checking doors and lights and windows and plumbing and the insulation in the attic. While Buck worked in the back bedroom and I sanded the floor in the hall, Bobby eased around me to get to the bathroom. "That's a nice claw-foot tub."

"Sure is." I could hardly wait until the house was ours so I could take a long soak in it.

He opened the cabinet under the sink. "Uh-oh. Looks like you've got yourself a leak here."

I sat back on my haunches and pushed my hair out of my eyes. "A plumber's coming out to take a look." While Buck, Owen, and I had learned from fellow contractors how to handle simpler tasks like installing drywall, we'd also learned it was best to leave plumbing projects to the professionals. One wrong turn of a wrench and you could find yourself knee-deep in water.

Bobby's phone burst into song, Kenny Rogers's classic "The Gambler." He pulled his phone from his pants pocket, greeted the person on the other end with "Hold on a minute," and eased past me again to head outside and take his call on the front porch. He probably thought going out front would give him some privacy, but with the windows cracked to air out the place, I could hear every word he said. Not that I understood all of those words. He said something about a "teaser" and an "under-over," neither of which meant anything to me. The only thing I knew was that, whatever they were, it was none of my business. Still, when he mentioned the Falcons, the Lions, and the Panthers, my curiosity was piqued. *Is Bobby placing a bet on the weekend's football games? Is that his bookie on the phone?*

A moment later, his tone changed, sounding strained. "I always come through, don't I? I'd hate to think what would happen if I didn't." He chuckled, but it sounded humorless.

What is he talking about? Money?

Bobby ended his call and came back inside, easing past me again to return to the bathroom, where he began testing the faucets.

Four hours later, the worst of the spots on the hardwood floors had been addressed, my elbow and shoulder ached, and Bobby had finished his inspection. He held out a hand to help me up from the floor.

After Buck joined us, Bobby gestured around the house. "There's a few issues, but overall you've got yourselves a solid, well-built house here."

"That was our take, too," I replied. "Glad you've confirmed it."

Bobby led me and Buck around the house, pointing out some of the problems, most of which we were already aware of. Kitchen cabinet doors gone AWOL. Missing doorstops and cracked switch plates in several rooms. Closet doors that had jumped their bent tracks. He pointed to the single smoke alarm, which was positioned on the hall ceiling by the bedrooms. "There's no battery in the smoke detector," he said, "so I wasn't able to test it."

Jackson or his fellow tenants probably removed the battery to use in another device. Then again, a couple of black holes on the wood told me someone had ground out cigarette butts on the floor. Maybe they'd removed the battery to keep the alarm from sounding when they lit up.

"You best get some batteries in the unit," Bobby continued. "I'd recommend getting a couple more smoke alarms, too. You can't ever be too careful."

"True. Anything else?"

He gestured for us to follow him out front, where he pointed out several rotting boards along the eaves. "See this wood?" He poked at a piece of trim with a long Phillips-head screwdriver. The end easily punctured the rotten wood. He pulled it out and used the tool to indicate the entire length of the board. "This whole piece will need to be replaced."

He proceeded to point out several other rotten boards. While replacing the wood would be an additional expense, it shouldn't cost much. Besides, I'd already been thinking about repainting the outside. The white paint the house currently bore was plain. A pale gray would bring out the nuanced tones in the stone and give the place a more elegant look.

Bobby showed us another rotten board out back, and noted that the handrail for the back steps was loose. "That's a safety hazard, but all it needs is to be screwed in tighter at the wall. Maybe add a little epoxy."

Our rounds complete, we returned to the kitchen, where

I made out a check for Bobby's inspection fee. As I handed it to him, I said, "I can't thank you enough for coming out so quickly. I'm really excited about the place."

He cocked his head. "You're not planning to live here, right? Mr. Dunaway said you were going to flip it."

"That's right. But I'm excited anyway. If this goes well, maybe Buck and I can do more flips."

"If you do," he said, "you'll give your favorite inspector a call, won't you?" He shot me a wink.

Chuckling, I said, "I sure will."

I held out my hand to shake Bobby's. Buck did the same.

As we walked Bobby out, he turned to look back over his shoulder. "I'll get your official report written up right away. And don't forget about those smoke alarms."

"I won't," I promised. "I'm planning to buy some supplies at the hardware store this weekend. I'll add them to my list."

"Good. You two take care now."

CHAPTER 7

FACE YOUR DEMONS

SAWDUST

The cat lay in the sunny sliver on the rug, stretched long to soak in what was left of the morning light. It was cold outside today, the glass panes in the door doing little to keep out the frigid temperature. Luckily, Whitney had turned the heater on. The warmth dried out the air and made his nose itch a bit, but it was better than being cold.

He opened one eye, just slightly, to glare at the demon in the back corner. As usual, the demon dozed like the dead during the daytime. It only came to life for twenty terrifying minutes each evening when it scurried about, sucking up crumbs and dust and cat hair for its daily meal. What kind of creep eats dust and cat hair? And if the monster ate cat hair, it would want to eat the rest of the cat, too! The demon looked weird, too. It was round and flat and dark, with no legs or paws. No ears or nose that Sawdust could make out, either. All around its body were short hairs that twitched when it moved. It had one big eye on top, though it kept the eye closed when it wasn't hunting. The demon's mouth was on its underside.

Sawdust was a runt. He knew it. His two siblings had squeezed him out when he tried to suckle from their mother alongside them. He'd had to settle for eating their leftovers once they'd finished. By then, their mother would be tired of being chewed and kneaded on, and would give him only a few quick minutes to get his meal in. He was tired of feeling small and scared. He was tired of the bad way that nasty demon made him feel. Today, he would muster up all the courage he could and check out the demon up close and personal. He opened both eyes. Slowly, quietly, he reached out one paw and rose to a crouch. *Look out, demon. Here I come!*

Slowly he crept, step by step, paw by paw toward the demon, stopping on occasion to make sure the horrific beast hadn't woken from its deep slumber. Sawdust knew that, without legs and paws, the demon couldn't climb. Thank goodness! But if he ended up facing the demon on its turf, the floor, he wasn't sure if he'd survive. Still, he'd had enough of this torment. He was going to get to know this devil monster so that, one day, he could conquer it.

As the cat crept across the floor, he felt his fur rise. Some of it was due to fear, but the rest was static electricity. He had no way of knowing that. He only knew that his fur seemed to have a mind of its own when the heater was running. Sawdust stopped a few feet from the demon to listen. There was no *whirr,* and the monster's eyeball was dark, unseeing. The cat took another step and stopped again. Still no signs of life. The demon was in a deep, deep sleep. He crept forward until he was mere inches from the demon. Bravely, he stretched out his neck to sniff the beast with his tiny pink nose. *ZAP! YOWLLLLL!* The evil demon had shocked him! And it hurt like the dickens!

Sawdust slashed at the beast and scrambled away,

inadvertently performing a backward somersault in his haste. He leaped up onto the bed, and from there onto his cat tree where he curled up into a tight, quivering ball on the upper perch, hoping the demon wouldn't open his single eye and search for the feline who'd dared to interrupt his rest.

CHAPTER 8

DIRTY DEEDS

WHITNEY

As Bobby and Buck returned to their vehicles, my cell phone rang. I didn't recognize the number on my screen, but the area code told me it was local. It could be related to my work for Home & Hearth. I tapped the screen to accept the call and put the phone to my ear. "Hello, this is Whitney."

"Hello, Ms. Whitaker."

The male voice on the other end of the line sounded familiar, but I couldn't quite place it. "Who's calling, please?"

"Thad Gentry."

My entire body went rigid. Thad Gentry was a powerful man. No doubt he was about to pull a power play with me. "What can I do for you, Mr. Gentry?"

"You can sell me that house on Sweetbriar once you own it. I'll pay ten percent over your price. You don't have to do a thing to it. I'll buy it as is."

"Excuse me?"

"You heard me. I know Rick Dunaway's giving you a

special deal. I offered him more than what it's worth and the man wouldn't bite. He's yanking my chain. Needless to say, I don't appreciate that. No point in me trying to negotiate with him when I can put money in your pocket instead."

As nice as easy money sounded, it would not sit well with Mr. Dunaway if I turned around and sold the house to Thad Gentry after Dunaway had refused his offer. Besides, even though I'd yet to wire any funds to the mortgage company, I'd already used up six dollars in sandpaper and felt invested in the house emotionally. My mind had pictured how beautiful it would look after Buck and I fixed it up. I'd already called in favors, made arrangements with other contractors. Of course, our discussions had been preliminary and nothing had yet been finalized. But nope, there was no going back now.

"Sorry, Mr. Gentry. But my answer is no."

"Fifteen percent."

Even at fifteen percent over my price, Gentry would still be getting the house well below market. "Sorry."

"Twenty."

"Look, Mr. Gentry. You could offer me ten times what the house is worth and I'd have to decline. It would put my relationship with Mr. Dunaway at risk." As a businessman, he'd understand that relationships were the key to success and that I couldn't jeopardize things with Mr. Dunaway for some quick money—even if it was *a lot* of quick money.

Gentry was silent for a moment before he spoke again. Unlike the jovial tone he'd used before, his voice now was low and menacing. "You're making a mistake, Ms. Whitaker. One you'll live to regret."

First Jackson and now Thad Gentry. *Why is everyone threatening me lately?* "Mr. Gentry, I—"

There was no point in saying anything else. He'd hung up on me.

I closed my eyes and heaved a loud sigh. This old house was already causing me trouble. *It's not an omen of things to come, is it?*

My phone buzzed again. This time it was the mortgage lender.

"You and Buck are approved!" she sang.

I squealed in delight.

"Even with your cousin cosigning," she said, "it took some convincing on my part to win over the underwriter. But when I mentioned all the business Home and Hearth sends our way, he finally got on board."

Thank goodness. "I appreciate everything you've done."

"Happy I could make it happen," she replied. "The appraiser will be out on Monday.

Let me know which insurance company you're going with. We'll need a quote to determine your escrow and monthly payments."

Escrow? This is really happening, isn't it?!? "I'll get right on it."

The appraiser came by Monday afternoon, and by Tuesday the financing had come through without a hitch. *Woot-woot!* With the great deal Mr. Dunaway was giving me on the house, there was no doubt it would appraise for above the contract price. Buck and I would be on our way to fame and fortune. Well, fortune at least. We'd leave the fame to the Property Brothers and those other folks who hosted home renovation shows on television.

Buck and I met at the title company at eleven on Friday morning to sign the paperwork. Though I'd attended closings before on behalf of Home & Hearth, this was the first time I'd been a party on the paperwork. By the time I'd signed the stack of documents my hand was cramping and a blister had erupted on the inside of my middle finger. Not that it mattered. Given that I worked part-time as a carpenter, my hands weren't dainty and delicate. They were covered in scratches and calluses, but it was a small price to pay for the joy of seeing raw wood evolve into a beautiful bookcase or gazebo.

After making copies of the documentation, the title company's agent returned to the room, gave me and Buck a smile, and handed me our copy of the paperwork. "Happy homeownership."

The deed was right there on top, a formal notice to the world that I, Whitney Whitaker, owned my own little piece of Nashville—along with my cousin, of course. Unable to hide my excitement, I hugged the documents to my chest. "Thanks so much!"

As Buck and I returned to our cars, he said, "I'm free tomorrow. Want to get started?"

"Sure! What time should I expect you? Eight? Nine?"

Buck groaned. "On a Saturday? Are you crazy, Whitless? It's the one day I can sleep in. I'll get there when I get there."

Buck might not be a morning person, but he was a hard worker. Despite his smart comeback, I knew I could count on him to put in a full day's work. We parted with an affectionate fist bump.

While Buck had a carpentry project he needed to work on that afternoon, I had nothing to do for either Whitaker Woodworking or Home & Hearth. I climbed into my car and headed straight to the hardware store to pick up a few small items. Cleaning supplies. A new pair of work gloves to replace the worn pair I'd been using. Batteries and a couple of new smoke detectors, as Bobby had suggested.

The sky grew dark as I swung by the pool house to

change clothes, pick up some tools, and pack some clothes and bedding. I figured I'd stay at the Sweetbriar house while we were fixing it up. Living there would enable me to put more hours into the project and keep an eye on our tools and materials, which were sometimes stolen during the night from unattended job sites. Sawdust could tag along with me. Given how busy my week had been, I'd been gone from home more than usual and I'd missed the little fella. He'd been extra affectionate when I was home, so I suspected he'd missed me, too. Besides, he'd have fun sniffing around the house and checking things out. The small space we lived in didn't provide much opportunity for exploration.

As I gathered up my things, Sawdust climbed into the suitcase I'd left open on the bed and settled in among my shirts and socks and undies. When my robotic vacuum whirred to life, Sawdust howled and hissed and burrowed deeper into the bag until he was hidden from sight.

"It's okay, boy," I told him. "That thing's not going to hurt you." No matter how many times I told him that, he never seemed to believe me.

Rap-rap-rap!

I turned to see my mother at the door. She poked her head inside. "Getting ready for a date?"

I fought the urge to howl and hiss and hide in my suitcase myself. I hadn't had a date in months. Unlike my mother, who thought my life wouldn't be complete unless it had a man in it, I wasn't in any rush to get hitched and felt perfectly content living alone, at least for now. Besides, I had Sawdust to keep me company. "Nope," I replied, doing my best to keep my irritation out of my tone. "No date tonight."

Mom spotted my suitcase and came inside, lifting her

foot as the robotic vacuum made its way past her, sucking up Sawdust's fur and stray toast crumbs. "Why's your suitcase out? Are you finally taking a vacation?"

"I'm moving into the house on Sweetbriar. Just until the work is done. We've left a lot of valuable tools and materials there, and Buck and I figured it was best if I stayed at the place to keep an eye on things. Thieves sometimes hit work sites looking for tools to pawn."

My mother's eyes flashed in alarm. "Thieves? Will you be safe there?"

"Don't worry, Mom. Thieves look for quick and easy targets. If a potential burglar sees my car in the driveway, he'll know someone's at the house and move on. He won't risk getting caught." Or *shot*. This was Tennessee, after all. Lots of people here owned guns. I did, too, though my arsenal included only a caulk gun and a nail gun, nothing that shot actual bullets.

"All right," Mom said on a sigh, clearly not liking my plans but knowing she was powerless to stop her hardheaded, hard-hat-wearing daughter. "Why don't you have dinner with me and Dad before you go? He picked up Indian."

She had my attention now. "Did he get samosas?"

She gave me a patronizing smile. "You know he did."

Dad lured me to dinner with my favorite foods, just like Mom lured her dog and I lured my cat with their favorite treats.

I reached into my suitcase and wrangled Sawdust out from under my clothes. He snagged a bra with his claw on the way out, and I gently removed it. "Come on, boy. I know you don't want to be left here alone with the scary vacuum."

While my parents and I enjoyed our meal, Sawdust and

Yin-Yang played an improvised game of tag, chasing each other around the couch. Sawdust always won because he could fit under the couch and reach out a paw to tag the dog as she galloped by. Of course he kept his claws in. He didn't want to hurt his best friend.

When dinner was over, I put Sawdust into his carrier and loaded him into the car, and drove to the Sweetbriar house. I pulled my SUV into the driveway. Without the porch light on, the walkway was dark and I had to make my way carefully as I carried Sawdust up the path in his plastic carrier.

The woman who'd peeked at me earlier in the week came out her front door. She held a watering can and promptly set about watering the yellow mums on her porch. When she spotted me, she raised a hand to shield her eyes from the glare of her porch light. "Who's over there?" she demanded.

"It's just me!" I called across the dimly lit space. "The property manager."

"Oh. Okay." She lowered her hand. "I noticed you got rid of those pesky boys."

"I hope they didn't cause you too much trouble."

"Too much?" she exclaimed, waving her watering can around. "They were nothing *but* trouble! Always throwing a party, playing their music too loud, cars coming and going at all hours. I called the police on them three times. The big one got into a fistfight with another boy right there in the front yard a while back. Had to turn my hose on them like stray tomcats."

"Those days are over," I assured her. "I bought the house."

"We'll be neighbors, then."

"Actually, no," I told her. "My cousin and I plan to fix the place up and resell it."

She wagged a finger at me. "Make sure you sell it to someone quiet."

"I'll do my best." Given that I'd likely see this woman again over the next few weeks, I figured we might as well get on a first-name basis. "I'm Whitney, by the way." I lifted the carrier. "This is Sawdust."

"Patty," she replied.

"Nice to know you, Patty." With a nod in good-bye, my cat and I went inside, the knocker ring swinging with the motion of the door to issue a soft metallic *tap* behind me. I promptly turned on the porch light.

After releasing Sawdust from his carrier, I set up water and kibble bowls in the kitchen, and a litter box in the bathroom. As I situated his things, he puttered around the place, sniffing along the floor and walls and climbing inside the lower cabinets to check them out, performing his own inspection that was nearly as thorough as the inspection Bobby had completed.

After lugging my things into the house, I retrieved the aluminum WHITAKER WOODWORKING sign from my SUV and rounded up my dead blow hammer from my toolbox. The signs were effective advertising, often generating new jobs from the client's neighbors, who'd come by to take a look at our work. We Whitakers took great pride in our projects, using only real woods, no fiberboard, and paying great attention to the details. We also guaranteed our work, both materials and craftsmanship. To date, not a single client had needed to put that guarantee to the test.

Tucking the hammer under my arm, I positioned the sign near the curb, where it would be the most visible. I pushed down, easing the metal legs into the hard-packed soil. I put my foot on the crossbar and used my body weight to force it down a couple more inches. When I'd done as much as I could with my human force, I tapped each end of the sign with the dead blow hammer to better secure it. With any luck, another sign would take its place soon, one that read:

FOR SALE
HOME & HEARTH REALTY
WHITNEY WHITAKER, AGENT

Back inside, I performed a detailed cleaning. I dusted the windowsills, scrubbed the claw-foot tub and disinfected the bathroom fixtures, wiped down the walls and doors to remove grime and fingerprints. The final task of the day was replacing the battery in the existing smoke alarm and installing the new ones. I positioned the stepstool under the existing smoke detector, reached up to remove the plastic plate, and attached the nine-volt battery to the prongs. After pressing the battery into place, I replaced the cover. The green light came on, indicating the unit was functional. Still it couldn't hurt to test the device, right? I pressed the button. *BEEP-BEEP-BEEP!*

Sawdust, who'd been snoozing atop a canvas tarp, woke with a howl and took off like a rocket into the back bedroom.

"Sorry, boy!" I called after him. *I should've covered his ears.* I climbed down from the stool and closed the door to the back bedroom. The alarm had scared the poor cat half to death, but at least he'd be safe in the closet while I installed the new detectors.

I attached the first of the new detectors to the kitchen ceiling, far enough away from the stove that it wouldn't be set off by everyday cooking. After inserting a fresh battery, I pushed the button to make sure it was working.

BEEP-BEEP-BEEP! I screwed the second device into place in the living room and jabbed the button to give it a quick test. Like the other, it beeped loud and clear. Finished, I hopped down from the stool, folded it up, and leaned it against the wall. Finally, I could get into the tub and take that nice, long soak I'd been looking forward to.

CHAPTER 9

FRAIDY-CAT

SAWDUST

The cat didn't think anything could be more frightening than the fur-eating floor demon that terrorized the pool house every afternoon, but that earsplitting sound from the ceiling demon had been even worse because he hadn't known it was coming. At least the fur-eating demon warned him with a *whirr* before it set out on its daily search-and-destroy mission.

Sawdust cowered in the back of the closet with his head down and his paws over his head, hiding from that horrifying, screeching monster. He hoped he'd never, ever hear its screams again.

CHAPTER 10

HOT PROPERTY

WHITNEY

Now that I'd finished installing the alarms, I opened the back bedroom door and switched on the light. The bulb flickered on and off. *Is the bulb loose?* I rounded up my stepstool and stood on it to check that the bulb was screwed in tight. It was. *Hmm.* It must be near the end of its life and making its last gasp. I made a mental note to buy new bulbs. The last thing I wanted was a potential buyer thinking the fixture was defective or the house was haunted.

I rounded up Sawdust from the closet, and attempted to console the frightened feline with murmurs of reassurance. "It's okay, boy. That noise was scary, but it could save someone's life."

The cat wasn't convinced. He tucked his head into my armpit as if to shut out the world. I carried him out of the room, switching off the light as I went. It had been a grueling few days and every muscle in my body ached.

I set Sawdust down and gathered up my pajamas, a cute set in baby blue with rubber duckies printed on them. They'd come with a pair of bright yellow duck-face slippers and a matching robe, which I hung on the back of the door. I couldn't resist the set when I'd come across it online. I started the tap and poured a capful of lavender bubble bath into the tub, draping a folded towel across the back of the tub to serve as a pillow. In minutes, I'd settled into the warm, welcoming water, my tired muscles crying *Hallelujah!* I placed my phone on the floor next to the tub and slid my earbuds into my ears to listen to the latest audiobook I'd downloaded, a lighthearted romantic comedy. Sawdust stood on his hind legs and peeked over the edge of the tub, reaching in to scoop up the scented bubbles and flicking them from his paw.

I closed my tired eyes, listened as the hero helplessly flubbed his first attempt to woo the heroine, and the next thing I knew, I woke to a pitch-black room, a tepid bath, and a piercing sound. *BEEP-BEEP-BEEP!*

What is that? my sleep-fuzzy brain wondered. *My phone? And hadn't I left the light on when I'd climbed into the tub?* I reached over the side of the tub to feel around for my phone, only to realize that the sound wasn't coming from the device.

BEEP-BEEP-BEEP!

Wait. Do I smell smoke?

I sat bolt upright in the water, splashing some over the edge and onto the floor where it landed with a *splat*. I leveraged myself up and out of the tub, slipping on the wet floor in the darkness, haphazardly sliding across the bathroom like a klutz learning to ice skate. When a foot found my duck slippers, I dropped to the floor on my bare behind, grabbed the slippers, and yanked them onto my wet feet.

BEEP-BEEP-BEEP!

My eyes had adjusted to the darkness enough for me to

see the door was open a few inches, enough to have allowed Sawdust to escape. I stood, grabbed my robe from the hook on the back of the door, and slid it on as fast as I could.

I whipped the door open and called for the cat. "Sawdust?" Big mistake. A cloud of smoke billowed into my face. I gasped in terror, which only sucked the filthy air into my lungs and made things worse. My lungs attempted to reject the bad air, causing me to cough and hack as I desperately called out for my cat. "Sawdust?" *Cough-cough.* "Where are you? Come to Mommy!"

BEEP-BEEP-BEEP!

There was a fire in the house, but I couldn't tell where. Unlike the movies, which show burning buildings lit by bright flames, this fire, wherever it was, was obscured behind a dense cloud of black smoke.

"Sawdust?" I cried again, again devolving into a hacking cough.

BEEP-BEEP-BEEP!

Unsatisfied with merely invading my lungs, the smoke claimed my eyes, too. They burned and watered, the involuntary tears no match for the smoke. The fire must be spreading fast. I had to get out of the house right away. But I wasn't about to leave without my precious cat.

"Sawdust!" I shrieked, unable to control my tone even though I knew my panicked voice would only frighten him more. "Where are you?"

BEEP-BEEP-BEEP!

How was I going to find my cat if I couldn't see?

My scrambled brain told me to look for him where he'd run the last time the alarm had gone off. Putting my hand on the wall, I felt my way into the small bedroom at the back, the bedroom where the light had been flickering.

The smoke was even thicker here. I could feel it billowing against my skin, feel my brain begin to fuzz from lack of oxygen. If I passed out, not only would I die, but Sawdust would, too.

I can't let that happen!

As my lungs coughed up smoke, my mind coughed up a tidbit from some long-ago fire safety course in elementary school. *Smoke rises. Stay low.* I fell to my knees and crawled toward the closet. Had I closed the doors earlier? If so, that meant Sawdust wouldn't have been able to get into the closet to hide and that he could be anywhere in the house.

BEEP-BEEP-BEEP!

I crawled several feet and reached out a hand. The right closet door was closed. *Oh, no!*

I felt along until my fingers reached the inside edge of the door. *Would I find the left door closed, too?*

When my hand moved into an empty gap, I knew the left door was open. *Thank the stars!*

I crawled forward and—*BAM!*—promptly smashed my face against the door. Looked like it had only been open a few inches.

BEEP-BEEP-BEEP!

I swept the door open and reached my arm into the closet to feel around.

Nothing.

Nothing.

Nothing.

Fur!

CHAPTER II

CRY OF THE DEMONS

SAWDUST

BEEP-BEEP-BEEP!

Sawdust could see nothing through the smoke, but he could hear the ceiling demons' piercing war cry. He hunkered down in the corner of the closet, shrinking back, trying to make himself as small as he could.

BEEP-BEEP-BEEP!

Though he could see nothing, he heard an odd sound coming toward him. It wasn't quite footsteps, but similar. *Had the demons grown paws? Were they coming for him now?* The smoke made it impossible for him to see or smell, and he had only his ears to rely on. He pricked them up as high as he could. Out of the smoke came something unseen, something that grabbed him in its cold, wet clutches. *It's got me!*

Sawdust whipped out his claws like little switchblades, ready to slash at the demon. But it had him by the middle and, no matter how hard he squirmed, he couldn't get into position to swipe at the beast. He did the only other thing he could. He bit into the demon's flesh with all the force his fangs could muster.

CHAPTER 12

SMOKE SIGNALS

WHITNEY

In his terror, Sawdust sank his fangs into my hand. The puncture wounds would probably hurt like the dickens later—*assuming I survived the fire, that is*—but, thanks to approximately fifty gallons of adrenaline flowing through me, I felt no pain at the moment. I clutched the cat in my grip, thankful the runt was small enough to be grabbed by one hand, and pulled him to my chest. He hissed and spat and wriggled like his life depended on it. Ironic when, in actuality, his life depended on me keeping hold of him.

Keeping low, I crawled out of the bedroom, through the small hallway, and into the living room. Fortunately, I bumped into Sawdust's carrier along the way. I pushed it along until it banged into what I hoped was the front door.

I stretched my hand up to feel around for the dead bolt. The windowsill told me I was several feet to the right of where I'd thought I was. Luckily, though, I was able to feel my way along the ledge and reach out until I found the door hinges. I felt for the dead bolt and turned it.

Click.

That sound is the sound of life.

Grabbing the doorknob, I turned it and pulled the door open. The porch light was out, too. I fell across the dark threshold, still clutching Sawdust to me. At least he'd stopped struggling, seeming to realize now that it was me who'd grabbed him out of the closet and that I was his only hope. Reaching back into the house, I felt for the handle of the carrier and dragged it out behind me.

On the porch, I opened Sawdust's carrier and shoved him safely inside. Smoke poured out the open door behind me. I slammed it closed, remembering that oxygen feeds a fire. This one could starve to death as far as I was concerned.

The night was cold, but like Sawdust's bite, I scarcely felt it. Putting a hand to the porch rail, I pulled myself to a stand, grabbed the carrier, and tripped my way down the steps.

Now that we were out of the house, I needed to call 911. But with my cell phone inside the burning house, I'd have to find another phone to use. I ran next door, jostling poor Sawdust around in his cage as I went.

I banged on Patty's door so hard it was a wonder I didn't break every bone in my hand.

Bang-bang-bang!

"Help!" I screamed. "My house is on fire! Help!"

Why was Patty always watching my house, except when I needed her to be?

Bang-bang-bang!

"Help!"

Seeing the lighted doorbell, I tried that, too, pushing the button in such rapid succession the *dongs* never got a chance to follow the *dings. Ding-ding-ding-ding-ding!*

"Help!" I hollered again. "Call 911! My house is on fire!"

Patty finally opened the door, wearing a flannel nightgown and a startled expression. "What's wrong?"

I gestured frantically with my free hand. "The house!" I cried. "It's on fire! We need to call the fire department!"

She glanced over at my house. Flames had erupted from the roof over the back bedroom. If only it was a big birthday candle, then I could blow it out and make a wish. *I'd wish that the fire had never started.*

On seeing the flames, Patty shrieked. "Oh, my!" Leaving her door ajar, she turned and ran through her den for the landline on her end table, jabbing at the buttons on the cordless receiver. "The house next door is on fire!" she cried into the phone. "Send help! Quick!"

With my neighbor summoning first responders, I ran back down her steps, once again tossing Sawdust around in his carrier. I dropped the carrier on Patty's lawn and grabbed her hose, turning the faucet until it could turn no more. I ran back to my burning house, yanking the hose along behind me.

I aimed the stream into the air, but there was no nozzle attachment on the end and all I managed to do was douse myself. Putting my thumb to the end, I created more force and sent a streaming arc of water up to the roof. By then the flames had spread, engulfing what had been the smallest bedroom. The single stream of water was powerless against the inferno. All I could do was stand there, hopeless, blinking my eyes against the acrid smoke and coughing to clear my lungs as the house I'd had so much hope for made the same noises as a bowl of Rice Crispies.

Snap.

Crackle.

Pop.

Within minutes, several of the street's residents had joined me outside with their hoses. But instead of aiming the water at my house, they wetted down their own roofs to keep stray embers from taking their houses down, too. I supposed I couldn't blame them. Besides, from the looks of it, my house was already a goner.

WOOOOOOOO!

The wail of the fire truck grew louder as the vehicle turned onto the street and approached the house. I dropped the hose and raised a hand to wave to them, though with flames shooting from the roof they'd have an easy time spotting which structure was in need of their services. It wasn't until then that I noticed the blood oozing from the puncture wounds on my right hand. I pulled the sleeve of my rubber-ducky robe down over the wound and applied pressure to stanch the bleeding.

The truck braked to a stop in front of the house. A broad-shouldered firefighter in a hard hat threw open the passenger door and hopped out, while several others emerged from the truck and swarmed like bees across the lawn.

"Is anyone in the house?" he demanded as he approached me.

I wrapped my hands around myself, embarrassed by my wet and whimsical attire. A duck smiled up at me from my sleeve. If I didn't know better, I'd think the bird was laughing at me. "No," I told the fireman. "My cat and I escaped. We were the only ones inside."

"Good." He whipped out a radio. "Any idea what caused the fire?"

I shook my head.

"Is there anything unusual inside the house?" he asked.

"Any chemicals or gases? Anything flammable or explosive?"

"No." Buck and I had moved the leftover paint into the attached garage, and none of the cleaners I'd been using were flammable.

The guy pushed a button on his radio and spoke into it, informing the other firefighters that they were good to go. In seconds, they had a much bigger stream of water aimed at the house, courtesy of the fire hydrant at the curb two houses down.

A female firefighter wrestled an axe from the truck and glanced over at me, noting me pressing on my hand. "Are you injured? Do you need medical assistance?"

"My cat bit me when I grabbed him." Feeling the need to apologize for Sawdust's bad behavior, I added, "He was scared to death. But I'm okay."

She gave me a nod and dashed off with the axe.

I retrieved Sawdust's carrier and made my way across the street to get out of the way of the firefighters. Alerted by the earlier sound of the siren and the shouts among the first responders, more of the residents had ventured out and we huddled together to watch.

Did I leave a candle burning? No, I hadn't lit a candle while soaking in the tub.

Had I left a tool plugged in? One that might have overheated? I had my doubts. All of my tools were in good working order and I didn't remember plugging any of them into an outlet. Besides, the tools were in the living room and the flames seemed to be concentrated in the small bedroom at the back left corner of the house.

Could that flickering light have had something to do with it?

Of course the cause of the fire wasn't the only question running through my mind. Many others were, too. *Will the house be a total loss? If not, how long will it take to repair the damage? Would Buck and I manage to make the mortgage payments in the meantime? Will the fire impact the resale value?*

I knew I'd have to give Buck the news, but I saw no point in ruining his night. He'd learn about the fire soon enough tomorrow. Besides, there wasn't anything either of us could do about it for the moment.

As the firefighters extinguished the fire, leaving only smoldering remains, my neighbors ventured back to their homes. Satisfied there'd be no flare-ups, the firefighters packed up and returned to their truck.

I stepped over to thank them. Putting out fires might be their job, but they risked their lives and safety doing it. "Thanks to all of you. I appreciate what you've done to save the house."

"Happy to help." The driver opened his door, but before climbing back up into the truck, he said, "The department will send out an inspector tomorrow to take a look, see if the cause can be determined."

Good. Maybe the fire inspector could discover what had gone wrong. Houses don't just go up in flames for no reason.

I wanted to know what that reason was.

CHAPTER 13

BETTER THE DEVIL YOU KNOW

SAWDUST

Even though there'd been three of them—*a pack*—the ceiling demons didn't move about. And after that first time they'd made noise, they'd been absolutely silent, content to simply keep an eye on the world with their single eye. Sawdust had decided that the ceiling demons were far less scary than the floor demon.

Until tonight.

Tonight they'd somehow filled the house with dark, choking air as they screeched their hunting cries. *Thank goodness Whitney had found him before the demons did!* He felt bad for biting her. He didn't realize it was her hand that had seized him. Not until he bit into her anyway. But he knew she'd forgive him.

He and Whitney were back in their small house now. The floor demon lay quietly in the corner. Sawdust eyed the beast, pulling back his lip to show off his fangs. *I'm not scared of you anymore. I've faced much worse and survived.*

CHAPTER 14

A FLICKER OF RECOGNITION

WHITNEY

I tossed and turned in bed for what remained of the night. Not only was I worked up about the fire and what it might mean for Buck and me, but the hand Sawdust had bitten began to throb and feel hot. Not a good sign.

Did that flickering light have something to do with the fire? Jackson, the former tenant, had threatened me. *Was the fire his doing?*

When the sun came up Saturday morning, I dragged myself from the bed and forced myself to face the day. I reached down to run a hand over Sawdust and gasped. My hand had swollen to half again its usual size and looked like an oddly shaped potato. But there was no time to deal with it now. The fire inspector was due at the house in just over an hour.

After taking a shower and getting dressed, I walked across the backyard and let myself into my parent's house to use their phone. The pool house didn't have a landline and my cell phone had disappeared last night. A fireman had brought my wet purse to me once the fire was out, so at least I'd been able to get my keys and drive back here.

My mother looked up from the kitchen table, where she sat with Yin-Yang on her lap. She held a mug in one hand and stroked the adorable bug-eyed dog with the other. She cocked her head, confused. "I thought you went to stay at your new property last night."

My father stood at the stove, flipping pancakes. Before I could respond to my mother, he asked, "Can I interest you in some breakfast?"

"No, thanks," I told him. "I'm not hungry." The anxiety twisting my insides made it impossible for me to have an appetite this morning.

"Have some coffee, at least," Mom said.

"Can you put it in a travel mug? I've got to get going."

"Anything for you, dear." She set the dog on the floor and rounded up a plastic to-go cup. "What time did you come back last night? Your car wasn't here when we went to bed at ten."

"Two or so," I told her.

"Two?" She paused, holding the coffeepot aloft, her face drawn in concern.

Dad likewise looked over at me. "What were you doing out so late?"

"Nothing much," I said. "Just fleeing a burning building."

"What?!?" Rather than pour the coffee, my mother set the carafe back down.

Dad turned off the burner and rushed over.

As the enormity of the situation struck me, warm tears welled up in my eyes. I supposed until then I'd been in shock. "The house that B-B-Buck and I bought," I blubbered, breaking down into a sob. "It c-c-caught fire!"

My mother's mouth fell open. She stepped forward and

enveloped me in her arms. My father, in turn, enveloped both of us in his. With my head resting on my mother's shoulder, I told them the whole story. How the fire alarms woke me from my bath. How Sawdust had run off and how I'd had to crawl through the smoke to find him. How I'd left my cell phone behind in the house and had to run next door and ask the neighbor to call 911.

Mom stroked my hair like she'd been stroking the dog's minutes earlier. "Oh, honey," she murmured. "Oh, honey."

Dad released us and pushed me back to arm's length, looking me up and down "Are you all right?"

"I'm okay," I reassured him. "So is Sawdust. But the house will need a lot of work."

Mom tried to console me. "Well, maybe it won't add too much to the cost of the renovations you were already planning."

I snagged a napkin from the holder on the counter and dabbed at my eyes, trying not to smear my mascara.

Remembering what she'd been doing before I'd dropped this bomb on her, my mother retrieved the coffeepot. "What caused the fire?" she asked as she filled the travel mug.

"I have no idea. I guess I'll find out when the fire inspector comes out this morning." I took the warm cup from her.

Alarm sparked in her eyes when she saw my wounded hand. She reached out, but stopped herself before touching it, seeming to realize the contact might cause me pain. "You're not all right. You're hurt!"

Dad rushed over to take a closer look.

"It's nothing," I said. "Sawdust bit me is all. He was terrified by the smoke alarms."

"Poor thing." She sighed. "That bite looks awful, though."

"Sure does," Dad agreed. "I'm calling in a prescription for you." Dad pulled his cell phone from his pocket to call the pharmacy. He was an ear, throat, and nose specialist, not exactly the kind of doctor a person thought of when they had an injured hand. Nonetheless, he had seen minor, routine injuries like this when doing his rotations back in medical school. Besides, even without medical training, I knew a round of antibiotics should clear things up.

"Can I use your landline?" I asked my mother.

"Of course." Mom retrieved the receiver from the cradle on the wall and handed it to me.

The first person I called was Buck. He answered with a groan. Clearly, I'd woken him.

"Any chance you can meet me at our house at nine?"

His voice was raspy with sleep and his tone was suspicious. "Why?"

"There was a small fire at the house last night." Calling last night's conflagration a "small fire" was a total understatement if not a downright lie, but I didn't want him to get freaked out and rush over, risk an accident on the road.

"Unbelievable," he snapped. "We own the house a matter of hours and already there's a problem."

Guilt joined the anxiety puckering my gut. "It's nothing that can't be fixed," I replied. At least that part was true.

As I ended the call and turned to go, my mother put her arms around me a final time and whispered into my hair. "I don't even want to think—" She stopped herself and released me. "I'm not going to let my mind go there." She fluttered her hand. "You go on now. Shoo." She turned away, but not before I saw her eyes grow misty, too.

"Pick up your pills as soon as they're ready," Dad said. "Take the first one right away."

"I will," I promised, giving him a peck on the cheek.

After dropping a couple dozen doughnuts at the station as a thanks to the firefighters, I drove to the house and waited outside as I'd been instructed. The worst of the damage was on the back slope of the roof, but the front bore telltale signs of last night's events, too. Ruts appeared here and there in the lawn. The WHITAKER WOODWORK-ING sign lay in the yard, dirty and dented. I picked it up and stashed it in the cargo bay of my SUV, trading it for my hard hat.

Buck pulled his van up to the curb, took one look at the house, and shook his head. He climbed out, hard hat in hand, and slammed the door. "I thought you said the fire was small."

"I was only looking out for you. If I'd told you the truth, you'd have driven over here like a bat out of you-know-where."

He frowned, but didn't disagree. He knew I was right.

Just before nine, a large white SUV bearing the fire marshal's logo pulled to the curb, a fortyish, sturdy red-head at the wheel. The inspector climbed out and introduced herself, offering me a handshake and a hard hat.

I gingerly took the handshake but declined the hard hat. "I've got my own," I said, holding it up.

"Me, too," Buck said. "We're carpenters."

"Good." She lifted her chin in acknowledgment. "Then I don't have to explain to you two how dangerous a site like this can be."

After walking the perimeter of the house outside, she ventured inside ahead of us to check things out. She looked up. "The ceiling in the living room looks stable." When she looked down again, she asked, "Where's your furniture?"

I explained that the house had been vacant. "We just bought the place yesterday."

"Yesterday?" She shook her head. "What are the odds a house would burn down the day of a sale?"

I shrugged. The odds were infinitesimally small, yet we hadn't beaten them. "I was planning to sleep here to protect our tools and materials. I'd brought an air mattress."

She nodded and waved us into the foyer. "Wait here until I take a look at the rest of the place."

Buck and I stopped just inside the door. My nose crinkled of its own accord when the lingering smell of smoke hit my olfactory glands.

Buck snorted. "I haven't smelled this much smoke since my last Boy Scout campout."

While the inspector made her way about, my eyes traveled around the room. The soaked blankets and deflated air mattress lay on the floor. All of the drywall would have to be replaced. So would the floorboards. With all the water that had been sprayed into the house last night, much of it still standing on the uneven surface, they'd already begun to warp. On the bright side, if there was one, the wooden window blinds looked intact, at least in the living room. I tried to remind myself that the house had needed a lot of work anyway. A look ahead told me the kitchen was largely untouched. Ditto for the bathroom. *And hey! There's my cell phone!* Surprisingly, it seemed to be working. Looked like those advertisements touting its water-resistant qualities were accurate.

The investigator came out of the largest bedroom and wandered into the smaller one at the front. A few seconds later, she came out and went into the smallest bedroom at the back. "Judging from the amount of damage to this room," she called "the fire started here."

She poked her head into the hall and gestured for me and Buck to come her way, stopping us at the doorway. The upper part of the walls had burned away, leaving only charred studs against a backdrop of ashy stone. The ceiling and roof were gone, too, only jagged edges of the shingles remaining. It was odd to see sunlight pouring into a room from above. The only other time I'd seen something like this was when my mother dragged a seven-year-old me to see ruins in some foreign country. At that age, I'd been unable to appreciate their sense of history and endurance. I'd only wanted to go back to the hotel so I could watch cartoons, even if I couldn't understand the words the characters spoke. The comedy of cats chasing mice was universal, breaking any language barrier.

A trio of birds perched on the edge of the open roof, their heads cocking to and fro as they curiously watched the inspector below. When a garbage truck rattled outside, the three took off in flight, one of them sending a stream of white poop down onto my hat. *Plop.*

As if I haven't been through enough.

Buck eyed the poop, his lip quirking in disgust.

The inspector looked up through the hole in the roof, her expression thoughtful. Being a fire investigator must be difficult. The fires probably destroyed a lot of the evidence.

She pointed upward but turned her gaze on us. "Was there anything in the attic over this room?"

"No," I replied. "The attic was empty, but the light in this room was flickering on and off last night."

"Flickering, huh?" Her brows arched in interest.

"I thought maybe the bulb was loose, so I checked it. It seemed fine. I figured it was about to go out, but I didn't have any replacement bulbs so I left it in and turned the light off."

"Hmm." The woman stepped out into the hallway, whipped a flathead screwdriver from her pocket, and used it to punch through a wet piece of drywall. She reached up with her fingers and pulled the material away, exposing the stud and a couple of ceramic knobs that were attached to its side. Thick wires encircled the knobs and ran up and down the wall, out of sight. She gestured to the knobs with the screwdriver. "You folks know what this is?"

"Not a clue," Buck said.

"Me neither," I added.

She filled us in. "This here is what's called knob-and-tube wiring. It was common in houses like this that were built in the early part of the last century. Don't hardly see it anymore, though. It's an outdated system and can become dangerous as it ages. Plus, there's no ground wire. Most knob-and-tube wiring was replaced years ago. It costs a few thousand dollars to have a house rewired, but that's a small price to pay compared to losing your life."

A small price to most people, but not to a cheapskate like Rick Dunaway. Given that he'd rented the place out rather than living here himself, he hadn't had to worry. Any life lost would not be his own.

I knew from researching the chain of title that there had only been two owners before Buck and I had purchased the place. The original owners had stayed in the house for over sixty years. They'd sold it to Dunaway's firm in the late 1990s. While I could understand how the original owners might never realize their electrical system was deteriorating, the issue should have come up when Dunaway had the house inspected prior to purchasing it.

The rest of me grew as hot as my infected hand.

Dunaway knew the electrical system was a potential problem, didn't he? Bobby should have caught the issue, too, when he inspected the house for me. *He knew, too. He must have!*

I closed my eyes as if doing so could shut out the thought. I didn't want to think it was possible, that anyone could be so reckless with other people's lives. Maybe with the wiring being inside the walls the home inspectors hadn't been able to see it. Maybe I was being too hasty in condemning Dunaway and Bobby. While I didn't trust Dunaway—he was as ruthless a businessman as they come—Bobby had never given me reason not to trust him.

Or had he?

My mind went back to Bobby and Dunaway speaking outside prior to Bobby starting my inspection, and to what Bobby had said to me after completing it. *"I'd recommend getting a couple more smoke alarms, too. You can't ever be too careful."*

He had certainly seemed concerned. But it could be mere coincidence, right?

Gulping down the lump of raw emotion in my throat, I pointed to the knobs and posed a question to the woman. "Would a home inspector be able to tell that a house had knob-and-tube wiring?"

"Any inspector worth his salt could have."

If Bobby was anything, he was worth his salt. But even seasoned inspectors like him could make an innocent mistake, couldn't they? Maybe forget an aspect of an inspection entirely? Perhaps something had distracted him and he'd totally forgotten to take a look at the electrical system.

Buck caught my eye. "I thought that inspector you hired was experienced."

"He is," I insisted. "He must have missed it."

"I don't see how." The woman pointed down to the outlet in the hallway. "See that? These outlets can only accommodate plugs with two prongs, not three. That's a sure sign of knob-and-tube wiring. The only thing you can plug into these outlets is smaller appliances."

I hadn't noticed, probably because I hadn't plugged anything in. No saw. No shop vac. No electric sander. Another day or two and Buck and I might have noticed the outlets, realized the wiring was deficient.

As she headed around the house, we followed after her. She glanced down at the outlets on the kitchen walls, as well as the two along the backsplash for counter appliances. Buck and I performed a quick visual check, too. All of the plugs in the kitchen had three prongs. On closer inspection, we discovered that there was also a three-prong outlet in the living room, in the wall that divided it from the kitchen. The bathroom also had a three-prong outlet.

The inspector frowned. "These outlets tell me that the wiring in the bath and the kitchen walls has been replaced, but the rest of the house was left as is. Mixing things up like that is a really bad idea."

Looked like buying this house had been a really bad idea, too. The sour expression on Buck's face told me he was having the same thought. At least he was nice enough not to say it out loud. He could probably tell how upset I was.

The woman wrapped up her inspection a few minutes later and we walked her back out to her vehicle. "Have your insurance company get in touch with me if they want a copy of the report." With that, she climbed into her car, closed her door, and drove away.

"Call Bobby Palmer," Buck growled. "*Now.* We need to have a conversation."

The conversation would be best done in person. That's the only way I'd be able to gauge the expression on his face and determine whether Bobby had made an honest mistake—*or whether he'd gambled with our lives.*

CHAPTER 15

THAT JUST BURNS ME UP

WHITNEY

Screech!

The sound of tires coming to a sudden stop drew our attention to the street behind us. Buck and I turned to see Bobby's pickup at the curb. He'd made it to the house in record time after I'd called him and informed him about the fire.

Bobby cut the engine, hopped out, and was on the porch in three seconds flat, taking the steps two at a time. His eyes were wide and frantic, his skin red, as if his heart were pumping overtime. As I eyed him, he took a deep breath. Was he trying to calm himself?

"Hello, Bobby," I said.

He removed his ball cap. "How bad is the damage?"

I exhaled sharply. "It's bad, all right."

Buck stepped aside to let Bobby into the house. "Come in and take a look for yourself."

As we stepped inside, the first place Bobby's eyes went was to the ceiling. He pointed up at one of the newly installed detectors. "Good thing you put those smoke alarms up like I told you to."

Was he trying to assuage his guilt, convince himself he'd saved my life rather than risked it? Or was he merely pointing out a fact?

I led him back to the bedroom with the hole in the roof. "The fire inspector said this is where it started."

Bobby looked up at the sky as a plane soared over us thousands of feet above. "Holy moly! The whole roof is gone!"

"You sure have a keen eye," Buck muttered, cutting Bobby a scathing look.

"The fire spread fast," I said. "I was lucky to get out. I had to crawl through the smoke to find my cat. He bolted when the alarm went off."

Bobby grimaced, as if the information personally pained him. *Hmm.*

I held up my potato-hand. "My cat bit me when I grabbed him. It's infected."

His brows formed a deep V of concern.

The three of us backed out of the room and I motioned for Bobby to come stand by me in the hallway. When he did, I pointed to the hole the inspector had made in the drywall, the hole that revealed the knob-and-tube wiring. "That right there? The old wiring? That's what caused the fire."

As Buck and I stared at Bobby, he, in turn, stared at the ceramic knob, a series of expressions contorting his face as he appeared to be struggling with his emotions. Finally, he turned to me. "I feel really bad about this, Whitney. I hope you know that."

Good. You should. At best, he'd performed a shoddy inspection and inadvertently failed to check the electrical system. At worst, he'd purposely misled me about a dangerous, potentially deadly condition in the house. *Which one was the truth?* I figured the best way to find out was to ask.

"Why, exactly, do you feel bad?" I cocked my head and watched him intently.

He frowned. "Because I must have missed this in my inspection, that's why. I looked at the electrical in the kitchen and bath. The garage, too. It's been updated. I assumed things had been updated throughout the house. I thought everything was fine."

Ironically, the level of detail he'd provided made me wonder again if he'd known things were *not* fine, if he had, in fact, performed a thorough inspection of the electrical system and knew precisely which rooms had been updated and which had not.

"Is that really why you feel bad?" I asked. "Because you accidentally botched the inspection? Or is it because you and Rick Dunaway were in cahoots and you intentionally hid the electrical problems from us?"

Rather than crinkling in confusion, his eyes went wide with shock, the kind of look kids get on their face when they were caught with their hand in the cookie jar. Yep, Bobby and Dunaway had cahooted, hadn't they? I'd only suspected it before, but now I felt much more certain. And there would be only one reason Bobby would be in cahoots with Rick Dunaway. *Money.*

My voice came out soft and cracked when I asked, "Why'd you do it, Bobby?"

Bobby gripped his ball cap in his hands, twisting it to and fro. His gaze darted between me and my cousin. Finally, he looked down at the floor and softly said, "I didn't mean for this to happen."

It wasn't an outright admission, but it was darn close. He seemed to realize that he'd made a stupid decision.

How could he have thought he'd get away with it? Didn't he realize that any potential buyer would have had another inspection, and that the second inspector would discover the faults with the wiring? That the buyer would insist we have the system updated before purchasing the house?

"Look, Bobby," I said. "I invested every penny I had in this house. Buck's money is needed for the renovations. Now we're facing an unexpected five-thousand-dollar insurance deductible. The least you could do is pay our deductible since you defrauded us."

"Defrauded you?" On hearing his dirty deed named outright, his face became hard. "I am not a crook!" he snapped. "I don't like what you've insinuated."

"And I don't like what you've *incinerated*." I pointed to the burned roof. "So? You gonna pay the deductible or not?"

Buck crossed his arms over his chest, which made his biceps swell.

Bobby instinctively took a step back. "I don't have that kind of money just lying around."

In other words, he'd already spent what Dunaway had given him.

"What did you do with the money Dunaway paid you?" I asked. "Bet it on a football game?"

His face reddened and he turned away. Looked like I'd hit the nail on the head. When he looked back, he found my angry eyes on him.

"How much did Dunaway pay you?" I demanded. The man had said he liked me, for goodness' sake! That I reminded him of himself. I wanted to know just how much Rick Dunaway had thought my life was worth.

Bobby didn't answer my question. Instead, his face brightened as if a light bulb had illuminated inside his head. "Five grand would be nothing to Rick Dunaway. You should ask him. I'd bet he'd give it to you."

Ironically, betting was just the thing that had likely gotten all of us into this mess. Still, Dunaway's pockets were definitely deeper than Bobby Palmer's. On the other hand, Rick Dunaway was a penny-pinching cheapskate who wouldn't spend a cent if he didn't have to. "Rick Dunaway would be more likely to cough up the five grand if he knew he could get in trouble with the law," I said. "Will you admit that he bought you off? Would you be a witness against him? Sign a statement?"

The frown returned and the virtual light bulb flickered off. Bobby put his hat back on his head. "I'm not admitting anything. How stupid do you think I am?"

Buck snorted. "Do you really want us to answer that question?"

Bobby cut Buck a final glare and stormed out the door, leaving me madder than a wet hen. A wet hen who'd been duped by someone she'd trusted. Bobby Palmer and Rick Dunaway had stolen my nest egg. Maybe it was the fever making me bold, but this wet hen wasn't going to take it lying down.

Buck wasn't, either. "We should sue that man for every cent he's worth."

"That's the problem," I said. "I don't think Bobby's worth much." Heck, from the conversation I'd overheard through the window before, it sounded like he was in debt to his bookie.

Buck and I walked back to the bedroom and looked up once again at the gaping, jagged hole.

Buck grunted. "The fire's going to set us back more than a few dollars. It's going to set us back timewise, too. I was hoping we'd have a contract by Christmas."

"Me, too." Instead, it felt like Santa had left coal in our stockings. Still, as angry as I was with Bobby, we wouldn't be in this situation if Rick Dunaway hadn't offered him a bribe. "If Rick Dunaway thinks he can get away with treating us like this, he's sorely mistaken." My voice rose along with my ire. "He should take out some insurance on his life because I have half a mind to put an end to it!"

Buck cut me a glance that was both amused and surprised. I wasn't a pushover, but I'd never had cause before to threaten someone's life. I hardly recognized myself, either. Being forced to flee a fire and getting only a few minutes' sleep had made me bold, brash, and brazen. *Hell hath no fury like a woman scorched.*

"Take your nail gun," Buck suggested. "A few framing nails in Dunaway's foot might help convince him to give you the five grand."

"Yep, that tool could do the trick." Of course this was all bluster on my part. I wasn't going to physically threaten the guy, though I had to admit the thought was darn tempting. I had to get myself under control before I could get the situation under control.

Could I even do it?

First, I had to come up with the insurance deductible. Repairing the fire damage and replacing the electrical system would add another few weeks to our flipping schedule, and that would mean more mortgage payments we weren't prepared to make. Even if the electrical system was completely updated, would anyone want to buy a house that had recently caught fire? We might have to discount the price to entice someone to take a chance on the place. And if we had to discount the price, that meant we might not make a profit or, worse, that we'd take a loss. *Ugh, ugh, ugh.*

As if the house weren't enough to worry about, I was supposed to take my real estate agent's exam soon, shortly before Thanksgiving. I'd figured a passing grade would give me something special to be thankful for. Between my usual duties and the renovation work, I'd have little time to study. I'd planned to cram over the next few days but, thanks to the fire, I'd be tied up with filing my insurance claim and dealing with an adjuster. The longer it sat there without a roof, the worse things would get. Raccoons or possums might make a home in the exposed attic.

My cousin and I headed outside and parted ways at the curb.

"Let me know how it goes," Buck called before closing his door.

I hopped into my SUV and headed in the opposite direction. After picking up my prescription at the pharmacy, I drove to the fast-food place next door and ordered an iced tea, downing the first of my pills right there in the drive-thru. *Take that, infection!*

Though I was hopped up on sweet tea and antibiotics and ready for a battle, I knew it would be best to check with the Hartleys before making any rash decisions. I called Mr. Hartley's cell phone and filled him in on my suspicions about Bobby and Mr. Dunaway.

"I don't mean to sound like I'm doubting you, Whitney," Mr. Hartley said, "but Bobby's been so reliable all these years. I find it hard to believe he'd put his reputation on the line for a few measly dollars."

"I had the same thought," I told him. "But I also overheard Bobby speaking with someone on his phone the morning of the inspection. He took the call on the porch, but the window was open. Apparently he hadn't noticed. I think he was talking to his bookie. It sounded like he was placing a bet on a football game."

"Well, shucks." Mr. Hartley sighed through the phone. "I wonder if he got himself into some trouble."

"I asked Bobby about it this morning," I said. "He didn't admit anything flat out, but he sure acted squirrelly." I took a deep breath. "In fact, that's why I'm calling. I put every penny I had into that house. I've got nothing left for the insurance deductible. Bobby suggested I speak with Mr. Dunaway, see if he'll cover it. I wanted to clear it with you two before I spoke to him. There's a risk he'll get angry and take his business elsewhere. Do you have any objection?"

I heard muffled voices on the other end of the line as Mr. Hartley filled Mrs. Hartley in.

"You go right ahead. We trust your judgment, Whitney. You've got a good head on your shoulders. If Rick Dunaway paid Bobby Palmer to hide a problem with the house, we wouldn't want him as a client anyway."

I appreciated their vote of confidence.

It was almost noon on Monday when I snatched a ticket from the machine at the entrance to the underground parking garage downtown. I drove in and circled the first level, which was mostly reserved parking for tenants. I passed a Mercedes that looked like Dunaway's. A few spots down in a public spot sat a plain white sedan. It looked like the one that had been parked down the street the day Dunaway had offered me the house. Of course, all white sedans looked pretty much alike. The car was backed into the space. Like the one that had been parked on Sweetbriar, it bore no front license plate. Because the car was backed in, the rear plate was not in view. A sunshade had been erected inside the windshield. Odd, given that the car was parked in a covered underground garage. Then again, the driver probably put the shade up out of habit.

I continued on, having to circle down to the deepest level before finding an available spot. As I rode the elevator up to the eighteenth floor, my stomach churned. I wasn't sure if it was because of my lingering infection or because I was about to confront Rick Dunaway, one of the most powerful men in Nashville. Probably both.

What would Mr. Dunaway say to my accusations? Would he admit that he'd bribed Bobby to falsify the inspection report? Would he fire Home & Hearth and find a new property manager? And even if he didn't, would the Hartleys want to continue to work for someone so lacking in scruples? Would I?

The only questions to which I had answers were the latter two. *No,* and *no.* If he admitted to bribing Bobby Palmer, Home & Hearth's relationship with Rick Dunaway was over.

CHAPTER 16

CHECKS AND BALANCES

WHITNEY

Ding. The elevator stopped on the eighteenth floor and the doors slid open. To my surprise, Rick Dunaway was standing right there in the hall, waiting for the car. Beside him stood Lance Abbot, the other half of Abbot-Dunaway Holdings, the silent partner who'd slid quietly into semi-retirement. Now, instead of working for his money, Mr. Abbot had his money working for him.

I'd seen Mr. Abbot only once before, when I'd come to the office to sign the property management contract all those years ago. Rick Dunaway had briefly introduced the two of us. I recalled my youthful exuberance, how I'd gushed about how wonderful it was to meet him. Mr. Abbot had responded by giving me a bemused smile and a barely perceptible nod in acknowledgment. I also recalled thinking it ironic that, while his last name was undeniably of Anglo-Saxon origin, his nose was one hundred percent Roman, with a pronounced curve and downward-sloping tip. Mr. Abbot had aged a little since then, his white hair a little thinner, the lines around his hazel eyes more pronounced. His nose was just as Roman, though, and he bore the same dignified demeanor I remembered, the kind that spoke of old money and manners and long-gone teenage years attending cotillions.

While I recognized Mr. Abbot, there was no sign of recognition on his part. I supposed I'd been far more impressed with the millionaire real estate mogul than he'd been with the scrappy young woman trying to become self-supporting.

But while Mr. Abbot had no reaction, Dunaway's eyes flashed when they met mine and he jerked back slightly in surprise. He quickly regained his composure and offered a polite smile. "Hello, Whitney. I wasn't told you'd made an appointment."

I put a hand on the elevator door to hold it open. "I didn't. But I need to talk to you."

"I'm sorry," he said, "but Lance and I are on our way out to lunch and my afternoon is fully booked." He hiked a thumb over his shoulder to indicate his office down the hall. "Check with Presley. She has my schedule and can set something up in the next week or so." With that, he attempted to step past me into the car.

"No!" I sidestepped in front of him, putting my right hand up now, too, my limbs forming a human-sized X in the doorway. "There's an urgent matter with the house on Sweetbriar. We need to talk *now*."

Lance Abbot raised a thick brow and looked at Dunaway.

Dunaway chuckled, turning to his partner. "You can see why I hired her to manage our properties. She's got spunk." It was the same thing he'd told Thad Gentry days before. He cut me a look that said, despite the chuckle, he was not feeling jovial. "Let's talk in my office."

As I stepped out of the elevator, Dunaway turned his

attention back to his partner. "I'll meet you at the restaurant in a few minutes, Lance. Have the server bring me a scotch."

Mr. Abbot nodded and stepped into the elevator. The doors slid closed without him uttering a word. He truly was a *silent* partner.

Rick Dunaway and I strode down the hall and into his offices. He pushed the door open and held it for me to enter before him. It was a gentlemanly gesture, and I had to fight the urge to tell him not to bother, that I was on to him, that I knew he was actually a ruthless creep who'd nearly put an end to my life just so he could earn a quick and easy buck.

Presley looked up from her desk, wearing another outfit straight out of a fashion magazine and greeting me with another not-so-warm smile. "Hello, Whitney."

She didn't ask how I was doing, didn't seem to care. I, on the other hand, remembered my manners. "Hi, Presley. How are you?"

"Busy." She swept her hand to indicate the pile of paperwork on her desk. Though she was replying to my question, her focus was on her boss, her response clearly intended as a nudge to Mr. Dunaway, a reminder of everything she did for him. Not that he'd notice or care.

Mr. Dunaway and I proceeded into his corner office. The windows offered a fabulous view of the Cumberland River, downtown Nashville, and the tree-covered hills in the distance. The trees were growing bare as winter approached, but a few orange leaves still hung on and a number of evergreens did their best to keep up appearances. Mr. Dunaway's oversized, hand-carved desk spanned the space between the windows, a credenza and bookcase gracing the walls.

He shut the door behind me. "Take a seat."

I sat down in one of his cushy wing chairs. Unlike the vinyl ones at Home & Hearth, these were real leather, probably from an endangered species.

He dropped into the high-backed rolling chair behind his desk and got right down to business. "What's so important you're making me late for lunch?"

"The house on Sweetbriar caught fire Friday night. With me and my cat in it."

His brows rose and his eyes went wide. "That's terrible!"

While his expression was what one might expect from somebody first learning about a fire, his verbal response was not. Yes, it had been terrible. But wouldn't most people want to know more? What had happened? Whether the cause had been identified? Dunaway, though, asked no questions, as if he already knew the answers.

I narrowed my eyes at him. "Aren't you going to ask me about it?"

He raised his palms again. "What happened? Did you forget something on the stove?"

"No," I replied. "The fire was caused by old, faulty wiring."

"Faulty wiring? Who determined that?"

"An investigator from the fire marshal's office. She said the electrical system had only been partially upgraded and that the older parts had become dangerous."

He was quiet for a brief moment before speaking again. "I can understand your concern, Whitney. But isn't this something you should bring up with your inspector? If the wiring was faulty, he should have discovered that fact when he inspected the house and disclosed it to you."

"I believe he did discover it," I said. "But he hid it from me." I hesitated a moment this time, waiting for Dunaway to ask the obvious question an innocent person would ask. *Why would he hide it from you?* But, again, the question never came. "I also believe you paid him to keep the information from me."

He scoffed. "That's ridiculous." He sat up straight in his chair before leaning forward over his desk, keeping his voice low. "You might want to be careful before you go throwing accusations like that around, Ms. Whitaker. I could sue you for slander."

"And I could sue you for fraud." Unlike him, I didn't keep my voice low. In fact, I raised it. I had no idea what had gotten into me, but whatever it was, it was angry and rabid.

He eyed me intently. "Did your inspector say that I paid him?"

"Not in so many words," I said, "but—"

"But *nothing*," he fired back. "As you know, Abbot-Dunaway Holdings owns seventy-eight residential properties. You think I know all the details about each one? Of course not. I had no idea the wiring was bad. Besides, rewiring the place would have cost a pittance compared to the discount I gave you. Talk about looking a gift horse in the mouth! I had no reason to mislead you about that house. For goodness' sake, I was trying to do you a favor!"

He made a valid point. The discount he'd given me was in the tens of thousands of dollars. Fixing the wiring would have been a cheaper way for him to go, assuming there weren't other defects with the property that I wasn't aware of.

Are there other defects? Or have I made a bunch of assumptions that aren't true?

He stared at me for a moment and seemed to sense I was wavering. I'd never been one who could hide her emotions. *Darn my sincerity!* "I sank all of my money into that house." My voice was feeble and faint. "Even my emergency fund. Insurance isn't going to cover all of the expenses to get things fixed."

Dunaway's face relaxed. "You're upset, so I'll give you a pass on your outlandish accusation. Heck, I'd be willing to cover your deductible if you feel like you got a raw deal."

My gut unclenched for the first time since I'd woken in the tub to a dark room and the beeping of the smoke alarm. "You would?"

"Of course, Whitney. I don't want things to be bad between us. If it takes a few thousand dollars to make things right, I'll do it."

It was a generous gesture, one that made me feel like a real nincompoop. First I'd accused Bobby Palmer of purposely falsifying the inspection report, and then I'd accused Mr. Dunaway of paying him off. I'd been hasty in my rush to judgment, hadn't I? Nonetheless, this hasty nincompoop could use the money. "Thanks, Mr. Dunaway. I'd appreciate that."

"Happy to help. How much is your deductible?"

"Five thousand."

I'd expected him to whip out his checkbook and take care of things on the spot. Instead, he said, "My lawyers will insist on a written agreement. I'll have them draw something up and bring it to you with the check. I've got some business travel the next few days, but I could swing by the house Friday evening around six."

I would have preferred to leave his office with a check today, but it was clear that wasn't going to happen. Men like him didn't do anything without running it by their lawyers first. This was the best I could hope for. "Okay."

The matter resolved, he stood, came around his desk, and opened the door for me. He gave me a nod in good-bye.

I stepped into the doorway and said, "See you Friday at six."

We exited his office to find Mr. Abbot standing by Presley's desk.

Dunaway stopped short. "What are you doing back here, Lance?"

Abbot lifted the black umbrella he held in his left hand and pointed it at the window. Though he'd said nothing, his actions spoke for him. He'd seen the clouds gathering outside and realized he'd forgotten his umbrella in the office. The gathering clouds might have told Mr. Abbot to grab an umbrella, but they had a message for me, too. *Buy an extra-large tarp, and quick!*

CHAPTER 17

ATTITUDE ADJUSTMENT

WHITNEY

After paying the parking attendant, I drove to a home improvement store and parked in a sea of pickups and flatbeds and cargo vans. Pulling out my phone, I placed a call to Bobby Palmer. He'd been the one to suggest I approach Rick Dunaway to recoup my deductible. I supposed it was only right to give him an update, especially now that my suspicions were in doubt. When he answered, I told him that Mr. Dunaway had agreed to cover my deductible. "He's coming to the house Friday night at six to give me a check."

Bobby exhaled in relief, the breath audible over the line. "Good. All's well that ends well, right?" he said with what sounded like forced joviality.

"I'm gonna have to disagree with you there," I told him. "This adds a lot to the work my cousins and I will have to do on the house. The delay means we'll have another mortgage payment or two to make, and we won't be able to take on other projects we'd be paid for. Mr. Dunaway might be covering my deductible, but I'm going to be eating peanut butter sandwiches until the house sells."

"I'll make you a deal," he said. "I'll take you out for a nice meal after the next inspection."

The man must have a screw loose. And if he did, I wasn't willing to tighten it for him. "There's not going to be another inspection, Bobby. Not for me, and not for Home and Hearth."

He exhaled again, but this time it was a huff of indignation. "One minor oversight and you're going to find another inspector?"

His oversight had hardly been minor, and the consequences had been disastrous and nearly deadly. Still, I could understand his reaction. He performed nearly every inspection for Home & Hearth. Without our business, he'd stand to lose around $25,000 a year in fees.

"Sorry, Bobby," I said.

"Sorry's not going to pay my bills!" He hung up without another word.

Ironic how the house that was supposed to produce a nice profit now seemed to be bankrupting everyone involved.

I texted Buck to meet me at the house in a bit. *Rain's coming. We need to get a tarp on that roof.* I slid my phone back into my purse, headed into the home improvement store, and bought the largest tarp they had, as well as several two-by-fours. I knew diddly-squat about roofing, but I'd observed that two-by-fours were often used on roofs to hold temporary covers in place. I also had three extra keys made for the contractors. Finally, I made my way to the garden department, where I bought several bags of soil and three flats of purple pansies. While the inside of the house was a mess, I could focus on the landscaping.

Back at the house, I sat on the porch and called contractors I'd worked with, trying to find someone who'd be able to get to work on the house ASAP, meaning as soon as the insurance company approved the repairs. I was in luck. Winter was the slow season for roofers, and they could come out as soon as Buck and I could replace the framing. An electrician could come out with a team as early as Thursday to start rewiring the place. Both could send representatives out tomorrow morning to prepare estimates while the insurance adjuster would be here. Buck, Owen, and I would handle the drywall and flooring once the others finished their work. More ducks had obediently gotten in the row. *Quack-quack.*

Buck arrived as I ended the call with the electrician. He climbed out of the car, looked up at the roof again, and heaved a fresh sigh. "What have we gotten ourselves into?"

"At least Rick Dunaway agreed to cover our deductible."

"It's hush money," Buck spat. "The stuff of presidents and porn stars."

"We can't be high-and-mighty about it," I replied. "I've got no solid proof they tried to mislead us." Only a sneaking suspicion that I couldn't completely shake.

We pulled the extension ladder from the roof of his van and together carried it to the back of the house where I'd stacked the tarp and two-by-fours. As he finagled the ladder into place, the first scattered raindrops came down.

Buck glanced toward the heavens. "The sky looks like it's about to open up. We best get a move on. Hand me the tarp."

I handed the covering to him and he headed up the ladder while I held the bottom in place. When he reached the top, he climbed off the ladder and onto the roof.

"Be careful up there!" I called. I'd dragged Buck into this. If my cousin got hurt on my account I'd feel horrible.

While I watched from the ground, he shook out the folded blue tarp and spread it over the hole, occasionally disappearing from sight over the slope of the roof. A few minutes later, he peeked over the edge and reached an arm down. "Hand the boards up here."

One by one, I held the two-by-fours up and he took them from me, positioning them across the roof to hold the tarp in place. He finished in the nick of time. Drops of rain began to pelt us. He climbed halfway down the ladder and hopped off, his leap saving him the last few steps. He rushed to collapse the ladder and we each grabbed an end again and scurried to his van to fasten it to the roof.

Darting among the raindrops, we dashed up onto the covered porch and went inside the house, heading to the bedroom to see how things looked from the inside. The tarp cast the room in an eerie blue shadow, but it seemed to be doing its job. No rain was coming through.

Buck gestured to the walls. "We better get the wet drywall out of here before we end up with mold."

He and I retrieved cutters from our toolboxes and set to work, cutting the drywall out. As it piled up, Buck braved the weather and hauled the soggy scraps out to the garage. When we'd removed all the wet drywall, we went back into the bedroom with the damaged roof and evaluated how much wood we'd need to frame it. Buck whipped out his measuring tape and stood on my stepstool to get an estimate, calling numbers down to me. I jotted the information down on the notepad.

When we were done, we locked the place up and headed out.

I was back at the house Tuesday morning, leading an insurance adjuster around the place. He was a dour, diminutive man in his mid-forties with pointy teeth, nose, and ears, like a goblin in wire-framed glasses and a cheap polyester sport coat. He said little as we took the grand tour, mostly grunting and *tsk*ing and *hmm*ing. While I was busy with the adjuster, the electrician and roofer looked about, too, determining how many workers their jobs would require and what would be needed in the way of materials.

The adjuster snapped photo after photo to document the damage. He read over the fire investigator's report and stopped in front of the hole she'd made in the drywall in the hallway. He took several more photos of the knob-and-tube wiring. When he was done, he turned to me. His eyes seemed to be narrowed, but perhaps it was just the rectangular eyeglasses making them appear that way. "There was no mention of knob-and-tube wiring in the report your home inspector sent us before we issued your insurance policy."

"I'm aware of that," I told him. "After the fire investigator mentioned the wiring, I spoke with the inspector and asked him why he didn't note it in his report."

"What did he tell you?"

"That he must have missed it."

The man stared intently at me. "I find that hard to believe."

You're not alone.

The inspector continued. "But what I don't find hard to believe is that a homeowner would mislead her insurance company to get coverage on a house with a dangerous defect."

It took me a few seconds to process the fact that the adjuster was accusing me—*ME!*—of unscrupulous behavior. My mind and mouth refused to cooperate with each other, their connection short-circuiting. "What? *Me? Why . . . ?* You think I would . . . *what*?"

"We see it all the time," he said. "Homeowners slip some cash to an inspector in return for the inspector leaving a known dangerous condition out of the written report. That way, the homeowner won't be refused coverage when something goes wrong."

My spine went perfectly straight. Finally, I had posture my mother would be proud of. "I would *never* do that!"

Though the antibiotics and aspirin had taken care of my fever, the adjuster's accusation reignited me with righteous indignation. I felt as if I were about to self-combust. I prided myself on my hard work and my integrity. How dare this man, who didn't know me at all, make these baseless accusations against me?

"If I'd known there was a problem with the wiring," I said, trying my darnedest to stay calm, "I would've insisted the seller take care of it before I bought the house. I certainly would not have risked my cat's life and my own by sleeping in a house that could go up in smoke." I narrowed my eyes back at him. "Seems to me like you're trying to get out of paying a legitimate claim. That's breach of contract." Stealing Dunaway's tack, I added, "And wrongfully accusing me of insurance fraud? That's slander."

The man and I locked gazes for a long moment, engaging in a stare-down. After a few seconds, my eyes began to water and I had to blink.

He slid his phone into the breast pocket on his jacket. "I'll need to talk with the fire investigator and your home inspector. I'll get back to you."

"You do that," I snapped.

If Bobby Palmer hadn't admitted anything to me, he sure wouldn't admit anything to the insurance company. He could be charged with criminal fraud. But would his denial be enough? Would they pay my claim? Or would I have to hire a lawyer and take the company to court? If so, where would I get the money for a lawyer? *Great. More things to worry about. As if I didn't have enough already.*

The man headed to the front door and, despite how angry he'd made me, I remembered my manners and walked him out. As he drove away, I sat down on the porch steps and put my face in my hands. *How had my dream of fixing up this house become such a nightmare?*

A woman's voice came from my left. "You okay?"

I looked over to see Patty positioning a festive stack of pumpkins on her doorstep, decorating for Thanksgiving. "Not really," I called back. "The insurance adjuster's being difficult." But this would all be sorted out eventually, right? Sure it would. I had to stay positive. I forced a smile and stood. "But I guess that's what they get paid to do, right?"

She frowned. "He better come around quick. That tarp's an eyesore." With that, she went back into her house.

The electrician and roofer gave me their written estimates as they left. I thanked them and snapped photos of the estimates with my phone, forwarding the information to the adjuster. Then I crossed my fingers and said a prayer to the god of home renovation that my claim would be approved, and soon.

I also called Rick Dunaway on his cell phone. While I'd been upset he hadn't issued me a check for the deductible yesterday afternoon, in hindsight it was a good thing he hadn't. Because he hadn't yet paid me, my legal claim against him had not yet been settled. His offer to pay my deductible might no longer be enough. If he didn't up the ante, he risked me and Buck filing a lawsuit against him.

Dunaway answered right away. I took that as a good sign. Usually I found myself routed into his voice-mail system with Dunaway returning my calls at his convenience.

"The adjuster has accused me of misleading the insurance company," I told him. "If the insurance company refuses to pay my claim, I'm going to have to consider other options for coming up with the repair expenses."

"Such as suing me, you mean."

"I didn't say that." I *meant* it, of course, but I hadn't actually *said* it.

"Attorneys can be quite expensive," he replied. "You'd have to pay a retainer up front."

He had to know that if I didn't have the money for the insurance deductible, I wouldn't have it for a lawyer, either. He was manipulating me, trying to make me feel helpless and desperate. But it wasn't going to work. *Not today.*

"Some lawyers take cases on a contingency," I told him. "You're one of the wealthiest men in town. Lawyers would line up for a chance to get into your pockets."

He chuckled. "You're not the woman I thought you were, Whitney."

"Not a pushover, you mean?"

He chuckled again, though the sound was mirthless. "The way I see it, I can either cough up the funds to pay you directly, or I can have one of my attorneys contact your adjuster and encourage him to pay your claim. I say we try option two first."

If his attorney could work things out, I'd take it. "I'd be okay with that."

"What's your adjuster's name and number?" he asked.

I rattled off the goblin's contact information.

"I'll let you know how it goes," Dunaway said, and *click* he was gone.

CHAPTER 18

TOSSED AND TURNED

SAWDUST

Whitney tossed and turned so much that night that Sawdust felt as if he were back in his carrier the night of the fire. Eventually he hopped down from the bed to sleep in the recliner. He wondered why Whitney wasn't sleeping well. Was she afraid the ceiling demon would start screeching? He'd noticed there was one on their ceiling here, too. Unlike the ones in the other house, this one had never made a peep. It seemed to be mute. *Good*.

He jumped up onto the recliner, curled up in the corner of the seat, and closed his eyes.

CHAPTER 19

LOOK WHAT THE CAT DUG UP

WHITNEY

The adjuster phoned me shortly after eight Wednesday morning. I was still in my parents' pool house, finishing my breakfast of cereal and coffee.

"I still have my doubts about your claim," he muttered, "but after hearing from your attorney, we've decided to pay it."

The attorney was Dunaway's, not mine, and my name hadn't been cleared, but as long as the insurance check did I'd be happy. I threw a fist in the air and turned to Sawdust, lying on the top perch of his cat tree. When I held up my palm, he stretched out a paw to give me a high five.

As soon as we ended the call, I phoned the electrician and the roofing company to let them know we could proceed. Of course I still didn't have the deductible Dunaway had agreed to pay me, but the new flooring, drywall, and paint could wait until after he gave me the check Friday night.

The next few days were a flurry of activity. While the

contractors worked at the Sweetbriar house, I performed my usual property management duties and spent the evenings cramming for my real estate exam, boning up on market analysis, land-use regulation, and, ironically, property condition and disclosures. On Thursday, while I was at the Sweetbriar house checking on things, I spotted Jackson coming up the street in his pickup. He slowed as he neared the house. I stepped out from behind my SUV. When he spotted me in the driveway, saw me point at my eyes then at him to let him know I'd seen him, too, he raised his middle finger, floored his gas pedal, and sped off. *What was he doing here? Planning to write another nasty message on the front door?* Maybe I should look into installing a security system at the house.

By Friday afternoon, things were looking up. The roofers had completed their work, and done a great job matching the shingles. If any birds had hoped to nest in the exposed attic, they'd missed their opportunity. The electricians weren't quite done, but they expected to complete the job on Monday or Tuesday. Maybe the fire wouldn't delay us as much as I'd feared.

I arrived at the house at five, pulled an undamaged WHITAKER WOODWORKING sign from my SUV, and retrieved my dead blow mallet from my toolbox inside the house to hammer it into the yard. I'd used permanent marker to write my initials, *W.W.,* on the handle. It prevented confusion as to ownership when I was on a job with my cousins or other contractors and we might be using and sharing similar tools. Good tools didn't come cheap, and while I didn't mind sharing them, I didn't want them walking off inadvertently.

Though it was fairly dark outside given that the sun set early this time of year and I couldn't turn on the porch light without electricity, the streetlight down the road provided just enough illumination for me to see that the pansies were beginning to wilt in their flats. I'd managed to find time to fill the bed with the fresh garden soil, but that's as far as I'd gotten.

I laid the mallet on the porch step to free up my hands and retrieved the garden hose. The electricity might not be working yet, but at least I had water. I turned the faucet until a gentle stream flowed from the end of the hose and gave the thirsty flowers a nice drink. After turning the hose off, I used the flashlight app on my phone to light my way to the door and went into the dark house. Might as well make good use of the next hour until Dunaway arrived.

I rounded up one of the battery-operated lights the electricians had brought with them, turned it on, and took it with me into the kitchen. After closing the blinds for privacy, I situated my real estate exam study guide on the countertop, plunked my rear end down on a tall stepstool, and went over the section on escrow accounts, occasionally checking my phone for the time. While the house had no light, the heat was gas, so though I sat in relative darkness, straining my eyes, at least I wasn't shivering.

I'd moved on to the specifics of time-shares when I realized it was 6:15 and there'd been no sign of Dunaway. *Hmm.* He was a busy man and had probably got hung up with something at the office or one of his commercial properties. Still, if he didn't show in the next ten minutes or so, I'd check in with him. I wanted to sign the settlement agreement, get my check, and move on.

At 6:28, a *thud* from out front drew my attention from my book. *What was that?*

I climbed down from the stool, walked to the front door, and peered out the peephole. With the porch light out, I could see nothing but darkness. I stepped to one of the windows and peeked out through a slat of the blinds. The glass reflected the portable light from the kitchen and again I saw nothing. I supposed I could turn off the light and come back to take another look, but it seemed pointless. Dunaway would knock when he arrived, and that thud had probably only been someone closing a car door down the street.

I returned to my stool in the kitchen and waited impatiently for a few more minutes before dialing Dunaway's cell number. After three rings, the call went to voice mail. "Hi, Mr. Dunaway," I said. "This is Whitney. I'm waiting for you at the Sweetbriar house. You said you'd swing by around six and it's well past the hour by now. Hope to see you soon."

Seven-thirty came, then eight, then eight-thirty. I left him a second message at nine. "I don't know what's kept you, but I'm going to head home now. Call me as soon as you can."

What's keeping him? Why hasn't he returned my calls?

I packed up my things, turned off the portable light, and used my cell phone to light my way out. To my surprise, as I opened the door, a large manila envelope fell into the foyer. It must have been leaning against the door outside.

I picked up the envelope, unclipped the metal brad, and pulled out the contents. Inside was a document entitled "Confidential Settlement Agreement." Rick Dunaway's signature appeared on the final page. The space for my signature was blank. There was also a check in the amount of $5,000 made out to me on the Abbot-Dunaway Holdings, Ltd., account. Rick Dunaway had signed the check, too. There were no instructions, though I suppose it was clear what I needed to do. Sign the contract, make a copy for my records, and return the original to Dunaway. The check, of course, would be deposited in my bank first thing in the morning.

But why had he left the contract and check on my doorstep? It seemed odd that he would leave such a large check. And what if someone had taken the envelope and read over the confidential settlement agreement? It wouldn't be confidential anymore. *Hmm*. Maybe he'd tried the doorbell and, because the electricity was out, it didn't work. But wouldn't a person try the knocker, too? Besides, my car was in the driveway. He had to have known I was here.

A silver Mercedes was parked at the curb between my house and Patty's. *Is that Dunaway's car?* I couldn't be sure. In a nice neighborhood like this, luxury cars were fairly common and, unlike Thaddeus Gentry, Dunaway didn't have identifiable vanity plates.

One way to find out.

I made my way down the walk and circled around the car so as not to startle Mr. Dunaway if he was sitting inside. I needn't have bothered. The car was empty.

I squinted to peer through the driver's window. There was nothing inside that pegged it as Dunaway's car. No business cards in the console. No monogrammed dress shirts in a bag from the dry cleaners.

I stood up and pondered the situation, coming to the only conclusion that seemed to make sense. The car wasn't Dunaway's. He'd swung by the house in a hurry and dropped off the envelope. Probably he had a charity event or some fancy dinner to attend with a business associate. Maybe he didn't knock because he was running late. Or maybe he'd had a local delivery service drop the envelope by and the courier hadn't bothered to ring the bell or knock. I supposed it didn't really matter. All that mattered was that I had my check and could move on.

Saturday dawned bright and sunny, the rain having moved on to other parts of the state. I donned a pair of yoga pants and a sweatshirt for extra warmth under my coveralls, loaded my cat into his carrier, and we were on our way.

Buck planned to sleep in. That would give me time to finish up the flower beds before he arrived. Sawdust would enjoy having some time outdoors. Of course I'd keep him on a harness and leash. Didn't want my precious baby wandering off and getting into trouble.

A half hour later, after making a quick detour by the bank to deposit Dunaway's check, I turned onto Sweetbriar. A small tractor was in the yard of the house on the corner, the one to the right of mine. The Infiniti with the vanity license plates was parked at the curb. Thad Gentry stood behind it, speaking with two men in hard hats. *Why is he here today?*

I eased over to the curb and unrolled my window. "Hello, Mr. Gentry. What's going on?"

He stepped over and leaned in my window. "Just reviewing things with my crew. They'll be grading the lawn and laying asphalt now that the zoning commission approved my plans."

"What plans?"

His mouth curved up in a sinister smile. "I had the property rezoned for commercial use. I'm converting it into a beauty salon."

He had the nerve to bark a laugh when I sucked in an involuntary gasp. "Does Rick Dunaway know about this?" I asked.

"Of course," he said. "He fought me every step of the way."

Though several of the houses on the corners of the busier cross streets had been rezoned commercial and converted to office space, boutiques, and the like, I'd had no idea the house next to the one Buck and I had purchased had been rezoned. I should've known better, should've looked into it, should've realized Mr. Dunaway's hurry to seal the deal was a red flag. The price Dunaway had offered me may not have been such a great deal after all. Having a commercial property next door would devalue my house by at least ten to twenty percent. Few people wanted to live next to a business, which were often bustling and noisy. That nice profit I'd hoped to make could disappear entirely. Buck and I would be lucky to break even. The appraiser apparently hadn't been aware of the matter, either, or it would have come up in the report. The designation must have been changed so recently that it had yet to be updated in the appraisal district's system. The five grand Rick Dunaway had left for me the night before seemed like nothing now, a mere pittance.

The fact that Gentry owned the adjacent property also explained why he'd wanted to buy mine. Owning the lot next door would give him room for expansion. His eyes sparked with mean-spirited merriment and his mouth spread in a snide grin. "I told you that you'd regret not selling to me. You should have listened."

Part of me realized he was right, but another part was more glad than ever that I hadn't sold the house to the smug son of a gun. I'd never run my business the way he—and Rick Dunaway—ran theirs. I'd never be able to live with myself. How they could look themselves in the mirror each night was beyond me.

"What did you pay for the house?" he asked. When I said nothing, he had the nerve to snicker. "If you paid more than three hundred, you got taken for a ride."

I jabbed the button to roll up the window, forcing him to back away.

"Have a nice day, Ms. Whitaker!" he called as I put my foot to the gas.

Fuming, I rolled on and pulled into the driveway next door, startling Sawdust with my sudden shriek. "No!"

As if this day hadn't gotten off to a bad enough start, both the front door and the WHITAKER WOODWORKING sign were covered in sticky yellow goo. Broken white eggshells littered the porch and yard. Someone had thrown three dozen or more eggs at the house.

I'd bet that someone was Jackson. When I'd evicted him and his roommates, Jackson had told me I'd be sorry. Egging the house seemed like just the type of juvenile prank an irresponsible punk like him would pull. Looked like he hadn't been satisfied by his earlier act of vandalism. At least this time he hadn't used profanity.

As I climbed out of the car, I noticed the Mercedes still parked at the curb between my house and Patty's. Perhaps Patty had a houseguest who'd spent the night, or maybe the car belonged to someone who was visiting another resident on the street. But why park here? There were plenty of places along the curb up and down the street.

I placed Sawdust's cage under the magnolia tree and gathered up the eggshells from the yard and porch. Though I was tempted to toss them into Gentry's yard next door, I tossed them into the garden instead. With their high calcium content, eggshells made a great natural compost. As an added bonus, coarsely ground shells deterred slugs and snails from invading the garden. And maybe having a beauty salon next door wouldn't be so bad. Maybe I'd sell the house to a supermodel or rising singing sensation who'd want a stylist and nail technician only yards away. Yep, I was trying to turn lemons into lemonade this morning. *Gallons and gallons of lemonade . . .*

Once I'd gathered up the eggshells, I retrieved the garden hose, turning it to a more forceful flow than when

I'd used it the night before to the water the flowers. I aimed the stream at the aluminum yard sign. The spray gave off a tinny sound as it hit the sign, but at least it washed away some of the goop.

Thad Gentry climbed into his Infiniti, backed out of the driveway next door, and gave me a wave and a *toot-toot* on his horn as he drove past. Clearly, he was trying to get my goat, and get my goat he did. I aimed the stream of water at his car and he gave me another *toot-toot* when it fell short, serving only to soak my mailbox. *Rats.*

Sawdust stood at the front of his carrier, watching through the metal bars as I carried the hose and rag up the steps to the porch and repeated the process. I hosed down the front door, including the Green Man door knocker. The face stared back at me as I used a rag from my toolbox to remove the stubborn, sticky egg whites from the grooves carved into the knocker. As I turned to head back down the stairs, I spotted my dead blow mallet on the ground next to the bottom step. I must have forgotten to put it away the night before. A dark reddish-brown substance coated the head of the mallet. Looked like the vandal had poured something on it, too. *But what is it? Barbecue sauce? Dark maple syrup?*

As I pondered the sticky substance, Patty came out of her house next door with a broom in her hand.

I called out "Good morning!" as she made her way down her front walkway.

She returned the sentiment. "Enjoying your new roof?"

"I am."

"I'm enjoying the peace and quiet," she said. "I thought those roofers would never finish. All that hammering gave me a whopper of a headache." She looked past me when the tractor revved up on the other side of me. Her eyes rolled. "Here we go again. I miss the good old days when all you'd hear in this neighborhood was the wind rustling in the trees."

"Did you know the house on my other side is being converted into a beauty salon?"

"Mm-hm," she sounded sourly. "A group of us from the street tried to fight it. The guy you bought the house from? He got us organized and hired lawyers and everything. We all went down to the zoning commission and had a hearing. They didn't listen. Not much, anyway. Thad Gentry promised he'd keep the outside intact and only remodel the inside so it would blend into the neighborhood. He also said he'd install a wall of bushes between your property and his so that the parking lot wouldn't be visible from our homes. The zoning commission bought his song and dance and approved his application. That man is *personus non grautin* around here."

Patty might not know her Latin, but she knew what a ruthless real estate developer could do to her property value.

As I debated what to do, whether to confront Rick Dunaway for his failure to disclose this material fact, I laid the mallet on the stone walkway and sprayed it off, too. I supposed I'd have to discuss the matter with Buck first. The Hartleys, too. Meanwhile, Patty swept her walk and drive.

When all the icky stuff was gone, I picked up the mallet and wiped it dry with a clean cloth. I returned the mallet to my toolbox, which I'd placed on the grass, and exchanged it for a trowel. Retrieving Sawdust from his carrier, I clipped the leash to his harness and carried him over to the flower bed. After securing the end of his leash to the porch rail, I set him free—or at least as free as he could be, tethered to a five-foot-long restraint.

The soil I'd poured into the bed appeared to have been

disturbed. Rather than smooth mounds, parts of it were flattened with footprints. The boys must've stepped into the beds when they'd thrown the eggs at the door. The flats of pansies looked as if they'd been kicked about, too. Rather than the orderly row I'd placed them in, they lay at odd angles. One of them was even upside down.

Sawdust sniffed the fresh earth, his head bobbing up and down as he made his way along, his leash stretching taut in his wake. After lining the flats up along the edge of the flower bed, I dropped to my knees, crumbled up the eggshells, and stretched out my arms to sprinkle them along the length of the bed. The eggshells dealt with, I began smoothing the dirt with the back of the trowel. Having become bored already of merely sniffing the dirt, the cat began to dig in it with his front paws, tossing loose soil to the sides and behind him. He was undoing my work, but he looked as if he were having a fun time. I'd let it slide for now and work on the other end of the bed.

A half-dozen pansies had made new homes in the soil when Patty came over and stepped up beside me. "I've never seen a cat that would tolerate a leash before."

"Many won't," I agreed, "but Sawdust is fairly docile." When he wasn't terrified by a piercing beep and thick smoke, that is. "I started training him on a leash and harness when he was only a tiny kitten. Starting him young helped, too."

"You're not going to let him off that leash, are you? I don't want him coming over and marking my bushes."

I looked up at her. "No need to worry. I wouldn't risk letting him roam free." There were too many potential dangers outside. Of course, the fire had shown that there could be dangers inside, too.

She gestured to the cat. "What's he got there?"

I turned to see Sawdust swatting at something sticking

up out of the dirt. It was a couple of inches long, and light in color. "Looks like he's got a root." I thought I'd dug up all the old roots from the half-dead, odd-shaped bushes that had been here before, but it looked like I must've missed at least one.

Patty moved closer to Sawdust and leaned in to take a closer look. "Lord Almighty!" she shrieked, shrinking back. "That's not a root! That's a finger!"

It took a second or two for her words to sink in. "It's a *what*?!?"

I sprang from the ground like a jack-in-the-box and rushed over. Sure enough, the thing I'd thought was a root had a fingernail on the end of it. The nail was short and unpainted.

Like Patty, I, too, instinctively shrank back, as if putting distance between the hand and myself would somehow make it less real. My mouth gaped as my gaze ran over the flower bed. While I hadn't discerned it before, my eyes now made out a human form beneath the soil, including a small mound at the top where the head would be.

Patty seemed to see it, too. "I'm calling the police!" she cried, bolting back toward her house.

Who was in the flower bed? Is there any chance the person could still be alive? Though my brain told me it was unlikely, my heart knew it would suffer guilt if I let a person die unnecessarily. I had to find out if there was any hope for him or her.

Forcing myself forward, I dropped to my knees again and grabbed the finger, pulling upward until the entire hand came free of the soil. Judging from the size and the light hairs on the knuckles, it appeared to be a man's hand. *Oh, my gosh!* The ring finger bore a white stripe where a wedding band had been removed. *No. No! It can't be. Can it?* In denial, I continued to pull up on it until the wrist appeared, along with the cuff of a now dirty white dress shirt and a gray suit jacket. I put the fingers of my other hand against the wrist to check for a pulse. I couldn't feel one, but I also realized the thick fabric of the gardening glove might be impeding the sensation.

Gulping down both fear and revulsion, I tugged off my gloves and put my bare fingers to the wrist—cringing at the cold, rubber-doll-like feel of the skin.

Nothing.

Both the lack of pulse and the temperature of the body told me that whoever was buried in my garden had gone on to meet his maker. There was no hope for him.

As I gently placed the hand atop the dirt, a watch peeked out from under the jacket cuff and glinted in the morning sun. It was a gold Rolex watch.

Just the like the one Rick Dunaway wore.

CHAPTER 20

OUTDOOR PLAYTIME
IS OVER

SAWDUST

When Sawdust went to sniff the hand Whitney had been holding, she squealed, unclipped the leash from his harness, yanked him away, and ran over to the big tree with the cat clenched to her chest. She opened the door to his carrier and shoved him inside, slamming the door behind him. She'd never been so rough with him before. Had something he'd done made her angry? What was it?

He crouched and cowered in the back corner, worried that he'd upset her and not knowing why. Human behavior could be hard to comprehend sometimes. For instance, Sawdust would never understand why Whitney liked to soak in water up to her neck. Sawdust hated baths. As far as he was concerned, water was for drinking only.

Meow? he asked. *Why are you angry at me?* He'd only been having a little fun, batting at the thing he'd uncovered. He couldn't help it if he'd been curious. Curiosity was the core of a cat's nature. She must know that by now. *Meow?*

But Whitney ignored his pleas. Instead, she put her face in her hands and began to shake.

CHAPTER 21

CRIME SCENE

WHITNEY

Unlike the door knocker, which could never hide its eyes, I kept my hands over my face for a long moment, trying to shut things out. But it was a futile effort. The image of that cold, lifeless hand would be forever etched in my mind.

I tried to think happy thoughts. Thanksgiving was next week, and that meant a feast at Uncle Roger and Aunt Nancy's cabin, including enormous slabs of Aunt Nancy's delicious sweet potato pie. Soon it would be time to decorate for Christmas. I always enjoyed that. Colette had recently sent me a link to a funny video of two kittens swatting cue balls around on a pool table. I tried to replay it in my mind, visualize the orange tabby swatting the eight ball into the corner pocket.

Sigh.

The happy thoughts weren't helping. My mind kept turning back to the body in the bed.

When I finally removed my hands, I turned my head away, pushed myself up from the ground, and walked on wobbly legs down the stone pathway to wait by the mail-box for the first responders. *I've got to notify Buck.* I pulled my cell phone out of my pocket and dialed his number. The first time I tried, it went to voice mail. No doubt he was still in bed, not yet ready to face the day. The second time I tried, he answered on the fourth ring, his voice gravelly with sleep.

"Somebody better be dead," he growled.

My voice quavered when I responded. "Somebody is, Buck."

There was a brief pause. "What are you talking about, Whitney?" He sounded fully awake now.

"I just found a body." My throat was so tight I had to force the words out. "In the flower bed at our house. The police are on their way."

"So am I," he said. "Hold tight, cuz!"

As I slid my phone into my pocket, Patty came back out of her house. She stayed on her porch rather than coming over. I couldn't much blame her. I'd just as soon jump into my car and drive as far away as I could, as fast as I could.

As I waited for the police, a litany of questions rolled about in my mind like loose ball bearings. *Is that really Rick Dunaway in my flower bed? Who had killed him? Had the murder take place here? When had it happened? Was he killed last night after I'd left? Or could that thud I'd heard yesterday evening have been the sound of Rick Dunaway falling to the porch?* Terror twisted around my spine at the thought of him being murdered right outside the door while I sat inside, unknowing, only a door sepa-rating me from the grisly action.

The first police car arrived with flashing lights on the top. While many city police forces drove black-and-white cars, the Nashville Metro Police cruisers were white with a thick blue stripe edged in gold down the side. Two female officers were seated inside. One of the officers was fresh faced, the other seasoned. Both were brown haired.

The flashing lights went off and the officers climbed out, stepping over to me.

The seasoned officer, whose name badge read HOGARTY, asked, "You okay, honey?"

Could she not see that I was performing an involuntary hokey pokey and shaking all about? But no matter how upset I was, I was infinitely better off than the person in my flower bed.

"My head's spinning," I told the officer, "but I'll be all right." My gut was churning, too, but that was too icky to mention.

"Where's the deceased?"

I pointed over my shoulder. "In the flower bed."

She glanced that way. "I see."

The two officers stepped gingerly toward the house, returning a few seconds later after getting a glimpse at the corpse. While the younger cop retrieved yellow cordon tape from the trunk of the cruiser, Officer Hogarty climbed back into the car, leaving the driver's door open and one leg on the pavement as she grabbed the dashboard microphone to contact the station. "Send a team from crime scene and a homicide detective."

After the dispatcher confirmed her request, she climbed back out of the vehicle. "Wait here," she instructed me. "We've got folks on the way."

With that, she went to help her partner cordon off the yard. When they finished, bright yellow tape spanned the length and width of my yard, like streamers at some type of warped birthday party. My toolbox sat within the perimeter, out of reach. Sawdust crouched in his carrier in the middle of the crime scene, asking more questions that went unanswered. *Meow? Mew? Meowww?* Not only did

Sawdust seem upset by the commotion, I knew from experience that holding him would calm me, too.

"May I get my cat?" I called to Officer Hogarty.

"Not yet," she called back. "We can't risk disturbing anything. You'll have to wait until the crime scene team has had a chance to comb over the area."

Sawdust looked pitiful and pathetic, an innocent prisoner in his cage. "Sorry, baby!" I called to him. "I'll get you out of there as soon as I can."

The officers remained by the flower bed, speaking softly and glancing around as if looking for evidence.

A few minutes later, a van pulled to the curb behind the cruiser. Like the patrol car, it was white with the blue and gold stripes. The side was emblazoned with the words CRIME SCENE UNIT. As the driver and passenger climbed out, the side door slid open to reveal a third technician. The techs stood next to the van, donning their specialized gear—booties, gloves, and white coveralls—before ducking under the cordon tape with their plastic toolboxes in their hands. They hurriedly erected a makeshift curtain around the bed to shield the body from view. *Thank goodness.* At least I could no longer see the poor person lying there, half covered in dirt.

A plain white sedan pulled up behind the van. It resembled the one I'd seen parked down the block weeks ago. With the van blocking my vision, I couldn't see the driver from where I stood at the curb, but a moment later he emerged from behind the vehicle. He was dark haired and stood around five feet eight inches, which meant we were nearly eye-to-eye—my blue eyes to his green—when he walked over and stopped in front of me. He wore navy blue pants and a heavily starched light blue button-down shirt under a nylon police-issue windbreaker. A light morning breeze brushed past, carrying his scent to my nose. He smelled woodsy, like cedar. Must be his soap.

"Are you the one who found the body?" he asked.

"Yes," I said softly.

He held out a hand. "Detective Collin Flynn."

I took his hand, which was warm and alive, much nicer than the last hand I'd held, the cold, dead one I'd pulled from the dirt. "I'm Whitney Whitaker."

He turned to address the uniformed cops, who were heading our way. "Good morning, Officers."

The two returned his greeting and came up next to us.

Officer Hogarty cocked her head. "You working homicides now, Flynn?"

"I am," he replied. "Just got promoted this week."

"Wow." She rocked back on her heels. "Seems like only yesterday I was your training officer, teaching you the ropes. You moved up the ranks faster than anyone I ever heard of. Congratulations."

With a humble nod, he accepted both the compliment and the hearty pat on the back she gave him.

"This is a big step," the woman added. "Dead bodies and such." She cocked her head and eyed him. "You sure you're ready for this?"

His jaw flexed, almost imperceptibly. "No doubt in my mind," he assured her, punctuating his words with a confident nod this time.

"All righty, then."

Hogarty and her partner set off to opposite ends of the sidewalk to control the gathering crowd of neighbors who'd come out to gawk. Detective Flynn whipped a pen and notepad out of the breast pocket of his jacket and returned his attention to me. "You up to talking now, Miss Whitaker?"

I glanced over at Sawdust again and bit my lip. All I really wanted to do at the moment was round up my cat and go home and have a good cry while I downed a gallon or so of rocky road ice cream, my go-to happy feel-good food. But I knew I couldn't. I had to do everything I could to help the police figure out how Rick Dunaway had ended up in my garden. I turned back to the detective and forced out a soft, "Yes. I can talk."

The detective angled his head to indicate the flower bed, where two of the crime scene techs were hunkered down behind the plastic drape, only the tops of their heads visible. "Any idea who that is lying in the flower bed and how the person got there?"

I gulped down the lump of emotion in my throat. "I don't know how he ended up in the flower bed," I replied. "I didn't see it happen." *He'd have to consult the door knocker for that information. Surely those dark, deep eyes had seen what transpired.* "But I'm pretty sure it's Rick Dunaway."

His brows drew inward in question. "Only 'pretty' sure?"

"I can't be certain. His head was buried when we found him. Still was when we called you."

"I see." He jotted a note on his pad and looked back up at me. "Who is Rick Dunaway?"

"He runs a real estate investment company. I work for another company called Home and Hearth. We manage his residential properties."

The detective gestured to the house. "Is this one of Mr. Dunaway's properties?"

"It was. He sold it to me a week ago."

"So you live here?"

"No," I said. "The house needs work. My cousins and I planned to fix it up and put it on the market soon."

"Flip it, you mean?"

"Yes."

He made another note on his pad. "When did you find the body?"

"About half an hour ago. I was working in the flower bed and my cat dug something up and started playing with it. I thought it was a leftover root from some bushes I'd removed. I was working in the other end of the bed and didn't take a close look until my neighbor came over and noticed the root was actually a finger."

Flynn looked around the area. "Which neighbor?"

"Patty." She'd come off her porch and huddled two yards over with a group of older folks from up and down the street. I pointed her out to the detective. "She's the one with the curly orange hair."

"Did either of you touch the body?"

"Yes. If there was any chance the person might still be alive, I wanted to help. I lifted up the arm and checked for a pulse." Thinking back to the cold, rubbery feel of Dunaway's skin caused me to shudder involuntarily.

The detective took in my reaction before glancing over at the bed, where one of the crime scene techs was standing behind the drape with a camera in hand, snapping photos of the body below. Turning back to me, he said, "What makes you think it's Rick Dunaway?"

"He's wearing a gold Rolex watch. Mr. Dunaway has one like it." I pointed to the Mercedes at the curb. "I think that might be his car, too. It was here last night when I left around nine. Mr. Dunaway was supposed to come by at six o'clock and bring me some paperwork but he never knocked on the door. As I was leaving, I tried to figure out if the car was his, but he wasn't in it and there was no way for me to tell for sure. I know he drives a Mercedes that looks like that, but I don't know his plate number."

Flynn's gaze swept over the car and swung to the techs before returning to me. "Wait here."

He ducked under the cordon tape and carefully made his way a few steps forward before summoning one of the crime scene techs. When the man stepped over, Flynn turned his back to me and ducked his head, talking too low for me to overhear. After a few seconds, they broke apart and the tech disappeared behind the screen. A moment later, the Mercedes came to life, its headlights flashing as the doors unlocked with a *bleep-bleep.*

They must've found Mr. Dunaway's keys. They were probably still in his pocket.

Flynn ducked back under the tape and retrieved two pairs of paper booties from the crime scene van. He slid one pair on over his shoes and held the other out to me. "Put these on. We need you to make a positive ID."

The blood in my veins went ice-cold. "You mean you want me to look at the body? At his face?"

"Yes."

Fear gripped my gut, spreading its cold, clammy fingers up to my heart. I'd already never get the image of that finger out of my mind. I didn't need a face to go with it. Hoping to preempt the issue, I said, "His wallet should be in his pocket, right? Can't you identify him by his driver's license photo?"

Flynn offered a soft, sympathetic shake of his head. "We need someone who's familiar with him to identify the body. I know it's not going to be easy, but it would be very helpful if you would do it for us. Otherwise, we'll have to call a family member. You don't want one of his loved ones to have to go through that, do you?"

I didn't. As hard as identifying a dead Mr. Dunaway would be for me, it would be infinitely more difficult for his estranged wife or one of his children. I closed my eyes and took a deep breath to steel myself. Forcing my eyes open again, I slid the booties over my steel-toed boots and followed the detective under the tape. He led me past my mewling cat over to the curtain. The female tech was crouched next to the body on the other side. A white sheet had been draped over his corpse and face. The woman took the edge of the sheet in her hand. "You ready?"

As ready as I'll ever be. "Yes," I croaked.

Apparently, I'd lied. As she began to pull the sheet back, my hands reflexively went back to cover my face again.

"Ms. Whitaker?" came the woman's voice. "You're going to have to move your hands. You can make it quick if you need to."

I most definitely need to make it quick.

I took another deep breath and opened my hands and eyes for a split second before closing them again, as if I were playing a sick game of peekaboo. But in that split second I'd played peekaboo with Rick Dunaway. He'd had a thin seam of soil running across his lips and in the lines around his vacant, unseeing eyes.

I stepped backward, out of range of the visage. "It's him," I squeaked. "It's Rick Dunaway."

The detective pointed back to the tape, indicating I could return to the sidewalk. As I made my way past my cat, the little thing mewed helplessly again. He was confused and scared and had no idea what was going on. He only knew I wasn't comforting him like I was supposed to. I hoped he'd forgive me. I bent down to look into his cage. "Not too much longer, baby," I told him, hoping it would be true.

"What's his name?" Flynn asked when I stood.

"Sawdust," I said.

"Because of his color?"

"That, plus the fact that he was covered in the stuff when I found him in my uncle's barn."

Once we'd circled back under the tape and stood again on the walkway, the detective resumed his interrogation. "You said you didn't see Mr. Dunaway last night. When was the last time you saw him in person?"

I thought back. "Monday."

"Here?" he asked.

"No," I said. "At his office downtown."

"What were you doing there?"

Accusing him of ripping me off, of knowingly selling me a house with an outdated, dangerous electrical system. I felt a little guilty about that now, even if it was almost certainly true. "I was talking to him about the house. It caught on fire right after we bought it. The very same day, in fact."

Detective Flynn ran his gaze over the house. "The house looks fine to me. Must have been a small fire."

"Actually," I replied, "it was a pretty big one. The entire roof over the back bedroom was gone."

"Really?" He glanced at the house again. "How did you manage to get it fixed so quickly?"

"I'm a part-time carpenter so I know a lot of contractors. My cousin and I did the framing ourselves. I found roofers who were able to get the repairs done right away."

"So roofers were on-site this week?" he asked.

"Yes. Electricians, too."

"Electricians? What were they doing?"

"Rewiring the house. They're not quite finished yet."

"Any other contractors?"

"No. My cousins and I planned to handle the repairs to the drywall and flooring ourselves."

Flynn asked for the names and contact information for the contractors and jotted the information down on his pad.

His note complete, he made a circular motion in the air with his pen. "Let's go back to your visit to Dunaway's office. You said you went there to talk to him about the house. If you owned the house when it burned, how would he be involved?"

It would be wrong to speak ill of the dead, wouldn't it? But it would also be wrong to lie to a detective. I decided to temper my language. "As it turned out, the house had an old style of wiring, a knob-and-tube system that can be dangerous. My cousin and I didn't know about it when we bought the place. I wanted to find out if Mr. Dunaway was aware of it. I was in the house when it caught fire. My cat was, too." I pointed to Sawdust, whose impatience had apparently overcome his fear. He watched us from behind the metal bars, sticking a paw through and pulling on the bars as if trying to open the cage himself. "My cat ran and hid when the smoke alarms went off. We barely made it out."

The detective nodded solemnly. "What did Dunaway tell you when you questioned him?" he asked. "Did he know about the wiring?"

"He said he didn't know of any problems with the electrical system."

He stared at me for a moment. "Did you believe him? Did you think he was being honest with you?"

I raised my shoulders. "I'm not sure. I wanted to. I mean, I hate to think he'd have knowingly put lives at risk, the tenants' and then mine. But . . ." I didn't finish the sentence, but had nonetheless made my point. Despite Dunaway's claims of innocence, I hadn't been convinced he knew nothing about the wiring.

"I see," the detective said. "Did you have an inspection when you purchased the house?"

"I did. The inspector didn't put anything in his report

about the electrical system. He says he didn't notice that there was any knob-and-tube wiring because the kitchen, the bathroom, and the garage all had more modern wiring and he'd assumed it extended throughout the house. But only part of the house had been updated. The living room and bedrooms still had the old wiring."

He mulled things over for a moment, twirling the pen in his fingers. "If I were in your shoes, I'd be very upset to find out the house I'd bought had a defect, especially if that defect caused a fire and could have killed me and my pet. You were upset, weren't you?"

Though his voice was casual, a muscle in his jaw flexed, telling me the question wasn't nearly as innocent as it sounded. But surely he didn't consider me a suspect. The mere thought was ridiculous!

"Who wouldn't be disappointed to see their investment go up in smoke?" I said in my defense. "But mostly I was angry with my inspector. He's done a lot of work for my employer over the years, so I thought I could trust him to inspect this house for me, too. He's supposed to be on the buyers' side, looking out for us."

"Did you confront the inspector after the fire?"

"Of course. We spoke the next morning right after the fire investigator left. I think he felt guilty. He didn't admit anything outright, but he left me with the distinct impression that Rick Dunaway had bribed him not to mention the wiring in the report."

Flynn's brows arched in interest. "A bribe, huh? Who was your inspector?"

"A guy named Bobby Palmer."

"Got his contact information? I may want to talk to him."

I took my phone from the pocket of my coveralls and pulled up Bobby's name in my contacts list. I held up the screen so Detective Flynn could jot down the information.

After he finished writing on his pad, he gave me a pointed look. "Do you think this Bobby Palmer is capable of murder?"

"Bobby? A killer?" A month ago I would have laughed at the suggestion, but now that I'd learned Bobby had a gambling problem and suspected he'd taken a payoff, I realized I hardly knew the man at all. I'd underestimated Rick Dunaway's heartlessness, too. Looked like I was an extremely poor judge of character. I shrugged. "I honestly don't know what to tell you. He always seemed like a friendly, upstanding guy, but I don't know him personally. We've only interacted on the inspections. I think he may have a gambling problem, though. I overheard him talking on the phone with someone that might have been his bookie. He mentioned several sports teams and also told whoever he was speaking with 'I'm good for it.' He also said something like 'I always come through. I'd hate to find out what might happen if I didn't.' I took that to mean he owed the person money and also that he was a little afraid."

His pen went to his pad to make another note. "Did Bobby know Mr. Dunaway planned to come by here last night?"

"Yes, he knew. When I was worried about having the funds to cover my insurance deductible, Bobby suggested I ask Mr. Dunaway for the money. I did and he agreed to pay it. I phoned Bobby afterward to tell him, and I mentioned that Mr. Dunaway planned to bring the check by Friday night. I also told him that Home and Hearth wouldn't be using him for inspections anymore. Bobby got pretty angry about that. He's averaged at least one inspection a week for us for years. It'll be a significant financial hit for him."

Flynn made another entry on his pad. "What about other suspects? Do you know anyone else who might have had reason to want to cause Rick Dunaway harm? To be angry with him for any reason?"

Heck, I was just getting started. "I recently evicted three college boys who were tenants here. They hadn't paid their rent and they'd trashed the place. One of them told me I'd be sorry I forced them out. His name is Jackson Pharr. I don't know that he'd be angry enough to kill someone, but when I pulled up this morning, there were broken eggs on the door and the yard sign. Someone had thrown them at the house. A juvenile prank like that seems the kind of thing a boy like him would do."

Flynn glanced around. "I don't see any evidence of eggs."

"Before I started working on the flower bed, I used the hose to wash down the door and the sign, and I crumbled up the shells in the soil. They're good for plants." Crumbling up the shells and mixing them in the dirt might have sullied any fingerprints the crime scene team would have been able to get from the eggs. I'd had no idea at the time that they could be important pieces of evidence.

When Sawdust issued a particularly pitiful cry, I cast a glance at him. He looked back at me, his eyes big as he opened his mouth in a silent cry this time.

Flynn drew my attention back. "Got contact information for Jackson?"

"I only have a phone number. He never provided a forwarding address after he moved out. I had to send the final bill for unpaid rent and damages to his parents' house. I've got his mother's number, too, though. If you can't get a hold of Jackson, his mother should be able to tell you where he's living now."

I pulled up Jackson's number on my contacts list and rattled it off for the detective. When he finished writing it down and looked back up at me, I added, "I believe Jackson might also be responsible for a threat that was scribbled on the door shortly after the eviction. It said 'Watch your back,' followed by the B-word."

"The B-word?" he repeated, looking slightly confused.

I cringed. "I think that threat was probably directed toward me. I was the one who handled their eviction. Jackson also drove by here in his pickup earlier in the week. When he saw me, he sped off. One of his roommates mentioned that he had a criminal record. I don't know what for. But Patty said she'd called the cops on him when he'd gotten into a fistfight with another young man on the lawn. It could have something to do with that."

He jotted more notes before looking up again. "Did Jackson ever meet Mr. Dunaway?"

"Not that I know of. As the property manager, I handled the interactions with the tenants."

"Seems the boy's beef is with you, then, not Dunaway."

He had a point. "I suppose you're right."

"Anyone else you know who might have a grudge against Rick Dunaway? Even a small one?"

Boy, did I. "Thaddeus Gentry. He's in real estate, too. He and Mr. Dunaway are competitors. Gentry owns the property next door." I pointed at the adjacent house to the right. "He's converting it into a beauty salon."

The detective glanced over at the house. "That explains the tractor."

"I heard from both Gentry himself and the neighbor on the other side that Rick Dunaway fought to keep the property from being rezoned. He got the other homeowners in the area involved and hired lawyers to represent their interests at a hearing."

"So he gave Gentry a hard time," Flynn said, appearing to be thinking out loud. "Probably cost him quite a bit in legal fees of his own."

I nodded and continued. "Mr. Gentry made an offer on this house, but Mr. Dunaway said he'd only sell the place to Gentry . . ." I had to swallow hard first to get the words out. "Over his dead body."

The detective's brows rose and he issued an accusing *hmm*.

"Dunaway gave me right of first refusal and a big discount," I said. Of course now I knew why. The house needed several thousands of dollars in electrical upgrades and would suffer a sharp decline in value when the house next door was converted to commercial use. "Mr. Gentry later offered to buy the house from me as is for twenty percent over my purchase price, but it didn't seem right for me to turn right around and resell the house to Mr. Gentry for a profit when Mr. Dunaway never would have sold the house to Gentry."

"So you felt a sense of loyalty to Mr. Dunaway," Flynn said.

"I did." Of course I now doubted Gentry had offered Rick Dunaway $450,000 for the place. Dunaway had probably lied to me about that to entice me to accept his offer. But I supposed that was water under the bridge now. "Rick Dunaway is a big name in real estate and landing the Abbot-Dunaway Holdings account made me proud. Truth be told, I was surprised when he chose Home and Hearth to handle his residential property management. Several of the bigger management firms had been vying for his business, too."

Flynn watched me intently and lowered his voice to just above a whisper. "Did you have a personal relationship with Mr. Dunaway?"

The mere thought made me recoil, but I tried to hide my disgust. No sense insulting the dead. "No. He's married." Not to mention that he was not my type at all.

"Why do you think he gave you the gig?"

I mulled things over for a moment. "At the time, I thought I'd won him over by telling him that he'd be our biggest client and our number one priority. But now, well, I hate to admit this, but he probably thought a smaller outfit like Home and Hearth would be easier for him to manipulate than one of the bigger management firms. He took advantage of me several times."

His gaze narrowed. "Took advantage of you?"

An instant blush blazed on my cheeks and I waved my hand as if to erase the wrongful impression I'd given the detective. "Not in *that* way," I assured Flynn. "He took advantage of me financially. He constantly complained about the maintenance and repair bills on the units, so I tried to keep the costs down by doing a lot of labor myself for free. I'm a carpenter. So is my cousin, Buck. He's an equal owner in the house with me."

Flynn made another note and twirled his pen some more as he mulled things over for a moment or two. "Let's talk a little more about the offer Thaddeus Gentry made you on the house. Seems to me that Mr. Gentry might have been angrier with you than he'd be with Dunaway. He offered you a quick, easy profit and you refused. Powerful men are used to getting their way. They aren't happy when they don't."

"That's very true." I'd learned that lesson quickly after Rick Dunaway had hired me. The wealthy man had often behaved like a spoiled, petulant child. "Mr. Gentry was next door earlier," I said. "I didn't know his plans for the house until he told me this morning. He rubbed in the fact that I would've been better off to have sold this house to him."

Flynn cocked his head and gave me a pointed look. "You think there's any chance that the college kid, Bobby

Palmer, or Thad Gentry came to the house last night planning to do *you* harm? Maybe you were the intended victim and Mr. Dunaway unintentionally got in the way."

The thought turned my knees to noodles and I had to put a hand on the mailbox to steady myself. "I hope that wasn't the case. I'd feel terrible if it was!"

Again, he eyed me closely before saying, "Let's explore that angle a little more. You mentioned that you had evicted this boy—" He glanced down at his notes to refresh his memory. "Jackson Pharr. That he'd written a threat on the door that seemed to be directed at you. It seems Palmer and Gentry are at odds with you, too. Who else might have it in for you?"

Sheesh. The detective was making me feel like some kind of pariah. Even so, he had asked a valid question. "There's a woman who works—" I quickly corrected myself. "*Worked* for Mr. Dunaway. I guess she still does. Works for Abbot-Dunaway Holdings, I mean. Her name is Presley. She was Rick Dunaway's right hand." Poor choice of words. Once again I was thinking of his left hand, the one that had been sticking up out of the dirt. I forced the thought to the back of my mind. "Presley has never warmed up to me, which is unusual."

Flynn's eyes seemed to spark. "Is it important to you to be liked?"

What an odd question. "Doesn't everyone want to be liked?"

He shrugged. "Go on. Why do you think Presley never warmed up to you?"

"At first it was because Dunaway hired me to manage his residential properties. He'd told me she had tried to convince him to keep the business in-house, to give the duties to her. She was looking to move up within the company, to learn more about the real estate business."

Flynn's head bobbed. "Makes sense."

"More recently," I added, "she let me know she was annoyed that Mr. Dunaway had sold this house to me without informing her first that he planned to sell the property."

"You think she would have wanted to buy it for herself?"

"We actually discussed the matter," I said. "But Rick Dunaway is notoriously cheap. He didn't pay her enough to afford this house on her own. He paid us below market rate for our management services and, like I said earlier, he routinely balked at making repairs, even small ones."

"That must have been frustrating for you." He gave me a pointed look.

"It was," I admitted. *Why deny something so obvious?* "But he owned a lot of properties so our management company was still making a profit on the account overall. And having him as a client gave us some clout, convinced other people to hire us, too. All in all, working for Abbot-Dunaway Holdings was good for me and Home and Hearth."

He bobbed his head thoughtfully.

"There's one other person," I added. "Though I'm not sure it's anything. The day I evicted Jackson Pharr and Mr. Dunaway met me here, there was a man sitting in a white sedan across the street a few houses down that way." I pointed down the street in the direction the car had been parked. "He was reading a newspaper. Mr. Dunaway seemed to hesitate when he spotted the car. I hadn't noticed the car until Mr. Dunaway pointed it out so I'm not sure whether it had been there before Mr. Dunaway arrived or not. When I went to the Abbot-Dunaway office after the fire, I might have seen the same car in the parking garage, down the row a little ways from Mr. Dunaway's Mercedes.

It was backed into its spot so the license plate wasn't visible. A sunshade was up inside. It seemed strange that the driver would put up a shade since the car was inside a garage, but I figured they did it out of habit. I wonder now if the shade was up to hide the fact that someone was in the car spying on Dunaway. Could he have been under government surveillance?" After all, if Dunaway had defrauded me, he might have been involved in bigger financial shenanigans, ones that had caught the government's attention.

"I'll have to check into it. It's also possible that Dunaway knew he was being targeted and had hired security."

"You mean the man in the car might have been a bodyguard?"

"It's possible."

If he had been a bodyguard, he hadn't done his job well. Otherwise, we wouldn't be here right now with Mr. Dunaway lying in my flower bed. And if Mr. Dunaway had been targeted, who was it that was targeting him? The mob? I'd heard the mob was involved in construction fraud along the East Coast, but I hadn't heard of such things taking place here in Nashville. Still, Mr. Dunaway was in the real estate business and worked with large contractors regularly on development projects. It seemed possible there could be a mob connection.

Parallel lines of concentration formed between the detective's brows as he readied his pen again. "What was the make and model of the car in the garage?"

"Sorry." I cringed. "At the time, the similarity just struck me as a coincidence and I didn't go over to look. My mind was occupied with the fire and getting the house repaired. I didn't even notice if the car was still there when I left."

Although his jaw flexed with what was likely frustration,

he seemed to forgive me for failing to make better mental notes. "Understandable. You'd been through a lot."

Having obtained all the information he could from me, the detective headed down the sidewalk to have a chat with Patty. I sat down on the curb and put my face in my hands. *What a morning this has been.* I hoped the detective would solve this murder right away. With all the trouble the house had been for me, I wanted to get it sold and never look back.

CHAPTER 22

SPRUNG FROM THE KLINK

SAWDUST

Finally!

A woman wearing latex gloves opened the door to the cage and reached in to pick him up. *It's about time!*

"Be a good boy," she told him, looking into his face. "No biting, okay?"

She held him up and looked him over thoroughly before kneeling down to peer into his cage. She picked the carrier up by its handle and looked underneath it. Sawdust had no idea what the woman was looking for, but whatever it was she hadn't seemed to find it.

She returned him to his cage and carried it over to Whitney, setting his carrier down on the sidewalk. "Here you go."

Whitney wasted no time opening his cage, taking Sawdust in her arms, and cradling him to her chest, murmuring how sorry she was that he'd been stuck in the cage for so long. He was so happy to get out of the joint that he gave her a grateful lick on the chin and his loudest, most appreciative purr.

PURR-URR-URR-URR!

CHAPTER 23

QUESTIONS AND ANSWERS

WHITNEY

As I stood and cuddled my sweet, furry baby, the detective spoke privately with Patty on her porch. The two glanced over at me occasionally as they talked. *What's that about?*

When the detective returned, he seemed stiff and cold, not unlike the corpse composting in my garden. "Is there anything else you'd like to tell me, Ms. Whitaker? Any detail you left out that might be important?"

"No," I told him. "Not that I can think of." Of course I was more than a little rattled at the moment. It was possible my mind had overlooked something . . . or some*one*. But I could always give the detective a call if something else came to mind, right?

He ducked back under the tape. He ascended the porch steps and looked the front door over from top to bottom, taking a moment to gaze at the Green Man door knocker. When he finished, he came back down into the yard and walked over to my toolbox. He called out to the female crime scene tech, and she promptly came over. The two spoke quietly, the woman bobbing her head as he spoke. The two crouched down and the woman opened the toolbox with her gloved hands. Flynn looked down at something inside. His eyes slid to me and held for a long moment, his expression assessing. When he stood, the woman closed the latches on the box and picked it up, carrying it over to the van.

"You're taking my toolbox?" While I was in no condition to work on the house today given the events that had transpired, Mr. Dunaway's death didn't relieve me of my obligations to Home & Hearth and its other clients. I wouldn't be able to go without my tools for more than a day or two. I used them routinely to make small repairs at the rental properties.

The tech and detective exchanged glances, and Flynn came back over. "Do you know how Mr. Dunaway was killed, Ms. Whitaker?"

Why is he asking me? Isn't that something he and the techs should figure out? Even so, it would seem rude to point that out to them, wouldn't it?

Sawdust rose in my arms as I shrugged. "I assume he wasn't shot or someone would've mentioned hearing a gun go off and would have called the police at the time." I swallowed hard before speculating further. "If he'd been stabbed here, there would have been a lot of blood on the porch or on the grass by the bed, wouldn't there?" *How else are people killed?* Poison was a possibility, but weren't most poisons put in food? And didn't poisons work rather quickly? I was no expert, but from what little I knew it seemed that if Mr. Dunaway had ingested poison prior to attempting the drive to the house, he would have perished in his car along the way. I could think of only one other option, a term that I'd heard in television crime shows and movies. "Was it blunt force trauma? Isn't that what you call it when a person is hit with something?"

"It is," he said. "And that's a really good guess." Flynn's pointed gaze drilled into me, as if he were trying to see inside my mind. He turned to the tech and called, "Bring it over."

I wondered what *it* would be.

The woman stepped over with a large plastic bag in her hand. She handed it to the detective and he held it up. Inside was my dead blow mallet, the one I'd inadvertently left outside the night before.

"Oh, no!" I cried, my arms reflexively retracting in shock, inadvertently squeezing Sawdust against my chest. "Is that the weapon the killer used?"

"We believe it might be. It's yours, isn't it?"

With the initials *W.W.* clearly written on the handle, there was no way I could deny it even if I wanted to. Then again, maybe I could say it belonged to Wonder Woman or Willy Wonka or Woodrow Wilson. But I had nothing to hide here, no reason not to be truthful. "Yes," I replied. "That's mine."

"When was the last time you used it?"

"Yesterday. I used it to pound the Whitaker Woodworking sign into the ground. I must've forgotten to put it away because I found it on the porch this morning." It seemed like hours ago that I'd discovered it covered with that dark and sticky substance. *Had the substance been Rick Dunaway's blood?* My intestines writhed at the thought.

"Your neighbor said she saw you out here cleaning the tool and washing down the porch. She said she didn't see any eggs. I saw no sign of the threat or the B-word on the front door, either."

Panic began to grip my throat, but I fought it. There was nothing for me to worry about. *The truth always prevails, right?* "I sanded the threat off the door," I told him. "If you look closely, you should be able to tell where it was. The paint will be smoother. As for the eggs, I'd already washed them off the sign and the door before Patty came outside earlier. Check the soil in the flower bed. You'll find pieces of shell mixed in."

"What about the tool?"

"The mallet had something wet and sticky on the head. It looked like syrup or barbecue sauce to me."

"Syrup?" Both his expression and tone were dubious. "Barbecue sauce?"

Holding Sawdust firmly with one arm, I tossed the other hand in the air. "Blood wasn't the first thing that came to my mind! It's not like I was expecting to find a body in my yard." I knew the detective had to perform a thorough interrogation of each witness or suspect, but, really. This was a bit much.

"The techs need to get into the house and take a look around," he said. "May we borrow your keys?"

"Of course."

I pulled my key ring from the pocket of my coveralls and handed it to him, pointing out the appropriate key. He passed it on to the crime scene team and stood silently by as they went inside. After a few minutes, they came back out. When Flynn looked her way, the female tech shook her head. I supposed that meant they hadn't found any further evidence inside.

He turned to me. "Okay if they search your car?"

I swept my arm toward my SUV. "Be my guest."

They wouldn't find anything incriminating, but I knew they weren't going to take my word for it. In the meantime, while they were wasting their time interrogating me and inspecting my property, the actual killer could be destroying evidence or putting more distance between himself—*or herself*—and the body. Maybe the killer was headed down to Mexico, or had gone into hiding somewhere in the Smoky Mountains to the east.

My cousin Owen pulled up in his van a short way down the street. Owen was a slightly younger, clean-shaven version of Buck. Through the windshield, I could see his face contort in question. Like Buck, Owen would have preferred to sleep in on the weekends. Owen's wife would've enjoyed the extra shut-eye, too. But that wasn't going to happen, not with them having three girls under the age of five who needed to be fed and dressed, and who liked their daddy to get up with them at the crack of dawn to watch cartoons, their Saturday-morning ritual. Heck, he'd probably been up for two or three hours already.

He climbed out and stalked over in double time. "What on earth is going on here?"

I filled him in. "I found a body in the flower bed this morning."

He glanced over at the makeshift curtain. "You really mean to tell me that on the other side of that blind there's a—" He whispered the next two words. *"Dead person?"*

Whispering the words wasn't going to the change facts, but I could understand Owen's reluctance to say them more loudly. Saying them in a normal voice would make it more real. But it was time for me to face the facts head-on. "Yes. It's Rick Dunaway. The man who sold the house to me and Buck."

Owen's mouth gaped open so wide he could've swallowed ten biscuits and a gallon of gravy all at once.

I went on. "It looks like Dunaway was killed with my dead blow hammer. The detective's acting like he thinks I did it."

Owen scoffed. "That's the craziest thing I ever heard! You wouldn't hurt anybody. You don't have it in you." He cocked his head and whispered, "But how did the killer get your mallet?"

"I left it outside last night after I used it to install a sign in the yard."

Buck's van came up the street and pulled to the curb on the other side. He threw his door open, leaped from his truck, and rushed over in his coveralls and cowboy hat.

"About time you got here," I snapped, anxiety making me testy.

"I came as soon as I could," he said. "I had to stop for gas. You okay?"

"Not really, Buck. It's not every day you find a corpse."

The detective returned, extended his hand again, and introduced himself to my cousins. "Good morning. I'm Detective Collin Flynn."

Buck shook the man's hand. "Buck Whitaker."

"Whitaker," Flynn repeated, looking from Buck to me and back again. "You're Whitney's husband?"

"Ew." Buck grimaced. "No."

I cut him a look. He'd be lucky to nab a woman like me—one he wasn't related to, of course.

The detective took another shot. "Brother, then?"

Buck shook his head. "Still no."

"He's my—" I began, but Flynn cut me off.

"Cousin," he said. "Your fathers are brothers."

"Good job putting the clues together, Detective." I rolled my eyes. Perhaps I should've behaved more politely, but I was fit to be tied. *Accuse me of murder, will you?* I wasn't going to show him any more respect than he'd shown me.

I might be a polite person, but even I had my limits and he'd pushed them.

Owen held out his hand. "Owen Whitaker."

Flynn took Owen's hand. "Another cousin?"

Owen replied with a dip of his head.

"Did Whitney call you two?" the detective asked Buck and Owen, looking from one to the other.

"Not me," Owen replied. "The three of us had already planned to meet here this morning to do some work on the house."

"She called me," Buck said. "I wasn't planning to get here until a little later."

The detective narrowed his eyes at Buck. "I understand you own an interest in the house?"

"Yes." Buck removed his cowboy hat. "'Course it's been one big fiasco from the start."

"The fire set y'all back, didn't it?" Flynn asked.

"Sure did. In more ways than one. We lost some time and it'll cost us some money, too."

Buck may not have realized it yet, but the detective was grilling him to see if he might know something about the murder, might have been involved in some way. After all, Buck was a big, brawny guy, someone who could have easily bested the lithe, lean Dunaway in a physical confrontation. Still, there was no way Buck had anything to do with Dunaway's death, either. Might as well let him speak his piece and clear himself.

Flynn readied his notepad. "Did you know Mr. Dunaway?"

"Nope," Buck said. "Never met the guy in person. Only heard about him from Whitney."

"What did she tell you about him?"

Buck cut me a nervous glance. I'd already told the detective that my relationship with Rick Dunaway hadn't been all Georgia peaches and cream. No need for my cousin to paint a prettier picture.

"I didn't sugarcoat things, Buck," I told him. "You don't need to, either."

Relief relaxed his features as he answered the detective's question. "Whitney told me that Dunaway could be demanding. Cheap, too. But she was learning from him, watching how he chose the properties he bought and sold. She fancies herself the future real estate queen of Nashville."

"Do you now?" the detective asked, directing the question at me.

"I most certainly do." Then again, it seemed Presley had the same ambition for herself. It would be funny if she and I ended up rivals one day, like Rick Dunaway and Thad Gentry had been.

The detective took a few seconds to digest the information Buck had provided. "Where were you last night?"

Buck went rigid, clueing in that the detective had him on the hot seat now. "I wasn't with Colonel Mustard in the conservatory, if that's what you're implying."

The detective skewered my cousin with a look. "You're part owner of this house. You've got skin in the game, too."

"In other words," Buck said, "I have a motive for killing Rick Dunaway."

"Exactly," Flynn said, not beating around the bush. "If you want to be cleared as a suspect, I'm going to need you to be more specific about your whereabouts."

"It was a Friday night," he said. "I was doing what I always do on Friday nights. Drinking beer with my buddies and flirting with the single ladies. Unsuccessfully, I might add. If you don't play guitar, you got no chance with the women in this town."

Flynn groaned. "I feel your pain."

Buck chuckled and offered the detective an empathetic fist bump. To my surprise, Flynn knocked knuckles with my cousin. *Men. Sheesh.*

"Where did you go?" Flynn asked.

"Up and down SoBro," Buck replied, using the name locals had given to the famous stretch of south Broadway. The area housed a dozen or more honky-tonks featuring up-and-coming country-western artists, cold beer for wannabe cowboys, and flavored moonshine for the ladies and hipster tourists. "We started out at Tootsie's, moved on to Tequila Cowboy, and finished up the night at one of them rooftop places that overlook the river."

The Cumberland River ran directly to the east of downtown Nashville, between the skyscrapers and the Titans' stadium, providing a scenic background for Music City.

"Were you aware that Rick Dunaway was planning to come here last night?" the detective asked.

"I was," Buck replied. "Whitney had said something about it, but I didn't pay it much mind. Seemed like she had things under control."

I usually *did* have things under control—which was precisely why I was having a hard time with my current situation. It felt as if my world were spinning wildly and dangerously, like a circular saw blade that had come off its shaft. I wasn't sure when the spinning would stop, where the saw blade would land.

Buck pulled out his wallet, opened it, and removed a couple of white slips of paper. He held them out to the detective. "Here you go. My bar tabs, paid by credit card. Proof positive I wasn't here last night. My Taco Bell receipt is in there, too. I stopped by and picked up dinner there around five thirty."

Flynn took the receipts and looked them over.

"That Taco Bell location is nowhere near here," Buck pointed out.

The detective bobbed his head and handed the receipts back to Buck. "I suppose I can cross you off my list."

Looked like Buck had been saved by the bell. The Taco Bell.

Having struck out with Buck, the detective turned to Owen. "What about you? Where were you last night?"

Buck snorted. "He's got three little girls. Hellions, all. I bet he fell asleep on the couch before nine."

While Buck's description of our darling, if sometimes overly energetic nieces was hardly flattering, Owen knew Buck meant nothing by it. Buck adored those little girls as much as I did, and that was saying a lot. Owen lifted his chin in acknowledgment. "You'd be right. Fell asleep watching a rom-com on Netflix. Can't even tell you which one. My wife picked it. 'Course she slept through most of it, too."

"All right. Thanks for the information." The detective closed his notepad and slid it back into his pocket.

"Are we done here?" I asked. "Can my cat and I go now?"

"Hang tight for a second." He stepped away to have a quick pow-wow with the crime scene team, returning a moment later with my keys. He handed them to me. "Here you are. You're free to go now, but don't leave town without checking in with me first, okay? I might have some more questions for you."

"Okay." I'd already told him everything I knew, and I didn't like having restrictions imposed on me, but fighting the detective would be futile. Given that I was a key witness in a murder investigation, he could probably get some type of court order requiring me to stay put if I didn't voluntarily agree to stick around. I'd rather he spent his time figuring out who killed Rick Dunaway and why. The sooner that person was behind bars, the sooner my life could return to normal.

CHAPTER 24

NAPTIME

SAWDUST

Whitney carried him into the pool house and promptly opened the cage door to release him. *Good.* He'd spent more than enough time in that little plastic box today. All the hubbub at the other house had prevented him getting any sleep. He normally took twenty to thirty naps a day. He was a half dozen in arrears already.

He hopped up onto Whitney's bed and curled up on her pillow. He liked how extra soft it was, how it smelled like her. He closed his eyes and was asleep in seconds.

CHAPTER 25

FIXIN' TO FIX
THINGS UP

WHITNEY

After dropping Sawdust back at the pool house, I rushed across the terrace and through my parents' back door. It being noon on a Saturday, they were relaxing on the couch, watching a travel show on TV. Well, my mother was watching the television, anyway. Both Yin-Yang and my father were asleep, the two of them lounging together on the sofa, snoring softly. Owen wasn't the only one who couldn't stay awake in front of the TV.

My mother looked up as I came in. "Hi, sweetie. Want some lunch? We had Greek last night. There's leftover spanakopita in the fridge."

"No, thanks. I don't think I could eat right now." I flopped down in one of their club chairs and put my feet up on the ottoman, trying to figure out where to start.

She sat bolt upright. "You're turning down free food. What's wrong?"

Might as well start with the big news, huh? "Someone's

done away with Rick Dunaway." I cringed at my unintended pun.

Her eyes went wide and she leaned toward me. "The man you and Buck bought the house from? Are you saying someone killed him?"

"Yep. They buried him in the flower bed at our house on Sweetbriar." *Buried* was a generous term. All they'd really done was plunk his body in the garden and toss some loose soil over him. "I found him this morning."

My mother's shriek jarred both the dog and my dad awake.

"What is it?" my dad cried, looking from my mother to me. "What's wrong?"

My mother stood from her chair, her arms fluttering like she was one of the baby birds from the backyard, trying to take its first flight. "Whitney found a corpse on her lawn this morning!"

"What?" My father reflexively stood, too. Yin-Yang took advantage of the situation to steal my dad's superior spot on the sofa. She slipped into place behind him.

I took a deep breath and ran through the morning's events, including the questions Detective Flynn had posed to me and the tool they'd asked me about. "The murderer must have used my dead blow mallet to kill Mr. Dunaway. The detective seems to think I might be responsible."

"How dare he!" My mother stamped a foot in righteous indignation, while simultaneously waving a dismissive hand and issuing a *pshaw*. "That's utterly ridiculous! You'd never kill anyone!"

Dad came over and put a supportive hand on my shoulder. "Don't worry, honey. I'm sure they'll sort this all out soon, find the killer, and clear your name."

I looked up at him. "I sure hope so."

"Until then," my mother said, "you're staying in the house with us."

She'd get no argument from me. I was too creeped out to sleep out in the pool house alone tonight.

The two came with me as I rounded up some clothes, toiletries, and my cat. Sawdust issued an irritated chirp when I picked him up. Poor thing hadn't gotten a nap in yet today and was clearly feeling cranky.

Back in my parents' house, I settled in my childhood bedroom, sitting at the small student desk I'd used when studying for American history and geometry and the SAT. I phoned the Hartleys and shared the bad news. They had the same reaction as my parents. Ms. Hartley called the detective's suspicions against me "the silliest thing I've ever heard," and Mr. Hartley assured me that Flynn would "realize how off base he was once he poked around a bit."

When we finished the call, I tried to study for my real estate exam. Only four days remained until the test and I was woefully behind. Unfortunately, I found it impossible to concentrate on the materials. The image of Rick Dunaway's ghostly face kept popping into my mind. *Eek*.

I mentally reviewed the list of potential suspects I'd given to Detective Flynn and the evidence against them.

Could Bobby Palmer have been the killer? He'd have every reason to want revenge on Rick Dunaway. If Mr. Dunaway hadn't offered him a bribe, he wouldn't have ended up losing Home & Hearth's business. Bobby had a gambling problem and was in debt to his bookie, for who knows how much. Desperate people do desperate things. Bobby also knew Dunaway was coming to my house last night. Maybe he'd confronted him out front while I'd sat unknowingly in the kitchen. Maybe he'd demanded more money from Dunaway and Dunaway had said no. Maybe he had flown off the handle, spotted the mallet, and whacked Mr. Dunaway with it. It was certainly possible. Still, having known and trusted Bobby for years, I simply couldn't see it. Then again, maybe I was fooling myself. How many times had people on the TV news said their homicidal neighbor had seemed like a nice person until bodies surfaced in the yard? Of course the people on Sweetbriar might be saying the same thing about me. *Ugh.*

It was also possible that Dunaway had pulled up when Jackson was hurling eggs at the house. Maybe Jackson had panicked when caught in the act, grabbed the mallet, and swung at Mr. Dunaway in an attempt to get away. But why not just run? It would be faster and easier. Besides, it was dark by six o'clock at this time of year. Wouldn't Jackson have seen Dunaway's headlights coming up the road and had plenty of time to hide or scurry off? Then again, Jackson wasn't the sharpest tool in the shed. Maybe he hadn't been paying attention to the road.

I wondered if Thad Gentry had been next door last night. Maybe he'd seen Dunaway arrive and had come over to start an argument about the house or gloat about Dunaway's unsuccessful attempt to prevent the rezoning of Gentry's property. With two powerful men going head-to-head, things might have gotten out of hand and become physical. It could happen. Even so, guys like Rick Dunaway and Thad Gentry seemed much more likely to take their battles to a courtroom than the streets. They weren't the type of men who liked to get their hands dirty. They hired people for that. *Wait. Could Gentry have hired a hit on Dunaway?* Though I supposed it was possible, it felt like my imagination was running wild, getting the best of me. Still, engrossed in my studies at the back of the house, I could have missed a disturbance out front if it wasn't too loud.

One possibility that hadn't crossed my mind until now

was that the crime could have been a totally random robbery. Mr. Dunaway's car and clothing sent an unmistakable message that the man had big bucks. Maybe someone had followed his car and mugged him on my doorstep. Maybe they'd clobbered him with the mallet when he'd put up some resistance. After all, if his wallet had been in his pocket, the crime scene techs could have identified him by his driver's license photo and they wouldn't have needed me to identify his body, right? Maybe the detective made up all that stuff about needing a positive ID because Dunaway's wallet wasn't on him. I wasn't sure of the police protocols, but it would make sense. I also knew police were sometimes hesitant to share information. Maybe they hadn't wanted me to know his wallet was missing.

Mr. Dunaway was in the process of divorce, too. Could it be that he'd liquidated the Sweetbriar property not to have money for his legal fees and his soon-to-be-ex wife, but that he'd sold it to have cash he could secrete away somewhere? Maybe his wife had found out and become enraged, followed him to tell him off and whacked him like a piñata when he'd expressed no remorse.

All of these scenarios were *possible,* but were any of them *probable*? I had no idea. Luckily, it wasn't my job to figure that out. It was Detective Flynn's. I could only hope the rookie homicide detective was up to the task. From what I could glean, the Dunaway case was his first murder investigation.

I spent the rest of the day fidgeting and worrying, but finally managed to eat a few bites of the spanakopita. *If only I could be whisked away to a Greek isle . . .*

When I called Colette that afternoon to tell her what had happened, she was incredulous. "I've got the night off. I'm taking you out for a drink. I know you need one."

"I do." *Or two . . . or ten . . .*

She picked me up at my parents' house and we drove to a quiet neighborhood bar nearby, taking a booth in the back corner. As soon as we'd placed our order with the waitress, Colette reached across the table and took both of my hands in hers, giving them a supportive squeeze. "Tell me everything."

So I did. I told her about finding Dunaway, Detective Flynn's interrogation, how Sawdust had been a temporary and very unhappy captive in the cordoned-off crime scene. She shook her head throughout the saga, her brown eyes wide in disbelief.

"So the real target might have been *you*?" She bit her lip. "I don't even want to think about that, Whitney."

"Join the club."

She sat back, chewing her lip as she pondered. "There certainly are a lot of potential suspects and motives. Who do you think is the most likely to have done it?"

"Honestly?" I raised my palms. "I have no idea. The killer could be any one of them, or someone else entirely. Dunaway has made quite a few enemies. He doesn't always treat people fairly." In fact, he rarely did. The man was only out for himself.

The wine arrived and, while I tossed back a big, nerve-numbing swig, Colette took a delicate sip. "My money's on Dunaway's assistant. What did you say her name was? Presley?"

"That's right." I set my glass down. "Really? You think she killed Dunaway?" The woman certainly had a motive, but I had a hard time seeing Presley picking up the mallet in her manicured fingers and conking Dunaway with it. Though she was among my mental list of possible suspects, she wasn't at the top of it.

"She kept Dunaway's calendar," Colette pointed out,

"so she would know he planned to go to the house at six on Friday. Besides, you've said he was an awful person to work for. Maybe all those years of working for the guy got to her."

My friend might be on to something, after all. Not only would our rendezvous be noted on his schedule, but I'd mentioned it aloud when I'd been leaving Dunaway's office the day I'd asked him to cover the deductible. I thought aloud. "He always managed to get on my last nerve, and I only had to deal with him in small doses." I could hardly imagine what it must have been like to work for him day in and day out, to put up with his constant demands and condescension. It had to be unbelievably frustrating.

"She seemed jealous of you, too," Colette said, "of your relationship with her boss. Her dedication hadn't gotten her anywhere, right? He hadn't brought her in on a deal. Maybe she was trying to frame you, to get back at both of you by killing Dunaway and making it look like you did it."

"Wow. You could be right." Killing her boss would kill two birds with one stone—or at least one hammer. I took another sip of wine. "Even so, if I had to hazard a guess, I'd say it was Jackson. He threatened me outright, not just once, but twice, the first time in person and the next time by scrawling 'watch your back' on the door of the house. Plus, he's young. People his age have poor impulse control." Not to mention that he seemed to be a natural-born nincompoop.

"Whoever did it," she said, "I hope the cops catch him or her soon." She reached a hand across the table to take mine. "Is there anything I can do in the meantime?"

"You can come with me and Buck to the home improvement store tomorrow afternoon to pick out things for the house. I need something to take my mind off the murder."

"You got it." She released my hand, giving it a soft pat.

"You can also help me look over some design Web sites to get some ideas." I pulled my tablet from my purse and circled around to her side of the booth. As we each finished our first glass of wine, I logged into the bar's Wi-Fi and the two of us went through page after page of photos on Isak Nyström's Web site. I'd hoped that reviewing the site would give us some thoughts for the house. Unfortunately, it gave us too many of them, some of the ideas being mutually exclusive.

When we'd reviewed everything on his site, Colette tipped back her glass to savor the last drop of her wine. "Too bad you can't hire the guy to design the space for you."

"I know, right?" Assuming the guy would even agree to design the house, there was no way Buck and I could afford even an hour of his time. "I guess we'll just have to see what catches our eye tomorrow." I put my fingers back to the keyboard.

Colette leaned in to take another look at the screen. "What are you doing now?"

"Pulling up Jackson Pharr's rap sheet." I'd learned how to run background checks at Home & Hearth. For a small fee, you could obtain someone's criminal records online. I logged into the site, paid the $19.95 fee with my credit card, and typed in Jackson's name.

"Whoa!" Colette said when his report popped up on the screen.

Whoa, indeed. Jackson had amassed an extensive and varied record, all of it since he'd applied to rent the house on Sweetbriar. He had a nonviolent offense for vandalizing a vehicle. He'd been assessed only a fine for that petty crime. He'd also been cited for driving under the influence. He was currently serving probation for that dangerous violation. Looked like he'd gotten off easy since it was his first charge for that particular offense. He'd also been recently charged with assault. Given the date of the incident, it appeared that entry related to the fistfight Patty had seen take place in the front yard. The charges were pending, no final adjudication having yet been rendered.

"He's no saint," Colette said.

"That's for sure." I downloaded the report so I could print it out later at home.

As we left the bar later, Colette reached into her purse, retrieved the small canister of pepper spray she always kept in the bag, and pressed it into my hand. "Until they catch the killer, keep this in reach at all times."

I looked at my friend. "I don't want you to be without it."

She stopped, wrapped her fingers around mine, and forced them to close around the spray. "And I don't want to be without *you,* Whitney."

I felt the same way. A genuine, long-lasting friendship like ours was rare. I accepted the spray but said, "When they arrest Dunaway's killer, I'm giving this back to you."

"Fine. Let's hope it's soon."

The following afternoon, Colette and I met up with Buck in the parking lot of the home improvement store.

I held out a printout to Buck. "Take a look at this."

"What is it?" he asked as he took it from me.

"Jackson Pharr's criminal record. I have a hunch he could be the one who ended Rick Dunaway. I was curious so I bought his record online. There's some interesting stuff in there."

Buck looked down and read over the document before looking up again. "He's off the rails."

While Jackson's criminal record didn't conclusively prove he'd been the one to write the threat on the door, egg the house, and attack Dunaway, it showed he was capable of such acts.

"I hope Detective Flynn took a look at Jackson's record, too, and followed up with him." I'd rest much easier once the culprit was caught and put behind bars.

Buck cracked his knuckles, as if warming them up for a fight. "I have half a mind to track that kid down, go 'round to his place, and encourage him to confess."

"I have the other half."

Buck lifted a determined chin. "Then let's do it. Now."

Colette was more hesitant. "It could be dangerous to confront him. Shouldn't you leave this up to the police?"

Buck frowned. "I'm concerned about that detective. He's still wet behind the ears."

Part of me agreed with Buck. Another part thought we should give the guy the benefit of the doubt. After all, his training partner had noted he'd moved up quickly. Surely the folks who were up the chain at Nashville PD wouldn't have promoted him if they didn't think he was ready. Still, the detective had a lot of leads to follow. Why not help move things along if we could?

There was just one small problem. "I don't have Jackson's current address."

Buck cocked his head. "Got his phone number?"

"He won't answer calls from me." I supposed we could try his mother, but she'd probably tip him off.

"I'll call him on my cell," Buck said. "That way he won't recognize the number."

I retrieved my phone from my bag, pulled up Jackson's name in my contacts list, and rattled it off. As I did, Buck typed it into his phone.

My cousin put his phone to his ear. Though Colette and I could only hear Buck's side of the conversation, we got the gist.

"Jackson Pharr?" Buck asked. He paused to listen. "I've got a package I'm trying to deliver to you. Looks like it's from some kind of electronics company. The box has an address on Sweetbriar Avenue, but a woman there told me you've moved." He paused again. "Uh-huh. So long as it's not too far, I can bring it to you. Where you at?"

Buck made a scribbling motion with his hand and Colette and I quickly rummaged in our purses until we came up with a pen and a grocery receipt he could write on. I turned my back to him so he could use my shoulder as a hard surface. "Got it. I'll be there in ten minutes or so."

Buck ended the call and the three of us piled into his van and drove to Pharr's new digs. As we climbed out, Buck opened his toolbox and retrieved his biggest wrench, slipping it into his pocket. "That kid tries anything, he'll be sorry."

After grabbing another wrench for myself, I pulled Colette's pepper spray from my purse and handed it to her. Armed with our makeshift defense system, we eased up to the door of the duplex where Jackson now lived. While Buck knocked on the door, Colette and I pressed our backs to either side of it so we'd be out of view if Pharr looked out the peephole.

We needn't have bothered. The kid pulled the door open and looked Buck up and down with bloodshot eyes. Looked like he was hungover again. "Where's my box?"

I whirled to face him. "Where were you Friday night?"

Pharr looked from Buck to me, his ruddy, unwashed face crinkled in confusion for a moment before he seemed to realize he'd been had. "Where I go is none of your business." He proceeded to call me some very loud and colorful names, the verbal equivalent of fireworks.

Buck pulled himself up to his full height and stepped

right up to Pharr. "You kiss your mother with that filthy mouth?"

"No." Pharr smirked. "I kiss *your* mother with it."

With that, he stepped back and slammed the door in our faces. *BAM!*

I sighed. "That didn't go well." We'd gained nothing by coming here. I should have realized the visit would be fruitless.

"The kid's a jerk," Buck said, "but I have to admit he had a pretty good comeback."

We returned to Buck's van and drove back to the home improvement store. While Buck rounded up a long, flat dolly for the larger pieces we planned to buy, I snagged a shopping cart for the smaller items we'd need, like nails and screws and paintbrushes. Fortunately, I'd heard from the crime scene team earlier. They had finished going over the house and we were permitted back inside.

Although Colette had come along primarily to offer her expertise on the kitchen items, we welcomed her opinion on the other decorative items, too, such as the lighting fixtures and bathroom cabinets. After spirited debate, we decided to go with brushed nickel over chrome or bronze, and a soft gray flat interior paint for the walls. We selected a dresser-style cabinet with feet and a curved front for the bathroom. The old-fashioned design would go well with the claw-foot tub. We'd add another cabinet over the toilet for extra storage, as well as new towel racks and a couple of hooks to hang robes or clothing items. After picking out new switch plates, again opting for the more expensive brushed-nickel style, we moved on to closet doors.

Finally, we came to the kitchen department.

Buck swept an upturned hand to indicate all of the options that stood before us. "Work your magic, Chef Chevalier."

She squealed, jumped up and down, and aimed right for the cabinets. After walking back and forth before the sample display and examining each option closely, she made her pronouncement. "I like the Shaker-style ones the best. They'd look great with glossy black paint and square knobs."

"As you wish, milady," Buck said with a bow. "Now. How 'bout countertops?"

When none of the standard, more affordable countertops met Colette's fancy, the saleswoman said, "Would you like to take a look at the granite and quartz slabs?"

Colette looked up at Buck. "Would quartz bust your budget?"

I'd been wondering the same thing. I was pretty sure we'd exceeded our budget already. But given that he was footing the bill for the renovations, it was his call.

Buck looked back down at her. "Don't you worry. Whatever you like, we'll make it work."

After looking over two dozen slabs of granite, marble, and quartz, Colette decided on a quartz piece that was primarily white with gray and silver streaks running through it.

I ran a hand over the stone. "It's beautiful." She'd chosen well.

When we were done in the kitchen section, Buck pointed down the main aisle that bisected the store. "Let's take a walk over there and see what they're offering in terms of security systems. In case the killer was really after you, we'd best put a system in at the house to keep you safe."

We made our way to the aisle and looked over the variety of security systems offered. They ranged wildly in complexity and price. After comparing the options and costs, we decided on a set of wireless units with motion-detection lights that would turn on anytime someone approached and record the activity. We also bought a wireless doorbell. It had a special function that would sound an alert via an app on our phones anytime someone rang the bell. We would be able to address the person through our phones. I hated that we had to spend the additional funds—*Buck's funds*—on a system that was almost solely for my benefit, but I wasn't about to turn my cousin down. Better safe than sorry.

After Buck placed the items in my cart, he said, "I don't want you at the house for an extended period of time by yourself. The killer could come back. Let me know when you'll be there so I can make sure to be there with you."

While I appreciated his concern, I knew he had much better things to do than play babysitter for me. "Colette gave me her pepper spray."

"That's good," he said, "but not good enough." He gave me a pointed look. "You heard me. Let me know when you'll be at the house. If I find out you've been there alone, I'll put an end to you myself."

"All right, Buck," I said. "Understood."

We turned and headed back through the store to the front checkouts, loaded down with the beautiful slab of quartz for the kitchen and bathroom countertops, two new sinks, the cabinets, the security devices, and more cans of paint and hardware than you could shake a stick at. On our way, Buck reached out and grabbed a new dead blow hammer from a peg in an aisle. He said nothing about it, but he didn't need to. My mallet, the one that had been used to kill Rick Dunaway, was in an evidence locker somewhere. I wouldn't want it back even if they offered to return it after the killer was convicted.

When we reached the checkout and the clerk had finished ringing up our items, Buck pulled out his credit card and held it aloft. "Everyone cross your fingers."

I gave him a pointed look. "You don't know your balance?"

"Nah," he said. "I like to live on the edge."

"The edge of bankruptcy?" I teased. Buck might not know his balances down to the penny, but he was responsible. Otherwise, the mortgage company wouldn't have approved him cosigning my loan.

He ran the card through the machine. When the word APPROVED popped up on the screen, the three of us cheered. I gave Buck a big hug right there at the checkout counter. The cashier smiled as he tried to wriggle out of my grasp.

"Stop that!" he said. "If you're going to keep hugging me, I'm going to have second thoughts about being your business partner."

"But I'm so grateful!" I gave him a final squeeze and let him go. "I couldn't have done this without you."

"Yeah," he agreed, cutting me a sharp look completely contradicted by the grin tugging at his lips. "Don't ever forget that."

CHAPTER 26

PRIME SUSPECT

Buck and I drove straight from the home improvement store to the house so we could unload the items and install the security cameras. Gentry's car was parked next door. The man seemed to work 24/7.

Though it had been only a day since I'd found Rick Dunaway's corpse in the garden, it felt like a lifetime ago. What remained of the yellow cordon tape drooped, some of it having fallen to the ground. A ribbon of it was picked up by the breeze and fluttered as if waving good-bye to a ghost. The warped birthday party was over.

I climbed out of my SUV. *First things first.* I circumnavigated the yard and pulled down all of the remaining crime scene tape, gathering it into a tangled ball in my arms. I carried it to the garage and stuffed it into the garbage bin as deep as it would go, leaning in to force it down.

"In a pickle, aren't you?"

The unexpected voice came from directly behind me and I reflexively jumped back. "Mr. Gentry," I said on a breath, my heart pounding against my ribs like an electric hammer. "I didn't hear you walk up." *Seriously, is the man part vampire?*

Gentry gestured around. "You can take that crime scene tape down, but people aren't going to forget. A man was murdered here. You'll be lucky to sell this house for half of what it was worth two days ago."

Gee, thanks. And good day to you, too, sir. "Can I help you with something?" My irritation came through in my words, but I didn't much care. Dunaway had been gone only a day and already Thad Gentry seemed to be trying to capitalize on the man's death.

"I'll take this place off your hands for three hundred and seventy thousand. Cash. You'd be able to pay off your loan in full."

"We'd be losing money." Most of our down payment, to be precise.

"You're going to lose money regardless," he said. "You'd be a fool not to take this offer."

I remembered Dunaway saying he'd only sell to Gentry over his dead body. Well, I wouldn't sell to Gentry even then. I crossed my arms over my chest and looked him directly in the eye. "I guess I'm a fool, then. But at least my heart isn't as cold as ice."

He glared back at me, flames virtually flickering in his eyes, before his mouth slowly turned up in what can only be described as an evil grin. "Call me when you come to your senses." With that, he walked away.

As I watched him go, a small part of me wondered if he might have killed Rick Dunaway here so he could snag the house for a song. But surely I was wrong. Gentry was ruthless, sure, but he wouldn't go that far . . . *would he*?

The tape and Thad Gentry dealt with for the time being, Buck and I unloaded his van, carrying our purchases into the house. He had a big job elsewhere that had to be wrapped up by the Thanksgiving holiday later in the week, so we wouldn't be able to work on our house again for several days. Although I could take care of some of the tasks by myself, I wasn't about to come back to this place alone. Not with a killer on the loose and Buck threatening to kill me himself if I did. It was frustrating. Every day the renovation work was delayed would cost us money—money we didn't have.

Patty watched from her window as we went about our business. She might have thought we couldn't see her behind her curtain, but I knew she was there. I'd seen the fabric move, caught a glimpse of her hand as she pushed it back. While I'd found her busybody tendencies a little irritating before, I actually appreciated them now. It would be safer around here with her keeping a close and constant eye on things. Maybe she'd even see something that could be helpful to the investigation.

I heard nothing further from Detective Flynn on Sunday, Monday, or Tuesday. It appeared that whatever suspicions he might have harbored about me had been quelled as he delved into the investigation. Unfortunately, though, there were no news reports of any arrests having been made.

While Rick Dunaway's death had been the feature story on the Saturday evening newscasts and in Sunday's newspaper, given that there'd been seemingly no progress in the case, the crime had already begun to fade from the airwaves and headlines. Keeping Colette's pepper spray close at hand and a close eye on my rearview mirror and surroundings lest the killer make an attempt on my life, I performed my usual property management duties. I showed a soon-to-be-available two-bedroom duplex to a young couple looking for more space as they anticipated their upcoming bundle of joy. I oversaw the installation of a new water heater at a rental house in east Nashville. I replaced damaged trim in a vacant town house and touched up the smudged paint. Of course I'd had to borrow tools from my cousins since my toolbox had been seized.

On Tuesday evening, my impatience got the better of me. I wanted Dunaway's murder solved, and I wanted it solved *now*. I phoned Buck. "Grab your wrench. Let's go talk to Bobby Palmer."

I found Bobby's home address in the county real estate records, and Buck and I headed over to his house. As we walked up his driveway, I took a quick glimpse into his truck, which was illuminated by a coach light between his garage doors. On his dash sat a lanyard with a collection of cards attached to a clip at one end. The cards were players club cards from casinos.

I angled my head to indicate the cards on the dash. "Looks like I was right about Bobby. He's a gambling man."

Buck eyed the cards and grunted. "Yep. Must've got himself into some trouble."

Bobby's wife, a sixtyish woman with a warm smile, answered the door. After we introduced ourselves, she called back to her husband. "Bobby? There's a Buck and Whitney here to see you."

Her cordial tone told me her husband might have been less than forthcoming with her about recent events.

Bobby scurried up, his eyes wide, though his tone was friendly, jolly even. "Hello, you two. My wife's watching *Jeopardy!* It's her favorite program. Why don't we step outside so we don't bother her?"

"Isn't he thoughtful?" his wife said with a smile.

"He's something," Buck muttered.

Bobby herded us out the door and onto the porch, closing the door behind himself. "Why are you here?" he hissed, sending furtive glances at the door.

"I take it you heard about Rick Dunaway?" I said.

"How could I not?" he replied. "It's been all over the news. Sad business."

Buck's hand went into the pocket that held the wrench as he stared the man down. "You have anything to do with it?"

"Me?" Bobby gasped. "Of course not!"

"You sure about that?" I asked. "It seems clear you've gotten yourself into some trouble with your gambling. Did you need more money to pay your bookie? Did you try to extort more funds from Rick Dunaway?"

"I did no such thing!" Bobby's expression was bewildered, as if he never would have considered the idea on his own. Heck, maybe he wouldn't have.

"If you didn't kill Rick Dunaway," I said, "maybe you know who might have."

Bobby's face contorted, an open display of the emotional struggle going on within him. "I have no idea who might have killed the man," he said, "but I will say this. A shady business doesn't yield a sunny life."

Had he just admitted something? "So you know Dunaway was shady?" I asked.

The door behind Bobby opened and his wife poked her head out. "The show's over now. Why don't you invite your friends in for some apple pie?"

"Thanks, hon." Bobby's tight face and closed expression told us he'd said all he'd intended to, and gave us our cue to go. "But they were just leaving."

On Wednesday morning, I downed an extra cup of coffee in preparation for my real estate exam. I hadn't slept well the last few nights, and I hoped the extra caffeine would keep me alert. Given the fire and Dunaway's murder, I'd had far too little time to study. Honestly, I wasn't sure I could even pass the test given the circumstances. But since I'd already paid my fee, I decided I might as well give it a shot. It would be horribly embarrassing to fail the test, but I could repeat it if I didn't pass this time around. At least with Thanksgiving tomorrow I had something to look forward to. Aunt Nancy's sweet potato pie was just the thing I needed to lift my spirits.

I picked up Sawdust and cradled him in my arms. "Be a good boy while mommy's gone." I gave him his usual kiss on the head and, with another quick kiss to my waiting mother's cheek, handed him off and headed out to my car.

As I'd done since the murder, I glanced at my rearview mirror every few seconds to keep tabs on the cars behind me, keeping a lookout for Jackson Pharr, Bobby Palmer, Thad Gentry, and Presley. I wasn't sure what Presley drove, but I knew Jackson and Bobby drove pickups and Thad Gentry drove a blue Infiniti. While I saw neither a pickup nor an Infiniti to my rear, as I neared the testing center, a metro police car pulled in behind me. My eyes immediately went to my speedometer. Nope, I wasn't speeding. I hadn't run a red light, either. Nevertheless, the flashing lights came on. *That's strange.* Had I made an illegal lane change? Was one of my taillights out? None of the warning lights on my dashboard were on. *Hmm.* I supposed I'd find out soon enough.

There was no shoulder on this part of the road, so I turned into the parking lot of a Methodist church and stopped my car. The cruiser pulled up sideways behind me, blocking me in. A moment later, both Officer Hogarty and Detective Flynn climbed out.

Uh-oh. I have a really bad feeling about this.

I rolled down my window as the detective stepped up beside my car. "Good morning," I said, forcing myself to sound pleasant.

His voice was firm and emotionless. "Step out of your car, please."

The bad feeling got even worse. I shut off the engine, removed my keys, and slid them into my blazer pocket as I climbed out of the car. My gaze went from the detective to Officer Hogarty and back again. "What's going on?"

"We need you to come to the station," Flynn said.

Alarms went off in my mind and my adrenaline spiked, raising my body temperature in an instant. "Why?" I squeaked.

"We need to talk to you about the Dunaway murder."

He'd already interrogated me up, down, and backwards. "I've already told you everything I know."

"We have some follow-up questions."

What could there possibly be left to ask me? "Could I come by the station this afternoon? I'm on my way to take my test for my Realtor's license." I hadn't studied nearly enough and would probably fail the test, but that was beside the point.

"Sorry about that," he said, not sounding sorry at all. "But we need to talk *now*."

"Can we talk here? I had to pay a fee to take the test and it's nonrefundable."

"Look." Hogarty pulled her handcuffs from her belt. "Are you going to cooperate or are we going to have to do this the hard way?"

I gulped and raised my hands in surrender. "I'll cooperate."

Hogarty made a circular motion with her index finger, directing me to turn around. When I did, she told me to put my hands on the roof of my car. I'd seen this play out before on television. *She was going to cuff me! Like a common criminal!* But there was nothing I could do about it.

She took my right hand by the wrist and pulled it down behind me. As she did the same with my left hand, drivers on the road slowed down to rubberneck, no doubt wondering what the benign-looking blonde had done to warrant her arrest. Cold, hard metal encircled my wrists, followed by two *clicks* as the officer secured the cuffs. *Worst bangle bracelets ever!*

After patting me down and finding nothing more dangerous than a tube of lip balm in my pocket, she took me by the upper arm and looked me in the eye. "You have the right to remain silent," she said. "Anything you say to us can be used against you in court. You also have the right to a lawyer. If you can't afford one, the court will appoint you one. Understand?"

I swallowed hard. "I'm being arrested?"

She scoffed. "What was your first clue?"

This can't be happening! my mind screamed as she escorted me to the cruiser and placed me in the backseat. Once I was seated, she buckled me in. She tossed my keys to the detective, who used them to open my car, remove my purse, and relock the vehicle.

The tasks complete, Officer Hogarty and Detective Flynn retook their seats in the front, separated from me by an expanse of metal mesh that felt miles thick. On their side was freedom. On mine was imprisonment.

Detective Flynn set my purse on his lap, unzipped it, and fished around inside. He pulled out the canister of pepper spray Colette had given me, examined it, and then dropped it back into my bag, continuing to fish around until he found my cell phone. He pulled it out and turned it on. "What's your passcode?"

"Five, six, eight, four."

He typed it in to confirm it was valid, then slid my phone back into my purse.

"May I call my parents?" I asked.

"Once we get to the station," Flynn said.

I wanted to cry and scream and stomp my feet and profess my innocence, but I only managed the former, a single tear journeying down my face and surely leaving a streak in my makeup. My eyes caught Detective Flynn's in the rearview mirror. *He saw me cry.* I felt ashamed and angry. Part of me wanted to cry harder. Another part wanted to kick the back of his seat and tell him that he was wasting everyone's time hassling me while Rick Dunaway's actual killer was still on the loose! What kind of detective was he that he'd think a woman like me would kill someone?

I realized at that moment that he didn't know me. Not at all. He had no idea that I'd once been a Girl Scout, that I'd received positive comments about my classroom conduct from all of my teachers on my report cards, that I'd volunteered as a teenager at the animal shelter cleaning litter boxes in the cat room. He didn't know that, more recently, I'd worked alongside other volunteers doing carpentry work for Habitat for Humanity. All he knew was that I had both a motive and the opportunity to kill Rick Dunaway. Maybe that was all he cared about, too.

I knew from the cop shows I'd seen that it was best to keep my mouth shut, but it was incredibly hard. I had to bite my lip to keep from talking. I wanted to profess my innocence. To tell him who I was. I wanted to ask why. Why had they decided to take me in today? What had they discovered between Saturday and this morning that, instead of clearing my name, had made them more suspicious of me?

People in adjacent cars looked over at me as we drove

along. An adolescent boy put his thumbs in his ears, wag-gled his fingers, and stuck his tongue out at me. As we drew near the station, we passed a billboard for Grumpy's Bail Bonds that featured owner Leah Hulan, the unbeliev-ably busty bleached blonde who called herself the "Bond Girl" and was considered a local semicelebrity. *Would I soon be needing Grumpy's services?*

At the station, Officer Hogarty opened the back of the cruiser and took me by the arm to help me out and lead me inside. We made a quick stop by Detective Flynn's of-fice, where he grabbed a manila folder from his desk. He and Officer Hogarty took me to an interrogation room that smelled like cigarettes and stale coffee and contained a metal table and four uncomfortable-looking chairs, two on each side. The table was bolted to the floor, though one of the bolts was loose. Leave it to a carpenter to notice. An old-fashioned desk phone sat on the table.

Hogarty led me to a chair. "Take a seat."

Once I'd sat down, she released my right hand from the cuff, and attached the loose manacle to a metal ring on the table so I couldn't attempt an escape. *Now I know how dogs feel when they're chained to a tree.*

Detective Flynn pushed the phone over in front of me. "You've got three minutes to complete your phone call."

With that, the two left the room.

I picked up the receiver and dialed my parents' number, fumbling given that my right arm had limited movement. My mother answered on the third ring. "Hello?"

"I've been arrested, Mom," I said without preamble, not wanting to waste any of the three short minutes I'd been given to make the call. "I'm at the midtown precinct po-lice station."

My mom's voice went up three octaves. "Are you kid-ding me, Whitney? If you are, this isn't funny!"

"I'm not kidding, Mom. I need you to get me a lawyer. The detective wants to ask me more questions about Rick Dunaway's murder and it's not smart for me to talk without an attorney to advise me."

"I'll get right on it!"

I hung up the phone and sat back in the chair. *All I'd wanted was to launch a home renovation business. How the heck had I ended up here, chained to a table?*

Officer Hogarty and the detective returned a couple of minutes later. Flynn held a small digital tape recorder, which he placed on the table as he took his seat. Rather than sit, Hogarty opted to lean back against the wall in the corner. I supposed she spent enough time sitting in her cruiser as she patrolled the streets of Nashville each day.

Flynn skewered me with a look. "Do you want to talk? Take this chance to clear yourself? Or do you want to wait for your attorney to arrive and tell you to keep your mouth shut and end up leaving us no choice but to charge you with Rick Dunaway's murder?"

Nice try, buddy. "I'll wait for my attorney."

Officer Hogarty heaved a sigh, pulled out her phone, and launched a game app. When a playful tune erupted from her phone, she tapped the volume button to turn it down. "Oops," she said. "My bad."

We sat there in silence for a full hour, my rear end going numb in the hard metal chair, before my mother arrived with an attorney in tow. The lawyer was black, boxy, and brash, with spiky dark hair and harsh slashes of plum-hued rouge down her cheeks.

When the officer and detective saw her, they exchanged glances and muttered under their breath. I took that as a good sign.

The attorney cut a look at Flynn and Hogarty. "Get out. I need a few minutes alone with my client."

They both raised their palms. Flynn rose from his seat.

"You, too," the attorney told my mother. "I want to speak to your daughter in private."

My mother hesitated and opened her mouth as if to say something, but seemed to think better of it and backed out the door, closing it as she did so.

The woman plopped down in the seat next to me and extended her hand. "Beverly Lewis."

I shook her hand as best I could. "Nice to meet you."

She laid her briefcase on the table and opened the latches. *Snap-snap.* She pulled out a legal pad and a pen, and turned to me, looking directly into my eyes. "Shoot straight with me," she said. "I can smell a lie a mile away and I won't tolerate anything less than the truth, the whole truth, and nothing but the truth. Got it?"

I found her no-nonsense demeanor to be oddly comforting. She seemed in control and in charge. "Understood."

"You don't say anything to these people, either. Nothing to the detective, the officers, anyone. You let me do the talking. Got that?"

I dipped my chin in acknowledgment. "Got it."

"Okay, hon." She craned her neck to get a better look at my face. "The police seem to think you killed this guy. Rick Dunaway. Why would they believe that?"

I gave her a quick but thorough rundown of the relevant facts. I managed the residential properties owned by Abbot-Dunaway Holdings. I'd done work gratis for Dunaway when he'd complained about repair costs on his units. My cousin and I had recently bought a house from him in a rushed sale, a house that turned out to be worth far less than I'd believed due to a faulty electrical system and the fact that the adjoining property had been rezoned commercial. Rick Dunaway had led a coalition of homeowners

from the neighborhood in an unsuccessful attempt to stop
the rezoning. The house I'd bought had caught fire due to
the aforementioned faulty electrical system, and I couldn't
afford my insurance deductible because I'd put every
penny I had into the house. I suspected Dunaway had
bribed my home inspector to overlook the ancient and de-
graded wiring. I approached Dunaway about covering my
deductible and he'd agreed to bring a check by last Friday.
Though I hadn't seen Dunaway that night, I'd found the
check and settlement agreement on the porch when I left
around nine. I found Dunaway's body the following morning, shortly after I discovered that Thad Gentry, the man
who'd offered to buy the property from me for a twenty
percent markup, had planned to turn the adjacent plot into
a beauty salon. I also found eggs that had been thrown at
the house and suspected that Jackson, a former tenant I'd
evicted from the property, could be to blame. Jackson had
a pending assault charge, as well as a conviction for vandalism. Though I didn't know for certain, I believed that
Dunaway's wallet might have been missing when his body
was found. I'd seen what might or might not be a suspicious white sedan parked both on Sweetbriar and in the
parking garage downtown.

When I finished, she asked, "Do you know how Dunaway was killed?"

"With a mallet. I found it on the ground that morning,
by the porch. I rinsed it off before I realized it had been
used to commit murder."

"Any idea who the mallet belongs to?"

"Yes." I swallowed hard but still squeaked when I spoke.
"It belongs to me."

Her brows rose in question as the eyes below simultaneously narrowed. "The mallet was yours? How did the
killer get hold of it?"

"I'd used it to hammer a sign into the yard, but I forgot to put it away. The killer must have found it."

She stared at me for a long moment before giving me a firm nod. "I think I've got what I need."

"You do?" I sat up straighter. "How are you going to prove my innocence?"

"I'm not."

Huh? "Excuse me?"

"You and I have no duty to prove that you didn't kill Rick Dunaway," she said. "The government has the burden of proof. It's their job to gather enough evidence to convince a jury beyond any reasonable doubt that you committed the crime. They won't be able to do that. Not under these facts."

I remembered thinking after I'd discovered Dunaway's body that it was the police department's job to find his killer. Now, though, it seemed like it might be a good idea to help them along in that process. Even if they lacked the evidence to charge or convict me, the thought of being under suspicion didn't sit well with me. "But if we can prove I didn't—"

She silenced me with a chop of her hand. "Don't make this harder on yourself than it has to be. In the last three days, that detective has probably spoken with dozens of people to try to collect enough evidence to pin this crime on you. He wasn't able to do it or you would have been charged with the crime already, not merely detained for questioning."

I took a moment to digest her words. I supposed it was good news, but even better news than learning that I'd likely go free would be that the actual killer had been caught.

She turned, went to the door, and opened it. Flynn waited in the hall.

"We're ready." My attorney waved the detective in and he took his seat again.

While I'd expected Detective Flynn to launch into a series of questions, before he could get the first one out of his mouth, Ms. Lewis seized the opportunity to interrogate him instead. "You didn't bring my client in on Saturday after you questioned her. Why are we here today? What's happened in the meantime?"

"I have since learned that Ms. Whitaker lied to me when I questioned her on Saturday."

"What do you allege she lied about?" Ms. Lewis asked.

"About the last time she saw Mr. Dunaway alive," Flynn said. "On Saturday, she told me the last time she'd seen him in person was Monday of last week. But I've got a canceled check here that says otherwise." He opened the manila folder and pulled out a copy of the front and back of the $5,000 check Mr. Dunaway had left on my doorstep. He slid the paper across the table. "See?" He pointed to the date at the top of the check. "That check was written on Friday and deposited in her account early on Saturday morning. That means Ms. Whitaker must have seen Mr. Dunaway alive sometime the preceding evening. The condition of the body that morning indicated Mr. Dunaway had been dead for several hours. She was likely the last person to see him alive."

"You'd be wrong about that," my attorney said. "Ms. Whitaker has informed me that she found the check and a settlement agreement in an envelope on the porch when she left the house a little after nine on Friday night. She wasn't sure why Mr. Dunaway hadn't come by at six o'clock as they'd previously agreed, but she assumed he'd gotten tied up with another matter. She had no reason to believe anything was seriously awry."

A muscle flexed in Flynn's jaw. "I spoke to Lance

Abbot, Mr. Dunaway's business partner. He told me that Whitney was extremely irate and rude and out of control when she came to their office on the Monday before the murder. Mr. Dunaway's bookkeeper, Presley, confirmed that Whitney appeared disturbed."

My cheeks blazed. *Disturbed? Seriously?* I'd been upset, sure. Angry, yes. But *disturbed*? Really? Talk about hyperbole.

My attorney answered for me again, leaning forward over the table. "No matter how Miss Whitaker might have appeared on that day, calm or agitated, the fact that Mr. Dunaway agreed to cover her deductible means she had no reason to be upset with him anymore. He'd given in to her request, given her exactly what she asked for." She sat back and raised her hands. "You've got no motive, Detective."

Again the jaw muscle flexed. "I've also spoken with Bobby Palmer, her home inspector. He says Whitney was extremely upset by the fire and looking for someone to blame and cover her losses because she's broke. He says there was no bribe and that he was shocked Whitney would accuse him of fraud given their long-standing business relationship."

"Oh, honey," Lewis said. "If you're surprised another potential suspect tried to place blame on Ms. Whitaker and soil her character, you aren't much of a detective, Mr. Flynn."

Ooh. That comment got a HUGE flex, one that involved the entire side of his neck. I fought the urge to snicker.

Despite the fact that he appeared to be boiling on the inside, Flynn's demeanor remained calm and cool. "Thaddeus Gentry told me much the same thing. Whitney exploded when she discovered he'd bought the adjoining property and had it rezoned for commercial use. He said she'd assaulted him with her car and attempted to spray him with her garden hose."

Assaulted him with my car? All I'd done was roll up the window! And as far as spraying him with the hose, I hadn't even thought of it until he'd tooted his horn to taunt me. Yet, regardless of how unfounded and off base the statements of these people were, they'd painted a picture of me as a vindictive, conniving, vengeful shrew. And that picture was a piece of art that Detective Flynn had bought and hung on his metaphorical wall, not realizing it was a forgery.

I had to defend myself. To tell him that he was wrong. "I didn't—"

Lewis threw her arm across me, like a mother protecting a young child when suddenly slamming on the brakes in a car. "I do all the talking, Miss Whitaker. Remember?"

My fight-or-flight instincts told me to fight. After all, with my hand attached to the table, it wasn't like I could escape. It took everything in me to close my mouth, to stop my verbal defense, to give her a nod of agreement.

She returned her attention to Detective Flynn. "None of this proves anything. And did you speak with Jackson, the former tenant? What did he have to say?"

"He admitted he threw the eggs at the house, but he said it was very late that night, around two A.M., after he'd been at a party nearby."

"And you believed him?" she asked, scorn in her voice. "A punk with a record?"

"Jackson Pharr didn't even know who Mr. Dunaway was, had no idea who owned the rental house. He said the only person he'd ever dealt with regarding their lease was Whitney."

Alas, that much was true. I'd handled all of the leasing arrangements and the rental agreement was in the name of Home & Hearth, not Abbot-Dunaway Holdings. Jackson had no reason to know who Rick Dunaway was. Still, it didn't eliminate the possibility that Jackson had actually thrown the eggs at the house earlier and come across Dunaway then. But surely I would've spotted the broken eggs when I left the house if they'd already been thrown, right? Would Dunaway have had a reason to return to the house later that night and maybe run across Jackson then? I had no way of knowing. Of course there was also the possibility that Jackson had swung at Rick Dunaway, thinking the man was me. After all, with the electricity out, the porch light had not been on and it was fairly dark outside.

The detective went on. "The next-door neighbor told me she overheard Whitney and Buck speaking through the hole in the roof the day after the fire. She heard Whitney specifically reference Rick Dunaway and suggested he might want to buy life insurance because—" He consulted his notes in an apparent attempt to get my quote right. "She 'had half a mind to put an end to him.' Miss Whitaker then referenced a tool that 'could do the trick.' She must have been referring to her mallet."

Actually, I'd been referring to my nail gun at the time, not my mallet, but I wasn't about to correct the detective and confirm that I had, in fact, engaged in a discussion about ending Rick Dunaway's life through violent means. It had all been a joke, for goodness' sake! A way to blow off steam, is all. I hadn't been serious.

"A carpenter having a conversation about tools is hardly unusual," Ms. Lewis said, but didn't belabor the point. Instead, she bombarded him with more questions. "Have you looked into the possibility that the attack may have been a random robbery? That someone might have followed Dunaway's fancy car to Whitney's house? His wallet was missing, right?"

Flynn hesitated a moment before revealing the information. "Yes. His wallet was gone. But his keys and watch weren't. If he'd been mugged, the thief would have stolen Dunaway's car. His Rolex, too. That watch is worth thousands of dollars."

"Not necessarily," Lewis said. "He might not want to risk being caught in a dead man's car, and he wouldn't have been able to pawn the watch. The robber would know the Rolex would be put on the stolen goods list that's supplied to secondhand shops. He'd have to find a buyer himself, or sell it at a big markdown to someone who deals in stolen property."

She certainly knew how crime worked. I supposed it came with the territory for a defense attorney. But all of this was new to me.

"Whitney mentioned a suspicious white sedan," Lewis said. "Have you confirmed that no government agency had Mr. Dunaway under surveillance? That he wasn't involved in dangerous illegal activity?"

"He wasn't being watched by Nashville PD, the Davidson County Sheriff's Department, or the FBI," he said.

"What about the IRS?" she asked. "ATF? ICE? Did you check with them, too?"

Another flex. In other words, he hadn't checked with those agencies. "I have no reason to believe Mr. Dunaway was involved with illegal firearms or smuggling. As for the IRS, I'll look into it."

Lewis continued relentlessly. "It's also possible the white car belonged to a hit man who took out Mr. Dunaway."

"It's not clear the white car is even relevant," Flynn said. "Miss Whitaker said so herself. Besides, none of the evidence I've uncovered points to Mr. Dunaway being the target of a premeditated hit."

"Maybe you're not digging hard enough," Lewis said, "or digging in the right places."

Digging. Ugh. The word had me once again picturing Dunaway's lifeless face as he lay in the dirt.

"Got anything else against my client, Detective?" my attorney demanded.

Flynn was quiet a moment. "That's it for now."

"You're going down a rabbit trail where Miss Whitaker is concerned," Lewis said. "You'll never get a conviction on this flimsy, circumstantial evidence. You and I both know that."

She rose from the table and I followed her lead before realizing I was still shackled to it.

She pointed to the handcuff. "You want to unlock that so she can go?"

Flynn stood and stared down my attorney. "No."

"No?" she repeated, her voice rising an octave. "Excuse me?"

"As you know, Ms. Lewis," the detective replied, "under Tennessee law Miss Whitaker can be held for questioning for seventy-two hours without charges."

Seventy-two hours? "But tomorrow's Thanksgiving!" I cried.

Lewis cut me a look that said *Shut that mouth of yours and shut it now!*

"Sorry," I told her. "It's just that I was really looking forward to it. My aunt Nancy makes this delicious sweet potato pie—"

Instead of telling me with her words and glances to be quiet, this time my attorney slapped her hand over my mouth and looked me in the eye. "You listen to me and you listen to me good, Whitney." She jabbed a finger in Detective Flynn's direction. "That man is keeping you here because he hopes to break you, to get you to confess to something you didn't do. Don't fall for it. Keep your mouth closed and don't say anything to anyone. I'll be back if and when he decides to question you again."

She was leaving me here? Now I knew how Sawdust felt that one time I'd had to board him at the kennel.

My attorney looked down at her watch then at Detective Flynn. "It's ten forty-three. My client better be out of here by ten forty-four Saturday morning or there will be consequences." She jabbed a finger on the table. "You'll be one of them."

She turned back to me, mimicked zipping her lip and throwing away the key, and left the room, slamming the door behind her. *Bam!*

Flynn tugged his radio from his belt. "I need a female officer to escort a person of interest to a holding cell, please."

Person of interest. That sounded slightly better than suspect, but not much.

Hot tears welled up in my eyes and my head felt as if it were full of helium, causing all coherent thought to float away. But an instant later, my resolve kicked in. I looked Detective Flynn in the eye. "This is your first murder investigation, isn't it?"

"That's none of your business."

"I answered your questions. You could at least answer mine."

"Actually," he reminded me, "you didn't answer any of my questions today."

"Point taken," I said. "But I answered them all on Saturday, at the house. Willingly and thoroughly."

"So?"

"So I can understand the pressure you're under to make a quick arrest, to prove to your boss that you know what you're doing. But throwing the wrong person in jail isn't going to impress your superiors. In fact, it'll do exactly the opposite."

He exhaled sharply. "Who says I have the wrong person?"

"*I* do. You said earlier you could smell a lie a mile away. Can you smell the truth, too?"

"What, exactly, would the truth smell like?"

I thought it over. "Cupcakes?"

His lip quirked as he fought a smile.

"Look," I said. "I know my attorney was a bit of a—"

"Ballbuster?"

I'd been thinking of another B-word, but *ballbuster* worked, too. "Don't punish me for it. She was only doing her job."

He grunted and stared me down for a long moment as if trying to look into my soul. The twitch around his eyes told me that maybe, just maybe, he was beginning to waver. "Nothing I've heard today proves your innocence. If you could prove to me that you didn't kill Dunaway, give me one incontrovertible fact, I'll let you go. But you can't do that, can you, Miss Whitaker?"

I couldn't. My heart felt as if it weighed a hundred pounds in my chest. Defeated, I looked down. And found just the evidence I needed.

I raised my unshackled arm. "Look at my sleeves. What do you see?"

He leaned in and took a look. "Cat hair. Lots of it."

"Exactly. I gave my cat a hug before I left the house. I love that furry little guy so much that I would never risk going to jail and leaving him behind. It would break my heart to be without him."

Flynn stared at me for another long moment. His gaze flicked to my mouth. "You kissed your cat, too."

"How do you know that?"

"You've got cat hair in your lip gloss." He reached out and plucked a stray fur from my lip.

We held each other's gaze for several seconds before the door opened. Officer Hogarty stepped inside and headed my way. "Let's get you to lockup, blondie."

Panic welled up in me, making my head feel like a helium balloon that would pop free from my neck and float away. *I'm going to jail! There's scary people in there!*

"Wait!" Flynn raised a palm. "I've changed my mind."

"You have?" *Hallelujah!* The tight knot my gut had tied itself into began to loosen and my brain began to defog.

Hogarty cut her eyes to the detective. "You haven't been swayed by a pretty face, have you, Flynn?"

"No," he replied, his eyes still locked on mine. "I was swayed by her arguments. She's not actually all that pretty."

My free hand went to my hip. "Hey!"

A subtle smile played over his face before he turned to the officer. "You can remove the handcuffs."

Hogarty gave a snort of disapproval. "You're the boss."

She unlocked the cuff from the table before removing it from my wrist. "There you are. Free to go. Just don't kill anyone else."

I heaved a sigh.

"You're still a person of interest," Flynn warned me, his tone all business again. "Don't leave the area."

"I won't. By the way." I pointed down to the floor. "There's a bolt missing down there. You might want to get that taken care of before some suspect rips the table out of the floor and whacks you over the head with it."

As Flynn bent over to take a look, I headed out the door.

"Enjoy your sweet potato pie!" he called after me.

I would. But first, I'd enjoy my sweet, sweet freedom!

CHAPTER 27

I SPY

WHITNEY

My attorney had told my mother that Detective Flynn had planned to hold me in jail, so my mother had left the station. She'd be pleasantly surprised when I showed up at her house later, a free woman once again.

Given that my cell phone was now in evidence, I had to beg the receptionist at the front desk to let me use hers. "Pretty please with sugar on top?"

"Make it quick," the stern woman barked as she plunked the phone on the counter and turned it my way.

Colette's place was the closest to the station, so I phoned her.

"Any chance you can give me a ride to my car?" I asked when she answered.

"No problem. What's going on?"

I gave her the rundown. Pulled over by police. Interrogated. Told I'd be held for three days, but eventually released. Car sitting at a church too far away for me to walk to.

"I'm on my way," Colette said.

I pushed open the station's front doors and stepped outside alone to wait for my friend. Even after the short time I'd spent in the dimly lit interrogation room, the autumn sun seemed extra bright, virtually dazzling. It took a few seconds for my eyes to adjust, but when they did, they took in several camera crews from the local television stations, as well as a notepad-sporting young woman who was likely a reporter for the local paper. I was headed toward them before I realized they'd come here for me.

"Roll the camera!" called a handsome man in a suit. I recognized him from the ten o'clock newscasts.

His cameraman activated his device and smoothly came toward me.

The reporter shoved a microphone in my face. "Miss Whitaker, why did you kill Rick Dunaway?"

"I didn't!"

"Were you and Mr. Dunaway having an affair?"

"No!" *Gross!*

"Are you sorry for what you did?"

"I didn't do anything!" I pushed my way past him only to find a different mic at my face now, a different reporter screaming questions at me.

"Did you act alone? Or did your cousin help you kill Rick Dunaway?"

Now they're dragging Buck into this? "I have no comment!" I hollered at the top of my lungs.

The reporters kept badgering me until I finally sat down on a bench, curled up in a sitting fetal position, and covered my head with my arms. "I said I have no comment! Go away!"

A couple of the more persistent reporters were still

lobbing questions at me when a horn sounded nearby.
Toot-toot!

I looked up to see Colette's car at the curb. She reached
over and threw the passenger door open. "Get in!"

"Who are you?" a reporter called to her.

"Beyoncé!" Colette called back.

I dashed over and all but dove into her car. She took off
before my belt was even fastened.

Once we'd cleared the station's parking lot, Colette
reached out and gave my hand a squeeze, concern in her
eyes. "You okay?"

"As okay as I can be under the circumstances, I guess."

She offered a supportive smile, but it morphed into a
grimace. "Whatever you do, don't look at social media."

An ominous statement if ever there was one. "News
travels fast, huh?"

"At cyber speed," she said. "You've been retroactively
designated as 'most likely to murder' on the high school's
Facebook page."

I groaned. Despite Colette's warning, I retrieved her cell
phone from the console and typed my name into the Internet browser's search bar. Several articles popped up, no
doubt written and uploaded on the fly by the reporters
who'd just been hounding me. Though the reporters were
careful not to designate me as a suspect, being identified as
a "person of interest" wasn't much better. Everyone knew
that most persons of interest eventually became suspects,
and that many of those suspects later became convicts.
Several of the stories of my arrest had included references to Home & Hearth, the business the Hartleys had
worked so hard to build up over decade after decade. I'd
brought shame on them, maybe even caused them to lose
potential clients.

I set the phone down and turned to my friend. "What

am I going to do, Colette? The detective doesn't seem to know what he's doing. This is his first murder case and, as far as I can tell, he's clueless."

She glanced my way before signaling to make a left turn. "If he can't figure out who the killer is, we just might have to do it for him after all."

I'd had the same thought. "That could be dangerous."

She shrugged. "It could be just as dangerous to wait and see if the killer strikes again."

She had a point. Still, I wouldn't even know where to start. When I said as much, she asked, "Have you checked the feeds from those security cameras Buck put up at the house?"

"Not since yesterday." So far, all the footage had shown was a couple of raccoons getting frisky in the yard and a neighborhood cat sauntering by, swishing its tail. "I'll take a look. See if anything interesting shows up."

After Colette dropped me at my car, I aimed straight for a Walmart, where I bought a cheap cell phone to use until mine was released from police evidence. My next stop would be Home & Hearth, where I would attempt some damage control. I wouldn't be surprised if the Hartleys decided to let me go, and I certainly wouldn't blame them a bit. This fiasco could bring down their business. No doubt they'd already received calls from concerned clients.

I zipped into the lot and hopped out of my car, hurrying inside. "I'm so sorry about all this mess!" I cried when they looked up from their desks.

"Don't you dare apologize," Mrs. Hartley insisted as she stood. "You have nothing to be sorry about. It's that young detective who's way out of line. That's what we've been telling the clients, too."

I dropped into a chair. "You talked to Detective Flynn?"

Mr. Hartley joined in. "He came by the office late yesterday afternoon and asked us some questions about Rick Dunaway and his relationship with Home and Hearth. We told him that Mr. Dunaway could be a tough cookie, but that you had a knack for dealing with him."

I wasn't sure that phrasing was the best response. It could be taken a number of ways. But that was water under the bridge now.

"I'll understand if you want to terminate my employment," I told them. Heck, maybe I should make it easy on them and tender my resignation on the spot.

Mr. Hartley wagged his finger. "No, no, no. We will not lose a valuable employee to baseless accusations!"

I felt tears well in my eyes again, but for a totally different reason. The fact that the Hartleys were standing by me said so much, gave me hope that all was not lost, that the truth would become known.

"I know I've gotten behind because of everything that's been going on," I told them, "but I'll catch up on things this afternoon. I can stay late tonight if needed." Leases on five of the Abbot-Dunaway properties would expire at the end of the year. I'd need to follow up with the tenants to see if they planned to renew their leases and, if not, begin showing the properties and evaluating rental applications.

The two exchanged an uncomfortable glance.

"There's not much to catch up on anymore," Mrs. Hartley said. "Lance Abbot terminated our management contract effective as of the end of the month."

"What?!?" The last day of the month was the day after tomorrow. I exhaled a sharp breath. "The contract with Abbot-Dunaway Holdings requires them to give at least thirty days' notice of cancellation. Did you remind him of that?"

"No," Mr. Hartley said. "It seemed best not to argue the point, given the circumstances."

The circumstances being that law enforcement had considered me the prime suspect in his partner's death. *Ugh.* Not only did I feel bad that the Hartleys had been forced to cover my duties while I dealt with the fire and the rehab and the murder investigation, but now the property management income—and my paychecks—would be cut in half. This situation was snowballing out of control. Heck, it wasn't just a snowball, it was an avalanche.

"Now that I've been released without charges," I said, "maybe Lance Abbot will change his mind."

"But you're still a 'person of interest,' right?" Mrs. Hartley said. "That's what the news is saying."

"Yes."

Mr. Hartley shifted in his seat. "I think it's best to let sleeping dogs lie."

"I understand." This turn of events meant I had nothing to do at Home & Hearth. Buck was finishing up a job at a house across town, and I wasn't about to go back to the Sweetbriar house by myself to work. It would be too creepy to be there alone. Buck had insisted I stay away unless he was there with me. What if the killer came back for me? The mere thought caused my toes and fingers to prickle in fear. I supposed there was nothing to do but go back to my parents' house.

An hour later, I was sitting on my parents' couch with my laptop on my thighs and Sawdust on his back next to me, his head tilted back so I could scratch under his chin. I logged into Facebook to see what fresh fodder the Internet trolls had come up with. Why I was choosing to torture myself was anyone's guess. I just couldn't help myself.

Scrolling down the feed, I saw the usual funny pet

videos, what everyone ate for dinner last night, and unlikely animal friends, today's best buddies being a hippo and the flamingo he allowed to stand on his hindquarters as he waded chest deep through a river.

I'd bypassed a couple of vacation pics when my face popped up in the feed.

Nooooo!

Someone had made a video of me, using a photo I'd posted on my page of me with a hammer in my hand. I'd been helping out on a project with Habitat for Humanity at the time. The photo had been tinkered with so that my hand moved up and down, as if I were pounding the hammer. A never-ending scroll of celebrity heads swept across the bottom, the pics cut and pasted from photos found elsewhere online. As the heads swept across the screen, each one stopped to receive a blow from my tool before exploding in cartoon blood spatter. Kim Kardashian. Zac Ephron. Mother Teresa. The cartoon face of Bob the Builder. The Rock. *As if I'd ever hit a man as attractive as Dwayne Johnson on the head.* The entire farce was accompanied by a score excerpted from MC Hammer's hit song "U Can't Touch This." As I brought the hammer down on each head, the singer belted out "Hammer time!"

My mother glanced back at me. "What are you looking at?"

I held up my computer to show her. Big mistake. She closed her eyes and put her hand to her forehead as if her head, too, was at risk of exploding.

"Is that on the Internet?" she asked. "For all the world to see?"

"Yes." My former schoolteachers and classmates. People from church. Neighbors. Clients. Anyone and everyone had access to the news and memes. I could only wonder what they were thinking. Were they shocked, telling themselves and others there was no possible way the mannerly and harmless Whitney Whitaker they knew would have ever killed someone? Or were they thinking back to the work I'd done at their homes or in high school shop class, the force with which I could bring a hammer down on an innocent smooth shank nail? They could be speculating whether I had lost control, used the tool for nefarious and fatal purposes.

The weight of the world settled on my shoulders, feeling as if I were carrying a load of four-by-fours on them. *When will this nightmare be over?* Part of me was tempted to climb into my childhood bed down the hall and pull the covers over my head, pretend this whole thing wasn't happening. But another part refused to let me take this humiliation lying down. It told me to do whatever I could to identify Dunaway's killer and see that person was put behind bars.

As long as I had my laptop out, I figured I should check the security camera feeds as Colette had suggested. I logged into the site where the footage from our system was stored. Buck had installed six devices. One on each corner of the house, and one over each door. One by one, I reviewed the videos. There was little activity on the cameras that faced the backyard, only the hoppity-hopping of a wild bunny as he traversed the yard, occasionally stopping to sample a scrumptious bite of clover. The front corner camera was a different matter. While the lenses were angled to primarily take in our yard, part of the side of Patty's house and a few feet of her front yard fell within the range, too. The feed showed her puttering around the edge of her lawn, raking the few leaves that had fallen since the last time she'd cleaned up her lawn. Rather than bagging the leaves, however, she looked around to see if anyone was watching and, apparently satisfied nobody was looking her way, dragged the dead leaves into our yard.

She looked toward the house and performed a quick double take, tiptoeing closer as she gazed up at the camera. Her face grew large and distorted as she stopped under it, squinting her eyes and bobbing her head as she checked it out. Once she'd given it a thorough lookover, she returned to her yard, leaving her leaves behind for Buck and me to clean up. "Thanks a lot, Patty," I muttered aloud.

The feed from the camera on the front of the house on the other side provided some more interesting fodder. The contractors performing the work on the beauty salon ventured onto our grass multiple times, and even used our garden hose to rinse dirt from their tools. *Maybe I should show them the footage and send them our next water bill, demand that they pay part of it.* But while that footage had caught my eye, what really got my attention was when Thad Gentry stepped into our yard from his own property next door. He wore his usual business suit. My guess was he'd stopped by to check on the progress at the salon between meetings and appointments and fancy business lunches. He walked to the porch, but didn't ascend the steps. He stood and simply stared at our house for a long moment, his expressionless face difficult to read. *Is he lamenting the fact that Buck and I didn't sell the property to him? Or is he reliving the memory of killing his competitor there, of getting revenge on Dunaway for fighting him at the zoning commission?* It was impossible to tell.

I downloaded the feed that featured Thad Gentry and e-mailed it to Detective Flynn along with a message. *Found this on my security camera feeds today. Thought you might find it interesting.* My attorney would probably be furious that I'd communicated with the detective again. But, at this point, I figured I had nothing to lose.

Thursday morning, after watching the Macy's Thanksgiving parade in our pajamas while sipping coffee and nibbling on pastries, my parents and I cleaned ourselves up, got dressed, and headed up Interstate 65, out of the city and into the woods and hills, taking the last exit before crossing into Kentucky. I'd brought Sawdust with me so he could visit his mother. It only seemed right that he spend the holiday with his family, too. After a few turns down country roads, we headed onto the inclined gravel drive that led up to the cabin. *Oh, how I love this place!* It was everything my parents' house wasn't. Casual. Cozy. Cluttered.

As I let Sawdust out of his carrier, his mother, aptly if not uncreatively named Mama, padded into the living room. She sauntered over and sniffed her son's face, welcoming him with a warm, wet lick between the eyes when she recognized his scent and realized he was one of her offspring. He responded with a loud purr and circled around her, rubbing himself up and down her sides.

Minutes later, my family was gathered around the long walnut dining room table Uncle Roger had lovingly made with his own hands. An assortment of mismatched bowls and pans crowded the center of the table. They held everything from green bean casserole to homemade corn-bread stuffing, along with what appeared to be at least a gallon of savory brown gravy. I was tempted to turn the gravy boat up and pour the stuff directly down my throat.

Everyone grabbed the closest item and passed it counterclockwise, using the system we'd worked out many holidays ago to make sure nobody missed out on anything.

Once the item you'd started with was handed back to you, you could place it back on the table. Soon, everyone had filled their plates and the conversation stopped as we all dug in.

Buck swallowed a mouthful of green beans and posed the question everyone had probably had on their minds but been afraid to ask. "What's it like in jail? Did you have to make a shiv out of your toothbrush to defend yourself?"

Now that I'd been freed without having even set one foot in a cell, I found I could laugh at the suggestion.

My oldest niece batted her big brown eyes at me. "Why did you go to jail, Aunt Whitney?"

"I didn't go to jail, sweetie," I told her. "Uncle Buck was joking. I only went to the police station."

"Why?"

"Because the police wanted to ask me some questions."

"Why?"

Because a business associate of mine had been bludgeoned to death. We adults exchanged nervous glances. Nobody wanted to be the one to introduce the concept of murder to a four-year-old. "The police thought I might know who used my hammer without permission," I told her. It was as close as I could get to the truth. *And now, for my second act, let's try some distraction!* I picked up the cranberry sauce and shook the bowl. "Look! It jiggles!" I spooned some onto my plate, took a bite, and wiggled around in my seat. "It jiggles on the inside, too!"

My niece giggled and clapped her hands. "I want some!"

Buck snorted. "Nice job, Witless."

"Shut your pie hole," I replied cheerily. I'd noticed that the girls tended to pay less attention to what was said when your voice sounded pleasant. They seemed to sense that the really good stuff was discussed in less congenial tones.

I passed the cranberry sauce across the table to my

sister-in-law so she could scoop some onto her daughter's plate. In seconds, my niece had swallowed a big spoonful and was shaking and giggling in her seat. Her two-year-old sister followed suit, nearly falling out of her booster chair. Fortunately, her mother anticipated the impending disaster and grabbed hold of her in the nick of time.

When we finished the meal, we gathered in the family room to let the food settle for an hour or so before attempting dessert. Some of us napped. Some of us watched college football on television. As for me, I plunked myself down in a beanbag chair and played game after game of Candy Land with my oldest niece, carefully watching that the younger two didn't steal the pieces and try to eat them.

Finally, my meal had settled enough that there was room in my belly to add a slice of Aunt Nancy's sweet potato pie. Of course she'd made pecan, blueberry, and peach pies, too, everyone's favorites. I packed up the game and stood. "Who's ready for pie?"

Unanimous and simultaneous shouts of *"Me!"* sprang from everyone's lips.

I went to the kitchen and prepared plates for everyone, carrying them back two at a time to the living room. Once the pie had been distributed all around, I eased back into the beanbag chair with my fork and plate, took my first bite, and closed my eyes to better savor the delicious flavor. *Mmm.*

At the end of the day, Aunt Nancy sent me home with a full pie of my own. She pointed a finger in my face as she ushered me out the door. "That's all for you. Don't share it with anyone."

"Not even me?" Buck asked.

She chucked her eldest son on the chin. *"Especially* you."

CHAPTER 28

MOMMY AND ME

SAWDUST

Sawdust knew Whitney wasn't actually his mother, though she served many of the same purposes. She fed him. Curled up next to him when he was napping to make sure he was warm enough. Kept him clean. She didn't lick him clean like his real mother had, though. Instead, she occasionally gave him a bath in the sink. It wasn't nearly as nice as a tongue bath.

It had been nice to see his cat mommy again today. She always seemed glad to see him, gave him a kiss or two. But those pesky little girls were a different matter, always following him around and picking him up awkwardly. He knew they meant well, but frankly he was glad to be back at the big house, stretched out on the bed next to Whitney, back to back. She was something he was truly thankful for.

CHAPTER 29

MANY HANDS MAKE LIGHT WORK

WHITNEY

Friday was the last day of November. Every year since we'd been old enough to venture to the mall on our own, Colette and I would go shopping on the day after Thanksgiving, snag some good Black Friday deals. Not this year, though. Until things turned around, my buying anything other than absolute necessities was out of the question. On the bright side, Buck and I could get to work on the house today.

As I drove over that morning after indulging in a nice slice of sweet potato pie for breakfast, all I could think about was that Buck and I had a mortgage payment due on the place soon. I could manage my half of the installment because my paycheck from Home & Hearth had just cleared the bank, but there would be virtually nothing left over. Now that we'd lost the Abbot-Dunaway Holdings account, there'd be less work for me to do and my next paycheck would be much smaller. I'd have to watch every cent I spent. No stopping for an occasional latte. No mani-pedis with Colette. No special tuna treats for my cat. My hair needed a trim, but that would have to wait, too. Maybe I'd get lucky and split ends would become the new rage.

As I pulled into the driveway behind Buck's van, I looked out at the house and heaved a heavy sigh. Despite all the awful things that had happened here, this was nonetheless a beautiful, classic house, exactly the type I'd want to live in myself if I could afford it. Surely someone would appreciate the home's timeless stone, the generous closet space, the beautiful kitchen we planned to install, the claw-foot bathtub. But could a potential buyer overlook the fact that a murder had taken place here? I wasn't sure. All I knew was that a body in a flower bed could devalue the home and put me and Buck underwater. An appropriate term, because it felt as if I were drowning.

I found Buck inside, ripping out the damaged hardwood. "'Mornin'," I said.

"'Mornin'," he replied.

He seemed to have things under control in the house, so I decided to start with the outside. Though I wasn't normally one to rush the holidays, I figured it couldn't hurt to go ahead and decorate even if it wasn't yet December. Christmas would soon be here, but the holiday spirit was eluding me. Maybe decorating would put me in the mood. I could certainly use some holiday cheer after everything that had transpired over the last few weeks. The events had left me feeling ho, ho, hopeless.

In addition to the inflatable snowman I'd bought at the home improvement store, I'd brought along several strings of icicle lights, three reindeer formed from twigs, and a half-dozen wreaths with red bows for the front door and windows. The latter items had been appropriated from my parents' garage. Rather than repeat a certain look for the house or tree as a tradition, Mom liked to shake things up and choose a new holiday theme each year. She planned to go with elves this time around. I'd had to fight a scream when the garage door went up and I found myself face-to-face with a dozen of the creepy little guys, staring vacantly out at me.

I summoned my courage and approached the flower bed, gathering up the plastic flats of purple pansies I'd been planting when I found Dunaway's body. The poor flowers were withered beyond hope, their leaves and blooms faded and dried to a crisp. I placed them at the curb for the trash men to take away.

Returning to my car, I opened the back hatch to retrieve Buck's old toolbox, which he'd loaned me. The thing was made of metal and maintained a few remnants of red paint where it wasn't dented, dinged, or scratched. The toolbox was also as heavy as a kettle bell. Merely carrying the thing was a workout. I had to lean to the left to keep from keeling over.

I set the toolbox down in the middle of the yard and went inside to retrieve an extension cord and the box that held the inflatable snowman. After spreading the snowman out on the lawn as per the instructions, I used my new dead blow hammer to pound four stakes into the soil to tie the inflatable down. Didn't want my new carrot-nosed friend going airborne and ending up in a Kentucky farmer's back forty. Once he was secured, I plugged him in and watched as he filled with air and came to life, like my own personal Frosty.

Buck came to the window and opened it. "That thing's as full of hot air as Detective Flynn!" he called.

"You got that right."

With the snowman lording over the left side of the center walkway, I decided the deer should have their own space on the other half of the front lawn. One by one, I situated the trio on the grass, trying different positions to see which held the most visual appeal. As I worked, a car rolled slowly by, the man at the wheel gawking at me. I recognized him as one of the residents from across the street. He seemed surprised to see me out of jail. I tried not to be offended by that fact. Like Detective Flynn, he didn't really know me. Nevertheless, it cut to my core. *I'm a nice person! Really!* I wanted to holler.

Perhaps I should bake a batch of gingerbread men for the neighbors and deliver them with a festive holiday card. Then again, the smiling cookies looking up at them from the plate might serve to remind them of the real man who'd been found lying on his back in my garden. Yep, those cookies could backfire, big-time.

Owen arrived as I finished placing the herd. He parked his van at the curb and climbed out. "What's all this?"

"I thought some holiday decorations would make the place look more homey, give it some extra curb appeal." Maybe they would help everyone forget about the house's horrible history, too. "Grab your stepladder. I need help hanging the wreaths on the windows."

I planned to affix the wreaths to each of the front windows using the double-sided magnets designed specifically for this purpose. I showed Owen how the magnets functioned. "I'll need to go inside so we can hang them."

"All righty."

While Owen held up each magnet on the outside, I matched it to its polar opposite partner on the inside. *Voilà!* As for the wreath on the door, I hung that with a good old-fashioned nail.

Owen climbed back up the ladder to hang the icicle lights. As he did, Patty happened to pass by her living room window, the movement inside her house catching my eyes. When she spotted me holding the ladder, she dashed to her drapes and yanked them closed. *Will I ever live down my arrest?*

When we were done decorating, we rounded up Buck and the three of us stepped back to the curb to take it all in.

"It looks great," Buck said.

"Sure does," Owen agreed.

"All but the flower beds." The beds contained nothing but soil, no foliage of any sort. But I wasn't sure I could bring myself to work in that cursed soil again.

Buck cut a glance my way and, as if reading my mind, offered to take care of the matter. "I'll put in some flowers. You want to go with purple pansies again?"

"No. Let's go with red camellias this time." The winter-blooming bushes would add a burst of vivacious color and maybe, just maybe, make my neighbors forget that the ground in which the flowering foliage stood had once been someone's shallow grave.

We drove to the home improvement store and selected eight yuletide camellias, four for each bed. As we returned to the house, I spotted several more vehicles lining up along the curb. Uncle Roger's heavy-duty pickup truck. The Hartleys' Chrysler sedan. Colette's Chevy Cruze. My mother's pearly white Cadillac. As I watched, my family and friends took turns wrangling panels of Sheetrock from the back of Owen's van.

My mouth fell open as Buck's van rolled to a stop in the driveway. "What's everyone doing here?"

Buck slid me a sideways grin from his place in the driver's seat. "They've come to help."

What a sweet gesture of support. *What had I done to deserve such good people in my life?* For what felt like the millionth time, tears began to well up in my eyes as I turned to my cousin. "I know you arranged this. Thank you, Buck."

He looked at my face. "Don't go getting all mushy on me, now."

"Too late!" I hugged him tight before releasing him and fluttering my hands around my eyes in an attempt to dry them. Finally, I got my emotions under control and slid out of his van. "Good morning!" I called to the crowd. "If I haven't said it before, I love you all!"

The group smiled and returned the sentiment.

While Buck planted the camellias outside, inside Owen gave the group a quick primer in installing drywall. How to measure it. How to score the paper before cutting it. How to anchor it to the wall with screws. When he was done, he distributed gloves, tools, putty knives, and other materials, and assigned each of the novices an experienced partner. Ready to get moving, we all got right down to work. Well, right to work after Buck came back inside, pulled out his phone, and launched his carpentry playlist. All of the songs were country-western tunes, a tribute to our hometown of Nashville. Each song had something to do with houses, too. Sam Hunt's lively if irreverent hit "House Party." Garth Brooks's upbeat melody "Two of a Kind, Workin' on a Full House." Miranda Lambert's more solemn ballad "The House That Built Me."

As the music played, we worked along, side by side. I'd been partnered with Mr. Hartley. He seemed to enjoy the task, whistling while we worked our way across the back living room wall. Owen oversaw my parents along the perpendicular wall. Mrs. Hartley toiled under my Uncle Roger's tutelage in the hallway. Buck and Colette were partnered in the back bedroom that had caught fire, their banter and laughter drifting through the door. The two seemed to be enjoying each other's company. I was glad my best friend and my favorite cousin got along so well.

Just a few hours later, new drywall was in place throughout the damaged areas of the house. I gave everyone a warm hug and a kiss on the cheek as they left. "Thank you so much!" I told them. "You're the best crew ever!"

Now that it was just me and my cousins left in the house, we completed the finishing work, applying the tape and joint compound needed to smooth the seams, cover the screws, and prepare the Sheetrock for painting. The mud compound, which would smooth and strengthen the walls, would need at least twenty-four hours to dry before the paint could be applied. It was after five by the time we finished. The three of us parted ways with an agreement to return tomorrow.

On Saturday morning, Buck, Owen, and I were back at the house by ten. Patty was in her front yard, hanging Christmas lights on her bushes. As my cousins headed inside, I said, "I'll be back in a minute. I want to talk to Patty right quick."

The woman cast me a wary glance and picked up a large plastic candy cane decoration as I stepped over to speak with her. I supposed she intended to use the candy cane in self-defense, if necessary.

I offered her a smile. "Good morning, Patty."

"Hello, Whitney." Her greeting was as cool as the outdoor temperature.

There was no sense beating around the bush. "I was wondering if we could talk about the night Rick Dunaway was killed."

She stiffened. "What about it?"

"I was wondering if you saw anything."

"I've already told the detective what I saw."

"I'm sure you did," I said. "But I'd really like to help him along if I can, to clear my name. We'll all be safer when the killer is behind bars. If you could tell me what you saw that night, maybe it would help me help him."

When she simply stared at me, I added, "Please, Patty. I had nothing to do with Rick Dunaway's death. I swear."

Her face bore a drawn, dubious expression. *How can I convince her?*

"Think about it," I said. "If I had killed the man, would I really have left him right there in the flower bed? In front of a house I owned? Of course not. That would be stupid. I would've done a better job of disposing of the body and the weapon. I would have taken them somewhere else, hidden the evidence. His body would have easily fit in my SUV. I could've driven right down the road and dumped his body in the Cumberland River."

She angled her head as she appeared to be thinking things over. Like Detective Flynn, she stared at me intently, as if doing so would tell her whether or not I was guilty or innocent. "All right," she said finally, apparently determining I was the latter. "I'll tell you what I saw."

Thank goodness. She believes me!

"Dunaway's Mercedes pulled up around half past six. I saw the headlights and peeked outside to see who was parking in front of my house. I didn't much appreciate that. People should park in front of the house they're visiting. What if I'd had guests coming?"

I had yet to see anyone come to visit Patty, but I supposed it could happen.

"Anyway," she continued, "I saw him get out of his car and head into your yard. Your place was dark, so once he set foot on your lawn I couldn't see him anymore. A few minutes later, another set of headlights drove past. By the time I got to the window, the car was gone. I don't know if it was someone just driving down the street, or whether they'd been parked and were leaving." She raised her shoulders. "That's all I know."

"Did the headlights sit up high, like they belonged on a pickup truck? Or were they low, like a regular car?"

Jackson drove a pickup. If the lights were higher, it could have been his vehicle that had gone past her house.

She raised her shoulders again. "My curtains were only open an inch or two, and I was watching the evening news on TV, so I didn't get a good look."

It wasn't much information, and it was nothing definitive. Even so, it told me that someone other than Rick Dunaway had been in the vicinity around the time he came to the house.

Patty set the candy cane down and reached into a plastic bin for two strands of green lights. She plugged the end of one strand of lights into the other. "Around eight o'clock that night, I realized I was out of coffee and had to make a quick run to the grocery store to pick some up. I'm an absolute grump if I don't get my morning coffee."

She was a bit of a grump regardless, but I wasn't about to point that out to her.

She paused to untangle the other end of the strand, which had tied itself into a knot. "When I came around the corner, I nearly ran into Thaddeus Gentry's car. You know, the one with his name on the license plates?" She shook her head. "What an ego that man has." She added a *tsk* of disapproval. "Anyway, he backed out of the drive at his place without bothering to look back and took off in a hurry."

Thad Gentry had been around the night Rick Dunaway was killed? That was certainly an interesting bit of information. "Did you tell Detective Flynn that you'd seen Thad Gentry that night?"

"Of course," she said. "I told him if he questioned Gentry, he should have a talk with the man about his driving habits, too."

"Thanks, Patty. Any chance you've noticed a man in a white sedan hanging around?"

"Not recently."

"But you saw him before?"

She nodded. "The morning you evicted those boys. The guy was just sitting in the car, reading the newspaper. I thought maybe he was waiting for someone, but he drove off a little later by himself."

"Did he talk to anyone?"

"Not that I noticed."

Hmm. I'd assumed earlier that the man might have been keeping an eye on Rick Dunaway, but was it possible that the man in the car had been spying on Thad Gentry instead? And, if so, who was the man and why was he interested in Gentry?

I gestured to the lights in her hands. "Need some help with those?"

She, in turn, gestured toward the dogwoods in her front yard. "I'd love to string some lights in my trees. Got a ladder handy?"

"I sure do." I went into my house next door, retrieved a stepladder, and carried it over to her yard. I positioned the ladder under her tree and strung the lights up, over, and through the tree limbs as she directed me.

"Can you get them a little higher?" she asked.

I tossed a strand over a bare limb above me. "How's that?"

"It'll do."

As the two of us put up the lights, one of the neighbors from down the street jogged by. He did a double take when he realized it was me, the "person of interest," helping

Patty decorate her yard. Another gawked from her minivan as she drove by. Still, I couldn't help but think that having the backing of the neighborhood busybody would convince the others I wasn't to blame for Dunaway's death.

Patty didn't thank me when we were done, but at least she gave me a lukewarm "see you." At that point, I'd take what I could get.

I set back to work, pulling the damaged closet doors from their tracks, carrying them out to the garage to be hauled off later. I removed the metal tracks, too, adding them to the pile of refuse on the garage floor. As I walked back out of the garage, a plain sedan pulled to the curb. Detective Flynn sat at the wheel. *What's he doing here? Has he come to arrest me again? Will he put me in jail this time?* My hands broke into a sweat inside my gloves, and I yanked them off.

I stood in the drive as the detective climbed out of his car and walked over to me.

"I went by your parents' place," he said. "They told me I could find you here." He reached into his pants pocket, pulled out my cell phone, and held it out to me. "You can have this back."

I wiped my hand on my coveralls and took the device from him. "Thanks." I had few phone numbers memorized, and not having access to my contacts list the past few days had been extremely inconvenient. "Any chance I'll be getting my tools back soon, too?"

"Possibly," he said. "The lab is still checking them for DNA."

I sighed. "For Dunaway's blood, you mean."

"Yeah," he said softly.

"What do the crime scene techs think I did? Whack Dunaway with my hammer and then attempt to disassemble him with a screwdriver? He was a man, not a mannequin."

Okay, so I probably shouldn't have made light of a serious situation. But I couldn't help myself. For them to think I had anything at all to do with a murder was absolutely ridiculous!

Fortunately, Flynn chuckled before cocking his head and eyeing me. "I reviewed your cell phone history. It corroborates your statement that you made two calls to Dunaway the evening he was killed."

"Because I told you the truth."

"Maybe." He shrugged. "Or maybe you placed the calls to a man you knew was dead, to throw off suspicion."

I exhaled a long, exasperated breath. "I did nothing of the sort."

"You might be interested to know we've got Jackson Pharr in custody."

"Really?" *Could this nightmare be over?* "You've arrested him for the murder?"

"No. I don't have enough evidence for that. He was brought in last night on a drunk-and-disorderly charge after getting into an altercation in a bar."

I shook my head. "That kid has no self-control."

"I'm inclined to agree with you. We're going to hang on to him as long as we can, see if we can get anything out of him."

"A confession, you mean?" My heart buoyed with hope in my chest.

Flynn nodded. "Whoever killed Rick Dunaway seems to have done so in the heat of the moment. If the murder had been planned, the weapon wouldn't have been left behind. I've talked to the district attorney's office and we're thinking if we offer Pharr a plea deal for involuntary manslaughter and a light sentence, he just might bite."

I was tempted to tell him that if he wanted to apply thumbscrews to the twerp, he was welcome to use any screws in my toolbox, which was still in police possession. My better judgment told me to keep that thought to myself. Instead, I said, "Good luck with that." I hoped that Jackson would sing like a canary, or like any of the dozen or so aspiring musicians who busked for tips around the city.

Flynn lifted a hand in good-bye as he backed away. "I'll be in touch."

I ventured back into the house to give Buck and Owen an update. "Detective Flynn just came by. He says they've got Jackson Pharr in custody."

Buck's mouth formed a smug smile. "I told you he was the one."

"You could be right. I'm not counting my chickens before they're hatched, though." Or before they confessed. "Right now, they've only got him on a drunk-and-disorderly charge, but they're going to work on him, see if they can get him to confess to killing Rick Dunaway."

Buck added the last piece of damaged floorboard to a stack in the corner. "I'll keep my fingers crossed they can wear him down."

Over the next hour or so, my cousins pulled the old, cheap cabinets from the kitchen and bath and carried them out to the garage, where they joined the closet doors I'd hauled out earlier. They dismantled the sinks and removed those, too.

Owen begged off at that point. "My better half has already texted twice asking when I'll be home. If I stay any longer I'll be in the doghouse."

The doghouse Owen had built for their oversized mutt had a raised floor, a ventilated roof, and Plexiglas windows on each side. It even had a front porch. He could live pretty well in that thing.

"We understand, bro." Buck gave him a pat on the back. "Thanks for your help."

"Yeah. Thanks, cuz." I gave him a pat of my own. "Give those girls a hug for me."

"Will do."

With that, he left the house.

Buck and I pulled out the old stove, dishwasher, and refrigerator, leaving the kitchen a mere shell. Improvising a little two-step, I cleaned up the dust and debris left behind, getting things ready for the new cabinets, sinks, and countertops to be installed tomorrow. With any luck, Detective Flynn would have a confession from Jackson soon, and Buck and I would have the house on the market. Things seemed to be looking up.

The two of us headed out around seven that evening, our muscles sore and aching. But pain meant progress, so that made it bearable.

On Sunday morning after church, while Buck and Owen installed the cabinets and countertops in the kitchen and bath, Colette and I replaced the damaged floorboards. It was sweet of her to help again. Surely she had better things to do than perform hard labor for free.

"I owe you," I told her.

She waved off the comment. "Nah. I'm sure I'll need you for something someday, and we'll call it even."

As the afternoon wore down, Buck emerged from the kitchen, a broad grin on his face. He waved us over. "Come take a look, you two."

Colette and I made our way into the kitchen. While the cabinets had yet to be painted, the majority of the work in the kitchen was complete. Even without paint, the space was beautiful, the quartz countertops gleaming under the new light fixtures.

"It's gorgeous!" Colette exclaimed, clapping her hands in delight.

Buck grinned. "You women sure do like your kitchens."

"You're one to talk," I shot back. After all, Buck made the state's best homemade barbecue sauce. He laced it with bourbon from up the road in Kentucky, and added just enough garlic, onions, and Tabasco to give it a nice kick.

"I don't like to *cook*," Buck said. "I like to *eat*."

Colette cut a coy look his way. "And women aren't just lining up to cook for you?"

"Nope." Buck shrugged. "I'm as baffled about that as you are."

She shook her head and laughed before looking from my cousin to me. "You have to let me cook here at least once before you sell the place. I'll test out the kitchen for you."

"That would be great," I said. "Will you make your bread pudding?" I *loved* Colette's bread pudding. She put both regular and golden raisins in it. Of course I loved everything she prepared. She was an incredible chef.

"Of course I'll make bread pudding," she said. "No meal would be complete without it." She checked her phone for the time. "Speaking of cooking, I gotta run. My shift starts in an hour."

We parted with a hug on the porch. While Buck and Colette didn't hug, Buck did lift his chin in good-bye and she lifted hers in return.

"Later," he said.

"Later," she replied. While Southerners often drew out their syllables, even adding an extra one or two to some words, we rarely spoke in complete sentences. It would sound uppity.

Buck and I got back to work, sanding the rough corners on the cabinets. By seven that evening, we had them ready for paint. We also had sore backs and tight arm muscles.

I tossed the worn sandpaper square into a trash bag. "Let's call it a day."

Buck put a hand to his sore back. "Amen to that."

I unplugged the snowman as we left. No sense running up an electric bill I couldn't afford. As the air left his body and he crumpled to the ground, I felt as if I'd ended his life. Luckily, unlike Rick Dunaway, the snowman could be resurrected by simply plugging him into an outlet.

CHAPTER 30

A KEPT CAT

SAWDUST

Sawdust gazed out the window, watching the squirrels scurry about, gathering nuts that had fallen from the hickory tree. He'd been watching them long enough to know their routine. They'd find a nut, choose a place to bury it, and hold it in their mouth while they dug a hole with their claws. When the hole was big enough, they'd drop the nut in and cover it with dirt.

Sure seems like a lot of work.

Sawdust pitied the rodents. He had never had to worry about where his next meal was coming from. Whitney made sure he had a never-ending supply of crunchy kibble, wet food, and his favorite tuna treats. Still, he liked digging, too. That was something he and the squirrels had in common. It had been a while since he'd had a chance to dig, though. The last time was that day at the stone house when he'd dug up that odd plaything in the dirt and Whitney had tossed him into his cage. He'd been stuck there for hours in the cold. What a miserable day that had been.

He wasn't cold now, though. It was nice and warm here in Whitney's parents house. He decided he'd had enough of watching the squirrels. He rolled over onto his back to get more comfortable. *Time for another nap.*

CHAPTER 31

INVOICES AND INQUIRIES

WHITNEY

Over the next week, between my duties for Home & Hearth and Buck's duties for the family carpentry business, we painted the cabinets, the remaining walls, and what wood there was on the primarily stone exterior. We installed the brushed-nickel switch plates. We poured our blood, sweat, and tears into our work and the project progressed at a rapid pace. Nothing motivates two people more than a looming mortgage they can't afford.

The plumber came and fixed the leaky pipe in the bathroom. The window guy replaced the broken glass in the kitchen window. We also installed the new closet doors and light fixtures. We trimmed the trees and seeded the yard. Buck added several bags of black bark chips to the beds to really make the red flowers on the camellias pop. Colette came by on occasion to cheer us on and fill us up with culinary creations from her kitchen, all with a New Orleans flair. Beignets covered in powdered sugar. Po'boy sandwiches. Thermoses of her super spicy gumbo.

Finally, the last brushstroke was complete. I took a minute or two to polish the door knocker with cleaner and a soft rag. The Green Man gleamed proudly.

My cousin and I stepped back to admire our work, standing on the walkway, gazing at the place.

Buck beamed with pride. "We done good, didn't we, cuz?"

I raised my hand to exchange a victorious high five. "We sure did."

I couldn't help but smile. In record time, we'd completed the renovations and the house was ready to go on the market. The place had undergone a metamorphosis, transforming from an unkempt eyesore owned by a penny-pinching landlord to a fresh and inviting cottage. It looked like the kind of place someone would be proud to call home. The only question now was *Who will that someone be?*

A car rolled to a stop on the street behind us. We turned to see Detective Flynn at the wheel of his plain, government-issue sedan. He climbed out.

"Did Jackson confess?" I asked as he headed our way.

Unfortunately, while things had progressed at the house, they seemed to be at another impasse in regard to the murder investigation.

"Jackson won't admit anything," Flynn said, "even with a generous plea deal on the table. His lawyers say he didn't kill Rick Dunaway and that they'll take the risk of going to trial if he's charged. We had no choice but to release him."

I sighed. Jackson might deny that he killed Rick Dunaway, but that didn't mean he was innocent. Guilty people lied about their crimes all the time. As far as I was concerned, he was still on the list of potential suspects. *Will Rick Dunaway's killer ever be convicted?* I was tired of looking over my shoulder, of having Buck babysit me, of living in my parents' house. I wanted my pool house back. I wanted my life back. Heck, I'd be happy just to get my tools back.

I was in luck. Flynn pushed a button on his key fob and the trunk popped open on his vehicle. He circled around and pulled my toolbox from his trunk. "You'll be pleased to know that no blood residue or other DNA evidence was found on your tools."

I was pleased, yes. But I wasn't surprised, of course. I accepted the toolbox. "Better late than never. We just finished the renovations."

He glanced over at the house. "Can I take a look?"

I cast a questioning glance at Buck. Our relationship with Detective Flynn was an odd one. He'd considered both Buck and me to be potential suspects in a murder, though he'd dismissed Buck quickly and had eventually let me tentatively off the hook. We weren't exactly friends, here. Still, we were proud of our house, of the hard work we'd put into it, proud we'd managed to get the place fixed up so fast amid very trying circumstances.

Buck's pride won out. He motioned with his hand for Flynn to follow him. "Come on in. We'll take you on the grand tour."

I followed the two men as Buck led Flynn around and pointed out all of the things we'd done to fix the place up. Buck stopped once we'd circled back to the front door.

The detective said, "The place looks great."

"We just need a buyer now," Buck said.

I eyed Flynn. "The murder isn't going to help move the place, especially if the killer isn't caught."

He met my gaze and held it for a moment before releasing a long breath. "I'm as frustrated as you are. I've talked with Dunaway's family and friends, interviewed all of the potential suspects you and the others have named, but none of the evidence seems to stick. Until something new comes to light, or the killer slips up, the case seems to be at a dead end."

A dead end wasn't good enough for me. I wanted a resolution, and I wanted it *now*.

"What about the video of Thad Gentry I sent you?" I asked. "He seemed unusually interested in this house, what with the way he was staring and all."

Flynn shrugged. "Maybe. But it could have been for any number of reasons. Lots of people are fascinated by crime scenes. There are businesses that even offer tours to murder sites."

"Really?" I shuddered at the thought of taking a vacation to see where grisly crimes had been committed. A long weekend at a cabin getaway in the Smoky Mountains was much more my style.

Buck had a slightly different take. "I bet Gentry was looking at the house, thinking what he'll do with it if we're forced to sell to him after all. He may be the only person willing to make an offer."

No doubt he'd lowball us if he was even still interested in the place.

I returned my attention to the detective. "What about the fact that Patty saw Gentry's car the night of Dunaway's murder? She told me that she mentioned it to you. He backed out in a hurry and sped off."

"I asked him about it," Flynn said. "He said he'd come by his property next door to make sure the contractors were proceeding on schedule. He rushed off when he received a call that the fire sprinklers at one of his other properties had accidentally activated. I looked into it. His story checked out."

"He could've still killed Dunaway before he left, right?"

"That's true. But without his fingerprints on the weapon or a witness saying they'd seen Gentry on your property, there's nothing to pin on him." The detective raised a shoulder.

"Did he tell you whether he'd seen any activity at our house?"

"I asked. He said he'd seen nothing. He'd noticed a light on inside your place, but that was it."

He must have seen the light coming from the portable lantern I'd brought along with me to study for the real estate exam.

We bade each other good-bye as we exited the house and aimed for our respective cars. As I opened the door to my SUV, Flynn called over to me, "Hey, Whitney?"

I looked in his direction. "Yeah?"

"Say hello to Sawdust for me."

On the following Monday morning, I went to the Home & Hearth office.

Mr. and Mrs. Hartley greeted me with their usual warm welcomes. Before they could say anything further, I circled around their desks and gave each of them a great, big hug. "Thanks again for helping out at the house. I can't thank you two enough."

"Shoot, hon," Mrs. Hartley said. "After all the hard work you've put in for us? You don't need to thank us at all." She waved a dismissive hand. "We were glad to help."

Mr. Hartley nodded in agreement. "It was the least we could do."

After pouring myself a cup of coffee, I sat down at my desk and completed the paperwork to put the Sweetbriar house on the market. Though the plan all along had been to sell the place once we'd renovated it, I found myself feeling wistful. The house seemed almost a part of me now, like a first love I wasn't quite ready to let go of even though I knew it had to be done. We'd been through a lot together. I'd poured my blood, sweat, and tears into it. Then again, some of Rick Dunaway's blood had gone into the place, too. *Eeek*. That thought made it a little easier to sign my name on the bottom line.

After sliding the paperwork into Mrs. Hartley's in-box, I went to the file cabinet, rounded up all our copies of the keys for the Abbot-Dunaway units, and typed up a quick list noting the status of each property. *Leased through May. Currently accepting applications. Homeowners' association fees due January 1.* Our contract didn't require me to provide the update, but it felt like the courteous thing to do. It would make things easier on whoever they hired to take over the management duties.

When I was done, I printed out the document, gathered up my things, and bade the Hartleys good-bye. "See you later."

Mr. Hartley pointed to the stack of aluminum HOME & HEARTH REALTY signs leaning against the wall. "Don't forget the sign for your yard."

"Oh! Right." I grabbed one of the signs and carried it out to my SUV.

On my drive downtown, I made two stops. The first was at the house. I placed the FOR SALE sign in the yard, trying not to think about the last sign I'd erected here, the one for Whitaker Woodworking, the one I'd pounded into the ground with the dead blow mallet I'd inadvertently left outside to become a weapon of death. On the handle of the front door I hung a lockbox containing keys to the house so that Realtors from other agencies could show the place. Buck wouldn't be too happy if he knew I'd come here alone, but I planned to make it quick.

I went into the house, locked the door behind me for safety, and turned on every light in the place so I could snap some pics. They'd come in handy for the online listing. *Our first flip!* I'd also add the photos to the Whitaker Woodworking portfolio of before and after pictures that highlighted our superior carpentry work.

My second stop was at a florist. While I had scant funds to afford flowers, I wanted to take something to the Abbot-Dunaway Holdings office as a sign of respect. I bought a nice peace lily in a white ceramic pot and wrote *"May he rest in peace"* on the sympathy card I attached.

I parked in the underground garage, keeping an eye on my surroundings as I exited my SUV and made my way to the elevator. I saw no white sedan today, but I supposed that made sense. If someone had been spying on Dunaway, they'd have no reason to continue after his death.

My heart pounded as I rode the car up to the eighteenth floor. I had no idea what type of reception I would get, but surely they'd realize I wouldn't show my face at their office if I were guilty, right? Besides, the police hadn't kept me in custody. The fact that I'd been released said something.

Ding! The doors slid open. As I stepped out, I saw a man in my peripheral vision climbing into the adjacent elevator. He was stocky and wearing a suit. *Wait. Was it Thad Gentry? If so, what was he doing here?*

I rushed over to the elevator, having a difficult time moving fast with the lily in my hands. By the time I got there the doors were closing, giving me only a glimpse of a gray suit before they fully shut. I reached out and jabbed at the up and down buttons, hoping to force the doors open again. But it was too late. The elevator had already begun to descend.

I turned and made my way down the hall to the door of

Abbot-Dunaway, using my elbow to push the handle down given that my hands were filled with the peace lily and paperwork.

While I could hear the whir of the copy machine from down the hall, the reception area was empty. I carried the plant over to Presley's desk and set it down. As I did, my eyes spotted an invoice in her in-box. The bill was from Isak Nyström for $32,000 in interior design services and furnishings. The invoice was dated the day of Mr. Dunaway's death, and noted *"Terms: Net Ten."* I knew from my own experience with various contractors that the term meant the bill must be paid within ten days. Given that Mr. Dunaway's funeral and the Thanksgiving holiday had fallen during the interim, Presley apparently had not yet had time to process the invoice. According to the document, the costs were purportedly incurred for services at 1212 Laurel Street. Though no specific unit number was referenced, I knew the address was for a high-rise luxury tower not-so-creatively named Twelve Twelve.

That's odd.

Twelve Twelve was a newer building in a trendy area of downtown known as the Gulch. The first condominiums had been put on the market in late 2014. Abbot-Dunaway had bought one of those units. It had been a smart investment. The Gulch had only grown in popularity since, and the value of the condo had increased substantially.

Just last month I'd leased the one-bedroom place to a professional couple in their mid-thirties. Both of them traveled regularly for work, and they'd wanted a convenient, upscale abode that was close to the Nashville nightlife and would allow for easy upkeep. Though they could have afforded to buy a place, they didn't want the hassles that came with home ownership.

Because the Twelve Twelve building was so new, the

interior featured the latest styles in fixtures, flooring, and other design features. There'd be no need to have the condo renovated. What's more, the unit had been offered unfurnished. None of the Abbot-Dunaway residential properties came with furnishings.

In other words, the invoice made no sense.

Before I could fully process the situation, the whir of the copier ceased. I snapped a quick pic of the page as Presley came down the hall looking like a fashion model on a runway in another fitted sheath dress, leather boots, and Gucci scarf. She held a stack of papers in her arms. When she saw me, she stopped in her high-heeled tracks, her lip curling back in a snarl. "You've got a lot of nerve coming in here."

Despite my complete innocence, my cheeks burned with a blush. "I'm sorry about what happened to Mr. Dunaway, Presley. But I had nothing to do with it."

"Nothing to do with it?" She set the stack of papers down on top of the invoice and threw up perfectly manicured hands. "You were brought in for his murder!"

"But the police released me," I insisted. "They haven't charged me with any crime."

She pointed to the door. "Get out right now or I'll call security!"

Clearly, there was nothing to be gained by arguing with her. The people at Abbot-Dunaway Holdings thought I was guilty. So much for my hopes of getting Lance Abbot to reconsider firing Home & Hearth.

I held up the manila envelope. "The keys for the properties are in here. I've provided a status summary for each of the rentals, too."

I set the manila envelope down on her desk and walked out, my head held high. No matter what she thought, I knew I was innocent. I refused to leave the place in disgrace.

As I rode down in the elevator, my mind ventured back to the strange invoice. As the manager of the condo at Twelve Twelve, I should've been told if Abbot-Dunaway had wanted to hire a designer to perform services at the property. In fact, it was my job to arrange such things.

Why had Rick Dunaway left me out of the loop?

Maybe he'd left me out because the matter was personal. It was possible that Dunaway had moved out of the house he shared with his wife and into a condo at Twelve Twelve. The two were in the middle of a nasty divorce, after all.

Once I was back in my car, I pulled up the Davidson County Property Assessor's Web site and ran a search in the name of Rick Dunaway. There was no unit at 1212 Laurel Street in his name. The only residential property in his name was the house in Belle Meade that he owned with his wife. *Hmm.*

I went back to the records for Twelve Twelve. There were 286 units in the building. Was it possible that Dunaway had a mistress who lived there? If so, maybe his mistress had killed him. The man was ruthless in business matters. Surely he could be ruthless in matters of the heart, too. Maybe he'd set his sights on another woman, negotiated a better deal with her, and decided to terminate his arrangement with his then-current lover.

Was one of the units in her name? If so, who might that girlfriend be?

Presley.

The name popped unbidden into my mind and my hands went unbidden to my mouth. *Could it be?*

If Rick Dunaway and Presley were involved in a romantic relationship, it certainly would explain a lot of things. How she could afford the expensive clothes and accessories she wore. Why the invoice had been sent to the Abbot-Dunaway office. Why she'd seemingly tried to hide it from my view by placing a stack of papers on top of it. Still, even though these facts pointed to Presley, the fact that she'd seemed to harbor some resentments toward her boss told me it might not be her. Then again, assuming she was his mistress, maybe the fact that she not only worked for Dunaway but was sleeping with him made her doubly angry with him for selling the Sweetbriar house to me. Or maybe her resentment was a ploy. Maybe Presley only pretended to resent her boss so that people wouldn't suspect the two of them of having an intimate relationship.

I ran her name through the system, but nothing came up. *Hmm*. I went back to the Twelve Twelve records for a third time and read over the list of all 286 owners, searching for units that listed a female owner. A couple of the names sounded vaguely familiar, but a quick search of the Web told me why. They were up-and-coming country singing stars. I'd probably seen them on the news or performing at a venue around town. There seemed to be a lineup in every bar and restaurant in the city. I'd even seen a guy playing guitar once in a frozen yogurt shop, probably hoping an agent or record-label executive would wander in for a cone. Anything to be heard and potentially discovered.

I typed Rick Dunaway's name into the search browser and skimmed over the articles about him that popped up, looking for any references to a woman he might have associated with who could have been a potential lover. I found a couple of photos of him with an attractive woman from the chamber of commerce, but when I compared her name to the list of owners of condos at Twelve Twelve, I found no match. *Darn*.

I pondered the information and decided that I could reach no definitive conclusions from it. Dunaway could have bought a condo in the building through a "straw man," putting the unit in the name of someone else so his wife wouldn't know about it. Or maybe he didn't own the unit, but was merely renting the condo. Still, if he had purchased or rented the condo for personal use, by himself or a girlfriend, he should have paid for the design services out of his own pocket. The expense should not have been run through the company. On the other hand, maybe he'd planned to pay for the service, but had the invoice sent to his business address so that his wife wouldn't find out about it.

I returned my phone to my purse and started my car. As I drove back to Home & Hearth, I continued to mull the situation over. The more I thought about it, the more concerned I became. The curriculum for my business degree had included several accounting courses. My Accounting 101 professor had taught us the importance of checks and balances in any accounting system. Part of those checks and balances involved splitting the accounting functions among several staff members. Separating the tasks was not a difficult thing for large businesses to do, but for a firm like Abbot-Dunaway Holdings with a small staff, it wasn't always possible to implement proper protocols. Unscrupulous employees could exploit the system for their own nefarious purposes, siphon off dollar after dollar before anyone else got wind of it. Some of them were never caught.

The invoice from Isak Nyström looked legitimate on its face, but was it? I had my doubts. I supposed it could have been an honest error. Maybe someone on the designer's staff had issued the invoice by mistake. But how would that person have had the address of an Abbot-Dunaway property they'd never been associated with? And if the bill was fraudulent, what did that mean?

It meant that someone was trying to pull a fast one on Abbot-Dunaway Holdings, that's what. That someone had to be Rick Dunaway, Isak Nyström, a member of the designer's staff, or Presley, right? Or perhaps some combination of these people working together?

If Presley had faked the invoice, it could explain why she'd shooed me out of the Abbot-Dunaway office so quickly this morning. Maybe she was afraid I'd spot the bill and realize something was out of order.

A sick feeling tiptoed into my tummy. *If that invoice is a fake, could it have something to do with Rick Dunaway's death? Had Rick Dunaway found out that Presley was processing fraudulent invoices and skimming money from the company?* She kept Mr. Dunaway's calendar, knew everywhere he'd be and when. She'd have known he planned to meet me at the house on Sweetbriar Avenue that fateful Friday evening.

Had Presley killed Rick Dunaway?

I pulled into the parking lot of Home & Hearth, parked, and went into the building. The Hartleys looked up from their desks as I came in.

"I might be on to something."

Mrs. Hartley tilted her head in interest. "What is it?"

I told the Hartleys about the invoice I'd spotted on Presley's desk. "The bill is suspicious, isn't it?"

Mr. Hartley's brows gathered above his nose. "It raises some questions, that's for sure."

I looked from one of them to the other. "What should I do?"

Mrs. Hartley provided an answer. "I suppose the right thing to do is give Mr. Abbot a call and let him know what you saw."

"Let me do it," Mr. Hartley said. "He might not accept a call from Whitney."

I mentally cringed, but had to agree.

Mr. Hartley picked up the receiver for his desk phone. "Got the number handy?"

I fished my cell phone out of my purse and pulled up Rick Dunaway's contact information. I had both his private cell number and the main office number for Abbot-Dunaway. I rattled off the office number and Mr. Hartley dialed it.

"Good morning," he said when the phone was answered. "May I speak to Mr. Abbot, please?"

He paused for a few seconds during which Presley must have asked who was calling.

"Marv Hartley," he replied, "from Home and Hearth." Another pause.

"He's not in? All righty, then. May I have his voice mail please?" Mr. Hartley gave us a thumbs-up to let us know he was being transferred to Abbot's voice mail. After another short pause, he left his message. "Hello, Mr. Abbot. Marv Hartley here. We think there might be a problem with a bill your firm received. It has to do with one of the properties we managed for you. It seems you might have been overcharged. Please give me a call back as soon as you can." He ended by leaving the Home & Hearth office number.

After he hung up the receiver he shrugged his shoulders. "Guess all we can do now is wait for him to call back."

I hoped Lance Abbot would return the call soon. While determination and tenacity were some of my virtues, patience was not among them.

While I'd been gone, Mrs. Hartley had processed the paperwork for the Sweetbriar house and it was ready to go public. I went to my desk to upload the information about the house into the multiple-listing service Web site. I took care of the easy part first, inputting the square footage, the year the house was built and the date of its most recent re-model, the number of bedrooms and bathrooms, the size of the lot. Next, I uploaded the photos I'd taken of both the exterior and interior of the home. Finally, I took a moment or two to formulate a description that would be sure to entice a buyer. It was no secret Realtors sometimes had to get creative when describing properties to potential buyers. There was a not-so-secret code. *Cozy* meant small. *Great location* meant the house was in a convenient area, but wasn't much to look at. *Handyman's dream* was the code for a fixer-upper. After some thought, I came up with:

> *The perfect blend of classic style and contemporary conveniences make this custom stone cottage a must-see for the discerning buyer. Located in the desirable Belmont-Hillsboro neighborhood, this home features exposed stone in the living room, a claw-foot tub in the bath, and a newly remodeled chef's kitchen. Fresh paint, new flooring, and lush landscaping round out this one-of-a-kind property.*

That sounded so much better than *Crime scene for sale. Your children can play where a corpse once lay!*

After discussion with Buck and the Hartleys, we'd deci-ded on a listing price of $499,000. I typed the price into the appropriate field on the screen. Objectively, the home should be worth every penny of the list price. All of the fire damage had been repaired and the wiring was com-pletely updated. All evidence of Rick Dunaway's murder had been removed, too. Subjectively, though, buyers might not want to pay market price for a house that had suffered a fire and served as a venue for violence. But we'd cross that bridge when, and if, it came to it. We could always negotiate the price down if we had to. I only hoped we wouldn't end up in a short sale situation. We'd have to get the mortgage company's approval to sell the house for less than we owed. A short sale would not only ruin my credit and Buck's, but it could get our loan officer in hot water, too. She'd stuck her neck out for me, convincing the underwriter that I was a safe bet. I'd hate to let her down, jeopardize her career, too.

I hit enter to submit the photos and information. Within minutes the listing was live. I crossed my fingers. *Somebody buy the house and soon!*

Things were off to a great start!

By the end of the workday, I'd received three calls about the house. *Woo-hoo!*

The first showing was that very night. While buyer's agents don't normally like their clients to interact directly with the seller or seller's agent, this agent had asked me to be on-site. His client was an executive who was being transferred to Nashville soon. The client was in town for only a short period of time, and the agent wanted to show him as many options as possible and seal the deal before the man flew out on Wednesday. If his buyer had questions, he wanted someone readily available to answer them. I was happy to oblige. I met them at the house at seven thirty.

The agent was on the younger side, in his early thirties. His client was in his mid- to late fifties. Both wore dress pants and jackets, but no ties.

"Good evening!" I called in greeting from the porch as they made their way up the walk.

We exchanged handshakes and I took them on a tour,

pointing out the features. We started with the outside. I showed them the spacious garage and backyard, pointing out that the stone spanned the entire outside of the house. No cutting corners by using wood or aluminum siding on the sides and back.

When we'd made our way back to the porch, I led them inside and took them through the rooms.

"My wife would love this kitchen," the older man said as he took a look around. "She loves to cook." As for himself, he liked the stone wall in the living room. "That's not something you see every day."

"That's true," I agreed. "This property is unique."

When we were done with the tour, the agent said, "May I have a moment alone with my client?"

"Of course," I replied. "I'll wait out front."

I stepped outside. The night was frigid, but the cold air smelled fresh and clean, like a new beginning. *This buyer's interested, isn't he?* My gosh! I might sell the house its first day on the market!

A minute or so later, the agent opened the door and invited me back inside. "We're interested," he said. "Of course we'll need to take a look at the disclosure statement. Do you have a copy with you?"

"I do." I pulled the statement from my bag and handed it to him.

He carried the document into the kitchen and laid it on the breakfast bar where he and his client could stand side by side and look it over together.

The agent flipped to the second page and looked up at me. "There was a fire here?"

"Yes," I replied. I'd disclosed the fire in the section where the seller was supposed to list any known repairs. "But it was contained to the small bedroom."

"What caused it?" the client asked.

"Old wiring," said. "No need to worry, though. The entire electrical system has since been updated."

The agent picked up the report and ventured into the back bedroom. His client and I followed him. "Is this where it happened?"

"Yes," I said. "As you can see, there's no evidence of fire damage."

"There's certainly not," the buyer agreed. "Whoever the contractor was did a really good job."

Thank you. I couldn't agree more.

The agent glanced back down at the report. "I don't see anything else that causes me any concern."

The buyer pointed in the direction of Gentry's property. "I saw a Bobcat tractor next door. What's going on over there?"

Ugh. Here we go. "That house was recently rezoned so that it could be used for commercial purposes. It's my understanding the owner plans to lease it to a beauty salon."

The buyer's *hmm* wasn't exactly encouraging. *Darn Mr. Gentry and his ruthless pursuit of the almighty dollar!*

I did what damage control I could. "It's my understanding that the developer has agreed to put in a privacy hedge between that property and this one. You won't even be able to see the salon once it's installed."

The buyer's second *hmm* sounded a little more positive. "I'll need to think on it tonight," he said. "I really like this place. I'd prefer to have people living on both sides of me rather than a business, but the salon's not necessarily a deal breaker. We live next to a branch library right now. It hasn't been much of a problem, but we've got a brick wall between us. That gives us some privacy and keeps the traffic noise down."

I stuck out my hand and we exchanged final handshakes. I gave the men my best buy-this-house smile. "I'll look forward to hearing from you in the morning."

With that, we exited the house and stepped onto the porch. As the men made their way up the walk to the agent's car, I followed after them.

The gawker from across the street was rolling his trash bin out to the curb. He looked over at the men. "You gonna buy the murder house?" he called.

The buyer and his agent stopped in their tracks, just like Presley had done when she'd come upon me this morning. I nearly ran into their backs, stopping only a couple inches behind them. Both of them turned around to face me and we found ourselves standing awkwardly close. The agent raised a brow in question while the buyer crossed his arms over his chest. *Defensive posture. Not good.*

"There wasn't a murder *inside* the house," I clarified. "A body was found outside."

"Outside where?" asked the agent.

"In the flower bed," I replied.

The potential buyer glanced over at the flower bed. "That bed there?"

I nodded.

"Whose body was it?" the client asked.

Eek. "The former owner's."

He muttered a few choice words and cut me a look so pointed I could have hunted buffalo with it.

I raised my palms. "It's not what you think. The owner didn't live here. The house was a rental."

The client grunted. "Like that's much better. Did they at least catch the guy who did it?"

"Not yet." *But they did drag me in for questioning.*

The client's jaw went slack in disbelief. "So the killer is still on the loose? He could come back at any time?"

"I suppose it's possible. I don't think it's likely."

The agent chimed in. "When did the murder take place?"

"A couple weeks ago." *Okay, so it was only ten days. But everyone knows it's okay to round up.*

"Wait a minute." The agent jabbed his finger in the direction of the house. "Is this where they found Rick Dunaway?"

There was no denying it. "Yes."

"Holy moly!" He shook his head and turned to address his client. "Sorry about this. If I'd known, I would've told you up front and not wasted your time coming by here to see the place."

Without so much as another glance in my direction, the two climbed into the agent's car and drove away. I climbed into mine, started the engine, and accidentally on purpose backed into my neighbor's garbage can, tipping it over on his lawn. *Cost me a sale, will you?*

CHAPTER 32

KITTY KISSES

SAWDUST

The cat could tell that Whitney wasn't happy when she came home that night. She kept closing her eyes and sighing. She'd also eaten an enormous bowl of ice cream. Sawdust had noticed she did that when she was sad or worried.

When she put it in the sink without washing it, he seized the rare opportunity. He leaped up onto the counter, waltzed over to the sink, and treated himself to the melted remnants, lapping it up as fast as his tongue could go.

When he'd licked the bowl clean, he figured he should go and try to cheer her up. After everything Whitney did for him, it was the least he could do in return.

First, he whacked his ball with his paw and sent it rolling across the floor. *Jingle-jingle-jingle*. He chased after the ball, performing a spin as he passed her chair. That move usually got a laugh out of her. Not tonight, though. Tonight, she reached down, snatched up his ball, and stuck it in the top drawer of the dresser.

Oookay.

Since the ball hadn't worked, he decided to try crazy

cat. She seemed to get a kick out of it when he sprinted around the room and bolted up and down his cat tree. Off he went. He made three dizzying trips around the room and still she hadn't cracked a smile. His little heart was beating so fast he could feel it in his ears!

He had one more trick he could try. He jumped up onto the bed and traipsed up to the top, where he wriggled under the covers. He wriggled all the way down to the end and back, but Whitney never tickled him through the sheets like she usually did.

Out of ideas, he decided maybe she needed love more than amusement. He hopped up into her lap, raised his chin, and stuck out his tongue to kiss her cheek. That seemed to cheer her up lickety-split. She wrapped her arms around him and buried her face in his fur.

CHAPTER 33

MONEY TALKS

WHITNEY

Word that the murder house was up for sale spread like wildfire. The next morning, both scheduled showings were canceled. Nobody else called about the property all day. Lance Abbot didn't call about the suspicious invoice, either. Wednesday was more or less a repeat of Tuesday. No calls. No movement on the house or the invoice. No news of an arrest in Rick Dunaway's murder.

Being a woman of action, and running out of patience, I decided on Thursday morning to seize the bull by the horns. I scheduled an open house from ten to six on Saturday, noting the event in the multiple-listing service online. Maybe that would lead a buyer to our doors. I also advertised the event by placing a sandwich board sign with changeable letters next to the FOR SALE sign in the yard. I'd arranged the letters to say FULLY RENOVATED DREAM HOME! DON'T MISS OUR OPEN HOUSE SATURDAY 10–6.

I also decided to go by the property in the Twelve Twelve building and speak with the tenants. They could tell me whether Isak Nyström had done any work there. Knowing the couple who leased the condo worked irregular hours, I took a chance and stopped by that afternoon. The lobby of the building was just as chic and stylish as I remembered. I rode the elevator up to the fifth floor, made my way to the end of the hall, and knocked on the door.

The wife answered. She was wearing yoga pants and a T-shirt. Her feet were bare. It wasn't clear whether she was actually exercising or if this was simply her go-to lounging gear as it was for so many women these days, including myself. She looked at me, her focus on my nose, her eyes squinting a bit as if she didn't recognize me.

"Hi," I said. "Do you remember me? I'm Whitney Whitaker. From your property management company?" *Former* management company, to be precise.

"Oh, right." Her eyes widened to normal, though her focus was still on my nose. "I don't have my glasses on so you're nothing but a big blond blur." She indicated my fuzzy form by making a circling motion with her palm, as if she were waxing an invisible car.

I glanced past her into the condo. As far as I could tell, nothing had changed here. The kitchen had the same appliances, the same tile, the same countertops. The flooring was the same, too. The walls were the same basic, neutral taupe color that I had the painters put in all of the rental properties when they needed to be repainted.

I hadn't come to the condo since handing over the keys, so I'd never seen the couple's furniture. But there was absolutely no chance that Isak Nyström had selected their furnishings. I'd visited his Web site umpteen times and attended enough tours of homes to know that he trafficked in rare, unusual pieces and bright, bold colors. The décor here was distinctly Crate & Barrel. Neutral tones. Standard styles. Everyday furniture fare, with nothing particularly eye-catching or conversation-starting.

Could the designer have ordered furniture, but not yet delivered it? Better to eliminate all possibilities.

I returned my attention to the tenant. "Can you tell me whether a designer has been by to take a look at the place? Was any furniture ordered for the condo?"

"No." Lines of confusion popped up on her forehead. "Why?"

I gave her a slightly altered version of the facts, but one that would serve to waste no more of her time and keep the name of Abbot-Dunaway Holdings out of the conversation. "Home and Hearth received an invoice from a designer that we can't match to a property. I'm trying to sort it out for our records."

Her eyes narrowed again. "Wouldn't the easiest way to sort it out be to talk to the designer?"

It would be, if I didn't want to tip him off that I suspected him of fraud. "I haven't been able to reach her," I said to cover my tracks, inadvertently giving the designer an impromptu sex change. "She's on vacation. But I'm sure she can clear things up for me when she returns. Sorry to have bothered you."

"No problem."

The door closed behind me as I turned and headed back down the hall. I returned to my car on the street to find a parking ticket on my windshield. *Ugh!* My mind had been going a million miles a minute when I'd arrived. I'd totally forgotten to feed the meter.

I snatched the ticket out from under the wiper and checked to see how much the infraction would cost me. *$75? Sheesh!* At this rate I was going to have to learn to forage for berries in the woods or force myself to eat crickets.

I'd heard they were a dietary staple in some countries. Sawdust had played with an errant cricket or two that had ventured into our pool house. Fortunately for the bugs, he hadn't seemed to have a taste for them.

I tucked the citation into my purse and climbed into my car. Pulling my phone from my purse, I called Buck and gave him an update. "I'm going to talk to the designer. Any chance you can play bodyguard for me?"

"I'll meet you there in half an hour."

After ending the call and using my phone to find for the address of Nyström's studio, I plugged it into my GPS and headed back out on the road. Fifteen minutes later, I pulled into the lot of a warehouse in east Nashville. The only thing identifying the place as Nyström's business were his initials, IN, which were spelled out in rust on the side of the metal building. Who knew rust could be forced? I thought it just happened naturally.

The designer was known for picking up odds and ends that caught his eye, whether they be at a garage sale in the hills of Kentucky or a chic boutique in Paris. The bay doors were open, revealing a smorgasbord of pieces. A collection of vintage food tins, ranging from a large red tin of animal crackers to a rectangular tin of Prince Albert tobacco. The dinged and dented front bumper of a circa 1955 car, the Tennessee license plate still attached. A vintage poster for a revival to be held at the Ryman Auditorium. The local tourist attraction had been built by a reformed riverboat captain to serve as a church, and had been originally named the Union Gospel Tabernacle. Years later, it had been converted to an entertainment venue. It served as the original home of the Grand Ole Opry for decades. I'd attended several concerts there myself over the years.

Buck pulled up in his van and took the parking spot

next to my SUV. We climbed out of our vehicles and met on the pavement.

He patted his pocket to let me know that, once again, he was armed with his wrench in case things went south.

As we wandered into the space, my eyes noted the handwritten price tags hanging from some of the items: $4,850 for a pair of worn whitewall tires on which a circle of glass had been placed to form a makeshift coffee table; $6,570 for an old-fashioned, precomputer library card catalog; $13,300 for a wall-sized painting of an airplane with a ceiling fan turned on its side as the propeller. *I've gone into the wrong business.*

Seeing nobody in the bay, we walked up to a solid metal door at the side of the room to see if we might find someone in an office. The words BY APPOINTMENT ONLY were spelled out in colorful plastic magnets, the kind people put on their fridge to teach their children the alphabet. *Amusing.* The designer had a definite sense of whimsy.

I raised a hand and rapped on the door. *Rap-rap-rap.*

After waiting for a full minute with no response, I tried again, knocking harder this time. *RAP-RAP-RAP.*

Still nothing.

"Can I help y'all?" came a voice from behind us. Despite the Southern phrasing, the words were tinged with an accent I assumed was Swedish. *Talk about a culture clash.*

Buck and I turned to find a young man with spiky platinum-blond hair. He wore bright red plastic eyeglasses and a black and white striped jumpsuit. If not for the fact that the stripes were vertical rather than horizontal, he could be taken for an inmate. And if not for the fact that he was wearing the eyeglasses, he could be taken for a zebra.

"We'd like to speak to Mr. Nyström. Is he in?"

"Is it about one of the pieces here in the shop?" The man swept his hand to indicate the items. "Because I can help you with anything here."

"No," I replied. "It's about his design services."

"Do you have an appointment?" He looked from me to Buck and back again.

"No."

"You will have to make an appointment. Mr. Nyström's time is valuable and he is beyond busy. I have been given strict orders not to interrupt him while he is creating."

I understood the value of time as well as anyone, even if my time might not yield as many dollars per hour as the designer's. *Hmm. That thought gives me an idea.* "I'm here to pay a thirty-two-thousand-dollar invoice for a property I manage." If that kind of money didn't open Nyström's door, I didn't know what would.

The young man held out his hand. "I can take it."

"I have some questions about the invoice."

He lowered his glasses and eyed me over them. "What are they? I can pass them on and get back to you."

"I would much prefer to discuss the matter with Mr. Nyström himself."

The young man scowled, clearly insulted. "Why should he spend his valuable time on something his assistant can handle for him?"

Money may talk, but it didn't speak loud enough for this guy. Thirty-two thousand dollars must be a mere pittance for the designer and his staff. *Must be nice to earn big bucks like that.*

"Go now." Done with us, the young man shooed me and Buck out of the place, waving the backs of his hands and coming at us until we had backed out onto the asphalt parking lot.

"What am I supposed to do about my questions?" I asked.

"Put them in writing and mail them in," he snapped before pushing a button to lower the bay door.

The guy's behavior and attitude had me wondering whether he was involved in the fake-invoice scheme.

After we'd walked back to our vehicles, I exhaled sharply and turned to Buck. "Looks like I'll have to find another way to get to Isak Nyström."

Buck gestured toward the building. "We know he's in there, right? Why don't we wait for him? He's got to come out sometime."

"You've got a point." We could only hope he didn't decide to put in a late night and keep us waiting until the wee hours.

So that the assistant would think we'd left, we drove our cars out of the lot and parked on the street, on either side of the narrow entrance into the parking lot of INnovations. I climbed into the passenger seat of Buck's van and we watched a movie on my phone while we waited, an action movie starring one of Hollywood's many muscleheads. Buck chose it. I would've preferred a lighthearted romcom, but since he was helping me out here the least I could do was let him pick the flick.

At ten minutes after five, the door from the administrative part of the building opened. The young blond man I'd spoken to before emerged. A couple seconds later, none other than Isak Nyström himself came out of the building. Though I'd never met the man in person, I recognized him from photos on his Web site and in magazines. Like his cohort, he sported platinum-blond hair, though instead of standing up in spikes his was tied back in a short ponytail. He was dressed head to toe in winter white, the only splash of color a royal blue scarf that encircled his neck and draped over the shoulders of his knee-length coat.

I wasn't about to miss my chance to ask the exclusive, reclusive designer about the invoice. I hopped out of the van and hurried over, raising a hand. "Mr. Nyström!" I called. "I need to speak with you!"

The slamming of a door behind me told me Buck had gotten out of his van, too, and had my back.

Nyström stopped in his tracks. His ice-blue eyes narrowed as I approached, his gaze traveling up and down my work coveralls. He said nothing, letting his assistant take the lead.

"*You* again," the assistant said, continuing toward us. "I told you to mail in the invoice with your questions."

Buck stepped up beside me. Ignoring the young man, I addressed the designer. "I'm Whitney Whitaker. I managed properties for Rick Dunaway."

While his assistant fumed next to him, Nyström put his palms together, as if in prayer. When he spoke, it was with the same Swedish accent as his assistant. "Tragic what happened to him, no?"

His use of *no* confused me. Did *no* really mean *yes* here? Rather than accidentally say the wrong thing, I avoided *yes* and *no* and simply said, "It certainly was."

Though this man knew of Dunaway's death, he didn't seem to recognize me as the person of interest whose face had been all over the news and papers. I supposed I looked much different in my coveralls and work boots than I did in the blazer and slacks I'd been wearing the day I'd been arrested. *Good.* Maybe he'd be more forthcoming.

I said, "I understand you did some work for Mr. Dunaway?"

Nyström nodded. "I designed the house for him and his wife in Belle Meade. The Venatino marble I installed transformed it into a masterpiece." He cocked his head. "You have seen the home, yes?"

"Unfortunately, I have not," I said. Though the Dunaways' frequent soirees had been featured often in the social pages of the local newspaper, I'd never been invited to one of them. Dunaway seemed to consider anyone who worked for him to be beneath him.

The man clucked his tongue. "Such a shame. You see such exquisite beauty, you are never the same. It touches you here." He clutched a fist to his chest.

"In your heart?" I asked.

"No." He closed his eyes and whispered. "In your soul."

Despite his melodrama, I could understand where he was coming from. Some of my carpentry projects had produced an almost spiritual reaction in me. But I had a much more mundane matter to address with him than the effect of a beautiful piece of real estate. "I had a question about an invoice from your office." I took my cell phone from my pocket and pulled the photo of the invoice up on my screen. "This one."

"Business," he spat, his nose wrinkling in disgust. "Such an ugly but necessary part of the process." Crooking one arm behind him, Nyström bent forward from the waist and ran his eyes over the screen. "Something is wrong." He looked up with a frown. "I designed for three others who live in the Twelve Twelve building. But never did I design there for Abbot-Dunaway Holdings."

"What about Rick Dunaway himself?" I asked. "Did you do some personal work there for him or maybe for"— *how could I phrase this delicately?*—"an *acquaintance* of his?"

The designer gave me a knowing look. He knew what I was getting at. "No," he replied. "Not for him. Not for an acquaintance."

"Are you sure?"

His assistant stood up straight and tapped one ankle to the other, like a soldier coming to attention. "Of course he is sure!"

What an odd duo. I slid my phone back into my pocket and dipped my head politely before turning to go. "Thank you for your time, sir."

CHAPTER 34

LEAD ME ON

WHITNEY

The following morning, as I drove to a rental property to look into a potential roof leak, I wondered why Lance Abbot hadn't returned Mr. Hartley's call. Wouldn't he want to know if there was a problem with a bill?

It dawned on me then that, just like the man I'd spoken with earlier served as Nyström's gatekeeper, Presley served the same purpose at Abbot-Dunaway Holdings. Presley might have deleted Mr. Hartley's voice mail. Depending on how secure their system was, it might not be hard to do. Maybe Colette's hunch was right, maybe Presley had had enough with her boss and delivered him a solid whack on my front porch.

After confirming the roof leak at the rental house, notifying the property owner, and arranging for a roofer to swing by and take a look, I drove to the midtown police station. My attorney had told me not to talk to the cops, so she wouldn't be happy with me right now. But if I called her and asked her to pass the information about the invoice along to the detective, she'd charge my parents a fee for her time. Essentially, they'd be paying hundreds of dollars for her to serve as a parrot, simply repeating what I'd tell her. It couldn't hurt for me to talk to the detective about the invoice, right? Besides, given that I'd spoken to him several times since he'd dragged me into this mess, that ship had long since sailed.

I went inside and checked in with the woman working the front desk. "Is Detective Flynn in?"

She pointed behind me. "There he comes right now."

I turned around to see Detective Flynn and Officer Hogarty coming up the hallway from the interrogation room. Bobby Palmer walked a step or two ahead of them. The look on Bobby's face was both enraged and terrified at the same time.

When Bobby spotted me, he rushed toward me. "Tell them, Whitney! Tell them I didn't do it! You know I wouldn't kill anyone!"

I didn't know what to say. I had a hard time thinking Bobby was capable of killing Rick Dunaway, but I hadn't thought he'd con me, either. Even though I'd crossed paths with him many times over the last few years, I felt like I hardly knew him now.

As Hogarty continued past me, the detective stepped over, his demeanor toward me far more congenial today. "Hello, Miss Whitaker."

I looked from him, to Bobby, and back again. "What's going on?"

The detective eyed Bobby. "Do you want to tell her, or should I?"

Bobby hung his head, avoiding my gaze. "You do it."

"All right," Flynn said. "You're free to go for now, Mr. Palmer, but stay in town. We might need to speak with you again."

Bobby nodded and headed out the door.

Once he was gone, Flynn returned his attention to me and waved for me to follow him. "Let's go back to my office."

I followed him down the hall and into the small, windowless space he'd been assigned. Stacks of files in various heights formed a makeshift skyline along the edge of his desk. A couple of takeout menus were thumbtacked to the bulletin board behind his desk, along with an astronomy-themed calendar featuring a photo of the crab nebulae and photos of two cats, one a gray tabby, the other a black-and-white tuxedo.

He caught me eyeing the cats. "The gray one's Copernicus. The other's Galileo."

"They're handsome boys." I had to wonder if his two feline friends were why he'd believed my kitty-cat defense and decided to let me go the day he and Hogarty had brought me in.

He gestured for me to take a seat in a blue vinyl chair that faced his desk. Once I did, he caught me up.

"When I was questioning the Hartleys prior to your detainment, I asked about the payments Home and Hearth had received from Abbot-Dunaway Holdings. They showed me one of the checks and I made note of the company's bank. I went by the bank today with a search warrant and learned that Rick Dunaway made a three-thousand-dollar cash withdrawal from the account late in the afternoon on the day before Mr. Palmer performed the inspection on your house. I called Mr. Palmer into the station. He admitted he accepted the money as a bribe to falsify your inspection."

"He did?" Though I'd suspected as much, it hurt to know that Bobby had confessed to ripping me off, to risking my life.

"He didn't come clean right off. He spilled the beans

after I informed him we'd arrested his bookie and that the bookie said Palmer recently paid him three grand in cash."

"You arrested his bookie?"

"No." Flynn's mouth curved up in a self-satisfied grin. "I only told Palmer we did. It was a ruse to get him to confess. You'd think a gambler would be able to recognize a bluff, huh?"

"A good gambler might," I noted, "but Bobby's not a good gambler. Otherwise, he'd be winning instead of losing."

"You've got a point," Flynn agreed. "Anyway, the bluff got Palmer to spill the beans. He said he couldn't believe 'Jack' had ratted him out like that." He raised his palms. "Now we've also got a lead on an illegal gambling operation."

It was an effective trick. Maybe I hadn't been giving Detective Flynn enough credit.

"You haven't arrested him," I said, "so I guess he didn't confess to killing Rick Dunaway?"

"No," Flynn replied. "He still claims he didn't commit the murder. But I'm thinking he may have gone after Dunaway for more money. He might've smelled blood after being offered the three grand and knowing Dunaway agreed to pay you another five for your insurance deductible."

"The same thought had crossed my mind."

"You'd also told Palmer that Dunaway would be coming by the house the night he was killed, so Palmer knew where Dunaway would be. He could have laid in wait, ambushed Dunaway when he arrived, and demanded more cash. Dunaway might've turned him down. Palmer could have lost his cool and hit the guy with the mallet. Or maybe Palmer threatened Dunaway with the hammer and issued a blow to try to persuade Dunaway to give in. Maybe he hit a little too hard." The detective shrugged. "There's several different ways it could have played out. But no matter which way it happened, Rick Dunaway could have ended up dead at Palmer's hand. If Palmer's alibi doesn't pan out, I'll bring him back in."

"What's his alibi?"

"He claims he was out of town that weekend, gambling at the Tropicana casino in Evansville, Indiana."

I remembered the player's club cards lying on the dashboard of Bobby's truck a few days after Dunaway was killed. I told Flynn about them.

"I'll need more than some cards to clear him," he said. "He's going to have to show up on video footage from the casinos."

"If you're looking into Bobby now," I said, "does this mean I'm off the hook?"

"Sorry, but no. You're still officially a person of interest."

"Gee, thanks," I said sourly.

He gave me a soft, sympathetic smile and leaned back in his chair, propping his feet on his desk. "Now, what were you here to see me about?"

"I have another potential lead for you. Two, really. The first is an odd invoice." I handed him a copy of the invoice that I'd printed out. As he looked it over, I continued. "I spotted it on Presley's desk Monday when I went to the Abbot-Dunaway office to return the keys to their properties."

He finished perusing the document and looked up at me. "What's odd about this invoice?"

"The address of the property where the services were supposedly rendered is twelve twelve Laurel Street."

"I know the place. It's the Twelve Twelve condominiums, right?"

"Exactly. Anyway, there wasn't a unit number on the

invoice, but Abbot-Dunaway only owns one condo there. To my knowledge, a designer had never been to the unit, and none of the Abbot-Dunaway residential properties come furnished. As the property manager, I should've been involved if any redecorating was taking place at a property. I've since gone by the unit and confirmed with the tenant that there were no design services rendered and no furniture delivered. I went by the designer's office, too, and he confirmed that he didn't send the invoice."

"You think the designer was telling the truth?"

"I assumed so." Of course it was possible that Isak Nyström had, in fact, issued the invoice, but had feigned innocence when Buck and I questioned him. *Ugh.* If only I could read minds and tell who was being honest and who was lying. It would make things so much easier!

Flynn tapped his ballpoint pen against his chin. "This invoice could have several implications. I'll look into it. What's the second lead?"

"Remember the white sedan I told you about?"

"Of course," he said. "I got nowhere with it. No other agencies were investigating Dunaway, so it wasn't undercover law enforcement. There were several white sedans that showed up on the security camera feed from the downtown parking garage the day you visited the Abbot-Dunaway office. All of them cleared but one. It was a rental. Given that it was a weak lead anyway, I didn't follow up." He raised his palms. "There just aren't enough hours in the day."

Given that I now speculated the man with the newspaper on Sweetbriar might have been watching Thad Gentry rather than Rick Dunaway, I supposed the car that had been in the parking garage at the Abbot-Dunaway office weeks ago didn't matter. Odds were it wasn't the same car anyway, just a look-alike.

"A thought crossed my mind," I said. "What if the man in the car had been watching Thad Gentry instead of Mr. Dunaway? Mr. Gentry was at the house next door that morning."

Detective Flynn sat up straight in his seat. "That's an interesting thought. I'll look into that, too."

"Also, I can't be sure, but I think I might have seen Thad Gentry getting onto an elevator today when I went to the Abbot-Dunaway office."

He nodded and jotted a note.

Our business concluded, he walked me to the doors, where we bade each other good-bye.

I'd taken just five steps out of the building when Bobby Palmer stood from the bench he'd been sitting on and approached me.

"I'm sorry, Whitney," he said, his expression anguished, "I want to apologize. I screwed up. I was desperate. I had to pay off my bookie. He'd threatened to put a bullet through my foot."

"I could've died, Bobby. My cat, too."

"I know, but I didn't think you'd be staying at the house. I thought the risk would be low, especially with additional smoke detectors to warn you if the wiring went up in flames. I figured that once you got the place ready to sell, whoever bought it would find out about the wiring and insist you fix it before the sale. You'd be out a few grand to update the electrical systems, but Rick Dunaway said he'd given you a great deal on the house, so I figured it was fair enough. I might look bad for missing the electrical problem, but that would be better than getting shot. Rick Dunaway seemed desperate, too. He said he needed some ready cash or his business would go under. He said his wife and her lawyer were taking him to the cleaners."

The man had used the same words with me.

"The guy got me feeling sorry for him," Bobby said. "I guess he played me."

I sighed. "He played me, too."

We stared at each other for a long moment.

"So if you didn't kill Rick Dunaway," I said, "and I didn't kill him, then who do you think did?"

He answered without hesitation. "Thad Gentry."

"What makes you say that?"

"I've been in this business a long time," he said, "and I've heard things. Those two men have been at each other's throats for years, figuratively speaking. Doesn't seem much of a stretch to think things might've turned physical for one reason or another."

He had a point. But was he right?

CHAPTER 35

CONFRONTATION

WHITNEY

Back in my car, I phoned Buck and Colette, getting the two of them on the line at once.

"Big news," I told them. "Detective Flynn brought Bobby Palmer in for questioning in Dunaway's murder."

Buck demanded details. "What did they find on Palmer? Did he confess?"

I filled them in. "Detective Flynn found evidence that Dunaway had made a three-thousand-dollar cash withdrawal the day before the inspection. He tricked Bobby into admitting he took a bribe to pay his bookie."

Buck scoffed. "So Bobby risked your life for only three grand?"

"Yep." It was incredibly insulting. My life was worth far more than three thousand dollars. Sawdust's was, too. "Bobby still claims he didn't kill Dunaway, but if he's been lying all this time about the inspection, Flynn figures he could be lying about the murder, too. Problem is, Bobby claims to have an alibi. He says he was gambling at a casino in Indiana on Friday night. Flynn's looking into it." I told him about the invoice, of my theories that Dunaway could have had a distraught mistress, that the mistress might possibly have been Presley. "What do you think?"

"You could be right," Buck said. "Rick Dunaway certainly wouldn't be the first man to have a little love nest somewhere. A pied-à-tush."

Colette corrected him. "It's pied-à-*terre*."

"You sure about that?" he asked.

"Absolutely," Colette replied. "I know my French."

"Ooh-la-la," Buck replied.

I forced them back to the matter at hand. "As angry as I am at Bobby for intentionally botching the inspection, it wouldn't be fair for him to spend the rest of his life in jail if he didn't actually kill Rick Dunaway."

"Maybe," Buck agreed. "But what can you do about it?"

"Actually," I said, "I thought *we* could do something about it."

Colette chimed in now. "Like what?"

"Like follow Presley home from work," I said, "see where she goes."

"I'm game," Buck said. "I can cut out a little early." A flexible schedule was one of the benefits of working for a family business.

"I don't have to be at the restaurant until seven," Colette said. "Count me in, too."

We arranged to meet at a public parking lot downtown at half past four.

At four thirty, we had our rendezvous in the lot.

Buck took in Colette's white chef jacket and offered her another good-natured ribbing. "When did you take up karate?"

She bladed her hands and improvised a kick. "Hi-yah!"

"If I didn't know better," Buck said, "I'd think you were Jet Li."

She rolled her eyes, contradicting the gesture with a grin. "Let's take my car," Colette suggested. "Presley might recognize your SUV, Whitney."

"Good idea." With the WHITAKER·WOODWORKING logo painted on its side, Buck's van was also clearly out of the question as a surveillance vehicle. It wasn't exactly subtle.

My cousin and I climbed into Colette's car, Buck in the front and me in the back. We parked on the street near the exit from the parking garage and waited.

"What kind of car does Presley drive?" Buck asked as he eyed the exit.

I shrugged and raised my palms. I had no idea what make and model Presley drove, so each time a car pulled out of the garage I had to quickly check the driver's face to see if it was her. Good thing I'd borrowed my mother's bird-watching binoculars.

"That's not her," I said as a Subaru exited the garage. "That's not her, either," I repeated in regard to a Toyota Camry. "Still not her," I said when a Chevy pickup pulled out a few seconds later.

This process continued for several minutes, during which sixty-seven cars exited the garage. We hit pay dirt with the sixty-eighth, an economical Ford Fiesta in a bright blue color. Presley sat in the driver's seat, her perfectly manicured fingers curved over the top of the steering wheel.

"Bingo!" I lowered the binoculars and slid on a pair of sunglasses to disguise myself. "That's her in the Fiesta."

Colette harrumphed. "If she was Rick Dunaway's mistress, he could've at least bought her a fancier car."

"Maybe," I said. "But maybe they thought an administrative assistant driving a luxury car would be too obvious, raise eyebrows." After all, her pricey clothes and accessories had caught my attention, made me wonder how she could afford them.

Colette started her car and eased out into traffic, following behind Presley's car.

"Oh, my gosh," I said, when Presley hooked a left onto Demonbreun. "Is she going to the Twelve Twelve building?" *Had I been right to suspect she could have a personal relationship with Dunaway?*

She slowed as she approached the turn she would need to take to go to the building, but then rolled on past it.

"Guess not," Buck said.

We followed her as she took the overpass above the interstate and hooked another left to enter the entrance ramp to I-65 south. We trailed Presley for several miles, heading south into Antioch, one of Nashville's suburbs. Presley made a stop at a dry cleaner's, where she emerged with several articles of clothing in clear plastic bags. She also drove through a Schlotzsky's, apparently picking up a warm deli sandwich for dinner.

Eventually, Presley turned into an expansive apartment complex with buildings composed of red brick and pale yellow siding. She parked in an uncovered spot, climbed out of her car, and walked over to the array of mailboxes situated under an overhang. After unlocking her postal box and pulling out a stack of colored paper that appeared to be mostly, if not entirely, junk mail, she headed up to the third floor, the lengthy climb having failed to deter her from wearing her usual designer heels. There, she let herself into a unit and closed the door behind her, leaving us staring up at it.

"Looks like she lives there," I said.

Buck groaned. "Well, this was real exciting, wasn't it? Following her on her commute?"

"Let's wait a while," I suggested. "See if she comes back out and goes anywhere."

Presley did not come back out of the apartment, despite my friend, my cousin, and I waiting around for an hour to see if she would.

Colette checked the time on her car's clock. "I hate to be a party pooper, but I'm going to have to get to work soon."

"Let's go up and have a quick talk with Presley," I said. "See if we can get anything out of her."

The three of us headed up the stairs and assumed the same positions we had taken at Jackson Pharr's duplex, Colette and I backed up out of sight on either side of the door while Buck stood in front of it and knocked.

A few seconds later, Presley's voice came from the other side of the door. "Who is it?"

Uh-oh. If she realized Buck was my cousin, there was no way she'd open the door.

Buck improvised, pulling the wrench from his pocket and holding it up in case she was looking out her peephole. "Maintenance. I need to take a look at your air conditioner."

There was a rattle and click as she released her dead bolt. The door swung open. Presley stood there in a pair of shorts and a T-shirt. She held a glass of iced tea in her hand.

I stepped up next to Buck, surreptitiously sliding my foot forward over the threshold.

She gasped. "What are *you* doing here?"

"I need to talk to you."

"I'm calling the police!" she cried. She attempted to slam the door shut, but with the steel toe of my boot in the way, met with no success. That didn't stop her from trying again, though. She opened the door a few inches and tried to slam it again.

I wasted no time, addressing her through the five-inch opening, though I could no longer see her behind the door. "Are you skimming from Abbot-Dunaway, Presley? Is that why you killed Rick Dunaway? Because he found out?"

Her face appeared in the gap and her mouth fell open. "*You* killed Mr. Dunaway!"

"No, I didn't. I saw the invoice on your desk. Did you fake it?"

"I have no idea what you're talking about!"

Was she telling me the truth? "Had Thad Gentry been at your office the day I brought you the keys?"

"That's none of your business!"

Buck grunted. "That's a *yes*."

"What did he want?" I demanded. Were the two of them in cahoots? Working together to undermine Rick Dunaway?

"Go away!" she cried. She tried again to slam the door on my boot.

"We're not leaving until we get some answers, Presley."

The next thing I knew, she whipped the door open and tossed the tea in my face, ice cubes and all. *Dang, that's cold!* Reflexively, I stepped backward. With my boot no longer blocking the doorway, she was able to close her door. *SLAM!*

I blinked and sputtered, swiping my face with my hand. Colette pulled a small packet of tissues from her purse and handed them to me. "Here. Use these."

Buck, on the other hand, turned away from me. His heaving shoulders told me he was laughing silently.

I dabbed at my wet bangs. "This isn't funny, Buck!"

Colette put a hand over her mouth in a vain attempt to stifle her giggle.

"You, too?" I spat.

She raised her palms in innocence. "It's just a *little* funny."

Once I'd dried myself as well as I could, we headed down the three floors to the parking lot. As we drove back to the parking lot where Buck and I had left our cars, Colette reminded us that she'd promised to cook one of her special meals for us in the new kitchen. "How's Saturday evening look for you two?"

"I'm free," I said.

"I've got a date with Kacey Musgraves," Buck said, referencing one of his favorite female country artists. "But I can stand her up."

Colette cut him a look. "Her husband would probably appreciate that."

As Buck slid out of Colette's vehicle, he raised a hand in good-bye. "See you in the mornin', Whitney."

We'd planned to hold an open house, see if we could generate some interest in the Sweetbriar property. "I'll bring coffee."

"You'd better," he said, "or you might find me asleep in that claw-foot tub."

CHAPTER 36

READY TO RUMBLE

WHITNEY

Saturday morning, Buck and I arrived at the house twenty minutes before ten. After handing him a large coffee as promised, I went to plug in the inflatable snowman and sweep the walkway. I changed the lettering on the sandwich board so that it read OPEN HOUSE TODAY.

Next door, Patty came out with recycling to add to her bin and saw me on the lawn. She looked from me to the house and back again. She wagged a finger at me. "Remember to sell that house to someone quiet."

I laughed. "Don't worry. We will."

Inside, I nudged the thermostat a little higher to make things warm and cozy. I turned on all the lights so the place would look bright and shiny, and lit a pine-scented candle to give the house a fresh and festive scent. I dragged two of the bar stools from the kitchen to the living room and situated them by the front window, where Buck I could watch for buyers stopping by to take a look. Finally, I released Sawdust from his carrier. A house isn't a home without a cat in it. I hoped any potential buyer would feel the same.

The first couple pulled to the curb at a few minutes after ten. They looked to be in their sixties and had no agent with them.

Buck and I met them at the door.

"Good morning," I said. "How are you folks today?"

"Just dandy," the man said, glancing around, his eyes wide. "Say, where'd they find that body? Was it in that flower bed? Or was it in the other one?" He pointed first to the bed where I'd found Dunaway, then to the one on the other side.

I lied. I wasn't about to indulge his morbid curiosity. "I don't know where the body was found."

"Shucks," he said. "We was wanting to know."

I decided to put him on the spot. "Why do you want to know?" *Creepy much?*

He shrugged. "I'm not sure. Just nosy, I guess."

At least he was honest. I supposed I couldn't blame them too much. I'd spent quite a bit of time Thursday night trying to dig up sordid details on a dead man. Maybe I was creepy, too.

Buck stepped up beside me and held out a hand to indicate the living room. "Would you like to see the inside?"

The wife's face lit up. "Was he killed in there?"

Ugh. "No. Nothing happened in the house."

"How can you be sure?" she asked.

Because I was here the night it happened. "The doors were locked the whole night." I'd leave it at that. They didn't need to know more.

They frowned, obviously disappointed their visit hadn't been more exciting, had provided no gruesome detail they could share with their friends over bingo or dinner at Cracker Barrel.

Several more lookie-loos came by later that morning, though most were people from the neighborhood who'd seen the police cars and crime scene van the morning I'd found Dunaway.

One of them, a man with stale burger-and-onion breath, leaned in toward me. "I heard you killed that feller. Is that true?"

I was tempted to say yes just to get him to back away, but it was probably never a good idea to admit to a crime, even in jest. "Of course I didn't kill him," I said.

He, too, looked disappointed.

Just before six o'clock, Detective Flynn's plain sedan pulled up out front. *What's he doing here?*

I opened the door as he came up on the porch. Sawdust came around, too, to see what was going on. "It's Saturday night, Detective," I said to Flynn. "Shouldn't you be on a date?"

"I am on a date," he said. "With justice."

Buck snorted. I groaned. Flynn grinned. Sawdust swished his tail in the cool air that drifted inside.

"How was the open house?" he asked.

Buck shook his head. "It was a total bust. Everyone who came by only wanted to check out the crime scene."

"If we'd had any foresight," I added, "we could've charged admission and made up some of the loss we'll have to take on the place."

The detective chuckled, but afterward his demeanor quickly became somber. "I've got some news. We've cleared Bobby Palmer. I reviewed the Tropicana's security feeds. The video and Palmer's credit card data verify that he arrived around four o'clock in the afternoon and didn't leave until ten the following morning. When I spoke with

Presley shortly after Dunaway's body was found, she told me that Dunaway had been at work until four thirty that Friday. And, of course, you found him before ten that next morning."

"So there's no way Bobby could have killed Dunaway, after all."

"I'm afraid not. He's been charged with making a false statement, though. I wasted quite a bit of time and energy chasing down that bribe. That time could have been better spent finding the actual killer."

I had to fight the urge to point out to the detective that he'd also wasted time interrogating *me*. But the last thing an investigator needs when handling his first homicide case is for someone to derail his confidence.

"What about Gentry?" I asked. "Was the man in the white car spying on him? Is he under investigation by another agency?"

"I can't give you that information," Flynn replied.

Buck and I exchanged glances. In other words, law enforcement had something on Gentry. I wondered what it was. Had he committed tax evasion? Hired undocumented workers? Buried someone in cement at one of his construction sites?

Instead, I asked, "What are you going to do now?"

"I'm going to look into that invoice that had you all hot and bothered."

I told him about our visit to Presley's apartment and asked him the question that had been dogging me. "Do you think Presley could have killed Rick Dunaway?"

"It's plausible," he replied. "There were no defensive wounds on Dunaway's body, so he either didn't see the blow coming or didn't consider his attacker a potential threat."

I thought out loud. "Dunaway might not have thought

Presley was capable of hurting him, and failed to defend himself."

"Exactly," Flynn replied. "I'm going to make a visit to the designer on Monday and see what else I can find out. In the meantime, I need you two to do me a favor. Don't say anything more to anyone about that invoice, okay?"

He looked to Buck and me for affirmation. Buck nodded, while I pretended to zip my lip and throw away the key, just like Beverly Lewis had taught me when I'd been interrogated at the police station.

Detective Flynn pretended to snatch the key out of the air and tuck it into his pocket. "I better keep this in case we need to talk later."

Sawdust watched from his perch on the interior living room windowsill as Buck and I walked the detective out and bade him good-bye at the curb. As Flynn drove off, Buck went back inside to blow out the candle, turn out the lights, and lower the temperature on the thermostat to keep the heating bill in check. I stepped over to the sandwich board with the plastic container in which we stored the letters and began to remove them one by one, dropping them into the bin.

As I was kneeling at the sign, a pickup roared around the corner. The driver slowed as the truck approached the house, switching from low to high beams. I had to put a hand to my eyes to shield them from the intense stream of light. Before I knew what was happening, the tires squealed, the engine roared, and the truck came straight at me.

Holy moly! It's going to run me down!

Acting on instinct, I threw myself to the right, rolling behind the stone mailbox at the curb. The truck careened into the yard, the tires missing me by mere inches. The truck took out both the sandwich board sign and the FOR

SALE sign, sending letters up into the air before circling the tree and coming back at me with another roar as the driver gunned the engine again. I had just enough time to lever myself to my feet and dart behind Buck's van before the truck crashed into the mailbox with a loud *BAM!* The truck came to a standstill, leaving deep ruts in its wake, its driver's side headlight now broken and dark.

What just happened? Is the driver drunk? Having a seizure? Trying to kill me?

When the driver's door swung open and Jackson Pharr leaped out, I realized it was the latter. He looked my way, called me a nasty name, and hollered, "You got me arrested for murder! I'll show you!"

As he stormed in my direction, my fight-or-flight instinct kicked in and I ran around the van, screaming for my cousin. "Buck! Help!"

Jackson had chased me around it twice and was gaining on me before the front door banged open and Buck appeared in the doorway. The knocker ring swung up and back, hitting the plate with a loud, metallic knock.

I ran toward Buck. "Help!" My cry was unnecessary. Buck had already assessed the situation, grabbed the porch rail, and vaulted over the front steps as gracefully as an Olympic gymnast. He ran past me to confront Jackson head-on. Literally. There was a sickening *crack* as skull met numbskull. I could only hope my cousin wouldn't end up with a concussion. The two men wrangled and wrestled on their feet for several seconds before Buck took Jackson down to the lawn, where they continued to wrangle and wrestle on their backs, the men equally matched in size and strength.

Roused by the noise and commotion, Patty came out onto her porch next door. "Goodness gracious!" she cried. "Here we go again." She placed a quick call to 9-1-1.

The next thing we knew, she'd turned her hose on full force and was spraying it at Buck and Jackson. She stepped closer, the coiled hose unwinding behind her like a snake. Sawdust paced back and forth on the windowsill as he watched the melee, clearly agitated. Meanwhile, I circled the men, trying to figure out how to help Buck best Jackson. Unfortunately, they were moving too fast for me to get in a kick without risking that I'd injure my cousin instead of Jackson. Ditto for Colette's pepper spray. There was no way to use it on Jackson without spraying Buck, too.

Screech!

I turned to see Detective Flynn's plain sedan pull up to the same spot at the curb it had left only minutes before. Flynn rocketed out of his seat before the car even settled back, leaving the door open. Patty turned her hose from the brawlers to her mums as he ran toward the men tangling on the lawn. He paused for a split second on the edge of the fray, determined who was who, and reached out to grab the back of Jackson's shirt. "Cut it out! Now!"

When he yanked Jackson back, it gave Buck the opening he needed to land a solid uppercut to the guy's chin. Jackson's head snapped backward, and he was momentarily dazed. Flynn seized the opportunity to grab Jackson's right arm and slap a cuff on his wrist. Before the detective could secure the other cuff, Jackson gathered what little wits he had and took a swing at him. Buck levered himself to his knees and launched himself at the boy, tackling Jackson back to the ground, landing a solid punch to the punk's gut this time.

Jackson retched and reflexively rolled onto his side, his hands grabbing at his stomach. Flynn used his foot to shove the punk's shoulder, momentum carrying the kid over onto his belly. With a quick *click,* the detective secured the second cuff, Jackson's hands now immobilized behind him.

I rushed to Buck. "Are you okay?"

He looked down as if trying to gauge how to answer that question. Given the ruts Jackson's truck had put in the lawn and the water Patty had sprayed, he was covered in mud and dried grass. But at least none of his limbs was bent in the wrong direction, and no blood was visible on him. "I'm all right. Nothing a shower and a washing machine can't fix."

Flynn put a foot on Jackson's back. "Don't move. You hear me?"

Jackson responded with a series of choice expletives, but remained facedown on the wet, messy lawn.

The detective looked up at Buck, Patty, and me. "I heard the call come in on my radio and turned right back around. Luckily, I hadn't gotten far."

A cruiser careened around the corner, lights flashing and siren wailing. As it approached, we could see Officer Hogarty was at the wheel. She extinguished the siren as she pulled to a stop behind Flynn's car, but left the lights on. She exited the vehicle and stepped over, where Flynn gave her a quick rundown.

She shook her head as she stared down at Jackson's back. "Just released from jail and he pulls a stunt like this." She bent down to look Jackson in the face. "You aren't too smart, are you?"

Jackson called her a name, too. She shrugged it off. "Eh. I've been called worse."

She, Flynn, and Buck hauled the boy to his feet. He made no effort to help them, intentionally going limp so as to be dead weight. *What a jerk.* I grabbed a leg to help and we eventually managed to lift and shove him into the backseat of Hogarty's patrol car.

When Jackson issued a fresh string of curses, Hogarty slammed the door on him. "What a potty mouth. Too bad I can't wash his mouth out with soap."

She climbed into the front and, with a wave in good-bye to the detective, took off to the station. Looked like Jackson's attorneys would be earning additional fees for defending him against an assault-and-battery charge. Maybe even more.

Detective Flynn watched until the cruiser's taillights disappeared around the corner before turning back to address me and Buck. "Pharr will be facing serious charges now. My guess is that, once everything is said and done, he'll be looking at some prison time."

"Good," Buck snapped. "It's time that brat got what he deserves."

I had to agree. I only hoped that while the things were being said and done, they'd keep him in jail. I had a feeling he might not be done with me.

CHAPTER 37

KITCHEN KLATCH

WHITNEY

Detective Flynn had barely driven off before Colette pulled up. She climbed out of her car and took in the damaged pickup sitting in the yard and the stone mailbox that now stood cockeyed, like a miniature leaning tower of Pisa. She raised her hands. "What in the world happened here?"

Her mouth gaped as we filled her in on the altercation that had transpired in the yard only minutes before. She looked Buck up and down, the caked mud on his wet clothing confirming our story. When we finished, she said, "I hope Jackson's arrest will put an end to this ordeal."

"Me, too," I said, though I still had a sick sense it wouldn't. Maybe I wouldn't feel a sense of closure until he was sentenced. Maybe that's why I still felt unsettled.

Colette turned, retrieved a bottle of wine from her car, and handed it to me. "I have a feeling you might be needing this about now."

I hugged the bottle to my chest. "You'd be right about that."

"I hope you two worked up an appetite," Colette said, "because I am going to stuff you silly."

She popped the trunk open and disappeared into it, emerging with a stockpot cradled in the crook of her arm and a bag of groceries in her hand. We made our way to the house. At the front door, I relieved her of the pot, while Buck grabbed the grocery bag. Her hands now free, she bent down and put one hand under Sawdust's chin, stroking the top of his head with the other. "Hi, boy. How ya been?"

He replied with a *mew* that said *I've been just fine, thanks for asking.*

After taking the pot and groceries to the kitchen, we returned to her car for more items. A large sauté pan. A rectangular baking pan. Mixing bowls and spoons. Cutting boards in two sizes. A colander and small plastic food storage container containing several jars of spices. By the time we were done, it looked like she had moved into the place, at least where the kitchen was concerned.

Now that the adrenaline had worn off, I had a nice case of the shakes, trembling from head to toe. I used a corkscrew to open the wine and poured three generous glasses, taking a large gulp of mine to calm my nerves.

Colette eyed me and bit her lip in worry. "You gonna be okay, Whit?"

"Honestly? I won't be okay until Dunaway's killer is caught and convicted." I'd been constantly on edge since I'd found the body in the flower bed. My nerves were shot.

She reached out and gave my hand a squeeze. "Maybe the detective will come through."

"He's trying," I said. "There's just not much to go on." Of course that fact could be my fault, for washing any potential fingerprints off the mallet. But no sense beating myself up over that fact. I couldn't change the past. *If only*

I had a time machine. Maybe I should look into buying a used DeLorean.

Having changed out of his muddy coveralls into a spare pair he kept in his van, Buck made his way to the breakfast bar. He took a seat on one of the stools to observe as Colette spread the bowls and dishes and utensils out on the countertop in front of him in preparation for cooking. "What's on the menu?" he asked.

She retrieved a long-handled metal spoon. "Red beans and rice. We're going full-out Louisiana tonight."

Sawdust and I peeked into the grocery bag on the counter. "I see the ingredients for bread pudding in here, too."

She brandished the spoon at me. "Hush, now! That was supposed to be a surprise."

Buck rubbed his belly. "Surprise or not, I can't wait."

"How can I help?" I asked.

She pointed the spoon at the bag. "You can start by cutting the bread into cubes and putting the cubes in the baking pan."

"Easy enough." I wasn't much of a cook, but I didn't see how I could screw that up.

She turned her spoon on Buck now. "Don't think you're off the hook, mister. I'm putting you to work, too." With that, she handed him a paring knife and the large cutting board, following up with a colander in which she'd placed a green pepper, an onion, and a stalk of celery. "Rinse the vegetables and dice them."

He rose dutifully from the stool. "Whatever you say, dear."

"I like the sound of that," she said.

"*Dear*?" Buck asked.

"No." She waved a spoon and grinned. "The 'whatever you say' part."

While Colette set her pot on the back burner and filled it with her homemade vegetable stock, I removed Sawdust from the counter, rounded up a knife and the smaller cutting board, and set about cutting the bread into small squares. The cat watched from the floor as I placed them in the baking pan. I dropped one to the floor for him. He sniffed the cube, his head bobbing. Having performed the sniff test and finding the bread unappetizing, he decided to see if he could make a toy out of it. He gave it a solid whack with his left paw and chased it as it rolled across the floor. The cat was nothing if not resourceful.

When I finished placing the bread cubes in the pan, I sought further instruction. "What's my next step?"

Colette made a circular motion with her spoon. "Round up the sugar, cinnamon, almonds, and raisins."

I gathered up the ingredients, along with a large mixing bowl. Meanwhile, she poured a small amount of olive oil into a pan and turned the burner to low underneath it. Seeing that I was ready to move forward again, she advised me to pour three cups of soymilk into the bowl, add the other ingredients, and mix them well. I poured the mixture over the bread cubes, slid the pan into the oven, and set the timer for thirty minutes. By then, she'd finished sautéing the vegetables and had added them to the beans and rice simmering in the stockpot. Also by then, Sawdust had seemed to realize that playing with a ball of bread and watching us cook was not nearly as interesting as watching the bugs flit about the back porch light. He lay on the windowsill, staring up at the swarm of moths warming themselves about the bulb.

Buck gathered up the dirty dishes and took them to the sink. "I'll wash these."

"Who *are* you?" I teased.

"What?" he said. "A man can't help clean up in the kitchen?"

"He *can*," I said. "I've just never seen you actually *do* it."

He cut me a narrow-eyed look. "What do you think I do at my own house?"

He had a point. Even so, I'd never heard him offer to help with the dishes after our holiday feasts at his parents' place. I'd only heard him offer to polish off a pie or what remained of the mashed potatoes. Not that he was a male chauvinist pig, by any means. It's just that Aunt Nancy tended to shoo her husband and sons out of her kitchen. She was outnumbered three-to-one when it came to male and female chromosomes, and the kitchen was the one room in her house she could claim as her own. The men had taken over her living room with their oversized chairs and big-screen TV.

As Colette stirred the pot, Buck washed the prep dishes and I dried them. When the food was ready, we sat down at the bar to enjoy our gourmet dinner from the stylish square plates my friend had brought with her. Sawdust wandered back over and hopped up to lie on my lap while I ate.

Buck shoveled a heaping spoonful of red beans and rice into his mouth and moaned in ecstasy. "I could get used to this."

I swallowed a delicious bite, myself. "Me, too."

Colette held a loaded fork aloft and turned the conversation to a more serious subject. "Do you think the DA will reconsider charging Jackson for the murder? Seems since Jackson tried to kill you tonight, it would make him a more likely suspect in Rick Dunaway's death."

As she took her bite, I shrugged. "I don't know if it changes anything. It's obvious Jackson has the potential to take a life, but he still hasn't confessed to taking Dunaway's."

Buck chimed in. "There's still that odd invoice to consider, too. Even if Pharr killed Dunaway, that doesn't explain the invoice."

She put her fork down. "Do you think Presley is up to something after all?"

Again, I shrugged. "Maybe. Maybe not. Isak Nyström could have lied to us. Maybe he did actually issue the invoice, but didn't want to admit it. He's an odd duck. The only thing that's clear to me is how unclear everything is."

She leaned back on her stool and mulled things over for a moment. "So Presley and Jackson are still possible suspects. Thad Gentry and Nyström, too. What about that guy you saw? The one in the white car that seemed to be spying on Rick Dunaway?"

I exhaled a long breath. "The police haven't been able to identity him, and I haven't seen him since Dunaway's death."

Buck took a swig of his wine. "That makes sense. If he had some kind of business with Dunaway and Dunaway is dead, there's nothing else for the guy to do now."

Colette raised her wineglass as well. "Especially if his business was killing Rick Dunaway."

"It's possible the man in the car was undercover law enforcement. Detective Flynn implied that Thad Gentry is the subject of a government investigation, but he couldn't give us any details. The longer this case drags on, the more complicated it seems to get." I let out a long groan and put my face in my hands. "Will this nightmare ever end?"

Colette picked up the wine bottle and poured what little liquid remained into my glass. "It will," she said, reaching out to rub my shoulder. "It's just going to take a little more time."

While I appreciated her attempts to console and encourage me, I knew her words weren't necessarily true. Many murders remained unsolved for years, decades even, some of them never resolved. Police departments were up to their holsters in cold cases. I could only hope Rick Dunaway's murder wouldn't be one of them.

Buck tossed back the last of his wine and set his glass on the countertop. "Maybe we should spy on Thad Gentry ourselves, see if we might catch a clue or two that law enforcement is missing."

An involuntary shiver ran through me. Thad Gentry gave me a bad vibe. Spying on him could be dangerous. Besides, we didn't have the manpower to cover him 24/7, and we didn't have any strong evidence linking him to Dunaway's death. Even so, sitting around and doing nothing didn't sit well with me, either. We compared schedules and agreed to meet Tuesday at five for a spy mission on Gentry.

The oven timer went off, letting us know the bread pudding was ready. Just in time, too. After thinking about cold cases, I could use something to warm me up.

Colette donned a pair of oven mitts and pulled the pudding from the oven. "This looks perfect."

"Smells good, too," Buck added.

"I didn't realize I was capable of cooking," I told my friend. "It was fun, too. You might have to give me more lessons."

"I'd be happy to. Cooking is always more fun when there's someone in the kitchen with you."

We finished the meal, washed the dinner dishes, and packed everything back into Colette's car. A tow truck had come by to haul Jackson's damaged pickup away, so the yard was empty now, the ruts from his tires forming deep grooves in the soil. *Ugh.* I'd see what I could do about the damage later.

"Thanks so much." I gave Colette a tight hug. "That dinner was really special."

"Sure was," Buck agreed.

Colette raised her hands to indicate the house. "This house is what's special. You guys have really done good here."

I couldn't help but smile. "We did, didn't we?" I could only hope it was the first of many houses we'd fix up and sell.

Buck pulled his keys from his pocket. "It's getting late. I think I'll head out, too."

I followed suit, making a quick run inside to round up Sawdust and lock the front door. After placing my cat's carrier into my car, I glanced back at the house. Dinner here tonight had been fun. We'd all felt right at home in the place.

It seemed a shame we'd have to sell it.

CHAPTER 38

MISTREATED

SAWDUST

It had been days since Whitney had given him one of his favorite tuna treats. He'd gone to the cabinet where she kept them multiple times and asked for one. *Meow? Meow?* But still she refused to give him a treat.

He'd tried again when she arrived home tonight, going so far as to try to open the cabinet with his paw. He'd managed to pry it open a little three or four times, but the darn thing kept shutting on him. *Meow?*

"Sorry, boy," Whitney said. "No tuna treats until mommy gets back on her financial feet."

Sawdust had no idea what her words meant, but he could tell by her tone that she was sorry. She opened the cabinet and showed him that there were no treats inside. She even let him climb into the cabinet and take a look around.

"I might not be able to give you treats," she said, "but I've got plenty of love. Love doesn't cost anything."

She scooped him up in her arms and cradled him, scratching his chest. Not quite as satisfying as a tuna treat, but not a bad alternative, either.

CHAPTER 39

MONEY TALKS, DEAD PEOPLE DON'T

WHITNEY

Jackson Pharr was released from jail again on Monday. Buck and I were at the house that morning, using a shovel and hoe to smooth out the ruts the lawbreaker had put in the yard when Detective Flynn called to tell me the news.

"Jackson's been charged with aggravated assault," he said. "His truck is considered a deadly weapon under Tennessee law. The DA is still considering whether to charge him with Rick Dunaway's murder, too. Even though Jackson came after you, his attorneys say it's only because your statements to the police are what led to him being held after his drunk and disorderly arrest. I can understand the DA's position. A lot of money and time go into a murder case. They don't want to bring one if there's not a reasonably good chance of a conviction. Besides, we're still not convinced Pharr was the killer."

I wasn't, either. "What's the penalty for aggravated assault?"

"Three to fifteen years," Flynn replied. "It's a class C felony."

Though the judge had set his bail at half a million dollars, Jackson's parents coughed up the funds to pay for their son's bond. Given the boy's history of violence, he was fitted with an ankle monitor so that law enforcement could keep track of his whereabouts.

Flynn assured me that Jackson's release posed no threat to my safety. "He'll be arrested immediately if he ventures away from his parents' house. Things are under control. You can sleep easy."

Easy for him to say. I wouldn't sleep easy until the Dunaway murder was resolved, his killer sentenced and placed in prison. Jackson Pharr could very well have been Dunaway's killer. He could have been coming after me that fateful night, and he definitely had it in for me now. Still, the fact that there was no conclusive evidence on him made me hesitant to consider the case closed just yet. As his defense attorneys had pointed out, all the evidence against him was circumstantial at best. Even if he was eventually charged and tried, a jury might be unwilling to convict a young man for murder without definitive proof. It seemed the best I could hope for was that he'd get the maximum sentence for the aggravated assault. What's more, I simply couldn't shake the feeling that the fraudulent invoice could be significant.

Around noon, I drove my parents to the airport so they could catch their flight to New York City. They were making their annual pilgrimage to see the Christmas tree at Rockefeller Center, take in a Broadway show, and shop at Macy's, like the characters in *Miracle on 34th Street,* my mother's favorite holiday movie. Normally, I made the trek with them. But given that Buck and I were underwater on the Sweetbriar house, I figured I'd better pass this year.

Instead, I'd stick around and work as many extra hours for my uncle as possible to make sure we could cover next month's mortgage. My mother had offered to cancel, but I'd insisted they go. No point in everyone missing out on the fun. Even though Dunaway's murderer had yet to be convicted, most everyone, my parents included, believed that Detective Flynn had his man, that the killer was Jackson Pharr. With his ankle monitor in place, Jackson Pharr presumably posed no threat to anyone outside his parents' home. Besides, other than Jackson, nobody seemed to be after me.

I took care of a heater problem for a Home & Hearth rental property in the early afternoon, then joined my uncle and cousins, who were building a gazebo at a wedding venue. We installed the roof on the gazebo, which required lots of lifting and holding heavy boards in place. Before long, my arms began to shake from muscle strain.

I had kept my phone in my pocket all day, waiting to hear more from the detective, to find out whether the odd invoice I'd seen had led him to discover any new evidence, a fresh clue as to who might have ended Dunaway's life, to prove or disprove that Jackson Pharr was the killer. It wasn't until three in the afternoon that my mobile vibrated in my pocket. I called out to my cousins, who were holding either end of the long board I'd been supporting in the middle. "I'm letting go. Y'all got it?"

"We've got it," they said in unison, only to nearly drop the thing on their heads when I removed my hands and stepped away.

I put a finger in my ear to block the noise of the tools and strode away from the worksite so I'd be able to hear the detective. "What did you find out?"

"I spoke with Isak Nyström," he said. "He confirmed what you told me, that he didn't issue an invoice for thirty-two grand for a property at Twelve Twelve. He allowed me to look at his financial records. Abbot-Dunaway Holdings is listed as a client in their system, but their only billings were for design consultations on a couple of commercial properties that needed renovation. They had a personal account for Rick Dunaway, but it was for work at his private residence years ago. Their billing system is simple. I saw nothing to indicate the invoice was sent in error."

"What does this mean?" I asked.

"I'm not sure," Flynn replied. "I went to the Abbot-Dunaway office to question Presley, but she had left early for a dental appointment. Only Lance Abbot was there. He said that since he's been a silent partner all these years, he doesn't have log-on credentials for their computer system and has no clue how their records are kept. He wasn't sure how Dunaway had been handling their payables, either, how tight a rein he had on their finances. But when I'd spoken with the bank staff earlier about that three-thousand-dollar cash withdrawal, I'd learned something interesting."

"What did you learn?"

"That Presley has signatory authority on the firm's bank account."

In other words, she could sign checks on the company account, checks Rick Dunaway might not have been aware of unless he was keeping close tabs on the firm's books. It wasn't unusual at all for owners of closely held businesses to bypass the normal checks and balances, to provide inadequate oversight over financial assets.

"At any rate," Flynn continued, "Abbot's been relying on Presley to carry them through until he can hire someone to take over the duties Rick Dunaway used to handle. I'm planning to go back in the morning to talk to Presley and take a thorough look at the company's financial records. As they say, money talks. In this case, the money will tell us whether there's something shady going on."

We ended the call there. Tomorrow, with any luck, Detective Flynn would find the smoking gun that would tell us whether Presley had been fleecing her boss. If she had been, and if Dunaway had discovered it and threatened to take action, she'd have had reason to put an end to the man's life.

I arrived home physically exhausted. My mind was exhausted, too. Though I'd pondered and pondered the idea of Presley killing Rick Dunaway, I had to admit I had a hard time seeing it. The image of her in her high heels and dresses simply didn't mesh with an image of her picking up the dead blow mallet and delivering a solid whack to Rick Dunaway's skull as if he were a rodent in a game of Whac A Mole.

Still, other than Jackson Pharr Thad Gentry, and the unidentified man in the white sedan, I'd been unable to pinpoint another plausible perpetrator who hadn't been cleared. Neither had the detective. Pretty much everyone who'd done business with Rick Dunaway disliked the man, but had any of them been upset enough with him to end his life? We didn't know and, of course, there was still the chance that the murder had been simply a random mugging gone wrong. There was also the chance the killer had been coming after me, and that Dunaway had simply gotten in the way. But if that were the case, wouldn't the killer have made another attempt on my life? The only person who'd done so was Jackson Pharr, and he was on house arrest now.

I let Yin-Yang out into the backyard to relieve herself and raided my parents' fridge, peeking into the takeout containers to determine my options. I supposed I should feel bad for stealing their food like some sort of holiday-hating Grinch, but I was too tired to cook and the leftovers would go bad before they arrived home later this week. Better not to let the food go to waste, right? My options included lo mein noodles, spinach enchiladas, and baked ziti. *Hmm . . .* Enchiladas it is.

I carried the box out the back door, locking the door behind me. I planned to return to the pool house tonight. With Jackson Pharr under electronic surveillance and no one else seeming to have set their sights on me, it seemed safe to return home. More than anything, I simply wanted my life to return to normal.

"Come on, girl!" I called to Yin-Yang. "You and Sawdust can have a sleepover."

Sawdust sat on his perch on his cat tree, watching as his mommy and best buddy approached. Cats can't smile, but the way he paced back and forth betrayed his excitement.

I unlocked the door to the pool house. "Look who's here!"

Sawdust hopped down to the floor and exchanged sniffs of greeting with his friend. He leaned against the solid little canine and rubbed himself on the side of the dog, circling under her nose and rubbing down the other. Yin-Yang's tail whipped back and forth at a rate of a hundred wags per second and she bucked up on her back legs. In seconds, the two were playfully wrangling on the floor while I transferred the enchiladas to a plate and warmed them up in my microwave.

After dinner, I washed my dishes, watched an hour of television to unwind, and changed into my rubber-ducky pajamas to go to bed. I laid my head on my pillow—*had it ever felt so soft and inviting?*—and in mere seconds was dead to the world. Looked like Detective Flynn was right. I could sleep easy.

My mind was still in snoozeville when, hours later, Sawdust's growl drew me out of my slumber.

Grrrrr . . .

"What's wrong, boy?" Eyes still closed, I felt around on the bed for my cat, but my fingers never found him. Instead, they found my parents' terrier, who was curled up behind my knees. I forced my eyes open. Yin-Yang did the same. Our gazes followed the sound of Sawdust's growl.

Grrrr.

Sawdust crouched atop his cat tree beside the French doors, his body rigid. My parents' back porch light provided just enough illumination for me to make out the dark shape of a person on the other side of the door. The person's hand was trying the knob. The motion gave off a soft, metallic rattle.

Yin-Yang leaped from the bed and promptly ran under it. In my hazy, half-awake state, it took me a few seconds longer to process the situation.

Someone is at my door, trying to get inside.

My cat is growling at that someone.

If that someone was a friend or family member, the person would knock at the door and call my name to let me know I had nothing to fear. This person, however, had neither knocked nor called my name. Therefore, I should fear this person.

Eeeek!

CHAPTER 40

COMING IN,
COMING OUT

SAWDUST

This man was a threat.

Sawdust sensed it, from the tips of his ears to the tip of his tail. People didn't normally sneak around at night like raccoons and possums and skunks did.

Instinct told him to run, to hide under Whitney's bed with the dog, where the man couldn't see him. But this was no time to be a fraidy-cat. Whitney was a sitting duck in her bed. Yin-Yang was no help. The dog hadn't even barked. Only Sawdust could protect Whitney now. Besides, running away from the ceiling demon at the big house had done no good, and he'd ended up hurting the woman he loved with all of his furry little heart.

Time to face his fears and redeem himself.

Good thing he'd spent time sharpening his claws on the recliner today. They were as smooth and sharp as they could be.

He raised his left paw and extended his claws like tiny little switchblades.

This man will be sorry he messed with us.

CHAPTER 41

VAC ATTACK

WHITNEY

I sat bolt upright. Yin-Yang whimpered from under the bed. *Some guard dog she is.*

I grabbed my cell phone from the end table between my bed and the recliner to call for help. The screen told me it was 2:48 A.M., but in my terror, I couldn't seem to enter my security code correctly.

What is it?

5-4-6-8?

5-6-4-8?

Oh, no! I can't remember!

A sickening *click* told me the lock had released.

As the door began to swing open, I realized that even if I could manage to enter both my security code and dial 911, there was no way law enforcement could get here in time to help me.

I have to defend myself!

My eyes frantically scanned the room. My toolbox was in my SUV in the driveway, so there was no chance of getting to a hammer or screwdriver. A pizza pan rested in the dish drainer on the counter. It could serve as both a shield and a weapon but, by the time I got to it, whoever was at the door would be inside and it would be too late. Ditto for Colette's pepper spray in my purse. I didn't have time to dig around for it. I had to stop this man before he gained entry, scare him away.

But how?

Out of the darkness, from the corner next to my bed, a tiny green glowing beacon beckoned to me.

My robotic vacuum.

The device was in easy reach and weighed over seven pounds. Not a perfect weapon by any means, but when it came to matters of self-defense a woman had to be quick and resourceful.

I slid out of bed and grabbed the device in both hands, yanking it from its docking station. I turned back to the door to see a hand easing through the opening. The hand held a gun. The length of the barrel told me a silencer had been attached.

This person could shoot me dead here and now, and nobody would hear it.

The door swung open a few inches wider, and a head covered in a black ski mask peeked through the opening. My cat and I seized the opportunity. Before the intruder could get his visual bearings, we both pounced.

Sawdust hissed, arched his back, and raked his claws across the mask, going for the exposed eye. The intruder yelped in pain and surprise and jerked back, throwing the door fully open. He raised his hand to his injured face, inadvertently smacking himself in the forehead with his gun. "Ow! Stupid cat!"

Is that Jackson Pharr's voice? Thad Gentry's? I couldn't tell, but in the light from my parents' back porch,

I could see the man was dressed all in black, including the ski mask. He wore long, dark pants, making it impossible for me to tell whether an ankle monitor was attached to his leg. He held a letter-sized envelope in his right hand.

My only chance of surviving the situation was to seize the moment, to rush the guy before he could gather his wits. I raised the vac, dashed forward, and brought it down on his head with all the force I could muster.

BAM!

The vac took the blow like a pro. The intruder, however, did not. He wobbled on his feet and dropped both the gun and envelope to the patch of grass adjacent to the walkway. When I raised the vac again to deliver another hit, he turned and ran back across the pool terrace toward the open gate.

He might be fleeing, but I wasn't done with him yet.

I whipped the vacuum back over my shoulder and, with a loud cry, sent it sailing after him like a Frisbee. The device hit him square in the back. *THUMP!* He stumbled for a few strides, but regained his feet and took off. Meanwhile, the vac fell to the concrete behind him, clattering and breaking apart, pieces of plastic and metal raining down beside the pool.

I turned and darted back into my little home, slamming and locking the door behind me. Not that the French doors would be any match for the gun if the intruder came back, but I didn't dare make the run across the terrace to my parents' house. I'd be too easy a target when I stopped to unlock their door.

Rounding up my phone again, I got my security code right this time—*5-6-8-4*. I dialed 911, peeking out from the edge of the curtain at the window. I figured I'd better keep an eye out in case the guy tried to come back.

Dispatch answered on the first ring. "Nine-one-one. What's your emergency?"

"Someone just tried to break into my house!" I cried. "He had a gun!"

She asked for the address and I gave it to her. "I live in the pool house out back."

"Is the intruder still there?" she asked.

"I don't think so. My cat scratched him and I hit him with my vacuum and he ran off."

"I'll get officers en route right away."

While I waited for the cops to arrive, I grabbed a spatula and the pizza pan from my kitchenette, simultaneously realizing a plastic utensil made a poor weapon and the thin metal had no chance of stopping a bullet. But it's not like I was trained in situations like this. I was acting on instinct—instinct that had been dulled by generations of civilized behavior. I also flipped the switches to turn on the lights in the pool and along the terrace. Though light couldn't stop an intruder, my underlying, if irrational, reasoning was that bad things happened in the dark. If I could make things as bright as possible, the illumination would somehow protect me and the pets.

As I waited for a police cruiser to arrive, my mind churned, trying to process the situation. It could be entirely unrelated to Rick Dunaway's murder. The intruder could have simply been looking for things to steal and thought the pool house, with its French doors, would be easy to access. Maybe he thought there'd be valuable tools or equipment inside. Still, the fact that he'd had a gun at the ready told me his primary motive hadn't been theft. More than likely, his motive was murder.

But why me? Was he a random creep who'd spotted me from the street going into the pool house and thought I'd be an easy target back here? Though it was possible, I doubted such was the case. It seemed too much of a coincidence that someone would try to kill me just weeks after taking out Dunaway. There must be a connection, right?

I dialed Detective Flynn. It took five rings to rouse him from sleep, and his voice was gravelly when he answered. "Whitney? Everything okay?"

The fact that he knew it was me calling told me he'd added my name to his contacts list. He probably did the same for all suspects, so I wouldn't flatter myself by thinking it meant something more.

"Someone just tried to break into my place!" I cried.

"What happened?" He sounded fully alert now.

"Sawdust was growling and it woke me up. Someone was outside picking the lock. The next thing I knew, the door was open and the intruder stuck his head inside." I told him about the gun, too, and Sawdust's heroic feat. "He swiped the intruder right across the face. It bought me enough time to grab my robotic vacuum and hit the guy over the head with it."

He paused for a beat. "You hit him with a what now?"

"Robotic vacuum."

"Just when I thought I'd heard it all." A jostling sound came over the phone, the sounds of someone hurriedly dressing while trying not to drop their device. "I'll be right there."

Now that the more immediate matters had been tended to, I scooped up my frightened little cat in my arms and cradled him to my chest, stroking his head and neck. "You were a brave boy," I murmured. "A brave, brave boy."

He replied with a soft purr.

In minutes, a cruiser pulled to a stop out front, its flashing lights playing about the house and trees. I slid my feet into my rubber-ducky slippers, ventured across the pool terrace to the open gate, and waved my arm to get the attention of the uniformed officers. They climbed out of the patrol car and headed up the drive. One was tall and thin, the other short and stocky.

I gave the officers a quick, condensed version of what happened. "Detective Flynn is on his way."

The taller officer's brows formed a V in question. "You know Detective Flynn?"

"Yes," I said. "I came across a body recently. He's the one handling the investigation."

His eyes narrowed further as he studied my face, and popped wide as recognition hit him. "You're the one they brought in for questioning in the Dunaway murder, aren't you?"

I heaved a sigh. "Yes. That's me. But I was released without charges. And I didn't kill Rick Dunaway."

The officer looked me up and down, his gaze lingering on my slippers. An odd look crossed his face. Dare I think it meant *Killers don't wear rubber-ducky slippers*?

The stocky one angled his head to indicate their cruiser. "I'll take a look around the area. See if the guy's still around."

He jogged back to the police cruiser, slid into the driver's seat, and turned on the spotlight, bathing us in a blinding, bright light. Now I knew how the performers on Broadway felt on stage. I felt a sudden urge to make jazz hands and perform a soft-shoe routine. The officer set off down the street with the spotlight on, shining it into my neighbors' bushes and trees, looking to see if the intruder was hiding somewhere about.

The tall officer stuck around. As I led him back to the pool house, he shone his flashlight about, noting the shattered remnants of my robotic vac. "You can kiss your warranty good-bye."

I cut him a look. "Better than kissing *my life* good-bye."

He raised his palms in acquiescence. "You got me there."

As we stepped up to the door of the pool house, he verified the location of the gun and the envelope. "Leave those be until the detective gets here."

Rather than continue to stand outside shivering in the cold night air, we stepped inside, where I promptly set about making coffee. Maybe not the best idea, given that my nerves were already jittery. But it gave me something to do with my anxious energy.

As the coffee dripped into the pot, the officer stared out the window, keeping an eye on the backyard. I took a seat on the raggedy recliner. Sawdust sat on my lap, leaning back against my chest as if trying to melt into me. *Poor thing.* Yin-Yang must have sensed that Sawdust was scared and upset. The little Boston terrier peeked out from under the bed. Once she'd assured herself that the danger had passed, she issued an empathetic whine and *clickety-clicked* over on the tile floor, standing on her hind legs to repeatedly lick the cat's face from chin to ear to comfort him. Sawdust responded with his steam-locomotive purr. *PRRR-RRR-RRR-PRR-RRR-RRR.*

Ten minutes later, the officer who'd been cruising the neighborhood returned with a report. I set my cat down on the recliner, and stood to address the policeman. "Any luck?"

"None," he said as he stepped inside. "Didn't see anyone lurking about. No suspicious cars, either. Looks like whoever came after you has gotten the heck out of Dodge."

Darn! I'd been hoping the officer would spot the intruder hiding in someone's azalea bushes and make a quick and easy arrest, clearing my name in the process.

Detective Flynn arrived on the officer's heels. Rather than his usual loafers, navy pants, and so-starched-it-could-stand-up-on-its-own button-down shirt, he'd thrown on a pair of tennis shoes, nylon running pants, and a fitted long-sleeved athletic shirt. His eyes went straight to my slippers. His upper lip quirked as he fought a smile, but he became all business once again as his focus shifted from my slippers to the gun and envelope lying just outside the door where he stood. He whipped a pair of latex gloves from the zippered pouch at his waist, slid his hands into them, and picked up the gun, dropping it into a clear plastic evidence bag. "We'll have crime scene check the gun for prints."

"I can't say for sure," I told him, "but I think the guy might have been wearing gloves, too." After all, he'd taken pains to cover his face so that he couldn't be easily identified. He'd probably made sure he wouldn't leave fingerprints, either.

Detective Flynn frowned at my response. *Was he thinking I'd faked this attack? Planted the gun and come up with the quick response about the gloves to explain why they might find no prints?* He could certainly be thinking exactly that. But the only thing I could do was tell the truth and hope he'd believe me.

He bent down again to retrieve the envelope. When he stood, he said, "Walk me through what happened."

"Okay." I gestured for him to come inside.

As he entered, he stepped over to give Sawdust a pat on the head. "Hey, boy. Heard you scared off an armed prowler. Nice work."

The cat's terror having dissipated, he now lay on the recliner, licking a paw and looking somewhat smug. It was almost as if he understood the detective's words and felt proud he'd scared off a human twenty times his size.

While the detective and the officers gathered off to the side, I climbed back into the bed to reenact the events. I pulled the covers up to my chin.

"I was lying here asleep," I said, "when Sawdust's growl woke me. He was crouched on top of his cat tree next to the door. I heard the sound of someone picking the lock. I could see the person's outline in the light on my parents' back porch. When I realized what was happening, I jumped out of bed and looked around for a weapon." I tossed the covers back, climbed out of bed, and acted out looking around the place. "The light on top of my robotic vacuum caught my eye, so I grabbed it. By then, the guy had opened the door and stuck his hand and head through, like this." I walked out the door and now played the part of the intruder, sticking my left hand through the door, my thumb and index finger forming an improvised gun.

The detective eyed my ad-libbed weapon. "The gun was in his left hand?"

"Yes." I shifted, playing the part of my cat now, standing by the cat tree. "Sawdust reached up and swiped his paw across the man's face." I swung my left hand in the air. "The man yelled *'Ow! Stupid cat!'* when he hit himself in the forehead with the gun."

The cops exchanged glances and chuckles. I only wished I could find the situation as amusing as they did. I supposed it was funnier when it wasn't your own life that had been threatened.

Flynn cut the officers a look and they immediately stopped laughing. The detective returned his attention to me and asked, "Did you recognize the man's voice?"

"No. It didn't sound familiar at all."

Of course the intruder had only said three words, *stupid cat* and *ow*. I wasn't sure *ow* even qualified as a word.

Maybe it was merely a sound effect like *pow* or *whammo*? But I supposed it didn't matter.

I continued with my story. "The door swung open further and I struck." I mimicked raising the circular vac and bringing it down on the intruder's head. "The intruder turned and ran back toward the gate. I hurled the vacuum after him. It hit him in the back and fell to the ground."

Flynn looked out across the terrace at the shattered remains of my vacuum before finishing the story himself. "Then you called 911 and me."

"Right."

He continued to look out the window, though his gaze shifted from the broken vacuum to the back door of my parents' house. "Did you warn your parents?"

"No. They're not home. They're on vacation in New York."

I'd be there, too, if I wasn't teetering on the verge of bankruptcy.

Flynn turned his head back my way. "What about the neighbors? The vacuum must have caused a racket when it smashed to the ground. Did anyone come out to investigate?"

"Not that I know of. But I came right back inside so it's possible I didn't see them."

The tall cop chimed in. "We didn't see anyone when we pulled up, and there didn't seem to be any lights on in the adjacent houses."

Flynn nodded slowly, as if mulling over what we'd told him, before turning over the envelope in his hand. "It's sealed." He glanced over at my tiny kitchenette. "What drawer do you keep your silverware in?"

"The top one," I replied.

He stepped over, pulled the drawer open, and retrieved a table knife, sliding the point under the seal to loosen it.

When the flap had been freed, he pulled a piece of paper from the envelope and read it over. He looked from the paper to me, his gaze intent.

"What does it say?" I asked.

"It's a confession," he said. "From the person who claims to have killed Rick Dunaway."

A confession? Could this case be over now? Would I no longer be a suspect? My heart lurched in anticipation and instinctively I straightened up and leaned toward him. "Who is it?"

He exhaled a sharp breath and gave me a pointed look. *"You."*

CHAPTER 42

THE END OF THE DEMON

SAWDUST

The demon was no more!

It had gone berserk. Whitney had grabbed the demon to try to control it, but it attacked the man's head and then flew after him. Sawdust had seen the demon crash to the concrete and break into pieces, not moving. The cat knew what that meant. *It won't be back to torment me ever again. Hooray!*

Now that he'd licked the prowler's scent from his paw, Sawdust hopped down from the recliner, padded over to the glass door, and looked out at the demon's remains. Crashing to the ground couldn't have been a pleasant way to die. The cat almost felt sorry for the demon.

But not quite.

CHAPTER 43

FRAMED FOR MURDER

WHITNEY

My mouth dropped open and I pointed a finger at my chest. *"Me?"*

Detective Flynn held the paper up and the officers and I stepped closer to read it.

> *I can't live with the guilt anymore. I didn't mean to kill Rick Dunaway but he made me so angry I lost control. Please forgive me.*
>
> > *Love,*
> > *Whitney*

It was both a confession and good-bye. *Eek!* While the body of the letter was typed, the signature was handwritten in ink.

That's my signature. How can this be?

I wagged a finger. *No, no, no.* "I didn't write that!"

"Then who did?" the detective asked. "Who would have

a voice you don't recognize and also know what your signature looks like?"

Who, indeed?

When I couldn't come up with the name of someone who would somehow know my signature but whose voice I wouldn't recognize, the detective scrubbed a frustrated hand over his face. "Did anyone really come here tonight, or did you make this whole thing up, Whitney?"

"What?" I cried. "I'm a suspect again? Why would I lie about being attacked?"

He shrugged. "To throw suspicion off yourself?"

It was more a question than a statement. Still, it rankled.

"That's nuts!" I scoffed. "I don't even own a gun. You can check every gun store from here to Chattanooga. They'll tell you I never set foot in their shop."

Flynn lifted another shoulder as he slid the letter back into the envelope and dropped the envelope into an evidence bag. "It's easy enough to get a gun on the secondary market. Or you could have had someone buy it for you."

My mouth gaped. *Is this really happening?* "I thought you had decided I was innocent!"

"I did," he acknowledged. "But I reserve the right to change my mind in light of new evidence."

I tossed my hands in the air. "If I were making this up, why would I bother to put a silencer on the gun?"

"Maybe you thought that would make things look more realistic," he said. "If someone was trying to frame you and planned to shoot you and make it look like a self-inflicted wound, that person would try to be as quiet about it as possible to get away undetected. You're a smart person. You'd have figured that out."

I rolled my eyes. "You give me more credit than I deserve." *Wait. Had I just insulted myself?*

"Look." The detective raised conciliatory palms. "I'm not saying you were or weren't behind what happened here tonight. If you weren't, I'm sorry to have implied otherwise. But I've got to look at the situation from every angle. It's my job."

Truth be told, I'd feel the same way if I'd been in the detective's shoes. Nevertheless, by the time he and the uniformed officers left, I was beyond furious. Furious and more motivated than ever to prove my innocence. At least I had some fresh clues to consider. I also had a fresh pot of coffee to fuel my thought process.

I poured myself a steaming mug, took a gulp, and, tongue and tonsils burning, plopped down on my stool to think. Sawdust wandered over and hopped up into my lap. I stroked his back as I pondered the clues.

The person who'd come by tonight to try to frame me knew what my signature looked like. With so many things handled electronically these days, I'd signed very few papers in recent years. The documents to purchase my SUV at the Honda dealership. A rare credit card slip given that I didn't like paying interest and preferred to use my debit card, which only required a PIN. An occasional greeting card, though most of those were sent to people I knew well and cared about, not anyone likely to make an attempt on my life.

Could I have signed something at work? I couldn't recall anything specific other than the W-4 form I'd signed years ago when I'd first been hired by Home & Hearth. As owners of the business, the Hartleys signed all of the leases and other contracts and documents relating to the property management business. The same went for my job at Whitaker Woodworking. Uncle Roger was the one in charge, and he signed all of the contracts with the suppliers and clients.

Of course my signature would appear on checks I'd written, but given that checks were virtually obsolete these days I couldn't even remember the last time I'd written one. The only checks I'd dealt with recently was the check I'd written to Bobby Palmer, who'd been cleared, and the check for my earnest money for the house. But rather than a personal check, the earnest money check was a cashier's check, issued by the bank. My signature didn't appear on it. I retrieved my purse, pulled out my checkbook, and perused the register. That last check I'd written prior to the one to Bobby Palmer was way back in February. It was made out to a Girl Scout troop in the amount of $15 for cookies. I'd come across the girls in their green uniforms outside the Harris Teeter store when I'd been shopping for groceries. Having no cash on me at the time, I'd written a check. Going home without a few boxes of thin mints would have been utterly unthinkable.

Given that I'd made out no recent checks to anyone who might be a suspect, I closed the checkbook. The checks were a dead end.

Or were they?

My brain flashed and flickered and fizzled like the light that had short-circuited at the Sweetbriar house. But then the light came on and blazed in full glory, illuminating the situation so that I could see things clearly.

While I'd signed only a small number of checks on my own personal bank account, I'd recently endorsed a check made out to me—it was in the amount of $5,000 payable from the account of Abbot-Dunaway Holdings, Ltd.

That check had made me a suspect in Rick Dunaway's murder, and that check could now clear my name!

I threw my hands in the air, thanking the heavens—and the strong coffee—for giving me the answer. Or at least a possible answer.

That answer was Lance Abbot.

Lance Abbot could have obtained my signature from the company's banking records and traced it onto the confession letter. I'd never heard the man's voice, either. He truly was a silent partner. Like the intruder, Abbot appeared to be left-handed. He'd held his umbrella in his left hand the day I'd gone to their office to confront Rick Dunaway about the faulty wiring.

Lance Abbot checked all the boxes.

But is he really a killer?

It was hard to picture the calm, sophisticated man doing something so base and vile. The last thing I wanted to do was wrongly accuse someone of murder. I knew how awful and degrading it felt to have others think the worst of you. Still, just as Detective Flynn had noted that I could have faked tonight's attack to throw suspicion off myself, Lance Abbot could have planned to kill me to throw suspicion off himself. The detective planned to go through the financial records of Abbot-Dunaway Holdings tomorrow. Maybe Abbot had decided to strike tonight to prevent that from happening. Maybe there was something in those financial records that he didn't want the detective to see.

There was one way to find out for certain. I could go to see Abbot. If he had a scratch on his face, it would mean he was the killer. Of course confronting the guy directly would be a dangerous and reckless move. If he was the one who'd killed Rick Dunaway and had tried to kill me a couple hours earlier, he might decide to finish the job right then and there.

I bolted out the door.

CHAPTER 44

CATNIPPED

SAWDUST

Whitney went out the door without saying good-bye or giving him a kiss on the head. *What had gotten into her?*

Maybe she'd been in the catnip. Sawdust only partook of the stuff on occasion, when Whitney sprinkled it around the base of his scratching post in a futile attempt to encourage him to sharpen his claws on the toy rather than the recliner. The herb made him feel wild and crazy, like he wanted to roll in it and run and jump and fly like the birds that lived in the houses in the backyard.

He looked out the glass and saw Whitney running across the terrace in her ducky slippers.

Yep, she's on catnip.

CHAPTER 45

THE TRUTH CAN'T BE CONCEALED

WHITNEY

My robe billowing out behind me, I ran across the terrace and threw the gate open. Flynn's plain sedan was pulling away from the curb. I sprinted down the drive as fast as my rubber-ducky slippers would let me and dashed out in front of the car, raising my hands to stop him.

The car screeched to a quick stop, coming to a halt a mere three inches from my knees.

Flynn frowned through the windshield and unrolled his window, sticking his head out. "You trying to get yourself killed?"

An ironic question if ever there was one.

I darted over to his window. "I think I know who came here tonight!"

"Who?" he asked.

"Lance Abbot!"

"Abbot?" Flynn repeated. "Rick Dunaway's partner?"

"*Silent* partner," I said. Lance Abbot had been silent both in theory and in fact. I'd never once heard the man speak. "I've seen him, but I've never heard his voice. He always just nodded or gestured. Abbot might have lied when he said he didn't have access to the holding company's banking records. If he'd seen the records, he'd know what my signature looks like because I signed the check Rick Dunaway gave me to cover my insurance deductible. Abbot is left-handed, too. At least I think he is. He was holding an umbrella in his left hand the last time I saw him."

Flynn's brows rose. "This could all be circumstantial. Then again, you might be on to something."

"Let's go find out."

I ran back around the car, yanked the passenger door open, and began to climb in.

"Whoa, whoa, whoa!" Flynn held up a palm to stop me. "It's *my* job to find out, not yours."

I already had one pajama-clad leg in the door. "Please?" I begged. "You interrogated me and humiliated me over this case, and now I've lost an expensive vacuum cleaner thanks to the killer. The least you could do is let me witness the arrest."

He cocked his head. "How do I know you didn't hide a weapon in your pajamas? Maybe you're planning on taking me out on the drive over."

"You can frisk me if you want."

He arched a coy brow, a grin playing about his lips.

I rolled my eyes. "Cuff me then," I suggested. "But *please-please-pleeeeease* let me see you arrest Lance Abbot!"

The detective groaned, then grunted, but eventually agreed. "All right." He circled around the car with his handcuffs in his hand. "Turn around and put your hands on the top of the car."

"Here we go again." I sighed as I turned around and did as I was told.

He reached up and took my right wrist in his hand, gently pulling it down behind me and attaching one end of the cuffs, closing them with a *click*. He repeated the process with my left hand. *Click*.

Rather than seating me in the front, he opened the back door of his car. "In you go."

"I might have just solved your case for you, and you're going to make me sit in the back like a suspect?"

He exhaled sharply. "Yes. I shouldn't be letting you come at all. It may not be safe. Either get in the back or stay home."

"Okay, okay," I said. "I'll get in the back."

He helped me into the backseat and pulled the strap over me to buckle me in. "All good?"

"All good," I replied.

He circled back around the car and climbed into the driver's seat. As he pulled away from the curb, the computerized voice of his GPS told him to make a right turn at the corner. Apparently, he'd already programmed an address into his system.

"Where were you headed before I stopped you?" I asked.

His eyes met mine in the rearview mirror. This time, the smile he'd been fighting beat him. His lips spread in a grin. "Lance Abbot's house."

"Really? You already suspected he could be the killer?"

"I'd determined it was a distinct possibility." His gaze left the mirror and went to the road ahead. "You'd told me he never returned Mr. Hartley's call about the questionable invoice from the designer. That seemed odd to me. What business owner doesn't want to know if he's getting ripped off? My guess is he'd already figured it out himself, that he realized his partner was behind it."

"That would explain why he killed Rick Dunaway!"

Flynn nodded. "Abbot was also the one who told me about the check Rick Dunaway had written to you, the one for the insurance deductible. He claimed Presley told him about it, but I suspected he'd been going through the company's financial records prior to Dunaway's death. It seemed to me that he might be looking for someone else to pin his crime on, and he realized that the check could make you an easy target because it indicated you'd seen Mr. Dunaway in person the night he was killed. I figured if Abbot found your check, he might have also found others that were fraudulent. If he realized his partner was skimming from the company, that would give him a motive to eliminate his partner. Of course all of this is speculation on my part, but the theory ties up all the loose ends."

Given that I was one of those loose ends, I liked his theory.

It was only a few minutes after four in the morning, so the night was still dark as we drove. I stared out the window, buoyed by the thought that Dunaway's killer might soon be behind bars and I could focus on other matters, such as trying to find a buyer for the Sweetbriar house.

We were within two miles of Abbot's home and driving down a four-lane thoroughfare, when the lights of a twenty-four-hour pharmacy caught my eye. With most of the neighboring businesses closed for the night, the place was like a beacon, a million-megawatt spotlight beckoning people to come see the show.

As we sailed past, my eyes spotted three cars parked at the edge of the lot. They probably belonged to the employees who worked the night shift. Store staff usually had to park away from the doors to leave the more convenient spots open for customers. A black Lexus was parked near the doors, which told me it belonged to a customer. That customer was on the sidewalk, dressed all in black, and heading toward the automatic doors.

That customer was none other than Lance Abbot.

"Stop!" I cried.

The man disappeared into the pharmacy as Flynn slammed on the brakes. The car stopped, but momentum carried my body forward. With my arms cuffed behind me, I couldn't use them to brace myself. Even with the benefit of the seat belt, my face nearly slammed into the back of Flynn's headrest.

"What is it?" he asked.

I couldn't point with my finger, so I had to use my head to indicate the building. "Lance Abbot! I just saw him go inside the pharmacy!"

"Are you sure?"

"I'm eighty-seven percent positive!"

Flynn turned around to look at me and frowned. "By definition, anything less than one hundred percent is not positive."

Sheesh. "I only saw his profile. But he had Abbot's nose. It's gotta be him!" *Right?*

Flynn punched the gas, sending me rocketing backward now. But whiplash would be a small price to pay to see Lance Abbot taken into custody.

Flynn backed in next to the employees' cars and cut his engine. He looked over at the Lexus. "Is that Abbot's car?"

"I don't know. I'm not sure what he drives."

The detective grabbed the mic off the dash and pressed the button to talk. "I need you to run a plate for me," he said to the dispatcher. He rattled off the license plate number.

Sure enough, a few seconds later, the dispatcher came back with, "The car is registered to a Lance Abbot."

"Told ya!" I cried.

He pressed the button again. "Send backup, please. I'm going to be taking a suspect into custody." He gave the dispatcher our location using cross streets for a reference.

"Are you going inside?" I asked when he slid the mic back into its mount.

"No. I don't want to put the employees at risk. But I don't want to lose the element of surprise, either. It would be less risky to nab him here, when he's not expecting it, than it would be to pull him over or confront him at his house. I'm going to intercept him on the sidewalk when he comes out."

He used his keys to unlock his glove box, reached inside, and retrieved a handgun. He climbed out of the car and lifted his shirt to tuck the gun into the waistband of his pants, simultaneously displaying a nice six-pack of abs.

He opened the back door. "Lean forward."

When I did, he reached behind me and unlocked the cuffs, pulling them off me.

I sat up and rubbed my wrists. "You're letting me free?"

"Only because these are my only pair of cuffs and I'll need them. Don't get out of this car under any circumstances. You hear me? I don't want you getting hurt."

He was probably concerned about potential liability if I were injured.

"Okay," I agreed.

Armed and ready, he strode toward the entrance and positioned himself on the far side of a Coke machine that sat outside to the right of the doors. Abbot wouldn't be able to spot the detective behind the machine, lying in wait.

As I peeked around the headrest, watching the door for Lance Abbot to emerge, my heart pulsed a thousand beats a minute in my chest and my breaths came fast. *This is so exciting!*

A minute passed.

Another followed.

Then came a third.

"Hurry up!" I muttered.

Another minute passed and I could tell that even the calm Detective Flynn was growing impatient. He leaned forward to peer around the vending machine every few seconds, anxious to pounce on his prey.

Finally, the automatic doors slid open. Lance Abbot emerged from the store with a white paper bag in his right hand, his keys in his left, and a stark white gauze patch over his right eye.

It was him who'd tried to kill me tonight! I knew it!

Abbot pushed the button on the fob to unlock his car. The headlights flashed. But there was another set of flashing lights, too. The second set sat atop the police cruiser coming up the block.

When Abbot spotted the cruiser, he aborted his plan to get into his car and instead scurried down the sidewalk, looking back over his shoulder to keep an eye—his good one—on the cruiser. With his focus diverted, he walked right past Detective Flynn without spotting him.

And he'd had the nerve to call my cat stupid.

Weapon at the ready, Flynn stepped right in behind Abbot. When Abbot caught the movement out of the corner of his eye, he spun around to see who was following him. Unfortunately, he was at the edge of the sidewalk as he turned. He stepped off the curb backward, lost his balance, and fell to his bum on the asphalt, dropping both his bag and his keys in the process.

Flynn pounced as Abbot reached for his hip. *Oh, my gosh! Is he going for a gun?*

The two struggled on the ground, Abbot putting up quite a fight for a man of his age. Just as Buck and Jackson had wrestled and wrangled on the ground only a few days earlier, Flynn and Abbot rolled about, first one, then the other, gaining advantage. A few seconds into the fracas, Abbot's hand emerged from the tangle of limbs and, in the dim glow of the streetlight, I saw the glint of a handgun.

"Look out!" I cried out the open car window. "He's got a gun!"

BANG!

The earsplitting sound was accompanied by a white muzzle flash. An instant later, a hole appeared in the soda machine Flynn had been hiding behind earlier.

Despite Detective Flynn having ordered me to stay in the car, I couldn't just sit there and watch him get shot. It wouldn't be right. Besides, if Abbot killed Flynn, he might come for me next.

Better to take the bull by the horns.

I slid out of the car and looked around for something— *anything!*—I could use as a weapon. I saw nothing. My hands fisted reflexively at my sides, touching the loose belt of my robe.

My belt! That's it!

I rushed over to the men, yanked my belt from my robe, and grasped it in my hands.

Flynn hollered, "I told you to stay in the car!"

"I have to help!" I shouted back.

I watched their movements, looking for an opportunity. Before I could find one, Abbot got off another shot. *BANG!* That one took out the rearview mirror on the passenger side of his car.

Finally, Abbot reared his head back as Flynn attempted to grab him by the throat. It was just the chance I needed. I looped the belt over his head, sliding it down to his neck, and yanked back as hard as I could, crossing my hands to cut off his air supply. He dropped his gun and reached up to claw at the belt choking him. It was all Flynn needed to best the man. He kicked the gun away and grabbed Abbot by the shirtfront. I released my hold on the belt and Flynn jerked Abbot forward, slamming him to the ground at his side. In mere seconds he had the man facedown with his hands behind him in handcuffs. Flynn panted from exertion as he knelt over Abbot, his knee in the man's back to keep him immobilized.

The detective looked up at me scowling. "You weren't supposed to leave the car."

"I might have just saved your life."

"And you might have lost your own."

I lifted my shoulders and raised my palms. "So we'll call it a tie, then?"

Before he could chastise me further, the squad car turned in to the lot. I waved my arms over my head to get the attention of the cop at the wheel of the cruiser. When Officer Hogarty looked my way, I pointed down to the men.

Hogarty pulled to a stop at an angle near Flynn and Abbot and climbed out of her car, casting a confused glance at my rubber-ducky slippers before turning her attention to the detective and his charge. "What in the world is going on here?"

Flynn gave Hogarty a quick rundown. Abbot was Rick Dunaway's partner. Abbot had killed Dunaway and attempted to implicate me in the murder. When charges against me didn't stick, he tried to frame me with a forged deathbed confession.

During the entire exchange, Abbot remained quiet as usual, his head turned to the side, staring straight ahead in defeat at my smiling slippers.

Flynn said, "I'm going to let you up, Abbot. No funny business." With that, he rose from his position across the man's back.

When the uniformed officer took Abbot's arm and pulled him to a stand, Flynn read him his rights and asked, "Is there anything you'd like to say?"

Remaining true to his title as Dunaway's "silent partner," the man said nothing, simply looking down and shaking his head, his one exposed eye avoiding our gaze.

Flynn retrieved the pharmacy bag and pulled out the contents—an over-the-counter antibiotic skin cream, eye drops, and a tube of concealer in buff beige. Looked like Abbot had planned to cover the scratches with makeup to avoid questions from his family or Presley.

Flynn frisked Abbot and found a folded receipt in his pocket from a nearby minor emergency center. The date and time stamp indicated he'd just come from the clinic. Abbot had provided a false name, Larry Abernathy, and paid in cash, probably hoping the visit wouldn't lead police to him if they contacted medical offices to inquire about patients coming in tonight with an eye injury.

With a final pointed look at Abbot, Detective Flynn turned to address Officer Hogarty. "Take him in."

The cop gave him a nod, took Abbot by the arm, and placed him in the back of her cruiser. She slid back into the driver's seat and raised a hand in good-bye. "See you later, Flynn!"

The detective and I watched as they drove away.

When the cruiser disappeared from sight, Flynn pulled out his cell phone to check the time and turned to me. "Loveless Café opens at seven. Why don't we start this day off right with biscuits and gravy? Maybe a hot cup of coffee?"

I moaned in buttery anticipation. "You had me at biscuits."

CHAPTER 46

HAPPY DAYS

SAWDUST

When Whitney returned a few hours after sunup, she was still acting a little strange, but it no longer seemed like a catnip high. She went about the pool house, singing and dancing as she opened a can of Sawdust's wet food, cleaned up his litter box, and swept up the fur he'd shed.

The cat wasn't sure what had put her in such a good mood. He could smell biscuits and gravy on her breath when she picked him up and cooed at him and scratched his chest. Maybe it was a good breakfast that had her feeling happy. But this seemed like more than just good-meal happy. No, he suspected it was something else entirely. But whatever it was, he was glad. She'd been worried and upset for the past few weeks. He was glad those days were behind them, and he looked forward to happier days ahead.

CHAPTER 47

HOME SWEET HOME

WHITNEY

With Dunaway's killer finally in jail, I returned Colette's pepper spray.

More details came out following Lance Abbot's arrest. While Bobby Palmer had been in cahoots with Rick Dunaway regarding the inspection of the house on Sweetbriar Avenue, Dunaway had acted on his own with regard to the fraudulent invoices. Because the invoices had looked legitimate, Presley hadn't had an inkling that Dunaway was skimming. Though she'd unwittingly processed the payments, she'd played no knowing part in the scheme and reaped no benefits. Dunaway had paid her such a paltry salary that she'd taken a weekend job doing bookkeeping at a consignment store. She earned a little extra money there, and was also given first dibs and an employee discount on items the customers brought in to sell. The arrangement explained how she'd been able to amass so many designer accessories on her modest pay.

Though Lance Abbot initially said nothing, his attorneys quickly realized that if he didn't offer some type of defense, he'd go down for first degree murder, which carried a potential death penalty. Detective Flynn phoned me after Abbot confessed to killing Dunaway.

"Apparently you were the first clue Mr. Abbot had that his partner was milking their firm," he said.

Me? "I was?"

"Abbot told me that Rick Dunaway always spoke very highly of you. Said you worked hard, charged reasonable rates, and had a good head on your shoulders. After you came by the office to talk to him about the fire, Abbot questioned him about it. Dunaway told his partner that he knew nothing about the old wiring in the house he sold you, but Abbot said Dunaway had always been a stickler for detail, so he didn't buy Dunaway's story. He realized Dunaway had tried to pull one over on you. And if Dunaway would swindle a young woman who'd been nothing but a help to him, Abbot wondered what Dunaway might do to a silent partner who'd been hands-off and trusted him to operate on the up-and-up. Lance Abbot looked over the financial records one evening after Dunaway had left the office, and got his answer. Dunaway had been fleecing the firm for years with false invoices, some of them purportedly from Home and Hearth."

"Home and Hearth?" I issued an indignant scoff. *Dunaway had unwittingly dragged the Hartleys' business into his scheme?* The thought burned me up.

Per Detective Flynn, Lance Abbot discovered that Dunaway had devised a system to skim funds without raising any red flags. Dunaway had Presley prepare the holding company's checks, but he would then sign and mail them. While the real checks were sent on their merry way through the U.S. mail, the fraudulent checks were never mailed to the parties they were made out to. Rather, Dunaway forged the payees' signatures using their actual signatures from legitimate payments. Abbot had stolen a play from Dunaway's playbook when he'd forged my name on the fake confession.

Flynn went on. "Dunaway countersigned the fraudulent checks in his own name and deposited the checks in an account he'd set up at another bank. The account was in the name of a shell business he'd incorporated in Nevada. He was the sole owner. Because Dunaway maintained a large balance in the account and because the checks he deposited were made out by another of his businesses, the staff of the second bank never questioned him."

It wasn't surprising. The bank employees wouldn't want to take a chance on offending a major client and having him take his banking business elsewhere.

"Abbot had only made it through the records for the past two years," Flynn said, "and already he realized Rick Dunaway had screwed him out of at least half a million dollars. Abbot went to the office to confront Dunaway around five o'clock on Friday of that same week, but Dunaway had already left. Abbot remembered overhearing that his partner planned to meet you at the house on Sweetbriar at six that evening. Abbot headed over to the house and confronted Dunaway on the walkway when he arrived. When Abbot told Dunaway he was going to sue him for every penny he was worth and report him to the police, Dunaway told Abbot he was off his rocker. Abbot became enraged, and that's when he spotted the mallet."

Though the detective didn't elaborate, it was clear what happened next. Lance Abbot had picked up the mallet, swung it at Dunaway's head, and killed the man as he came up onto the porch.

Flynn drew a deep breath before continuing. "When he couldn't rouse his partner and realized Dunaway was dead, Abbot panicked. He dragged Dunaway over to the flower bed, spread dirt over him, and took his wallet, hoping it would make the crime look like a robbery gone wrong. Abbot didn't think anybody else suspected that Rick had been stealing from the firm. As long as nobody knew, no one would have a reason to suspect that Abbot might have killed his partner. When you saw the designer's invoice on Presley's desk and had your boss call Abbot about it, he thought you'd let it drop if he didn't return the call. He didn't realize you'd be so tenacious." Flynn offered a soft chuckle.

"It's not the first time someone has underestimated me," I acknowledged. It rankled, but it also gave me the joy of proving them wrong.

"When I got in touch with Abbot about taking a look at the financial records, he panicked. He realized he had to do something that very night if he wanted to save his hide."

Again, the detective let me fill in the blanks. *Lance Abbot had tried to save his hide by pinning his crime on me, like a warped game of pin-the-tail-on-the-donkey.*

None of the parties to whom the fraudulent, counter-signed checks had been payable realized Dunaway had been issuing duplicitous checks in the names of their businesses.

"I've also identified the man in the white sedan," Flynn said. "He's an investigator for the divorce attorney Dunaway's wife hired. The lawyer had him follow Dunaway. Dunaway's wife suspected her husband had been squirreling money away, but she didn't know where. She knew her attorney was looking into the matter, but she wasn't aware his investigator was keeping an eye on her husband. The investigator trailed Dunaway to the bank a couple days before he was killed. Turns out he'd been funneling money from his shell corporation's account to an offshore account he hadn't told his wife or the IRS about. The offshore account was in Dunaway's name only, but since the divorce hadn't been finalized before his death and he hadn't revised his will to remove his wife as his heir, the funds are all hers now."

She was probably laughing all the way to the bank.

Given Abbot's confession, his lack of premeditation in Rick Dunaway's murder, and his lack of success killing me or Detective Flynn, the charges against Lance Abbot relating to Rick Dunaway's death were reduced. Lance Abbot's attorney worked out a plea deal with the district attorney. In return for a guilty plea for voluntary manslaughter (of Rick Dunaway) and attempted murder (of me and Detective Flynn), he'd receive a sentence of twelve years.

No one in Abbot's or Dunaway's families was interested in taking over the business, nor were outside parties interested in buying a company whose very name was synonymous with murder and fraud. Lance Abbot's and Rick Dunaway's wives decided to liquidate the holdings, take the money, and call it a day. Thad Gentry offered to buy the entire portfolio of properties for eighty cents on the dollar, but they turned him down and held out until he raised his offer another fifteen percent. At that point, they decided to accept. After all, they'd spend five percent or more in closing and administrative costs if they sold the properties separately rather than in bulk. And speaking of Thad Gentry, it turned out he'd been under investigation by the feds for suspicion of paying an influential member of the zoning commission for the favorable ruling on his Sweetbriar property. The authorities hadn't been able to prove anything—*yet*. Rather than risk a conviction and public humiliation, Gentry agreed to have the property rezoned back from commercial to residential, and to make a sizable contribution to the city's beautification fund. In return, the feds dropped the investigation.

Bobby Palmer was convicted of making a false statement to a police officer for lying to Detective Flynn about whether he'd taken a bribe from Rick Dunaway. He was ordered to perform a hundred hours of community service. I'd seen him collecting trash at the city's Christmas parade, a garbage bag in one hand, a grabber in the other.

All in all, justice was served.

Mulled cider was served, too. Buck and I had gotten in the habit of meeting up at the Sweetbriar house to hang out. Its convenient, central location made it the perfect meeting spot for friends from all over the area. We carted in my parents' card table and folding chairs for impromptu playing of board games or poker. We'd even erected an artificial Christmas tree and dressed it in blinking lights to keep everyone's spirits merry and bright.

One Saturday evening in late December, just before the Yuletide holiday, Buck and I were at the house, working on plans for custom shelving in a client's garage. While Buck stood at the stove, slowly stirring a fresh batch of spiced apple cider, I sketched out a crude diagram that included a designated space for both the client's golf clubs and his fourteen-foot canoe.

A knock sounded at the door. I peered out the peephole. Colette stood on the porch looking solemn, yet relieved. I let her in the door, frigid air sneaking in behind her. We warmed each other up with an affectionate hug before heading to the kitchen.

She gave Sawdust a pat on the head, did the same to Buck, and placed her cell phone and purse on the breakfast bar. She slid onto one of the barstools and heaved a sigh. "It's over."

"What's over?" I asked.

Buck looked over his shoulder as he stirred.

"Me and Shane," she said. "We finally faced facts. If we've been together this long but never felt motivated to take the next step, we owe it to ourselves to see if there's someone else better suited for each of us." She shrugged. "It was mutual and amicable, not bad as far as breakups go."

As Buck retrieved mugs from the cabinet and ladled cider into them, I reached out and gave her hand a squeeze. "Where will you go?"

Her boyfriend owned the condo the two had been living in. She'd have to find a new place to live.

"I'm not sure yet where I'll live," Colette said. "One of the waitresses has been looking for a new roommate for her apartment. Emmalee and I get along great, but I'm just not sure I'd be happy there. The kitchen is tiny."

Buck turned around with three mugs of steaming cider in his hands. He placed one in front of Colette, another in front of me. The third he sipped from himself. "Maybe you should move in here."

Colette and I exchanged glances.

"What are you suggesting exactly?" she asked, cradling the warm mug in her hands.

"There's been no movement on the house," he said, which was unfortunately true. Despite putting every effort into selling the place, we hadn't received a single offer, not even a lowball offer from Thad Gentry. Nobody wanted to buy a house where a corpse had once been buried. "Maybe it makes sense for you to move in here. Whitney, too. Lord knows she's lived in that doghouse long enough."

I rolled my eyes over the top of my mug as I took a sip. "It's not a *dog*house. It's a *pool* house."

"That's not much bigger," he said, which wasn't a lie.

I looked over at Colette. "He might be on to something. If Emmalee's interested, we could all three move in here."

Colette's eyes brightened and she ran her hand along the quartz countertop. "You mean I could cook in this kitchen every night? That would be a dream come true!"

If three of us lived here, and the other two paid a reasonable rent, I'd be able to cover the monthly mortgage without Buck's help. I'd accepted that my money would be tied up in this house until we could sell it, but would Buck be okay with that?

When I asked, he waved a dismissive hand. "I'll think of it as an investment. We'll split the equity fifty-fifty sometime down the road when people have forgotten about Rick Dunaway's murder and it makes sense to put it back on the market."

His proposition seemed like the perfect solution to our financial dilemma and would solve Colette's housing problem as well.

I turned to Colette. "I'll take the small bedroom."

She grinned. "I'll take the big one."

Buck pointed to Colette's phone on the countertop. "Call your coworker. See if she wants to take a look."

Colette phoned Emmalee. Luckily, she wasn't working that evening.

Emmalee showed up a half hour later, using the door knocker to announce her arrival. She had hair the color of mahogany, fair and freckled skin, and a warm smile. After introductions were exchanged in the doorway, she pointed to the knocker. "That's an interesting touch."

"It is, isn't it?" I said.

The three of us took her on the grand tour, showing her the mid-sized bedroom that could be hers if she wanted.

When we were done, I asked, "What do you think?"

"I love the place!" she replied. "There's much more space than my apartment. I like the idea of having a yard, too. The only place I can get outside at the apartment is by the pool and it's always loud and crowded when the weather is nice."

"One question," I said. "Are you allergic to cats?" If she was, it would be a deal breaker. Where I went, my cat went. Sawdust would be moving into the house with me.

"Not at all," Emmalee said. "I grew up with cats. I've been wanting one myself. The complex where I live now doesn't allow pets, but maybe I could adopt a kitten if I moved in here?"

"Of course!" I said. "Sawdust would love the company."

Colette and I moved in the following day. Buck offered his van and flatbed trailer, as well as his muscle in relocating our furniture to the house from our former abodes. Colette thanked him by whipping up a batch of hearty potato soup for dinner. To her delight, he downed three bowls and declared it the best potato soup on earth.

Emmalee moved in right after Christmas. By New Year's Eve, the three of us had arranged, rearranged, and re-rearranged the furniture until we were all satisfied that we'd found the best spots for each piece. We'd worked out our routines and were settling in nicely. Sawdust was, too. He'd already decided on his favorite places to nap—on Colette's cushy couch, curled up in Emmalee's Papasan chair, and, for some unknown reason, in the bathroom sink.

We three roomies decided to usher in the new year in our new place. We invited several friends to join us. Buck was invited, too, of course. A veritable buffet of gourmet snack foods stretched across the breakfast bar. Colette deserved most of the credit for the delicious spread, though she had delegated some chopping and measuring to me and Emmalee.

We shared jokes and funny stories, sang along with Emmalee's karaoke machine, and stuffed ourselves silly until midnight neared. Sawdust was the belle of the ball, weaving in and out of our guests' legs, collecting belly scratches and ear rubs as he worked the crowd.

Before we knew it, the ten-second countdown to midnight began.

"Ten!" we hollered in unison. "Nine! Eight!"

We continued on until we reached, "Three! Two! One!"

As midnight struck and those with dates turned to their partners to plant a big kiss on each other, Sawdust put a paw up on my leg and mewed up at me. *Meow?*

Colette looked down at my cat. "I think he's asking for a kiss."

"Then a kiss he shall have." I scooped my cat up in my arms and planted a loud one on his furry cheek. *Smoooch!*

All in all, not a bad way to ring in the new year. And I already knew the new year would be better than the last. After all, what were the chances I'd find another body?

When I returned to work at Home & Hearth after the holidays, Mrs. Hartley waved me over to her desk and patted the chair she'd pulled up next to it. "Take a seat right here, hon, and look at this new listing we got today."

Once I was seated, she scrolled slowly through a number of digital photos on her computer screen. The photos showed a rectangular white colonial, a type of house ubiquitous in Nashville where traditional residences ruled. A tall trellis reached from the ground all the way up to a small, octagonal window on the third floor, near the pinnacle of the gable. An attic window would be my guess. A climbing rosebush with an abundance of scarlet blooms ascended the trellis and had reached out in an attempt to claim the gutter as well. What shutters remained were painted black, as was the front door. Much of the paint was peeling, revealing weathered boards underneath. A covered porch spanned the front of the house. Several wide balusters were missing from the porch railing, making the house look as if it had taken a punch in the mouth and lost several teeth. At least it appeared to be smiling.

"What's the story behind the house?" I asked Mrs. Hartley.

"It was owned by an older woman who couldn't afford the upkeep," she said. "The woman passed away." She raised a palm. "Don't worry. It was natural causes, and it didn't happen in the house. She'd been taken to the hospital." She put her hand down again. "Anyway, her children don't want the place and they can't afford to fix it up, either. They want to put it on the market as is." She gave me a pointed look over her reading glasses. "You know how these listing things go. The house will sit on the market and continue to deteriorate until the government seizes it to pay back taxes or some developer offers peanuts for it and the desperate family has no choice but to take the offer. We'll end up with a pittance in commission."

Given what she'd told me, I had to ask the obvious question, "Then why did you take the listing?"

She gave me a smile. "So we could sell the house to you."

"Excuse me?"

"It's the perfect fixer-upper for a carpenter like you. It's in a good neighborhood. The lot is large. And just look at those roses! A little bit of trimming and they'd be gorgeous."

My gaze moved back at the screen. Yep, the house definitely had potential. But I, just as definitely, had no ready money to buy it. "Wish I could," I told Mrs. Hartley. "But every spare cent I had is in my house on Sweetbriar. With the mortgage on my credit report, no bank would give me a loan."

"We're well aware of your situation," Mr. Hartley said, rising from his adjacent desk. "That's why we prepared this."

He handed me a single-page document that read PROM-ISSORY NOTE across the top. The note provided that the Hartleys would loan me an amount equal to the offering price in the listing, $139,000. Interest would accrue at the ridiculously low rate of 1 percent per annum. Payments would be payable over thirty years in the affordable monthly amount of less than $450.

My heart swelled as I looked up at the Hartleys. "You'd do this for me? Really?"

Mrs. Hartley reached out to pat my hand. "We believe in you, hon."

"Besides," Mr. Hartley said. "We know it'll end up being a short-term thing."

True. If I took the loan, I'd pay it off early with the proceeds from the sale of the house once it was fixed up. The rest would be mine to keep.

Mrs. Hartley chimed in again. "It'll be our way of putting more money in your pocket without taking it out of ours."

"Yup," said Mr. Hartley. "One of them so-called win-win situations."

"You two are the best!" I stood from my seat and gave them each a warm hug and a firm handshake.

Mr. Hartley fished a pen out of his breast pocket and held it out to me. "Does this mean it's a deal?"

I took the pen from him, signed my name to the note, and handed both the pen and the page to him. "It is now."

After we shared another hug, Mrs. Hartley got on her phone to call the seller and tell them she'd received an offer on the house.

I, too, placed a call. "Grab your toolbox, Buck. We're back in business."

Read on for an excerpt from

DEAD IN THE DOORWAY

the next installment in Diane Kelly's new House Flipper series, available soon from St. Martin's Paperbacks!

WHITNEY WHITAKER

Click.

My breath fogged in the frigid January air as I stood on the cracked concrete driveway and snapped cell phone pics of the dilapidated white Colonial. Later, I'd look the pictures over and make a list of the repairs to be done and the materials needed.

Click. Click-click.

Sawdust, my sweet but spoiled cat, performed figure eights between my legs, wrapping his leash tightly around my ankles as if he were a cowboy at the rodeo and I was a calf he'd roped. Buck, who was both my cousin and business partner, stood next to me. Given that our fathers were brothers, Buck and I shared the last name Whitaker. We also shared a tall physique, blue eyes, and hair the color of unfinished pine. But while Buck sported a full beard, a monthly waxing at the beauty salon kept any would-be whiskers away from my face.

I slid my phone into the pocket of my coveralls, leaned down to extricate my legs from the tangled leash, and picked up my cat before turning to my cousin. "What do you think?"

Buck's narrowed gaze roamed over the structure, taking in the peeling paint, the weathered boards, and the missing balusters on the front porch railing. Several shutters had gone AWOL, too. A wooden trellis stretched up the side of the house, looking like an oversized skeleton trying to scale the roof. Several of its slats hung askew, like broken ribs. The climbing roses that graced the trellis had withered in the winter weather, awaiting their annual spring rejuvenation.

The home's former owner, a widow named Lillian Walsh, had lived a long and happy life here before passing from natural causes. Her fixed income hadn't allowed for much upkeep, though, and her children had put the place on the market as-is rather than deal with the cost and hassle of repairs. That's where flippers like me and my cousin came in.

Buck cocked his head as he he continued his visual inspection. "We've got our work cut out for us. But I don't see anything we can't handle."

House flippers maximize their profits by investing not only their money, but also sweat equity, in their properties, fixing up the homes themselves rather than hiring the work out at a markup. As a professional carpenter, Buck had the know-how to spruce the place up. Having regularly helped out at Whitaker Woodworking over the years, I'd grown adept at carpentry, too. What's more, thanks to my property management work and YouTube tutorials, I'd learned how to handle all sorts of repairs. If you need drywall patched or a sticky door re-hung, I'm your gal.

Looking back at the house, I felt hopeful. *A new year means a new beginning, doesn't it?*

Buck and I sure could use a fresh start. Last year had

been rough. I'd convinced my cousin to partner with me on our first house flip, certain we'd make a quick and easy profit. But after I'd invested all my savings in a stone cottage in the Belmont-Hillsboro neighborhood of Nashville, I'd discovered the seller had intentionally misled me about the property's condition and value. Never mind that I'd worked for peanuts as his property manager and had provided him untold hours of uncompensated carpentry work. *No good deed goes unpunished.* Of course bad deeds don't go unpunished, either. My cat had later dug up the man's body in the front flower bed. *That's a morning I'd like to forget.*

I took a deep breath and forced the thought to the back of my mind. My new year's resolution had been to put the past behind me and look forward. To that end, I motioned for Buck to follow me. "C'mon. I'll show you the inside."

We ascended the crumbling brick steps to the front porch. A ceramic frog with a fly on his unfurled tongue greeted us from his spot next to the door. I could understand why the frog was smiling—he was about to enjoy a snack. But why the tiny fly was smiling was beyond me. He seemed clueless about his fate.

"Fancy door," Buck said as he stopped before it.

Indeed it was. The door was made of heavy, solid wood with an ornate oval of frosted glass to let in light yet provide some measure of privacy. Once it was sanded and treated to a new coat of glossy black paint, it would really add to the curb appeal.

Setting Sawdust down on the porch, I unlocked the door and the three of us stepped inside, stopping on the linoleum landing of the split-level house. To the right of the landing was a coat closet with a rickety folding door that was either half closed or half open, depending on how you looked at it. But optimist or pessimist, you couldn't miss the smell of mothballs coming from inside. So many dusty jackets and coats were squeezed into the closet that the rod bent under the weight, threatening to break. The outerwear shared the lower space with a mangled umbrella and a hefty Kirby vacuum cleaner circa 1965, complete with attachments. The shelf above sagged under the weight of a reel-to-reel home movie projector, around which mismatched mittens, scarves, and knit caps had been stuffed. Lilian's family had cleared the house of everything of value, leaving the worthless junk behind for the buyer—*yours truly*—to deal with. *Sigh.*

After closing the front door behind us, I unclipped the leash from Sawdust's harness, setting him free to explore. Noting that the house felt warmer than expected, I checked the thermostat mounted next to the closet. 72. *Huh. Hadn't I turned it down to 60 the last time I'd been here?* I supposed I'd forgotten to adjust it when I'd left. I reached out and gave the lever a downward nudge. The three of us wouldn't be here long. No sense paying for heat nobody would be needing.

I swept my arm, inviting Buck to proceed me upstairs. "After you, partner."

We ascended the steps with Sawdust trotting ahead of us. On the way, Buck grasped both the wall-mounted railing and the wrought-iron banister and gave each of them a hearty yank, testing them for safety. While the banister checked out, the wooden rail mounted to the wall jiggled precariously. One glance at the support brackets told us why.

"It's got some loose screws," Buck said. "Just like you."

I rolled my eyes. "Ha-ha."

He circled a finger in the air. "Put it on the list."

"Will do." I pulled my phone from my pocket and

snapped a photo of the loose bracket as a reminder to my-self.

As we topped the stairs, Buck came to a screeching halt, one work boot hovering over the carpet as he refused to step on it. "Yuck."

Couldn't say that I blamed him. The carpet was hideous, an old, worn shag in the same greenish-brown hue as the goo that coated the hairballs my cat occasionally coughed up. Ripping out the carpet would give us no small plea-sure. Still, I wasn't about to let some ugly, balding carpet spoil my enthusiasm. I gave my cousin a push, forcing him forward. "Go on, you wimp. It's not going to reach up and grab you."

"You sure about that?"

To our left, the living and dining areas formed a rect-angle that ran from the front to the back of the house. The master bedroom and bath mirrored the layout to the right. In the center sprawled the wide kitchen.

"Wait'll you see the kitchen!" I circled around Buck and pushed open the swinging saloon doors that led into the space.

Buck proceeded through them and stopped in the cen-ter of the room to gape. "What is this place? A portal back to 1970?"

Between the harvest gold appliances, the rust-orange countertops and the globe pendant light hanging from a loopy chain, it appeared as if we'd time-traveled back to a much groovier era. But while the kitchen was hopelessly out of date, it was also wonderfully spacious. Plus, the cabinets would be salvageable if the outdated scalloped valances over the sink and stove were removed.

"Replacing the appliances and countertops is a no-brainer," I said. "But look at all this space! And the cabinets just need re-facing. They're solid wood. That'll save us some time and money."

Buck rapped his knuckles on the door of a cabinet. *Rap-rap.* Satisfied by the feel and sound, he nodded in agreement.

The counters bore an array of Lillian's cooking implements, including a ceramic pitcher repurposed to hold utensils. Cutting boards in a variety of shapes and sizes leaned against the backsplash. A recipe box nestled between an ancient toaster and a blender. A quaint collection of antique food tins graced the top of a wooden bread box. Hershey's cocoa. Barnum's Animal Crackers. Arm & Hammer Baking Soda.

As Buck and Sawdust took a peek at the plumbing under the sink, I walked over to the end of the cabinets and spread my arms. "Let's add an L-shaped extension here." An extension would increase the counter space and storage and, after all, kitchen renovations were the most profitable rehab investment.

Without bothering to look up, Buck agreed. "Okey doke."

My cousin and I had an implicit understanding. He left the design details up to me, while I gave him control over the structural aspects of the renovations.

While he continued his inspection, I meandered around the kitchen, snapping several more pictures before stopping at the fridge. A dozen blue ribbons were affixed with magnets to the refrigerator door, proudly proclaiming Lillian as the baker of the "Best Peach Pie" and "Best Peach Cobbler" at various fairs and festivals throughout the state.

A hutch on the adjacent wall was loaded with more cookbooks than I could count. I eased up to take a closer look. One book was devoted entirely to potato recipes, another to casseroles. A quick glimpse inside told me the recipes were as likely to clog the arteries as fill the tummy. Some of them sounded darn delicious, though.

I returned the books to the shelf and turned to find Sawdust traipsing along the countertop, while Buck peered into the drawers.

My cousin pulled out what appeared to be a caulking gun, along with a heavy metal lever-like tool with a rubber-coated handle. The latter resembled an airplane throttle. He held them up for me to see. "What the heck are these gadgets for?"

"You're asking the wrong person." While I loved working *on* kitchens, I didn't particularly like working *in* them once they were complete. Boxed mac-and-cheese marked the pinnacle of my culinary skills.

"Have Colette take a look," he suggested. "She might use some of these things."

My best friend worked as a chef and, unlike me, loved cooking. As her roommate, I was the lucky beneficiary of her skills. Colette kept our fridge stocked not only with raw materials, but also with finished meals to share. While she already had an extensive complement of kitchen equipment, this room contained items that probably hadn't been produced in half a century or more. If nothing else, she'd find these relics intriguing.

Having fully explored the kitchen, Buck and I moved on to the master bedroom. Like the kitchen, the room was dated but spacious. The walls bore lima-bean green wallpaper in a flocked fleur-de-lis pattern. Only the bed and a night table remained, all other furniture having been removed from the room. A stack of books towered on the night table, some hardcover, some paperbacks. Sawdust hopped up on to the bed to inspect the random items that had been placed there. Several pairs of ladies' shoes. A stack of Sunday dresses still on the hangers. A small jewelry box. A quick peek inside told me it contained only a few pieces of what I assumed to be cheap costume jewelry.

We continued into the master bath, which featured a once-fashionable pink porcelain tub, toilet, and sink. Wallpaper in a gaudy yet charming rose pattern adorned the walls. Fresh, if faded, towels filled the under-sink cabinet, along with an assortment of medications and beauty products. A tin box sat next to the sink. The top was open, revealing a trio of pink soaps in the shape and scent of roses.

Sawdust leapt up onto the edge of the tub and circumnavigated it with the ease and agility of a tightrope walker.

I snapped a pic before turning to Buck. "Let's replace that old bathtub with a walk-in shower, and add a jetted garden tub over there." I pointed to an open space under the window.

He pulled out a measuring tape to size up the space and, satisfied the tub would fit, issued an "mm-hmm" of agreement.

Having completed the tour of the master suite, we made a quick pass through the living and dining rooms, which contained only a slouchy velveteen sofa, a framed still life painting depicting a bowl of assorted fruit, and a glass-top coffee table that bore the sticky tell-tale fingerprints of spoiled grandchildren. A small wooden box sat atop the table, its cockeyed lid revealing two yellowed decks of playing cards nestled inside. Sawdust seized the opportunity to sharpen his claws on the couch before following us downstairs.

Creak. Creak. The bottom step complained under my weight, then Buck's. *Looks like we've got a loose tread.*

Sawdust stepped soundlessly down, too light to elicit a response.

Other than a couple of wire hangers on a rod, the laundry room was empty. The guest bedroom contained a full-sized bed covered in a crocheted afghan and a basic bureau with three empty cans of Budweiser sitting atop it. They appeared to be only the latest in a long series of beers enjoyed in the bed, as evidenced by a pattern of ring stains roughly resembling the Olympic symbol. I wondered who Lilian's beer-guzzling guest had been.

The other bedroom had been converted to a sewing room and appeared untouched. A white Singer sewing machine sat on a table, while a bookshelf to the right sported a selection of thread and rickrack, as well as a pincushion in the quintessential tomato motif. A plastic box filled with spare, shiny buttons sat open on one of the shelves like a miniature treasure chest filled with gold. Swatches of fabric draped over a quilt rack.

After a quick trip to the garage, the tour was complete. The bottom step creaked again as we made our way back up to the front doorway. There, I shared my overall vision for the house. "Classic black and white tile in the baths and kitchen. Paint in robin's egg blue for the walls." The look would be neutral and timeless, and would tie in well with the exterior colors. "Black hardwood floors would be a nice complement, too."

"Works for me," Buck said.

After noting that the thermostat reading was on its way down, I reattached Sawdust's leash to his harness and we headed out the door into the gathering winter dusk. Buck and I agreed to meet at the house at noon the following day to take measurements and start on the demolition.

He raised a hand out the window of his van as he backed

out of the driveway and drove off. I, on the other hand, looked up at the house one more time. *Yep. A fresh start.*

Too excited to wait until noon, I arrived at the house at nine the next morning. I'd need Buck's muscles for the heavy lifting later, but for now I could get started on that hideous carpet. I set my toolbox down on the porch. Cradling Sawdust against my chest, I unlocked the front door and went to push it open. It barely budged.

What the heck?

I pushed harder, putting my shoulder into it this time. The door opened an inch more but that was it. Something inside was blocking the doorway.

Unable to see anything through the small gap, I cupped my hand around my eyes and put my face to the frosted glass. Though I could see something lying on the landing inside, I couldn't make out exactly what it was. My eyes could only distinguish several blurred colors. *Had the coat closet's overburdened rod or shelf given way?* It seemed so. It also seemed any effort to get through the front door would be futile, so I pulled the door closed and relocked it.

Sawdust looked up at me. *Mew?*

"Something's blocking the door," I explained. The fact that he couldn't understand me was no excuse for ignoring his question. "Let's try the garage."

Returning to my SUV, I retrieved the remote and jabbed the button to raise the bay door. I ducked under it as it squealed and rattled its way up. Once inside the garage, I strode to the interior door and pressed the doorbell-style button to send it squealing and rattling back down again. *A squirt of WD-40 should do the trick.* I had a can in my toolbox, which I'd left on the porch. I'd grab it once I got the front door open.

I set Sawdust down and unclipped his leash. "There you go, boy." I ruffled his head, tucked his leash in my pocket, and headed after him into the house.

From the bottom of the staircase I could see a pile of mixed fabrics on the landing. Looked like I'd been right. Either the coat closet rod had broken or the shelf had collapsed. Maybe both. *The list of repairs keeps growing.*

The bottom step creaked as I stepped onto it. Above me, Sawdust hopped up onto the clothing heap, climbing down the other side. As I ascended the stairs, my eyes spotted something white and fluffy among the fabric. *Had the stuffing come out of a torn coat?* As I drew closer, my foot involuntarily stopped and hovered over the final step, much as Buck's had done the day before.

That's not stuffing. That's hair!

What's more, the hair was still attached to a head—an elderly woman's head. Her head was bent at an unnatural angle. The rest of the woman was bent at odd angles too, as if she were playing a solo game of Twister and giving it her all. She lay on her stomach, her right cheek pressed to the floor, her right arm crooked out of sight under her belly. Her eye was closed, thank goodness.

There's no way the woman could still be alive.

Still, what kind of person would I be if I didn't make sure she was truly beyond hope? Taking a deep breath, I bent over her and pressed my hand to her neck to feel for a heartbeat. "Ma'am? Are you okay?"

The lack of response along with the cold, stiff skin and absence of a pulse told me the woman was anything *but* okay. My mind went woozy, my vision tunneled, and my heart and stomach fought to see which could occupy my throat first. *Who is she? What happened? How did she end up dead in the doorway of an unoccupied, locked house?*

Sawdust, on the other hand, was unfazed. With feline curiosity, he poked the woman's cheek with his paw.

I gasped. "No, boy! No!" As I reached out to grab my cat, an unmistakable and terrifying sound met my ears.

Creak.

Someone was coming up the stairs behind me. . . .